ADAM

By

C. P. Schweikhardt

Dedication

ADAM is dedicated to my lovely wife and life companion, Patricia, who made valuable contributions to the completion of this work of fiction.

Preface

ADAM encompasses the full range of human feelings and emotions related to love, sex and happiness. It is totally fictional and does not represent any person or persons dead or alive. All characters depicted are completely imaginary as are the plot and all circumstances described.

Acknowledgement

I thank my daughter, Christy Schweikhardt Powell, for her assistance and critique which made this work possible. I thank my good friend and golfing buddy, Ramon Gonzalez, for suggesting that I write a novel otherwise I might never have undertaken the task even though I had developed the plot for this work several years earlier.

Prolog

Jacob Angleton, a south Texas rancher, and his son were building a new fence around their property which up until that time had been open grazing. The son placed a post in a posthole he had just completed. When tamped in the depth of the hole proved to be inadequate to support the fence post properly. The father explained to his son that the posthole needed to be dug deeper. He then added.

"If something is worth doing, it's worth doing right!"

Table of Contents

Chapter 1 Concept

While lying in his hospital bed recovering from double bypass heart surgery, George Angleton passed the time between sleep and alertness reviewing his life and accomplishments. During one of his alert periods, George suddenly grasped that he had acquired enormous wealth, but his single-minded devotion to making money had been at the exclusion of having a personal life, he had never married, had no family and no descendants. His coming years looked bleak except for making more money. In dismay George asked himself

"So, what the hell was the point?"

Although George had never allowed time for romance, not to say he never had sex, he disliked the thought of not having descendants to carry on his bloodline. He began to consider possible methods to correct this oversight before it became too late. At the time, he was approaching seventy years old and nearing the age of reduced reproductive ability. After much consideration and exploring many options open to him, George came up with a novel idea that he felt would offer a suitable solution to his dilemma.

George lapsed into a deep sleep and did not awake again until the nurse startled him the next morning when she checked his blood pressure and heart rate. George spent the rest of his time in the hospital looking back at his life and career all the while working on a method to carry out his plan once he was released.

George Angleton, the only child of Melva and Patrick Angleton, was born at home in Falfurrias, Texas. A small town named after the unique Hearts Delight flower which grows there and is found nowhere else on earth. George was born in midafternoon delivered with the aid of a local midwife he weighed in at a robust eight and one half pounds. The midwife didn't bother with the customary slap on the butt, it was unnecessary, George entered the world screaming at the top of his lungs angered by being rushed into reality too soon. Of the millions of babies that came into the world that day none, other than George, possessed the innate talents and abilities he inherited as a part of his genetic makeup. Mother Nature bestowed a unique gift on George the day he was conceived, although neither his mother nor his father were special, the onetime combination of their genes produced an exceptional individual unlike any other. Within a few days of his birth, George became accustomed to the outside world and with the tender warm touch of his mother's caresses he adapted to his new surroundings. He soon found that by applying certain skills he could manipulate his mother as well as others to satisfy his wants and needs. A naturally acquired skill in most babies, but one George used far into the future eventually leading to his accumulation of great wealth and a financial empire extending throughout the world.

His father, Patrick Angleton, worked as a head roustabout in the oil fields of south Texas, where he was employed by Oil Lease Services, Inc. an independent oil field contractor that provided manpower, tools and transportation for small jobs primarily related to the production of oil and natural gas. He and his roustabouts built tank batteries, laid flow lines, installed pumping units, and performed various other types of construction and general oil field work required by their customers. As gang pusher, or head roustabout, Patrick was by necessity a planner with many skills and diverse knowledge. His responsibilities included arriving at the location with the right number of people and tools for the job assigned. He planned and directed the crew's work which changed daily as they moved from one job to another. His work area included the counties surrounding Falfurrias, but his crews worked mostly in Brooks County. Patrick often quoted his father's and his grandfather's favorite saying to both George and his workers.

"If something is worth doing, it is worth doing right."

He lived his life by that saying as had his father and grandfather before him.

Falfurrias, the county seat was by far the largest town in Brooks County, it had a population of 4,550 hardy people made up almost equally between Hispanics and Anglos. There were no blacks in the town, or in the county for that matter, there had never been any slaves in this part of Texas it was ranch land derived from the old Spanish land grants which prohibited the trade in slaves. The town had the only high school in Brooks County which was home of the Falfurrias Jerseys football team. On rare occasions the Jerseys won the district championship, but they were never good enough to contend for the State championship against the much larger schools located in the more populated areas of Texas.

George managed to master the twelve steps of grade school and high school with a least of effort surpassing his classmates both in scholastic achievements and in outside accomplishments. By age ten, George had become a self-motivated money maker, he began mowing lawns and pulling weeds out of flower beds after school and on weekends to earn money on his own. He rarely took time to socialize or make close friends with any of his contemporaries, he was too busy working and trying to figure out how to make more money. George was addicted to the thing he liked and enjoyed most, making money. He was thrilled to feel the nickels and dimes he earned in his hand before putting them in his pocket for safekeeping. George had little time or inclination to spend his money instead he put most of his earnings into an interest bearing savings account at the local bank where it could grow even larger with time.

Upon graduating from high school, George was proud of his accomplishments as a student scholar, but he was particularly proud of the balance in his savings account which totaled $113.29 in deposits and interest. There had been no withdrawals, still he managed to buy all of his school supplies and clothes while going to high school using money he had earned. During this time, when the other boys were kissing girls, George hardly noticed there were people of the opposite sex mixed in with general population of Falfurrias.

Spanish became a second language for George he was fluent in Border Spanish conversing with his Mexican American classmates as one of their own. He had easily learned the language from schoolmates and the guys he worked with during the summer months when he was out of school. His last two years in high school, George worked with his father's gang during his summer break because he could earn more money working in the gang than at any other job available. Most of his coworkers were Hispanics forcing him to become proficient in Spanish to understand what they were saying on the job without requesting them to repeat themselves in English. George made no distinction between Hispanics and Anglos, they were all people trying to secure a place in the world around them.

George's parents coveted education believing it to be the path to a better life, but they could not afford to pay George's way to college. George did not consider this as an obstacle to his plans for the future. Since eighth grade, George had planned to attend the University of Texas

Business School to learn about the business world and to acquire the tools necessary to broaden his money making capabilities. Two weeks after graduating from high school, at the age of eighteen, he kissed his mom shook his father's hand and cashed in his savings account before hitchhiking to Austin to begin his quest to obtain a college education at UT.

The trip took George three days in all, he caught a ride the first day from Falfurrias to San Antonio with a truck driver hauling fruit from the Rio Grande Valley. His luck ran out on the second day. He caught a ride to Seguin with an elderly couple travelling there from San Antonio, when George told them he was headed to Austin, they were nice enough to drop him off on the north side of town. He thumbed for six hours straight without getting another ride ending the day tired and hungry. That night he slept on the ground under a bridge to save money it was inconvenient, but cheap. On the third day he was more successful catching a ride to Austin shortly after breakfast, he arrived downtown Austin just before noon. By day's end, he had rented a single furnished room for ten dollars a month and found a job waiting tables in a café near the University of Texas campus.

In September, George enrolled in the Business School at UT which at the time had no quotas, any Texas high school graduate who could pay the tuition was accepted. With hard work and taking an overload in credit hours each semester, George graduated three and a half years later with a degree in Business Economics. He had accumulated $215.30 in his savings account which made him very proud, he had worked at the café the entire time he was attending UT paying his living and educational costs from his earnings, yet he had managed to add to his savings. George had learned at an early age that to accumulate wealth an individual could not spend all of their earnings, a rule he followed, without fail, during his long and illustrious career. At the café George, advanced from waiter to cashier by the time he graduated from UT. Working at the café, he learned about the rewards of long hours and hard work, lessons he would use to his advantage during his long and successful business career. Because of his seven days a week job and his attending UT full time, without taking any summer breaks, he had not seen his parents or returned to Falfurrias since leaving for UT. He corresponded with them occasionally by postcard, but never had time off to go home or money to waste on an unnecessary phone call. George was overjoyed as he wrote to his parents telling them he had graduated at the top of his class and as the outstanding business student he had successfully landed a much coveted, high salaried job with an oil company in Houston. Upon receiving four days off for Thanksgiving at his new place of employment, George caught a Greyhound bus to Falfurrias to visit his parents. The first thing he heard as he stepped off of the bus was his mother's lyrical voice.

"George, is that really you? You have grown so tall since I last saw you."

George hugged his mother and shook his father's hand before he said anything.

"It's so good to see both of you, I've missed you."

Motioning toward the car his father replied, "Come on, George. Let's go home we can talk once we get there."

Over the following five years, George worked hard learning everything he could about how deals were structured, how money was raised to finance drilling prospects, how other companies were acquired, and how to make the most out of the least in the oil business. He worked long hours asking many questions about every project in which the company participated. Most of all, George paid attention to the smallest details involved in each project he and the other employees worked on for the company.

While working on one of his projects located in south Texas, George discovered the company had been trying for years to acquire an Oil and Gas Lease on a large ranch not far from Falfurrias, his hometown. Unfortunately, the rancher and his wife had rejected every offer the company had made. Although his discovery was totally unrelated to his assigned task, George found out through his associates that Investment Oil's President coveted the right to drill on the ranch. The geological department's studies in the area indicated the potential for enormous oil and gas reserves at a moderate depth across most of the ranch. Acquiring a lease from the ranch owner meant huge profits for the company if their geologist's assessment of the reserves were correct. George was well aware of the company's earlier failures to obtain a lease, but repeated past failures did not deter George he went directly to the president with a proposal.

"Sir, I am confident that I can deliver a lease on the PVX Ranch property if given a chance. All I need is to know the most we can pay for the lease. I can take care of the rest."

The president smiled at George saying.

"Well, George, everyone else we have sent has didn't obtain a lease, so have at it. We are willing to pay up to $2,000,000 for a three year lease, show me what you can do."

George called the ranch owner setting up a meeting the following afternoon in Benavides. Anxious to get started, George left the office at once driving to Alice nonstop where he spent the night in a cheap motel on the south side of town. The next morning, he drove to Benavides where he met the rancher in the local café for lunch. After devouring two large chicken fried steaks with mashed potatoes and gravy, they drove in their separate vehicles to the ranch which was several miles to the south of town. George followed the rancher's pickup allowing a modest distance between them to avoid the dust cloud boiling up behind the pickup. To George's relief, they arrived at the ranch house in less than two hours, the drive had been dirty and rough on the caliche road which wound through the mesquite brush for miles after they left the paved farm to market road outside of Benavides.

The rancher, a tall lean man, invited George into the house where they each enjoyed a cold beer while discussing the cattle business. His host was proud of his operation and liked to talk about his achievements since coming to the ranch.

"I have only Santa Gertrudis cattle in my herd. The wife and I raised Brahmas for years, but switched to Santa Gertrudis after the King Ranch developed the breed. They do well in this scrub brush country and fetch a higher price at the auctions. Once you get your own breeding stock built up, it's not so expensive, you don't have to rely on outside purchases to support the herd."

"That is very interesting to know. Did I mention, I grew up near here? I was born in Falfurrias, but my family was not in ranching dad worked in the oil field."

"What is your name?"

"George Angleton."

"You any relation to the folks who had the Angleton ranch?"

"Yeah, that was my grandfather, he sold out during the big drought, lost most of his savings."

"I knew your grandfather, he gave me my first job as a cowhand I was sixteen at the time. I learned a lot from him he was a good man. Do you know his favorite saying?"

"I sure do, my dad said it too."

"If something is worth doing, it's worth doing right."

"Yep, that's it. What can I do for you George?"

"My company has made several attempts over the past few years to lease your ranch to drill for oil and gas and for some reason you have turned them down every time. I was wondering if you and I could work out a deal to your satisfaction."

"George, it's a complicated thing you are asking me to do. I inherited the ranch from my wife when she died last year. I met her at Texas A & I when we were students about forty years ago. She was an only child, so when her parents died I took over running the ranch, but it still belonged to her. Her parents had always been against leasing their minerals they were convinced that drilling on the ranch would interfere with their ranching operations and they didn't want a bunch of strangers on their land. My wife felt the same way and was so adamant in her belief that we never leased."

"I think you and I can make it work to both of our advantages," insisted George.

"My late wife and I heard all of these complaints from our neighbors about the oil company workers leaving their gates open letting their cattle run wild and how the oil workers had no regard for their ranching operations. They were a damned nuisance and rounding up the cattle and separating them was an unnecessary pain in the ass for the ranchers! Frankly, she got pissed off every time leasing became an issue. We refused to lease because that is what she wanted!"

"Do you have any children?" asked George who was stalling for time. He wanted the rancher to cool off before pressing him to lease the ranch.

"We have two grown sons, who are both married, one is a doctor living in Corpus Christi and the other is a lawyer living in Houston. Why do you ask?"

"I was just wondering. I don't suppose either of them are planning to return to ranching. Are they?"

"No, they have their own careers, neither one of them is interested in running the ranch. After I'm gone, they will probably hire someone to run it for them."

"What if I could guarantee that your gates would never be left open by our workers and that interference with your ranching operations by drilling and production operations would be held to an absolute minimum? Would you consider leasing to us?"

"Maybe, how can you guarantee your workers won't leave any gates open? You can't put guards on all the gates twenty four hours a day!"

"Our company, at its expense, will replace every road gate on your ranch with a first class cattle guard which we will maintain at our expense. That way there will be no gates to open or close and your cattle won't be getting out and it will cost you nothing. I mean all the gates whether we use them or not! In addition, we will agree that no drilling operation will be commenced without your approval sixty days in advance that way you can plan your operations in the area around our drilling program to reduce any conflicts. Not only that, I am prepared to pay top dollar for a three year paid-up lease. What do you think?"

"You know, George, I am going to sell you a lease provided the money is right. I need to get all of this set up before the boys inherit the ranch otherwise what they do might not be to my liking or my wife's either I might add!"

George closed the deal with a handshake and had a signed lease in the president's hands within two weeks paying a bonus of $1,500,000 to the rancher for a three year paid-up lease providing for 1/8 royalty to the Lessor. Other terms of their agreement were contained in a side letter which was reference in the lease, but unrecorded at the courthouse. This arrangement was George's way of preventing the public from discovering his commitment to give the free cattle guards and the drilling restrictions he had signed off on buying the lease.

Success was in the making following George's acquisition of the lease, Investment Oil made a huge oil discovery on the ranch six months later which led to their drilling 346 producing oil wells over the next ten years. George's endeavors were well rewarded, he rapidly moved up the management chain at Investment Oil becoming Vice-President of Planning and Acquisitions. George became known as the "deal maker" by his peers in the oil industry and among the employees and management at Investment Oil. George's uncanny ability to find and make deals, made enormous amounts of money for the company stockholders and their outside partners in ventures he originated and put together. He proved to be a valuable asset to the company because of his ability to find quality deals. George knew he had a special talent for deal making he was surpassed by none and equaled by few in business.

Once he reached his goal of $150,000 in savings, George was ready to capitalize on his ability, he quit his job to start his own business in the process he raised another $200,000 from former business associates to whom he had sold successful drilling ventures during his employment with Investment Oil. His investors received a total of 15% of the stock in George's new company while he retained the remaining 85% and maintained absolute control of the company. Thus began the saga of Imperial Enterprises, one of the most successful investment companies ever created exceeding even the renowned Goldheim and Goldheim investment group headquartered in Boston. George Angleton became one of the most discussed, admired and copied self-made billionaires of all time. He and his career were often mentioned by the news media and was often featured in the Wall Street Journal as an example of the opportunities available to every American. His business techniques were discussed in business publications worldwide as were his letters and remarks to his stockholders. Everyone was looking for a clue to his next acquisition trying to cash in on the deal. He was emulated by many would be billionaires, but none matched his ability to find and close on good deals. George was the ultimate model for success in the business world. Through hard work using his uncanny skills in making deals, he amassed a fortune of 328 billion dollars over the course of thirty years. George insisted on honesty from all of his associates and employees, shady deals were not allowed, Imperial Enterprises was never involved in an investigation or law suit by the Securities and Exchange Commission or any other governmental body in the years George was at the helm of the organization.

Following a short rehab period after being discharged from the hospital, George called a special meeting of his five long time advisors all of whom held top management positions in Imperial Enterprises or its subsidiaries. These were men George trusted, he had known most of them throughout his business career and he knew from experience that any topic discussed or anything said in the meeting would not be revealed or repeated outside of the meeting room. There had been many such sessions over the years with never a leak or hint of disloyalty among his advisors these men were friends who had also become wealthy through their association with George. It was well known throughout the business world that George was a strong proponent of rewarding associates and employees based on performance and loyalty to him and the company. He insisted that they share in the rewards garnered from their ideas and contributions to Imperial Enterprises. George was aware that superb performance as well as absolute secrecy would be necessary to make his plan succeed. He intended to use the diverse talents and knowledge of his trusted advisors to make his plan become a reality. The participants were seated in their customary positions at the conference table when George began.

"You are probably wondering why I have called a meeting when we are not making an acquisition or sale. Gentlemen, this meeting has nothing to do with our business rather it concerns a personal project that I consider being my number one priority. To carry out this project and for it to reach a successful conclusion we must use of all of our talents in business, science and advertising and possibly the talents of a few outsiders."

George paused briefly to allow his statement to be digested before continuing.

"The key to attaining my goal is complete secrecy, not only now, but well into the future possibly beyond our lifetimes. Gentlemen, simply put, my goal is to father four children by four different women within the next twelve months."

George paused again to allow his advisors to grasp the significance of his statement. No one spoke, all of them were stunned by George's revelation.

"I shall not meet the mothers or the children, so obviously conception will be by artificial insemination. My requirements for the mothers are simple: they must be American citizens living in Texas, they must never have been married, have no known inheritable detrimental genes, be between twenty and thirty years of age, have at least a high school education, be from a low to middle income environment, have no criminal record, have no children and be employed."

The advisors were in shock, some slumped forward in their seats in complete disbelief while others became stone-faced. George had never mentioned any wish to have children, and certainly not four. None of them had any idea that procreation was one of George's concerns or that he wanted to extend his genes into the next generation. George did not wait for comments or questions he forged ahead.

"I want to make certain these children are raised in a middle class environment and reach adulthood. The aim for this meeting is to devise a detailed method to select the mothers and provide income and protection for them and their children. My identity as the father must stay unknown and be protected from detection in the future. In addition, I want to make it impossible for the children or anyone else to determine that they are related because of any actions taken as a part of this plan."

George glanced at each of the five to assess their reception of the new project, satisfied his associates understood he stated.

"Cost in not a consideration for this project, please present your plan as soon as possible. I'm not getting any younger, you know."

He smiled as he left the conference room certain that a workable plan would be forthcoming. He could still see the shock on their faces as he entered the elevator on his way out of the building.

None of the advisors laughed or even considered doing so, to a man they realized George was serious and, as always, determined to reach his objective. In the past, they had all labored long and hard using their special abilities to make George's wildest ideas become big money makers for the company and themselves. Jerry, the most senior of the group, took over the meeting following George's departure.

"It appears we have several key problems to overcome in formulating a plan of execution for this project which I suggest we give the code name ADAM. How do we find and select women who are willing to bear a child by artificial insemination using sperm from an unidentified donor and what other criteria will be needed in selecting the prospective mothers other than those expressed by George? Ed, you have worked with screening companies in the past, could you develop a plausible scenario for a person, group or company to conduct such a screening?

18

Keep in mind that neither we nor the company can be implicated or traced to the screening."

Ed thought a moment then replied.

"Since we are taking the first step in implementing ADAM, I am sure a workable plan can be devised which allows screening following George's desires. The prerequisites for selecting the potential mothers need to be clearly defined, so I am starting with them first. I will be ready for a full presentation on Friday."

Satisfied with Ed's reply, Jerry moved on to the next topic.

"Secondly, how do we convince the selected candidates to take part in ADAM?"

Harry quickly volunteered.

"I already have a few ideas along those lines which can be developed to fit several situations. Ed and I can work to gather avoiding conflicts later."

"Agreed, Harry you and Ed work together on those issues. The rest of us will work on the other three requirements necessary to complete ADAM, financing, protection and secrecy. Secrecy now and in the future being the prime issue for ADAM as George so clearly stated. Aaron, finance is your specialty, so that part is up to you. Frank will handle the protection phase while security will be my contribution. We will meet here in two days at 9:00 a.m. on Friday the 13th to review our preliminary findings and to finalize ADAM for presentation to George on Monday."

Jerry ended the meeting with a reminder to the others.

"Gentlemen, do not take this task lightly. This project is vitally important to George, and he expects us to make it happen just as he has visualized!"

Jerry did not leave the conference room until well after the others, he sat alone at the conference table allowing his mind to consolidate and analyze the day's events before moving forward with developing his security program.

"For us to formulate a fool proof and totally secure plan for ADAM is not going to be easy it could be the most formidable task we have undertaken during my long career with George. Well, if that is what

George wants? I am going to give it everything I've got to make it work!"

On Friday, the advisors began arriving at 8:30 a.m. Ed and Harry were the last of the five to take their seats before Jerry brought the meeting to order.

"Good morning gentlemen, I hope the last two days have been productive for all of you, shall we begin?"

Ed and Harry commenced removing their exhibits and associated papers from their bulging briefcases each of them were eager to present their recommendations to the group for their consideration. Ed, the youngest member of the team, took the lead.

"In considering the specifications and possible restrictions applicable to the women selected to be the mothers of George's children, two important questions must be answered. Are they allowed to have more children? And are the mothers going to be allowed to marry after giving birth to George's child? Regardless of the answers to these questions enforcement and complete secrecy present an almost insurmountable challenge. From a social point of view it will be beneficial to both the mother and the child for the mother to be allowed to marry, otherwise, the child will be raised in a single parent home which we know is not the best of all environments for producing a well-rounded individual. I do not think George would consider allowing the mothers to have more children if so his children could have half-brothers and half-sisters none of whom would be related to George. George will ultimately make that decision. A no more children ban can be achieved by sterilizing the mothers, without their knowledge, at the time George's children are delivered. My recommendation is to include a no more children ban and allow marriage for the mothers. Our screening program for applicants should be limited to those prerequisites stated by George. I think this will offer reasonable secrecy after the selections have been made while allowing our screening to cover the greatest number of potential candidates."

The others unanimously agreed with his recommendations. Ed was pleased his work was appreciated by these peers he glanced at Harry saying.

"The floor is all yours."

Harry opened his folder and began to speak in his slow south Texas drawl, which had captivated so many investors over the years.

"As Ed stated before, we agreed to limit the screening program to those categories set forth by George in our meeting last week. This not only simplifies the technique it, also, allows us to create a reasonable and morally acceptable reason for the screening and the later choice of four final candidates. Our program will be presented to the potential candidates, and the public, as an ongoing genetic study being conducted using unique beneficial genes detected in only a handful of males worldwide. We will position our program as a low key and benevolent scientific undertaking to avoid suspicion by the media, but should our efforts come to their attention we will take whatever steps necessary to assure they support and promote our program as being beneficial for mankind. Secrecy will be maintained throughout."

"How will that work, Harry? Please explain the program to the rest of us?"

"Jerry, the program will work like this. During the screening phase we will find those women who meet our requirements and who might be willing to take part in the study. Once those who are qualified have been separated from the others, we will move on to the next stage in which we find those who are willing to have a child through artificial insemination as part of the study in exchange for defined monetary and social benefits for themselves and their child. We will then select the final four from this group."

Harry was gratified as he sat down to the resounding approval from the other members of the group.

"Frank, please tell us about your protection plan for ADAM?"

Frank, a burly specimen of a man who looked more like a wrestler than an intellectual spoke slowly and deliberately.

"Protection for those participating in ADAM will start once the final four are chosen and continue for George's children until they reach the age of thirty. The mothers will have protection for life. Participants in the program will be protected from harm from all sources. By this I mean harm of both a physical and social nature. No one will be allowed to kill, maim or inflict physical harm or to threaten any of the ADAM group, nor will they be allowed to steal from them or entice them into harmful habits or relationships which would prevent them from leading a normal life growing up and later in life. In order to do this, all beneficiaries under ADAM will be under constant secret surveillance using electronic devices and visually by a person or persons capable of intervention if necessary. Except for extreme and eminent life threatening situations, our intervention will be without the knowledge of the beneficiary and even then it will be disguised to conceal the source. We will also set up an organization to support the efforts and functions of the ADAM group. To give undetectable protection, we will set up a company to offer both manpower and funding for this purpose. Gentlemen, this will be a very expensive endeavor because of the secrecy requirements imposed on all parties associated with it. I am sure that Aaron can help in organizing the company as well as funding it."

Jerry and the others indicated their satisfaction with Frank's protection proposal as well as his plan for supporting the other parts of ADAM.

"We will need at least two separate financial vehicles to support ADAM, both of which need to be funded in such a way that they are not traceable to us or to George or any of our affiliates. I will set up a company to fund the screening, testing, and insemination and to provide the funding to the mothers for life including medical care and future testing of the children. I suggest we name the company, Gentex Research, which I will register as an offshore company to avoid excessive examination of its funding. The second company which will provide funding for protection will, also, be an offshore company which I recommend we name, Abe. These companies will initially be funded with cash deposits made by wire transfers from George's personal account into offshore bank accounts which, through a series of manipulations, will make the funds untraceable to George. An investment account for each company will be established for the purpose of providing sustained income to the companies themselves. Over a short time interval, the cash will be invested in dividend paying securities and the dividends paid into their respective accounts for use in paying the costs of ADAM. Surplus funds in the investments accounts will be reinvested in dividend paying securities selected by our investment team to make the companies self-perpetuating. To avoid any obvious connection to us, all of this will be performed by paid third parties, with whom we have had clandestine relationships."

After Aaron's presentation, Jerry pointed out.

"Upon completion of the various components needed to carry out ADAM I will make a detailed security study of the project to decide what if any changes are needed?"

He adjourned the meeting confident George would be happy with their proposed plan on Monday.

George asked a few questions, he listened intently to the entire presentation outlining the plan and implementation of ADAM. Once the last detail about security had been explained, George addressed the group.

"I must commend each of you on your attention to detail as well as to my wishes in developing ADAM. At this point, it has my approval to move forward as quickly as possible, but, I want to make some restrictions in the overall program. I shall have no black descendants! Sterilization of the mothers is forbidden. I do not wish to punish these women for having been a part of the program, on the contrary, they should be able to lead full and happy lives as a consequence of their participation. Whether they have more children will be their decision not ours. George shook hands with each of his advisors and congratulated each of them again for their excellent work in creating ADAM emphasizing that its success was more important to him than all of their past projects combined."

Gentex Research and Abe were fully operational two months following George's approval of the plan to support ADAM. He was pleased with their respective reporting systems and structural management teams and the fact that they were in place and ready for business.

Gentex had a tight organization consisting of a three man management team, two doctors and a director appointed from among the five advisors. The doctors were responsible for all things medical including tests and genetic screening of women applying to take part in the Gentex program. They made agreements with selected independent doctors to conduct individual tests of the applicants at various locations across Texas. Although the fees paid by Gentex under these agreements were triple those normally received, not all doctors approached agreed to participate. Only those agreeing to complete secrecy on both the results and identity of the women were accepted, all information collected by the doctors belonged to and was the exclusive property of Gentex the doctor's records reflected none of the information gathered and provided to Gentex. Four specialists in the field of artificial insemination were selected by the doctors for use when needed, each of these specialist owned their own clinic and had a staff experienced in handling special clients. Secrecy was not an unusual need for these clinics they were accustomed to having well known clients who demanded anonymity. Many of their special clients were kept in isolation and were attended by selected staff members who were proven to be discreet and trustworthy. Once screening had been completed and the final four selected, the Gentex doctors were charged with selecting insemination specialist and obstetricians to deliver their babies. These selections were to be made depending upon the final four and their respective locations across Texas and all were subject to ADAM's strict secrecy code.

The director in charge of the overall operation of Gentex conducted the screening and selection programs and, in the process, established an office and control center in the Energy Corridor of west Houston to house his staff and their equipment. By design, the office was located on the top floor of the building to keep incidental traffic to a minimum and to provide tight security for its operations. Jerry, the head of ADAM'S security, was making a tour of the facility to insure it met his standards he was accompanied by Aaron the director of Gentex who gave a running commentary as they toured the layout.

"We have a fake entrance located midway down the hall from the elevator, with no number, just the word ACE on the glass door."

They entered the fake entrance finding a small sparely furnished room inside occupied by a pretty, well-dressed receptionist. The reception area had a blank opaque door with no sign of what lay on the other side. Aaron pointed toward the desk saying.

"The receptionist has a phone, but it has no outside number because there are no incoming calls. She is not a receptionist at all, her job is to get rid of peddlers and others who might come by and to alert the control center of their presence. When a person enters or passes outside her door on their way down the hall, she presses a button under her desk which triggers an alert signal in the command center."

Jerry indicated his approval before asking.

"Is there adequate security in the hallway?"

"The hall and reception area are viewed by invisible cameras which show images in real time on monitors in the command center. The alert signal prompts the command personnel to look at the monitors which run constantly. Should any of them recognize a person or persons in the hall as potential intruders a full lock down will be ordered barring entrance to the inner office and alerting our armed guards who are stationed next to the command center."

"Very good, very good, indeed!"

"The actual entrance to Gentex is located down the hall past the reception area it consists of a heavy unmarked door which can only be opened from the inside by anyone other than myself. I have an electronic pass key. To gain entry, staff members send their personal code names on their cell phones to a computer inside which then prompts them to enter their passwords. After confirmation of their password, they take a picture of their face with their cell phone. The photo is sent to the computer for final identification verification, the computer then unlocks the door."

"I understand the cameras' role to show people in the hall, but to make it clear to me let's go through the procedure to unlock the entrance using a cell phone again."

Aaron repeated his explanation in detail before opening the door with his electronic pass key. Inside the control center Jerry saw a large area consisting of offices equipped with computers and other sophisticated electronic equipment. A massive array of electronic devices, computers, displays and data storage devices dominated the main room. The director and his staff occupied the command center 24/7, when the director was away, his assistant directors were in charge depending on which one was on duty at the time. Highly trained agents with special areas of expertise worked in the individual offices they performed extensive and detailed background checks on applicants to the genetic program and those individuals working for Gentex as contractors. Some were sales experts hired specifically to sign up the final four for the Gentex program once they had been selected. These people were experts in the field of persuasion who were accustomed in making tough sales to doubting clients.

Frank chose a building across the street from the Tmex Hotel for Abe's headquarters it was within walking distance of Imperial Enterprises' home office where he spent most of his time. Frank frequented the bar at the Tmex it was convenient and his favorite watering hole in all of Houston. For maximum security, he had one-way glass installed in the exterior windows, occupants could see out, but no one could see into the building. Abe's headquarters occupied the entire second floor of the building and had a single unmarked entrance located near the elevator. The entrance was protected by three armed guards stationed at the unmarked door. It was impossible to enter Abe without passing the guards and showing an identification card which was placed face down on a scanning machine for identity verification by Abe's computer. Unknown, even to the armed guards, every Abe employee wore a hidden microchip transmitter whose signal identified them to the agents inside of Abe's headquarters. Should that identity be missing or differ from their scanned card identity, Abe was alerted that an imposter was trying to enter the building.

The elevators did not stop on the second floor, the actual second floor was not shown on the elevator menu at all, it didn't exist. The third floor was numbered two on the elevator menu to support continuity for the other occupants of the building and to shield it from the public. In order to enter Abe, one had to walk up one of the two stairways to the second floor then down the hall to the entrance at the blank elevator shaft. Hidden cameras recorded and stored images of everyone who entered the stairways and halls this information was, also, viewed in real time by agents inside of the Abe complex. Much of the electronic equipment was unique to Abe, Frank had it designed for specific uses such as continuous surveillance of objects and individuals. He retained computer experts to design the special software required for the needs of Abe and also to select the best equipment to do the job. His protection plan for ADAM included stationing special Alpha teams near each of the final four and their offspring. These teams were made up of young specialists trained in surveillance and intervention, many were ex-Navy Seals, and roughly half of them were women. Their assignments were to observe and record the actions of their specific charges around the clock seven days a week and to report their status to Abe. Each of the four Alpha teams operated independently of the others and were unknown to each other they also did not know members of the Abe staff in headquarters. A cadre of agents had been recruited to man the central command post around the clock with a managing agent in charge of each shift. There were special agents located in central control assigned to each of the final four, their duties included viewing the videos and surveillance reports from the Alpha teams for their specific assignments on a daily basis to become familiar with their habits, likes and dislikes. These special agents were charged with knowing everything there was to know about their assigned individuals, they were to analyze all the information in detail looking for any danger or threat which the on-site agents might have missed or overlooked. Teams were to be assigned to George's children once they were old enough to be away from their mothers. Because of the secrecy required by Abe, all agents were screened by an outside agency with a complete background check made on each before they were hired. The final decision on hiring all employees at Abe was made by Frank after he conducted an in depth personal interview. Although all of this took time, Abe was operational and fully staffed in less than two months.

Screening for the right surrogate mothers took much longer than anticipated due to the overwhelming number of young women who applied to participate in the Gentex Research program. No one associated with ADAM dreamed there would be over a hundred women in contention to make the final four. After many interviews and assessments by the genetic experts and Gentex agents, a consensus of the advisors was reached and the final four selected along with four alternates. There was always a chance that one or more of those selected would refuse to sign the final Gentex agreement which required them to produce a baby through artificial insemination. ADAM was prepared for any eventuality.

Chapter 2 Final Four

With his ADAM team assembled following selection of the final four, George spoke first, as was usual, in all of his meetings with his advisors.

"Gentlemen, I want you to know I have been doing my part. I have donated sperm to the project fourteen times in the past six weeks my genetic contribution has been completed. When, where and how are we going to impregnate the ladies within the confines of the rules established for ADAM?"

Jerry was prepared for George's question he immediately responded.

"All paperwork has been completed and the final four have been selected currently we are monitoring the fertility cycles of the women to determine the best time to inseminate each of them. Obviously, this process may take up to three months before they all become pregnant assuming that the first try is successful for each of them, otherwise, the time period could be extended several more months."

George gestured for Jerry to continue.

"Importantly, each of the procedures are being conducted in separate clinics, located in different cities, by different doctors, so there is no chance of breaching our code of secrecy. The security teams are in place each team will be working independently and unknown to the others."

George interrupted.

"Have you made certain that none of the five people making up each of the teams were not previously acquainted or knew anyone on the other teams? We need to take every precaution to avoid prior relationships between our field agents which could create problems later!"

"Absolutely, we have checked for prior relationships and our investigations also show each agent to be trustworthy and capable professionals who will keep their activities secret."

"Considering the expected long term duration of ADAM, what happens if one or more of the agents die or are unable to perform their duties?" Inquired Aaron.

"All the agents are in their late twenties and early thirties, hopefully, we will be able to complete the program with the same people we are starting with. Should something unforeseen happen, we are prepared to replace any of the agents on short notice. Abe's surveillance began for each of the final four at the time they consummated their final agreement and will continue to the end of their individual lives."

"In conclusion, gentlemen. All aspects of ADAM are functional and currently operating as planned," added Jerry.

"Thank you, Jerry, for that excellent report."

Looking around the table George spoke directly to Jerry.

"Keep me up to date on the pregnancy situation, once the children are conceived, I do not want to hear about them again until they are born. Remember, I do not want to know the names of the mothers or the children or where they are located just that they are alive and ADAM is functioning as planned."

Nods from all around acknowledged George's wishes.

Satisfied with the progress on his project George thought to himself.

"If I get to know my children and their mothers, I'll probably try to manage their lives. I want them to make their own decisions and find their own destinies without my interference, it's their birthright. All I want to do is give them life the rest is up to them!"

George left without saying another word.

The final selections to participate in the Gentex program were a diverse group consisting of Clare Cook, Darlene Strong, Peggy Wilkerson and Rachel Garcia. Each had completed their preliminary indoctrinations and were in their individual Gentex facilities awaiting insemination. It took a full three months before all the women rotated through their fertile cycles allowing the insemination procedure to be completed, another three months passed before it was known with certainty that all four women were pregnant.

George was delighted upon hearing his sperm had done its job.

"I hope my decision to sire these babies will prove to be a good thing for me, them and mankind in general."

In the latest report from Gentex concerning the status of his genetic contributions, George learned he was the father of two sons and two daughters all of whom were healthy normal babies. There had been no complications with the births, the mothers were well, and were in the process of entering into the new routine of being mothers to their babies. As originally planned only five people, other than George, knew that he had contributed sperm to the program and was the father of the four children, these were his five trusted advisors who had helped devise and would administer ADAM.

CLARE'S STORY

Clare had always been a wild thing, according to her parents, she didn't fit into their orthodox way of doing things she had her own view of life and how it should be lived. Her parents were not the least bit surprised, or shocked, when she first revealed she had been selected to participate in an ongoing genetic study which required her to have a baby by artificial insemination. They were upset when they learned the father would be an unknown male that Clare didn't even know. Her mother was against Clare's joining the program altogether, it was just another wild thing their daughter was doing that did not fit into the normal order of doing things, but then Clare had lost contact with being normal when she turned thirteen.

Clare's selection to the final four was not without controversy, several of the members of the five man selection committee were opposed to her being one of the finalist because in their minds, she had not demonstrated a commitment to anything before applying for the Gentex program. Her eventual selection was determined by arguments presented in her behalf by Jerry, who pointed out to the committee that she had an exceptionally high IQ and had the potential for extraordinary future achievement. Jerry successfully argued that Clare was the one person being considered for the final four who could produce a child with an intellect approaching that of George and that her good looks almost assured George would have one good looking child if she were the mother. In the end the committee selected Clare over her alternate based on Jerry's strong support and recommendation.

Clare's mother was skeptical of Clare's plan to enter Gentex's program as she had been of most of Clare's bizarre actions since she graduated from high school.

"Clare, since you have never made a long term commitment to anything, what makes you think you can rear a baby by yourself?"

"Mother, it's something I want to do, I think the program is a good thing. It will help a lot of people."

"You realize, it's not like your modeling job in Dallas or the job you had singing in that night club, you can't just quit after the baby arrives. You will have to be responsible for it. Raising a baby is time consuming and a lot of work."

"Yes mother, I am well aware that I haven't stuck to anything very long in the past, but this is different. You need to understand, I am committed to this program because I think it will do a lot of good for mankind."

Her response surprised both of her parents, it was difficult for either of them to believe how enthusiastically she embraced the idea of rearing a child alone, Clare seemed singularly dedicated to the success of the program. Clare had lived a jumbled life the last few years moving from one job to another without settling on a permanent career or adopting a set life style. Much to her parent's consternation, she had live-in boyfriends, from time to time, none of whom lasted very long either, Clare discarded them once they became boring or were no longer useful.

Before the Gentex program, Clare had not found anyone or anything that kept her engaged for long, after an initial burst of fervor, she lost interest and moved on to something new. The Gentex program presented a pragmatic cause to which she could dedicate herself, as if a light had been turned on, Clare suddenly wanted to make a worthwhile contribution to society. She embraced the idea of having a baby as part of the scientific program Gentex was conducting. Not knowing the father did not bother her at all, in her view, an unknown father was superior to having a baby with any of the guys she had dated. This way she would not have to put up with their nonsense and could get on with raising her baby as she saw fit.

Her parents were in their early forties living in a rent house near the Oklahoma border north of Denison when Clare was born. Both of her parents worked at a local assembly plant, which manufactured valves for the oil and gas industry, John Cook was a shift foreman while Mildred worked in the office as an invoice clerk. Together they made a comfortable living which allowed them to purchase a three bedroom, two bathroom home in Denison by the time Clare reached her third birthday.

Clare was a normal child doing the things all young girls do until she reached thirteen, at that point, her personality changed along with her physical appearance she grew tall and willowy with straight black hair and large blue eyes. She had a small mouth with full lips that curved into a sexy hint of a smile when she was amused. By age seventeen, Clare no longer listened to her parent's suggestions without question, as she had done in the past, she sometimes did the opposite of what they wanted. If she decided to stay out late, she stayed out late, if she wanted to go dancing, she went dancing whether or not her parents approved. They considered this type of behavior by a young girl to be on the wild side and ill-mannered at best. It was difficult for them to believe their own daughter could act this way. Although they disapproved of her actions, her parents loved Clare and avoided unnecessary confrontations out of fear of alienating her. They knew she loved them and they did not want to lose her completely in spite of her different outlook on life.

As she grew older, Clare became a very attractive young woman who invariably got a second glance from young and older men alike. She dressed well and in fashion, rarely wearing pants or jeans, which gave her an ultra-feminine look that set her apart from the other young ladies her age. Her well rounded breasts were of modest size, however, they were always standing at attention, which elicited a lot of attention from the opposite sex. In her circle of friends and acquaintances the more aggressive men were continually hitting on her no matter where she was or what she was doing. Clare never lacked for male attention whether she wanted it or not. On rare occasions, usually after she had been drinking, she gave in to her sexual desires allowing one of the young men to spend the night in her apartment. These liaisons had nothing to do with love, Clare sought pure physical gratification and, more often than not, she was disappointed. These young guys thought of themselves as studs, but most of them either knew nothing about taking care of a woman's needs or didn't care, so long as they got what they wanted out of the encounter.

Clare was twenty four at the time she entered the Gentex program, it was a new beginning and a turning point in her life she was tired of her old life style and wanted something more meaningful. The program offered a meaningful way for her to make a contribution toward making the world a better place, Clare was proud to be a part of the program.

Verona Elise Cook was born in the middle of a Sunday afternoon, the delivery room annex was empty, except for Clare, who had been having labor pains since early morning. "Is it ever going to happen?" She wondered as the pains became more frequent and powerful in intensity. She was nearing exhaustion by the time Verona finally arrived. Clare knew in advance she was having a daughter, she had chosen Verona for her name several weeks earlier in anticipation of her birth. Later in the day, Clare's mother and father were presented with a beautiful granddaughter who had straight black hair and big blue eyes just like her mother. Clare's parents were overjoyed, yet did not condone Clare having a child out of wedlock. In their minds, there was no legitimate reason to do such a thing, even if there was no sex involved, it was a part of their moral upbringing. John and Mildred had accepted that Clare had a right to her own opinions, and that she was going to live the way she wanted. Even though they did not agree with her choice, they could not help admiring her new found dedication to the Gentex project. In spite of their previous reservations, they loved Clare and Verona and planned to enjoy seeing their daughter and granddaughter grow up together. They were determined not to let Clare's past history deprive them of a close relationship with her and their granddaughter.

After Verona's birth, Clare with Gentex's aid, located in the rolling hills northwest of downtown Austin. Upon becoming pregnant, Clare had resigned from her clerical job with the intention of moving to a larger city which provided greater opportunities for a person her age. Clare liked the Austin atmosphere where most of the working people were young adults. Living in Austin afforded her an opportunity to find a job with one of the many tech companies which employed mostly young people about her age. As she and Verona neared their new home for the first time, Clare thought.

"Living here, I might meet a man my age who meets my criterion for a husband."

Gentex had purchased Clare's new ranch style home it was built on a large lot near the top of a hill overlooking a well-formed valley below. From the deck of their new home, they had an unobstructed view of the narrow winding stream which had carved out the valley over the course of thousands of years. The stream itself was bordered by a narrow swath of greenery, made up mostly of trees, which provided the deer and other wild animals cover during the daylight hours. A range of higher hills could be seen in the distance when looking to the west toward the Edwards plateau. The hills around Austin were beautiful, in Clare's opinion they were indeed living in paradise.

The thin top soil in this area of Austin is underlain by a white, chalky, lime based rock sometimes referred to as Austin stone. Many houses in Austin and across Texas are constructed of this material, it is also in demand in other parts of the country because its light yellow-brown creamy color creates a beautiful distinguished and lasting exterior that cannot be duplicated with other materials. Home sites are leveled once they are gouged out of the hillside resulting in a series of flat building pads used for home construction. This technique, which results in a terracing effect, provides one side of most homes with a beautiful scenic view of the hill country. From a distance, one can hardly distinguish the houses from the hillside because the cedar, mesquite, live oak and scrub oak trees, which are native to the area, grow profusely where there is enough top soil. These trees produce a canopy for the homes making them nearly invisible to the naked eye. Deer and other wildlife roam freely throughout the hills and often come into the yards of homes located on them, the wild animals sometimes eat the flowers, gardens and other yard greenery. Although an annoyance they are mostly tolerated and cherished by the residents.

Within a week, Clare found a receptionist job in the Research Department of MyTeeTech, a local technology company, located not far from her new home. She was starting a new career and a new life as a mother.

DARLENE'S STORY

Looking toward the Sabine River from the main road, one could see a tattered house standing on the side of a hill near a winding dirt road. The house was, perhaps, a quarter of a mile from the river itself, yet on the high ground. The decrepit structure served as home for the Strong family. A more frazzled group could not be found anywhere in the State of Texas. Jessie and Gerta had lived in the run down house ever since they decided to start living together some fifteen years earlier. Jessie's dad had owned the property since the great depression, but he had made few repairs or improvements before it passed to Jessie. In addition to Jessie and Gerta the Strong family included four children ranging in age from eight to thirteen years. All the family members were fair skinned and had long blond hair as did Jessie and Gerta.

They were a tight knit group, out of necessity, each of the children attended to their assigned daily chores and helped with extra work when Jessie killed a wild hog or deer for meat to feed the family. The Strong family lived mostly off of the land with Jessie and the boys providing meat with their rifles, snares and traps. Hunting seasons did not exist for the Strong family they hunted whenever they needed meat. The Game Warden intentionally stayed away, knowing they needed to hunt in order to eat, the Strong family relied on his cooperation to sustain themselves. He had no intention of giving them a citation for hunting out of season just because they were hungry.

A wild boar hog can weigh up to three hundred and fifty pounds or more which presented a problem for Jessie and the boys when taken down a long distance from the house. In most cases, the hog had to be dragged from the kill site to a clearing where it could be loaded on a hand cart then hauled to the house to be butchered, cleaned and prepared for storage. Sometimes, the pickup could be driven to the hog's location, when it was near the house and there was an opening through the trees, otherwise hard manual labor was required to convert the dead animal to edible meat.

The house had no electricity or refrigeration their meat was preserved, the old fashioned way, by salting and curing in a smokehouse. This often gave the general area an aroma of burning hickory or oak depending on the type of meat being cured. Their neighbors always knew when Jessie and the boys had made a kill, the telltale emissions from the smokehouse drifted downwind for several miles spreading the news that they were curing meat. The only store bought-meat the Strong children ate was that served at the school cafeteria. They ate it, but found it to be inferior to the wild meat Gerta served at home.

Originally, Jessie was the top cowhand in the cattle operations for the nearby Dalton Ranch, an eight thousand acre layout, owned by the Dalton family in Dallas. Years of declining cattle prices convinced the Daltons that ranching was more trouble than profitable, as a result, they sold their cattle herd and leased their land to a local rancher. Jessie would have been out of a job had not the Daltons decided to keep the ranch house, along with the lake, as a family weekend retreat. They kept Jessie on as a caretaker, he not only maintained the property he also became their servant when they scheduled visits and events at the ranch. The Strong boys helped, mowing the grass, painting, doing any other odd jobs to maintain the ranch house and keep the place functional for the Daltons and their guests. Neither Jessie, nor the boys liked working at the ranch house they much preferred hunting, trapping and fishing. Just being in the woods made them happy it had the feel of mystery and adventure invigorating and exciting them. There was never a dull moment in the woods, anything could happen, and often did, such as the time Jessie stepped into a swarm of copperheads. His high topped boots were all that saved him from being bitten multiple times before he beat the entire swarm which numbered more than thirty snakes, to death with a long makeshift club he fashioned from a large sapling. The Dalton's arrangement provided Jessie and Gerta with a steady, though meager, income to buy clothes and other necessities, such as flour and propane, which couldn't be gleaned from the land.

The Daltons needed a way to communicate with Jessie for scheduling their visits and for him to report on his progress in performing his duties as caretaker. He often needed to purchase supplies and materials to maintain the property and to provide for their comfort when they came to the ranch for a weekend. They decided to provide Jessie with a new battery operated wireless telephone, which he was required to keep with him at all times, for their convenience. Jessie recharged the batteries at the ranch house always keeping a charged spare with him when he left for the day. Jessy's cell phone became the Strong family's first method of direct communication with the authorities in case of an emergency. Before the advent of Jessie's wireless phone, they would have had to drive or walk to the nearest neighbors' house to use their telephone in case of an emergency.

The Strong children attended school catching the bus at its stop, on the paved road at the top of the hill, then riding to Joaquin where the school was located. The routine was burdensome for Darlene, yet she enjoyed going to school, while there, she could be with other girls her own age who talked about things not mentioned at home, such as dating and fashionable dresses. She was very interested in learning about other places and other cultures. Travelling to foreign places became her hidden dream, while attending school became her escape, a haven from her onerous life at home. Being an only daughter was difficult and lonely for Darlene, she could not talk with her mother, Gerta, about her concerns and girl things is general.

Near the end of her senior year in high school, Darlene told her mother she planned to find a job in town. She liked her family, but she did not want to live like they did, nor did she want to get married just to become mired in her mother's lifestyle. She had tried to discuss the subject with her mother more than once, unfortunately, her mother did not understand why she was so dead set on moving away and living in a big city. These failed attempts to communicate only reinforced Darlene's determination to make a better life for herself. Darlene looked at herself in her small mirror thinking.

"You sure are not a great physical beauty, a bit chunky with oversized arms and short legs, but I like those brilliant green eyes and that long straight blond hair."

She laughed, realizing her straight golden blond hair complemented her green eyes making her a striking young woman to behold despite her other physical shortcomings.

Upon graduating from high school, Darlene took a job as cashier at the Uptown Café located on Main Street in downtown Joaquin she moved her meager belongings into a single room she rented from a widow woman. At first, she kept to her room, but in a short time she and the widow became fast friends the two of them shared the entire house except for their bedrooms which remained private. They watched television together, discussed the local news and gossip, and discussed their problems and aspirations. Each of them enjoyed the other's company immensely they shared a mutual affection for one and other. Working at the Uptown Café for six years, allowed Darlene to accumulate a few nice dresses, a good winter coat, a small bank account, and a used Volkswagen. Otherwise, she was not much better off than when she took the job, there were no better paying jobs at the café, or in town for that matter. She visited her family once or twice each month delivering ten percent of her monthly pay to Gerta to help buy supplies for the family. They always needed ammunition to hunt and propane for the cook stove.

She and the widow woman often talked about the dead end of opportunity for a single woman in Joaquin.

"Darlene, the only solution I can come up with is for you to marry a rich man."

"The only problem with that is, where am I going to meet a rich man?"

37

They laughed at the idea since there were no single rich men in town, anyway.

When the widow woman read about the Gentex Research program in the Sunday newspaper, her first thought was of Darlene's limited opportunities in Joaquin and what it could mean to her. The widow was hesitant to bring up the subject because of the companionship and pleasure Darlene brought into her house and life. Darlene filled the void of loneliness that came after the death of her husband, this was not something that she wanted to give up, but in the end her desire to help Darlene won out. Tuesday morning, she handed Darlene the article about Gentex Research and their upcoming program. Once Darlene had completed reading the article, the widow said.

"Darlene, I think you should consider applying to participate in this program."

Darlene was surprised by the widow's remark responding.

"What makes you think they would accept me?"

"Well, you fit all the requirements listed in this ad, so you ought to apply. Who knows, you may be just what they are looking for!"

"If it will make you happy, I'm going to apply. What was that phone number?"

Darlene called the Gentex number listed in the paper and was pleasantly surprised when the gentleman on the other end of the line asked for her mailing address saying, "You seem to fit our requirements, I'll put your application in the mail today."

Following intensive screening by Gentex and a thorough investigation into her background, Darlene was selected to be one of the final four for the Gentex project. She was relieved when all the papers had been signed and she was officially one of the participants. Although Darlene did not understand all the technical points, she was more than willing to have a child as part of the program in exchange for the economic benefits that came with it. She liked children.

"It will be great to raise one of my own", she thought as she envisioned living in her own home with a steady income far greater than she had ever experienced or expected to make in Joaquin. She had no objection to becoming a single mother without benefit of knowing the child's father or his identity.

Darlene emerged from the delivery room the mother of a blond haired, blue eyed, baby boy who weighed an even nine pounds, a rather large baby for someone of her size and stature. All was well with Darlene, she was in good shape physically and delighted that her baby was a boy. She had grown up with three brothers, so she knew a lot about young boys and their behavior. The entire experience of artificial insemination and birthing a baby without having sex, had seemed unnatural to her, it was a weird dream that came true. Darlene dismissed any feeling of misgiving about the method of conception naming her new boy Alan Charles Strong.

Darlene and Alan moved into the new fully furnished home purchased for them by Gentex, their new home was located in a new housing development on the southern outskirts of Dallas near the neighboring town of Waxahachie. The home had three bedrooms, one of which, was outfitted as a nursery for Alan. There were bright pictures of playing children painted on the walls and boxes of new toys filled one of the three large closets. A new modern baby bed, located near the windows, dominated the room. Darlene had never seen anything like it in her entire life such beds could not be bought in Joaquin. Most things a mother would want were provided including separate closets for the toys, bedding and clothing, and another for supplies such as Pampers. At first sight, Darlene knew she and Alan were going to be happy living here, it was the nicest house she had ever seen from the inside.

Darlene's parents and brothers had no idea what had happened to her even though she had explained the Gentex program to them as best she could. Once Alan was born, she called her dad to let them know she was all right and that he and Gerta were the grandparents of a beautiful new grandson. The Strong family was bewildered, yet happy to hear Darlene was doing well with a new baby, a new home and, most of all, a good steady income. The fact that she had a baby without being married was a non-issue in the family no one brought it up or gave it a second thought. The widow read Darlene's letter with delight, she was happy for Darlene and her new son they would be happy and prosperous because Darlene participated the Gentex program. She called Darlene right away after reading the letter, she could hardly wait to talk with Darlene even if it was on the phone rather than face to face.

"Darlene, because of Gentex, you and your son Alan will have a good life. I'm happy for you both."

Darlene responded grateful to hear from her dear friend the widow.

"Without your friendship and insistence on me calling Gentex, I would not have been in their program and I would not have this beautiful baby, I cannot thank you enough for contributing to my good fortune. Alan and I will always love you for helping to make this happen."

Darlene never forgot the widow's friendship, she paid her long visits each time she journeyed to Joaquin to visit her family. The widow marveled at the beautiful blond boy they had created she took some of the credit calling herself his second grandmother. She and Darlene stayed in touch exchanging letters and phone calls until the widow's death several years later.

Once Darlene established her monthly cost of living, she began sending her parents $500 every month to help make their life a little easier as they grew older. She and Alan managed to visit two to three times a year, Darlene felt it was important for Alan to know his grandparents and uncles, since they were the only family he had outside of herself.

PEGGY'S STORY

Abilene is best known as the home of three Christian denominational universities, Abilene Christian (Church of Christ), Hardin-Simmons (Baptist) and McMurry (Methodist). The city was originally planned as a new town on the frontier west of Ft. Worth, its primary purpose was to serve as a cattle loading center on the railroad which had bypassed the existing settlement of Buffalo Gap located twenty miles away. Over the years the population of Abilene grew to nearly 100,000 people aided by extensive oil and gas operations in area and the location of an Air Force base nearby.

In spite of the large contingent of oil workers and military personnel in the area, Abilene was a "dry" city, no alcoholic beverages could legally be sold within the city limits, except in private clubs, which were exempt under the law because they were open to members only and not to the public. Those ordinary Abilene residents who wanted to buy beer for home use, or for a party, had to drive forty miles to reach the County Line liquor store which was located in the next county to make their purchases. Most users, as they were called in Abilene, took turns with friends in driving to the County Line to buy beer and other beverages for the group. These mini-coops were organized to save on time and gasoline for the members.

In 1960 a business man named Dallas Perkins incorporated his chicken farm and twenty seven acres located nearby to create the village of Impact located just outside of the Abilene city limits. The city of Abilene, fearing Impact might go "wet", appealed its validity in the State courts. After a ruling by the Texas Supreme Court upholding the incorporation, Impact, which had a population less than one hundred people, voted "wet" allowing the sale of alcoholic beverages within the city limits. During 1963 two liquor stores opened in quick succession. Pinky's, the most renown of the two, was owned by Mr. Perkins and his associates.

James Wilkerson was glad to see the liquor stores open, the long periodic drives to the County Line were no longer necessary, he became a frequent customer at Pinky's buying Coors beer by the case and an occasional six-pack of Lone Star for his wife. James worked as an accountant for a nationally known oil company in their district office located on North Willis Street. Originally from Louisiana, James did not like living in Abilene he hated its dust storms which without warning turned the sky red and deposited red dust all over and into everything. Another thing that really bothered James about Abilene was the crank calls he got at home in the evenings. He didn't know what to think the first time he received one of these calls, when he answered the phone about 9:00 p.m. on a Thursday evening, the caller inquired.

"Is this Mr. James Wilkerson?"

"Sure is. What can I do for you?"

"The bible forbids the use of alcohol. If you continue your evil ways using spirits, you will be damned and sent to straight to hell. Give up your evil habit now before it is too late!"

It took James almost a year before he learned not to throw beer cans or bottles in the trash, otherwise, he would get these irritating calls at night. The trash pickup crews were dedicated members of the Church of Christ who adamantly opposed the use of alcohol. They routinely noted the names and addresses of those people depositing liquor bottles or beer cans in their trash. These names were later furnished to their fellow evangelical church members who made nightly calls in the hope of convincing the alcohol users to give up their evil ways. His neighbor, an Abilene native and staunch member of the Church of Christ, was always preaching to him about drinking, so just for the hell of it, James started putting his beer bottles in his neighbor's trash late Wednesday evenings after the sun had gone down. He smiled as he eased each beer bottle into his neighbor's trash barrel he could almost hear the phone lectures his asshole neighbor received the next evening.

His daughter, Peggy Rae, was born at the Medical Center with no undue complications for either the mother or baby. She was the first of three children born to James and Joan, over the next three years, Tammy and June were added to the Wilkerson family. Peggy, being the oldest, set the standards for the Wilkerson girls, she loved people and enjoyed doing things with them she laughed constantly with an infectious laugh which caused those around her to laugh as well. In school, Peggy moved along in the middle of the class, neither excelling nor falling behind, she always had a good time no matter what was going on around her. In high school, she was popular and dated some, but never had a steady boyfriend like most of her friends. The guys liked Peggy Rae, she joked and laughed all the time and was a fun girl to be with, but she was no beauty just an average looking girl with a big smile and a winning personality.

By the time she reached college age, Peggy had dropped the Rae and was known simply as Peggy. After graduating from high school, Peggy left Abilene for Dallas where she planned to work part time and enroll in Richland College to continue her education. Her ultimate plan was to graduate from Texas A&M with a BS degree in Business. Upon arriving in Dallas, her most pressing problem was to find a part time job which paid enough to support her and still have money for tuition, books and other college supplies. She had several interviews with retail outlets and soon learned they paid much less than she needed to carry out her educational plan. After a week of searching without success, Peggy changed her tactics and began making inquiries at upscale restaurants with large bars hoping to get a job as a part time barmaid.

She found the perfect job at Bobby's Restaurant in downtown Dallas. Bobby's, had a huge bar which was usually packed in the late afternoon and early evening hours with diners and non-diners alike. It was a favorite destination for downtown professionals who often stopped for a drink or two after work to unwind following a tedious day at the office. Peggy found the big advantage of working at Bobby's was she was paid a fixed salary and she was allowed to keep all of her tips which turned out to be more or equal to her weekly paycheck. The bar manager was happy to set her work schedule to accommodate her attending Richland. As an accommodation to meet her school schedule, Peggy worked from 5 p.m. until 10 p.m. five days a week from Monday through Friday. Once acclimated into the work-school routine, Peggy was happy with her life in Dallas. She was doing well in school and enjoyed working at Bobby's bar talking and joking with everyone there and having a good time while paying for her college education. She also received a free evening meal on those nights she was on duty which saved time for studying and the expense of providing a meal for herself. "It's fantastic," she thought as she prepared to leave for work at the beginning her second month at Bobby's.

Peggy became the favorite of all the waitresses at Bobby's bar, many of the regulars looked forward to seeing her every day, being a part of the cheer and laughter that surrounded her was enjoyable and relaxing. They forgot their problems of the day when she was laughing with them, happiness followed her wherever she went. John, one of the regular bar patrons, waived his hand in the air to get her attention.

"Peggy, please bring us another round. Put this one on my tab. Will you?"

She returned with five drinks even though there were only four of them at the table.

John looked at Peggy for a moment then asked in a loud voice.

"What is this for?"

"Since you bought the last two rounds, I thought you deserved a tip."

They all laughed as John stood up and performed a make believe tip of his hat to Peggy who laughed with the others at his antics. At the end of their drinking session, each of the guys gave her an enormous tip in appreciation of the service and the happy atmosphere Peggy created.

All of this merriment and lavish spending was not lost on the bar manager, he concluded shorty after she came to work that Peggy was one of those rare people who made everyone feel good and that she was a gold mine for the bar. Over time, more and more regulars came in after work. They enjoyed Peggy's company as much, or more, than their drinks and most were big spenders, very good for business. The manager called her aside one evening following an extraordinary spending spree by the regulars saying.

"God, Peggy, I don't know how you do it, we have more business when you are on duty than I have witnessed in all the time I have managed the bar. Whatever it is, please keep it up."

"Oh, Ron, it's nothing special. I'm just laughing with the guys and being me."

Peggy never thought of herself as being special or outstanding just one of the crowd. She was doing well in her studies at Richland and was happy that her grades were slightly above average in all of her classes because she had never been a scholastic standout in high school. Toward the end of her second year, she had essentially achieved her goal at Richland. In a short while, it would be time to move on to Texas A&M University in College Station to complete her degree. Even though she loved her job, she would be leaving Bobby's bar behind to find another job in College Station or Bryan.

Peggy discussed her plans with Ron, the bar manager, with whom she had become close friends she trusted his judgment and wanted to enlist his help in finding a job when she left for A&M. To her surprise, Ron proposed a completely wild, far out alternative he handed her a Gentex brochure outlining their search for young single women to participate in a long term genetic study.

"I don't know the details surrounding this study, but listen to this, it provides for a lifetime income and other benefits for those selected to participate."

"That sure sounds interesting, Ron, I wonder what would be required for me to get in the program!"

"I don't know, but think what the program could mean to you. Why don't you call these people to see if you qualify?"

"Let me see. Is there a telephone number in there somewhere? I'm going to call them today, Ron. Thanks, this could turn out to be a great opportunity for me."

"Peggy, you have nothing to lose, you might be just right for their program. If you make the team, you will have plenty of money to complete your degree without having to work at all. If not, we can always find a job for you later."

44

The Gentex application form came in the mail at her apartment two days following her phone call. Peggy filled out the questionnaire and application mailing them back the next day. To her surprise, she received a phone call from a Gentex representative two weeks later asking her to visit a company doctor's office the next day for some preliminary tests. A week later a Gentex representative called saying that she was definitely qualified for their program and that they were nearing their final selections.

When the phone rang, Peggy though it was Ron, but it became obvious the voice on the phone was not his it was a Gentex representative requesting a face to face meeting the following day. He explained that she would be one of their final selections, provided, she agreed to the last part of their program, which he was required to review with her personally. The Gentex representative arrived at her apartment, as scheduled, on Saturday. Upon answering the doorbell, Peggy's heart skipped a beat before she asked him inside. She poured him a hot cup of coffee before he started explaining the contract requirements to her in detail going over several of them twice to make sure she understood.

The idea of having a baby by artificial insemination, without being married, had never entered Peggy's mind. Her initial reaction was to reject the proposal on the spot. Sensing her resistance the Gentex representative said.

"Please consider our proposal overnight before making up your mind then call me in the morning. This is the only remaining requirement for you to become one of our final selections to participate in our program."

Peggy spent a sleepless night agonizing over whether or not she should, or would, join the program. She called the Gentex representative early the next morning accepting their proposal.

Then she called Ron.

"Can you believe it? I have been accepted into Gentex's program my money problems to complete my degree have been resolved."

"Congratulations, Peggy. I'm glad it worked out for you."

"I thank you, Ron, for all you have done for me. Without you, I would never have known the program existed. I'll love you until I die!"

"Don't let my wife hear that she's the jealous type. Seriously, Peggy, let's keep in touch."

A huge storm produced lightning and thunder during Bruce Raymond's delivery, Peggy could not have cared less. Her main concern was that her son was here and in good shape with all of his limbs where they were supposed to be. Much to her relief, he was crying and healthy. She was OK, although a bit tired, she was relieved that it had gone so easily for she had feared the worst. There was no anxious father outside in the waiting room, still she was elated as this cute little fellow wiggled in her arms. His black hair was curly and long which with his blue eyes gave him a look somewhat like Peggy when she was an infant. Her parents looked on Bruce Raymond with reserved approval it did not seem right to them for Peggy to have a baby without being married.

"He is such a sweet child, but it is so strange not to have a father here," volunteered her mom as she and James stood side by side outside the viewing room.

"He is still our grandson, whether we like it or not, he is going to have our name, so it counts how we accept him. Let's do it right, it's not his fault he's a bastard. As you well know, there have always been a lot of bastards born in Louisiana, so one more born in Texas won't make any difference."

"He is such a beautiful baby. James, don't you ever call him a bastard again! I won't put up with it! Do you hear me?"

"Woman, this was Peggy's choice. I didn't like it when she made it and I still don't like it, but we have to make the best of things as they are."

There were two things James Wilkerson was not going to do, alienate his daughter or abandon his grandson. He declared out loud to himself and his wife Joan.

"They are family, that's all that counts!"

As Peggy's parents entered her room, she was glowing, happy to see them and grateful they accepted her decision to join the Gentex program. It was clear they wanted to be a part of her and her son's lives. Bruce's birth status was not mentioned by either James or Joan during their visit, or at any time thereafter. They were a family.

Peggy did not enroll at A&M in the fall as she had originally anticipated, rather she moved to Houston where Gentex's purchased a three bedroom home for her and Bruce it was located in a gated community just off of Memorial Drive in far west Houston. She decided to take two years off to be with Bruce before returning to school to complete her degree. Peggy made a point to meet all the nearby neighbors on her street talking to them regularly on a first name basis. Both the women and their husbands enjoyed her company she made them laugh and feel good about themselves. She was universally liked by her neighbors because of her outgoing nature and friendly personality.

There were few single people living in the neighborhood most of her neighbors were married parents who had selected the area because of the five superior schools located nearby. Peggy didn't go out much at night, she disliked leaving Bruce with a nanny, or a babysitter she took him with her wherever she went. With the passage of time, Peggy became more and more pleased with her decision to join the Gentex program she enjoyed Bruce marveling at how fast he changed as he grew. First, he learned to crawl and then to walk, after that he was a bundle of energy demanding all of her attention. She loved little Bruce he made her exceedingly happy. She had no misgivings about her decision, Bruce was the center of her life.

RACHEL'S STORY

Rachel was delighted upon learning she had been selected by Gentex Research to be a part of their genetic study. She was so excited she hugged the Gentex representative kissing him on the cheek while repeating.

"Thank you. Thank you."

Unable to believe her good fortune, Rachel kept reminding herself she was awake, and it was true. At age twenty-three, Rachel was going to have her own baby a desire which she had considered unachievable just a few months earlier. The economic advantages which came with the Gentex package were secondary to Rachel they were never a consideration in her decision to enter the program. Her sole motivation was to become a mother, to have he own child to love and cherish, to give to another what the Schubers had given to her.

"I am so glad God has chosen me!"

In her happiness, she thought.

"Can it be possible, at long last, to put aside the memory of the *no mas* I uttered in horror so many years ago?"

Her mind drifted to the tarp covered truck bed she and her four brothers shared with her parents as a home while picking tomatoes in the fields

47

of Indiana. They and her uncle's family of six, plus four others, had traveled from the Rio Grande Valley to the tomato fields of northeastern Indiana for the summer harvest. Uncle Hector, was *el jefe* of the group, he made all the arrangements with the farmers, collected all the money and distributed it to the pickers keeping a small part for his services. He also determined their assignments to the various farms each day and how many hours they would work. Each worker was paid on a piece work basis at the rate of two cents per crate of tomatoes picked, so the faster they worked the more money they made each day. It was backbreaking work, but efficiency paid off.

Rachel was eight years old, not yet strong enough to pick tomatoes all day, her job was to watch the trucks and the family's meager belongings in the encampment while the others were working in the fields. It was an easy job since there had never been an incident or any mischief in the camp over the years they had come to this place. Nevertheless, Rachel took her job seriously, she was vigilant at all times watching for anything out of the ordinary.

She saw her uncle's pickup coming up the lane to the camp and wondered why he would be there in the middle of the day. As the pickup neared, she jumped out of the back of the tarp covered truck bed and rushed to meet him. He laughed as he opened the pickup door motioning for her to come near. He reached toward her saying.

"Little one, you put a smile on your uncle's face, come with me to your truck I have a gift for you."

He lifted her into the truck bed climbing in behind her pulling the tarp together after him. It was still light in the truck, yet a person could not see in from the outside. Uncle Hector, pulled a small beautiful red and white rag doll from his pocket offering it to Rachel who immediately hugged the doll and loved her uncle for giving it to her. She held the doll tight to her cheek feeling very happy and secure in the presence of her loving Uncle Hector.

"Now *Chiquita,* you must do something for me," he said as he slipped his hand between her legs and removed her underwear. At first she was not overly alarmed by his actions, it was not until he pulled down his trousers and began to rub her with his large stiff penis that she guessed something was terribly wrong! She had never seen one this size before only those small ones on the young boys. He spread her legs then put his organ against her and began to push, gently at first, then harder as it began to enter her. She screamed in pain as his pushing became harder and faster then finally it was over. She was in pain, she had been hurt and was tormented by Uncle Hector's brutality.

"How could Uncle Hector do such a thing? How could he hurt me like this?"

She kept saying to herself over and over again.

"N*o mas, no mas.*"

Uncle Hector was not finished with her. After a short rest to rejuvenate, he repeated his attack with much more vigor and brutality. All the while in anguish and fear Rachel silently repeated to herself as Uncle Hector brutally raped her.

"N*o mas, no mas.*"

Then he was gone leaving her in pain, unsure of what might happen next and frightened. Rachel wanted her mama, but she was far away working in the tomato fields. Rachel was confused and angry, even though she was hurting, she tried to put aside the pain thinking.

"I don't want this to ever happen again. What can I do? What can I do?"

Her first thought was to tell her parents, but they were indebted to Uncle Hector for finding them work and he was taking care of them on the trip. Telling them what he had done to her, seemed impossible. Through her tears, it became clear she must somehow get away from Uncle Hector, he had hurt her and she was afraid he would do it again and again because he liked it. She decided to leave, to run away, as soon as possible, but to get away she would need money. She knew Uncle Hector kept cash in his covered truck because she had seen him put money is a small box under the seat on more than one occasion. The truck door was unlocked and after searching for a few minutes, her fingers grasped the money box which she deftly opened. It contained sixty five dollars in small bills with a couple of tens, she didn't dare take all of it for fear Uncle Hector would harm her parents once he discovered she was missing along with his money. She stuffed twenty three dollars in her pocket leaving the rest in the money box which she carefully replaced in its hiding place.

Rushing as fast as she could, Rachel ran to her parent's truck, reluctantly climbing back into the covered bed, where she placed her other dress and a pair of pants and socks in a brown paper bag. She then climbed down and began her long walk to the bus station in Muncie where she bought a one way ticket to Indianapolis. Within three hours of the "*no mas*" incident, she was gone riding the bus into the unknown safely away from Uncle Hector.

"Uncle Hector will not come looking for me or the money for fear I will tell the police what he has done. Then it could not be kept a secret from my parents and once they know, papa will have to kill him. So I must leave," she thought as she laid her head on the space between the seat back and the bus window. Even though the pain had subsided, she tried not to think about what had happened to her, but she kept reliving the pain and torment, still not understanding why Uncle Hector had done this horrible thing to her.

"I hate him! I was happy with a loving family and now that is gone, I am alone and will have to take care of myself as best I can."

Rachel was no longer the eight year innocent she had been yesterday, today she was a frightened eight-year-old woman alone.

She got off of the bus in Indianapolis, not knowing what to do next, she followed the other passengers into the bus station where she looked around before sitting on one of the wooden benches in the waiting area. As chance would have it, this was one of the most significant random decisions Rachel would make in her lifetime. From a small snack area, a middle aged woman happened to glance in her direction and was struck by the beauty of the young Mexican girl sitting alone on the bench. She watched Rachel for several minutes before concluding that the girl was, indeed, alone and seemed to be distressed and possibly lost. After a few more minutes of observing the young Mexican girl, Martha, who was a loveable big hearted woman, made contact with the girl thinking she might be of some help.

"Good afternoon young lady. My name is Martha. I noticed that you are alone, so I was wondering, would you like to join my husband and me for a small snack at our table over there? It will be good for you and we can talk if you like."

Rachel was more than a little surprised by this woman's invitation, which made her feel better, but she was leery of talking to an Anglo stranger because of her circumstances. She reluctantly agreed to accompany the seemingly good woman to her table for a snack. She was hungry and scared of what might happen to her next.

"I am Rachel Garcia. Thank you. I am hungry and I would like very much to join you for a snack."

Martha reached out her hand to Rachel helping her up from the bench. She did not release Rachel's hand, instead, she held it reassuringly in her own while they walked to the snack area.

"My husband and I are from Texas. We have been to my only sister's funeral and will start driving back to Texas once we are sure that my nephew has boarded his bus to Ft. Wayne. My husband, Burt, is putting him on the bus right now, or within a few minutes, depending on when the bus get here."

"This is so strange, I am from Texas too." Replied Rachel looking wide-eyed at Martha as though she had made a heartwarming discovery.

Martha was not surprised to hear Rachel was from Texas most of the seasonal workers in this part of the country were Texas Mexicans. She ordered a snack, consisting of two pieces of cheese and a glass of milk, for Rachel making sure to pay in advance to keep Rachel from spending any of her own money. The two of them talked at length about thing they liked to do.

"One thing Burt and I really like is being around children. We never had any of our own."

"There are four boys and me in our family, I am the youngest."

"What is your favorite thing to do, Rachel?"

"I like to read, but we never had many books. I read whatever I can find, usually what someone has thrown away."

"Where do you come from, Rachel?"

"My family is from Rio Grande City, I am trying to get back to Texas, but I probably don't have enough money to buy a ticket all the way there."

Rachel knew she could not go back to Rio Grande City because her uncle would be returning there as well, but she had no idea what to do next. Martha liked this young Mexican girl more and more as they talked, she was fascinated by her straight forward approach to life in a world she was hardly old enough to understand.

Martha and Burt Schuber had always wanted children, unfortunately, none were conceived, so there were none. They did not consider

51

adoption until after they were much too old to qualify under the rules. There were no rules governing people having children no matter how unqualified they might be to raise and provide for those children. For those wanting to adopt, it was different, the governmental agencies made it difficult for older couples to adopt without regard to their qualifications or ability to provide a good home for the child or children. In their case, this quirk in the law prove to be counterproductive, both Martha and Burt had an affinity for children and they possessed the means to provide a good life for them. Children who knew the Schubers wanted to be around them as much as possible they were fun and made them feel important, loved and wanted. The fact that the Schubers were good role models made no difference they were too old to adopt.

Martha wanted to know why Rachel was travelling alone on such a long trip prompting her to ask.

"Rachel, why are you travelling alone? Don't you have family here in Indiana?"

Rachel could hardly believe herself as she replied.

"I am alone because my uncle attacked me this morning, if I tell my parents, papa will kill him then the whole family will be lost. I don't want that to happen and I can't stay. So I left."

Martha was outraged to hear Rachel had been attacked that very day by her uncle. The thought of a relative attacking a child, angered her to the point she muttered under her breath, "That bastard." At the same time, Martha rationalized that Rachel was a young girl who in spite of her own hurt was thinking of those she loved when she decided to run away. Although they would experience anguish over losing a daughter, her family would be better off than had she stayed. At that moment, Martha decided she must help this beautiful Mexican child, no matter the future consequences.

"Rachel, this is not the end of the world even though you are hurt, confused and angry because of what happened today."

Rachel put her arms around Martha squeezing her tight saying.

"Thank you. Thank you for your kindness."

Martha put her arms around Rachel patting her tenderly before she replied.

"Every day you spend being unhappy is a day of your life wasted."

Martha then held Rachel tight against her bosom while whispering with tears in her eyes.

"Rachel. If you are willing, from this day forward, I will take care of you as my daughter. What do you say, Rachel? Shall we do it?"

"Yes, I would like to be your daughter."

Before Rachel finished eating her snack, Burt returned announcing that Martha's nephew had just departed. He introduced himself to Rachel as though he expected to find someone at the table when he returned. Martha explained briefly what had happened while he was taking Jimmy to catch the Ft. Wayne bus. He nodded and smiled a few times looking at Rachel while listening to the saga of the day's events. When Martha finished, Burt said.

"OK, Martha, Rachel, let's get in the car and go home to Orange Grove, Texas."

What a turn of events in the life of Rachel, she had been raped twice, stolen money from her uncle, ran away leaving her family, was found by a couple who wanted her and was on her way to Texas in a car all in less than eighteen hours. Rachel never forgot her family, although she never saw them again, nor did she return to Rio Grande City in search of them.

The three of them arrived in Orange Grove three days later. Burt and Martha took turns driving during the trip home making it a leisurely drive with stops for food and fuel as well as sightseeing and a motel room at night. Rachel loved it, she had never been on a trip in a car as a passenger, she and her family had always ridden in the back of a covered truck, filled with themselves and several others, making the journey crowded and unpleasant. The only scenery they saw was out of the flap on the back of the tarp covered truck bed and when the truck stopped for gasoline. At that time, all the passengers unloaded to go to the restroom and to stretch before reentering the crowded truck bed to resume the trip.

The Schubers owned a 160 acre farm located just off of a paved farm to market road about one and a half miles to the north of Orange Grove. Their farm was small by Texas standards, yet it was no ordinary farm, it had four oil wells located on it producing a total of 150 barrels of oil per day. Burt retained a one eighth royalty interest when he leased the farm to an oil company for drilling, meaning the Schubers received one eighth of the value of the oil produced from the farm. They paid none of the cost of drilling or production only their share of the 4.6% of the gross value of the oil produced paid to the State in production taxes. Their royalty income allowed the Schubers to live a comfortable middle class life with little disruption due to poor crops or lack of other income.

Martha enrolled Rachel Garcia as a fourth grade student in the local school listing herself and Burt as guardians. Everyone in the community accepted the fact that Rachel had come back from Indiana to live with the Schubers after Martha's sister's funeral. No other explanation was offered, or expected, thereafter, Rachel was a part of the social fabric of Orange Grove where she quickly made new friends and became one of the best liked and outstanding young girls in the community. As the years passed, Rachel, and the Schubers enjoyed their life together very much, they loved each other dearly. Rachel became the child Martha and Burt had always wanted with their love and guidance she exceeded their wildest dreams. Rachel excelled in school, helped Martha with work around the house, learned to cook and helped Burt with the daily chores and above all returned their love many times over. For Rachel, life with Martha and Burt became her greatest learning experience, an unexpected pleasure, she loved and admired both of them. Becoming a part of their lives was akin to going to heaven without having to die first, she could not have been happier.

The beautiful young Mexican girl that Martha first met remained a strong willed and determined person as she gradually acquired the characteristics of a middle class young lady with a stable family who loved her. Martha and Burt provided Rachel the opportunity to become educated a station unreachable before she accidentally met the Schubers. She not only accepted her good fortune in becoming their surrogate daughter she embraced it with a ravenous desire to assimilate into their lives and culture. By her eighteenth birthday, Rachel had graduated from high school in the upper ten percent of her class and, in addition, she was voted the most popular person in school. She was a stunning, well-spoken, beautiful young woman with a magnificent body and an air of self-sufficiency and determination that characterized her personality.

In the fall she enrolled in the Engineering School at Texas A&I, located in Kingsville, Texas, where she became a sensation on campus because of her intellect and stunning beauty. Few women chose to enter the Engineering School, one of the more demanding disciplines offered at A&I, an extensive understanding of advanced mathematics and science are required to pass the curriculum courses needed to obtain a degree. The male students and a few of the professors appreciated her statuesque beauty each lusting for her in their own way, but to no avail. Rachel kept a charming and reserved distance between those interested males and herself. She remained an elusive and unattainable beauty the entire four years she spent at A&I while working toward her BS degree in Petroleum and Natural Gas Engineering. Rachel went to dances and other function involving both males and females. She was a favorite of the males with whom she danced and shared conversational interests she had an all-around good time while attending college, except there was no dating. Female students welcomed Rachel to their midst, she was a happy person with an outgoing personality who added something unique to any gathering. At the same time, she did not make them feel insecure or threatened she was not competing for the attention of their boyfriends, or the other single males present at their gatherings.

By the middle of the first semester, it became apparent in the Petroleum and Natural Gas Engineering School that to place in the upper portion of the class one had to study hard because Rachel excelled in every facet of the curriculum. The big question in the Engineering School and across the spectrum of the males on campus was.

"How can she be so damned sexy, good looking and so smart?"

They all agreed as did their female counterparts.

"It wasn't fair!"

Rachel graduated with a BS degree in Petroleum and Natural Gas Engineering at the age of twenty two accepting a position with an oil company in Corpus Christi where she later learned of the Gentex project. Rachel was sure she wanted to participate in the program upon reading their brochure. Before applying to participate, she made a trip to Orange Grove to discuss the project with Burt and Martha their approval was important to her. She had made up her mind to apply, but only if they approved. Her concern proved to be unwarranted, Burt and Martha not only approved they were very supportive encouraging her to follow her dreams and to be happy no matter what. Martha repeated the Schuber precept which Rachel had heard many times since their first meeting in Indianapolis.

"Every day you spend being unhappy is a day of your life wasted."

During her years with the Schubers, Rachel had come to believe in being happy which reinforced her decision to join the Gentex program. Upon her acceptance, Rachel told the Schubers she had been thinking of legally changing her name to Rachel Donna Schuber. She had obtained a copy of her birth certificate from the Gentex representative when she signed her contract with them. With their consent, she planned to make the name change official when she returned to Corpus Christi. The Schubers were overcome with happiness at Rachel's revelation.

"This is the most wonderful gift you could ever give Burt and I," cried Martha as they all embraced. One month later, Rachel Donna Garcia legally became Rachel Donna Schuber in honor and respect for the couple who had made her a part of their family and given her a new life.

Rachel named her baby girl Martha Rachel Schuber, she was a dark haired, light skinned little bundle of Joy with large liquid brown eyes and an infectious smile. She laughed and smiled much more than she cried, little Martha was a happy baby from the onset of her life. Rachel could not have been more pleased she loved to cradle Martha in her arms and to feel the squirming little warm person next to her breast. It was her dream come true, Rachel found it difficult to realize that it had really happened, she had her own baby and was a mother. The first thing Rachel did, once she and Martha could travel, was to take little Martha to Orange Grove to introduce her to Martha and Burt. Martha was enthralled with the baby she could not hold her enough. Burt was equally enamored with their granddaughter, he smiled in adoration every time he held her in his arms. Burt was a happy man, he loved their daughter Rachel and their new granddaughter. Rachel had a loveable daughter who made their lives complete. He held her hand saying.

"Martha and I would never have had a grandchild, if you had not become a part our lives. Rachel, we thank you for your wonderful gift."

Rachel savored every minute of motherhood as if it were the ultimate joy of life itself. Martha saw how happy Rachel was to have her baby girl which nearly made Martha pop with pleasure herself. The Schubers were thrilled to have a granddaughter named Martha born by their beautiful daughter Rachel.

Rachel returned to work six weeks after Martha's delivery, out of necessity, she hired a nanny to take care of Martha during the day while she was away at work. Upon her return to work, her fellow employees greeted Rachel with hugs and congratulations, all of them were glad to have her back in the office. They had missed the affable atmosphere she brought both in private and in company meetings. Among the envious males and curious females there was mass speculation as to who might be the father of Rachel's child, yet no one dared to ask for fear of upsetting her? Everyone knew that one of their fellow employees, Phil Jensen, was seriously attracted to Rachel. He could not refrain from talking about how beautiful she was and how she would be the catch of a lifetime for some lucky guy. But, they had never been seen together, except in the office or the coffee bar where they were always in the company of others. In desperation, one of Phil's friends approached him directly.

"Phil, there has been a lot of speculation since Rachel's pregnancy, we have been wondering, are you the father of Rachel's baby?"

"I wish to hell I were. We have never had a date, much less had sex. I must admit I have thought a lot about both, it hasn't happened. I have no idea who the father could be, unfortunately it's not me. I bet he is one happy guy though."

Rachel told no one she was involved in the Gentex Research program or that she also did not know the identity of her baby's father. She had no need to speculate since she knew in advance the father's identity was unknown even to those doctors working in the Gentex program. None of her friends broached the question because they knew Rachel would not divulge any information she wished to keep private instead they speculated quietly among themselves.

Rachel returned to her duties as an engineer devoting herself to reviewing the company's properties for new development and exploitation. Every day, Phil looked longingly at Rachel, in spite of his feelings for her, he could not bring himself to approach her other than in the course of their interactive work schedule. No matter how hard he tried, Phil could not get Rachel out of his mind he too speculated about the father of her baby, but he did not ask. In spite of her becoming a mother, Phil remained in high spirits because Rachel was still single and unmarried.

By Martha's second birthday, Rachel had built a new home on Ocean Drive using money provided by Gentex she thought Corpus Christi would be a great place for her and Martha to plant permanent roots. The house was built on a small bluff next to Corpus Christi Bay providing an uncluttered view of the morning sun as it peeked over the horizon and slowly began its ascent above the water. Rachel's house was constructed on the bay side of the street giving its occupants a view of the near shoreline and the full expanse of the bay itself. Its most opulent features were a huge picture window looking out over the bay and sliding glass doors that opened onto a large bay side patio. The view was beautiful every day and breathtaking on special days. When the wind calmed the water became crystal clear and flat without a ripple to be seen across the entire expanse of the bay.

Rachel was extremely pleased with the progress she had made following Martha's formula.

"Every day you spend being unhappy is a day of your life wasted."

She had her daughter, Martha, and was ready to broaden her career.

Chapter 3 Cappuccino Romance

Austin turned out to be a perfect location for Clare the city suited her personality while providing great schools and an education dominated environment for Verona. Clare initially went to work for MyTeeTech as a receptionist in the research department. After taking night classes in advanced computer programming and operation for a year, she was promoted to special assistant to the head of research. Her career move not only increased Clare's income it also gave her a better insight into the company's operations and objectives. Her new position put her in direct contact with the young researchers most of whom were male engineering graduates with advanced degrees. The head of research picked Clare as his special assistant because her efficiency as his receptionist had caught his attention and he appreciated her dedication to furthering her education while working full time. He also needed someone with her computer skills to aid him in planning and evaluation of the various programs administered by his department. In a short time, he found her to be brilliant and highly effective in her new assignment, Clare became a prominent figure in the operation of the research group because of her special organizational abilities. Clare kept the department running smoothly with a minimum of problems and interruptions which allowed her boss to concentrate on initiating new ideas to be explored by his engineers. He considered her extraordinary abilities essential to the success of the department and the company.

The younger men viewed Clare through completely different eyes than her boss, in their view, she was an attractive young woman who exuded sex and stirred exotic desires when she smiled at them. Just looking at her raised their testosterone levels and heart rates as they invariably fantasized about having sex with her. These young men could not help themselves, she was devastatingly sexy without trying to be. Clare was a truly beautiful and extremely sexy woman with her long straight black hair, blue eyes, a kinky smile and a lovely sensuous body that flowed as she walked. Her sexy rear end provoked men when they viewed her walking, usually creating mental fantasies of her walking naked on her way to their bedrooms. Clare's walk was tantalizing driving the young males to erotic thoughts of sex as they watched her put one foot in front of the other on her way to anywhere.

After giving birth to Verona, Clare's breasts still stood at full attention they were tantalizing and beautiful to behold she was even more stunning than before Verona arrived. Clare knew from previous experience what was on the minds of these young male professionals, but she was a changed person since joining the Gentex program and the arrival of Verona. She resolved not to make the same mistakes she had in the past, no one night stands, or having sex with someone she didn't love. Until the right one came along, she was not giving in to her impulses, there was Verona to think about she was the most important thing in her life.

Verona was four years old and attending a local Montessori School when Clare first met Ned, he was a new engineer who had been recruited from Apple and had been working at MyTeeTech for only a short time. He joined MyTeeTech as a senior engineer in research designated for their fast track to a management position. Ned had been around for more than a month before he got round to introducing himself to Clare. She was interested the moment he spoke to her there was something about him that turned her libido switch to full on. He wasn't overly good looking, yet he had a mysterious sensual effect on Clare. This had never happened to her before, even when she was swinging it with the opposite sex years earlier, it was a strange almost frightening feeling. During their brief conservation, Clare was having difficulty containing herself, so she just smiled coyly and told him her name.

Ned did not come around again for a couple of weeks. When he did show up, he cheerfully engaged Clare speaking as though they were old acquaintances, maybe even close friends, who had not seen each other for an extended period.

"Hi, Clare how have you been? I'm sorry I missed coming by last week, but I've been out of town on business and couldn't make it!"

"I'm sorry too, it's good to see you again."

Not wanting him to leave, Clare asked coyly raising her voice slightly.

"What was your last name again? I seem to have forgotten."

She finished with a devious little smile which, though unintended, signaled I'm interested. She was thrilled Ned showed a concern for missing her the week before, she was definitely interested in him. He turned her on!

Ned wasted no time making it clear that he had more on his mind than incidental conversation.

"Clare, do you think it would be possible for the two of us to meet for coffee after work?"

Clare's heart was racing as she replied.

"I think we can do that. How about the Starbucks off Research Boulevard at five?"

"I'm looking forward to it, I'll see you there Clare," responded Ned in his unassuming manner.

Clare could not believe what had just happened, she was trembling with excitement her hand was shaking uncontrollably when she tried to open her company email account.

"It's only for a cup of coffee, get Shelia to pick up Verona and keep her for a couple hours after school," she told herself as Ned walked away.

She watched him for a few seconds as he made his way to the exit, his walk excited her even more, she was breathless by the time he disappeared from sight. Clare calmed down, but had difficulty keeping her mind on work the rest of the afternoon she kept thinking about having coffee with Ned and her heart rate increase every time she thought about being with him. He was exciting!

"Let's just play it by ear, don't do anything foolish or stupid," she kept telling herself even though her arousal was clouding her good judgment.

She arrived slightly before five o'clock selecting a table with a view. She purposely did not to order, instead, she waited for Ned to arrive wanting to make a good first impression. Clare definitely did not want him to think she was a self-centered female who thought only of herself, not only that, she wanted him to feel he was needed.

"Good God! What if he is married?" thought Clare, in her excitement the possibility had not occurred to her before.

Ned arrived a few minutes later, he walked in smiling broadly as he made his way to her table.

"Pardon me beautiful lady, is this seat taken?" He asked as he sat down next to Clare.

"Not if your name is Ned," she said smiling her sexy little smile.

"Have you ordered?"

"No, no! I want your advice before making a choice."

Clare was very pleased with herself in the way the opening conversation played out she had planted a paramount thought in Ned's mind, she wanted his advice.

"In that case, let me suggest we have their special cappuccino it's one of my favorites."

"That is exactly what I would have ordered, did you read my mind?"

Ned went to the counter to get their coffees returning to the table in a few minutes carrying two cups of hot special cappuccino. While sipping her coffee, Clare kept looking at Ned her interest growing with every passing moment.

"Ned, I assume that you are single. Is that right?"

"You could not be more correct, I have always been single, but the right person could persuade me to change that sometime. How about you?"

"Well, I am currently single and as you put it, I have always been single. I also could be persuaded to change that, as well, should the right person come along. It seems we have that in common." Said Clare as she studied Ned's reaction.

Clare cautioned herself, "This is getting personal and moving faster than I planned, I had better keep control of myself!" Clare gave a sigh of relief as she said silently to herself. "Thank God, he is available. Play it cool girl. Don't do anything stupid."

They talked and laughed for over an hour, the ease with which they found subjects of mutual interest encouraged them to keep talking on and on they both enjoyed the others presence and conversation. Ned and Clare exchanged bits of information about themselves they rarely revealed to anyone, in this case it felt right. Clare discussed her earlier experiences as a model and a night club singer before becoming a computer geek. The time passed quickly as they talked, to Clare it was clear they could become more than just good friends who worked together.

She decided to set the record straight before she became any more emotionally involved she did not want to suffer heartbreak and disappointment later if the facts turned out to unacceptable to Ned. Clare turned toward Ned speaking softly slightly above a whisper.

"This may be a shock to you, I have a four-year-old daughter named Verona who lives with me. It's not what you might think, she is legitimate, conceived by artificial insemination as part of a voluntary scientific program. Verona and I are permanent participants in the program. Ned, I can't tell you much more than that about the circumstances or the program."

Ned showed no visible reaction to Clare's statement replying in a smooth unaltered tone of voice.

"It must take real commitment for a person to participate in a program like that, I admire you for it. You are a more complicated woman than I realized."

He paused as he thought to himself.

"She's not only beautiful and sexy, but also a complex and interesting woman totally unlike any that I've ever known. Don't let her slip through your fingers. Play it low key."

In the beginning, Ned had been attracted to Clare by her beauty and sensual body now there was much more he liked about her. She was smart and intriguing, a woman he found irresistible, both for her mind and her body an unusual combination he had not often encountered. Ned was fascinated by Clare he found her allure far exceeded his earlier expectations he was totally and completely captivated by her uncommon qualities and rare personality.

Their relationship grew like an aggressive weed over the next few months engulfing them in an affair of growing desire, both yearned for more intimacy and physical interaction, but neither wanted to appear interested in sex alone. Clare laughed a lot while Ned was around, she enjoyed his talking about his work and the world in general. She was happy and carefree being with him, their discussions were diverse touching on many subjects ranging from child care to race horses. Their touching and kissing kindled an unquenchable fire in both of them the flames of passion were raging hotter with every encounter. Containment was an issue testing their restraint to the limit of human endurance, but neither wanted to cross the line for fear of losing the other.

Ned was very good with Verona interacting with her on a child's level often playing games with her for hours on end while spending time with her and Clare on the weekends. He genuinely liked Clare for who she was she excited him in a way other women had never done either mentally or physically. Ned loved this exceptional woman and her daughter, Verona. He could not spend enough time with them. Sometimes, Clare wished he would be a little more forward she wanted him to make sexual contact so much that she considered making the first move herself.

After four years of routine reporting of minor events, Alpha-1 sent its first Red Alert to their contact at Abe.

"Clare has been seeing a fellow named Ned Stanley for four months. Our knowledge of his past is incomplete other than he graduated from UCLA with a master's degree in computer science and formerly worked at Apple. He is now employed at MyTeeTech where Clare works. According to the State records, he is thirty three years old and was born in San Diego, California. Our surveillance team and spying operation indicates Clare and Ned are on the verge of a sexual relationship probably within the next month or so. At this time, marriage appears to be a distinct possibility. You may want to do a comprehensive background and character work up on Ned. In the meantime, we are intensifying our surveillance and will keep you apprised of any new developments or changes."

Abe's reply came early the next day.

"Ned Stanley is a person of good standing we found only one unusual item in his background. To pay his expenses the last two years at UCLA, Ned worked for a male escort service serving the rich and famous from the Los Angles and Hollywood areas. There were no complaints of any kind against him during his employment there he was considered a valuable and outstanding employee. He is clean, Ned Stanley meets Abe's standards. No remedial action required continue your surveillance."

Clare and Ned returned to her home at eleven o'clock on Friday night after sharing dinner at a nearby restaurant specializing in sea food, steaks and wild crazy drinks. They each had two Mexican Martinis, made with *tequila* instead of gin or vodka, these large drinks were served in the shaker rather than in a glass. They contained an extra shot of high quality Mexican *tequila,* designed to loosen up the customer's purse strings and to provide a feeling of comfort, but they also had another side effect. After consuming two of these drinks a person's actions became somewhat erratic and unpredictable. Clare was unleashed after finishing her second drink, she became a young tigress in heat the *tequila* warmed her blood and loosened her control. She urged Ned to skip dessert and to take her home early, the sooner the better. Ned was more than agreeable to Clare's proposal sensing urgency in her voice when she repeated the request in a pleading voice. Once they were in the car, Clare giggled as she draped herself around him with her lips pressed against his. As Ned started the engine, Clare began kissing him on the neck before nestling against him for the drive home. He was a little light headed too, but still managed to drive to Clare's house without running off of the road in spite of her clinging to his body and kissing him repeatedly. Clare sent the baby sitter home as soon as they arrived then checked to make certain Verona was fast asleep in her room. Clare and Ned embraced upon her return from Verona's room, in her uninhibited state, Clare kissed him passionately then giggled before throwing all caution to the wind whispering in his ear.

"Please stay the night. I need you now."

Ned latched the door and without a word from either of them Clare took his hand leading him into her bedroom where they kissed again and again while undressing. Ned moved behind Clare as her panties fell to the floor pressing himself against her back while putting both arms around her. His left hand was on her breast and the other touching her just above her navel on the other side. Caressing Clare delicately with each hand he began kissing her softly on the neck just below her left ear moving his kisses ever so slowly down her neck to her shoulder. Clare became electrified with Ned's every move her whole body tingled at his touch. She suddenly turned facing him, his delicate kissing continued until, Clare, in her excitement, pulled him down on to the bed. Hours later they fell asleep naked with Ned snuggled up to her backside with his right hand on her breast which was still at attention.

When they awoke the next morning in each other's arms they kissed again, then Clare whispered.

"Ned you were absolutely fantastic."

Ned began caressing her gently, but Clare interrupted his foreplay.

"Please don't get me excited we have to stop for now. Verona will be awake soon and she will be hungry I need to prepare her breakfast."

Ned got out of bed and dressed quickly kissing Clare again on his way out. As he drove to his apartment, on the other side of Austin, Ned tried to put the night in perspective.

"We were made for each other. What a beautiful and brilliant woman, she is absolutely fantastic in bed too."

Alpha-1 reported to Abe, "It happened, Ned and Clare had sex last night. He spent the night at her place and left this morning. Our video shows him leaving at 8:35 a.m."

While feeding Verona breakfast, Clare thought to herself half in panic.

"God, I hope the Mexican Martinis didn't make me so crazy that I have scared him away with my impulsive desire to have sex. I almost attacked him last night, what have I done?"

She fretted the rest of the morning not relaxing until she answered the phone and heard Ned's voice.

"Good morning my beautiful, Clare. I had to call, last night was the most wonderful thing that ever happened to me. I want you to know, Clare, I love you."

Clare was so overcome by his statement she had difficulty speaking finally managing to reply.

"I love you too, Ned. We were perfect together. Would you like to come over this afternoon to be with me and Verona? We could have an early dinner here before her bedtime."

Clare tucked Verona into bed then read to her until she fell asleep. Once certain Verona was not going to awake up, she and Ned went to Clare's bedroom locked the door and began undressing. Ned interrupting their kissing, stepped back and while holding Clare at arm's length said.

"Clare, before we start I want to ask you something. Will you marry me?"

"Yes, I love you, Ned. We were meant for each other."

Clare replied pulling him against her waiting body. They were consummate lovers each attending to the needs and desires of the other while enjoying the mutual rapture of two people in love. They fell asleep happy that they had found each other.

Clare and Ned had been married just under two years when she announced beaming.

"Guess what? I am pregnant!"

They were going to have a baby and Verona was going to have a brother or sister. The whole family was enthusiastically looking forward to a new baby in the house. Clare was radiant, as usual, she had a glow about her that was vaguely different. She was so glad she and Ned were having their baby they loved each other and the baby would be a product of that love. This time it would be much different from when she had Verona, Verona had been conceived without love it was an impersonal thing the love came after Verona arrived.

She loved Ned more every day he adored her and was attentive he took great care of both her and Verona. He knew and did the right things at the right times, Ned was a loving husband and a masterful lover, no woman could hope for a more perfect partner to be the father of their child. He loved Verona and was not the least bit upset or concerned about her unorthodox origin. Clare knew from the beginning of their relationship that Ned accepted Verona without reservation. Other than her physical attraction to Ned, his response to Verona's existence had drawn Clare to Ned even more following their first encounter at Starbucks. Verona had been the center of her life before Ned and she did not want her love for Verona to be diminished because she was having their child. Clare was determined to never allow that to happen she loved Verona.

"Had it not been for her, I would probably still be flitting around with no objective or meaning to my life and I would never have met Ned, the love of my life."

Their baby arrived in the fall, Verona was six years old and excited to have a new sister. To her delight she was allowed to hold Angel in her arms once she and her mother came home from the hospital. Clare had no problem bearing another child, but since she was over thirty years old, she doubted she and Ned would be having more children two were probably enough.

Her overriding desire was to become a full time mom to both Angel and Verona, so she decided to become a stay at home mother. Ned was more than supportive, he had wanted her to give up her job when Angel arrived, but out of consideration for Clare's career he had avoided bringing up the subject. Her decision reinforced Ned's conviction that Clare was not only beautiful and fantastic in bed she was also a brilliant mother and wife.

Ned had been promoted to Vice-President at MyTeeTech which was expanding rapidly in the electronic technology business. He felt strongly that Clare was needed at home with the kids, it was his desire to have their children raised by their mother, she would give them the love and guidance they needed since he would be traveling a good part of the time. He and Clare were in full agreement on the subject she happily retired to be a mother to their girls.

Alpha-1 sent a request to Abe.

"Verona will be starting high school next month an event which will increase our surveillance load considerably. We could use help. Is there anything Abe can do to provide more manpower?"

Abe's replied as expected.

"An additional team will be added to your staff before school starts, we are aware of the risks associated with this age group. Verona is your primary assignment her protection comes first she is vital to our program."

"This is going to be a difficult assignment going forward. These teenagers are hard to keep up with and there is no telling what they might do," said Alpha-1's chief speaking to his staff. He continued. "Despite the uncertainty, we cannot lose contact with Verona at any time. Is that clear to everyone?" No one spoke instead they all silently indicated their agreement by nodding their heads.

Shortly after entering high school, Verona became more aware of the sexual attraction between men and women she had observed her parents hugging and kissing when they thought she was not watching, but she had not considered having sex herself. Her mother made a great effort to explain these things to her, so she knew the facts about sex rather than having to rely on the half-truths and myths passed around by her friends. She liked boys and found that she preferred some to others. At one time, she had a crush on one of the younger teachers, but her infatuation passed without incidence when he transferred to another school. Verona was smart, she excelled in mathematics, science and the arts. At her parent's direction she was taking a preparatory curriculum intended for a college bound student.

Half way through her freshman year, Verona met Thomas at a school dance following the final Friday night football game of the season he was a sophomore and a year older than Verona. She was standing by the dance floor with two of her friends when a tall, nice looking boy approached them, to Verona's surprise, he asked her to dance.

"My name is Thomas, could I have this dance?"

"My name is Verona. I am happy to meet you, Thomas. Shall we?"

Thomas was a really good dancer which pleased Verona immensely. She and Clare had practiced dancing, starting when she was eight years old, so she was more than a proficient dancer herself. Thomas and Verona danced several dances, their bodies barely touched, which wasn't necessary dancing the new modern dances popular among the high school kids, still it was exciting for Verona. Thomas was the first stranger who had ever asked her to dance. She got the idea that Thomas asked her to dance because he liked her, which was a new experience for Verona, she had liked certain boys before, but this was the only time a boy showed an interest in her first. She liked it. Her friends were envious they wanted to know what she had done that they were not doing. Verona's explanation was simple and factual.

"I don't think I did anything. I was just standing there, he came up and asked me to dance and I said yes. I don't know, maybe he likes me for some reason, really I don't know why he asked me, whatever. I'm glad he did."

"Are you going to see him again?"

"I think so."

"Did he kiss you?"

"No, we just danced and talked. Why would we be kissing? We just met."

"Are you going to let him kiss you next time?"

"Probably if he wants to," replied Verona with a mystic smile on her face.

She had dreamed of her first real kiss with a boy for a long time, but for her Thomas did not exist before he unexpectedly asked her to dance. It was exciting for Verona to have an interesting boy interested in her. She was sure her mother would not allow her go on a date alone with Thomas, they would have to meet somewhere after school maybe for a treat on the way home. It was arranged the next day, they met at the Dairy Queen after school to share a milk shake. Their drink finished, the two of them sat a while talking about school and their friends before walking down the street together. Upon reaching the dividing point in their homeward routes, Thomas took Verona's hand.

"You know, I really like you, Verona, can we meet again tomorrow?"

"I don't know about tomorrow. We will see."

He kissed her full on the mouth then while walking away said.

"Think about it, see you at school tomorrow."

Verona had barely recovered from his kiss before Thomas disappeared around the corner and was out of sight. She walked briskly the rest of the way home, almost skipping at times, as she thought about Thomas' kiss and what it meant.

"He likes me a lot. This dating is more fun than I thought. I liked being kissed too. It was exciting."

As soon as she arrived home, Verona told Angel about her boyfriend and her first kiss explaining how exciting it was. Angel was eight and beginning to notice boys herself she was happy for Verona.

Verona's first kiss was of concern to Alpha-1. When the operative assigned to Verona reported for the day, he could not help adding.

"She is going to be far harder to keep track of than her mother ever was. She is just starting to fill out in the right places and the boys are going to be flocking around her from now on, I hope we can keep up and keep her safe. For your information, she has not told her mother about Thomas, but she did tell Angel who is going to be another problem for all of us at Alpha-1. Keep your seat belts buckled it's going to be a bumpy ride from here on."

Clare suspected something was going on with Verona she kept coming home later and later after school let out. It was unlike Verona to keep secrets from her, but looking back at herself at this age Clare knew most anything was possible once girls passed puberty. Their whole outlook changed, in fact, their whole world changed from a benign society to one charged with explosive feelings and desires urging them to do things they shouldn't. It was time for them to talk, Verona needed to understand she was not alone in dealing with these new found demons, her friends were experiencing the same things, almost all women had at some time or other.

"Verona, have you been seeing someone after school? I notice that you are getting home later each day."

Verona was reluctant to discuss Thomas and their relationship, but Clare was persistent.

"Verona, you are at an age when everything is changing for you. I only want to help you understand what is happing. Is there anything we should discuss?"

"I have this friend, Thomas whom I like a lot. We have been meeting after school for a treat and sometimes we hold hands and kiss afterwards."

"That's to be expected Verona. Is anything going on that is bothering you?"

"Lately, he has been feeling my breasts and touching my legs. I know I shouldn't allow him to touch me, but I liked it. It makes me feel good all over."

Clare understood exactly what her daughter was going through, she had the same experience at about the same age unfortunately Clare had been unable to discuss anything about sex with her own mother. She hugged Verona holding her in her arms saying gently.

"Dear, Verona, you are unique in most things, but among humans there is a thing called sex that plays a large role in the lives of both women and men. These urges you feel are natural and real, a part of being a woman, sex is also a part of life and love, the ultimate physical pleasure that you can give or receive from the one you love."

"I like Thomas a lot and letting him touch me is exciting. What's wrong with that?"

"Ideally, you should control those sexual desires until you meet that one special person you cannot live without. Verona, women are not meant to remain sexless all of their lives, but I think fourteen is much too early for you to start having sex no matter how much you might want to. You should talk with Thomas and establish limits on touching if he really cares for you he will accept these conditions as part of being with you."

"Thanks mom, I feel better now. I'll tell Thomas what you said."

"Verona, please come talk to me anytime you want to or need to I love you and want to help you cope and to be happy in this changing world of yours."

Verona and Thomas continued to enjoy each other's company. Over the following year, they became close friends sharing minor sexual touching, but they never had sex together out of mutual respect for each other. Verona was proud of herself, she knew a lot about sex without going all the way as several of her friends had boasted of doing. She and Clare were closer than ever they understood each other. Knowing that she could talk with her mother about any problem was reassuring to Verona. Clare loved her and she loved Clare together they could handle any problem that might come up now or in the future.

Verona developed into an unusual young woman, by the time she reached her junior year in high school, she looked a lot like Clare the one thing she lacked was the sinuous exotic walk which set Clare apart from most other women. Instead, Verona had a more stately walk which gave her a classical look, not too dramatic and not too forward, not totally hidden from view either, but a little mysterious. Her physical qualities were readily apparent to those who looked even though she didn't flaunt them like some of her girlfriends. Verona was very popular with the boys in her class partly because she was good looking and partly because she was smart and a fun loving person. She was an accomplished dancer who enjoyed dancing, no matter who happened to be her partner, she danced with those who asked rather than with a few preferred guys.

Midway through the Friday night dance, Johnny, a short boy who barely came up to her shoulders asked.

"Verona, do you think we could dance one time together?"

"Sure, maybe we can dance two dances if you are willing," replied Verona holding out her hand to Johnny.

The other girls had already turned Johnny down because he was short and not a very good dancer. Verona's consideration for others made her especially popular among the physically less gifted males in her group of acquaintances.

When she and her friends gathered around the pool, Verona's magnificent body became a major topic of observation and conversation. She was beautiful with near perfect body lines she had long legs, a narrow waist, a well-rounded booty and perky breasts all accentuated by her dark black hair and blue eyes. In a bikini she was ravishingly sexy. John Paul noticed Verona when he first entered the pool area, she was more than just an attractive girl, she was the sexiest female he has ever seen she definitely turned him on. John Paul had paid little attention to Verona in the past, but now that he had seen her in a bikini he had an unquenchable desire to become acquainted and more. He headed across the pool area in Verona's direction intent on striking up a conversation. She was lying back on a pool side deckchair sunning herself when he approached.

"Are you saving this chair for someone?"

Looking up, Verona saw a handsome young man, in a bright colored bathing suit, looking down on her with searching eyes and a big smile.

"No, that chair is not being used. Help yourself. Do I know you?"

"I don't think so. My name is John Paul, I am a senior at your school. We haven't met before, but I think it's time we did. What is your name, beautiful?"

"My name is Verona Elise, but you can call me Verona. I seldom use Elise."

Laying his towel on the deckchair, John Paul pulled it as near as possible to Verona before laying back to enjoy the sun.

"Oh, there is a bit of devil in this guy he's is good looking too," thought Verona. Before John Paul could say a word, Verona asked.

"How is it that we have not met before?"

"I don't know, Verona. I don't see how I could have missed anyone as good looking as you."

"John Paul, I think maybe I saw you at school once. Were you on the track team?"

Verona knew John Paul was not on any of the school teams. She knew quite a lot about him his good looks had caught her attention earlier in the school year even though she did not know him. She had been interested in meeting him for several months until now she had not found a way to make it happen.

"You must have mistaken me for someone else I've never been on any of the school teams." Replied John Paul somewhat deflated that Verona had mistaken him for someone else.

"My mistake," replied Verona. She continued in her most seductive voice.

"Well, we have met, so what do you like to do other than pick up girls in bikinis?"

John Paul was taken aback by Verona's remark he didn't know what to make of her forwardness and teasing attitude.

"There aren't many girls that look the way you do. I'm trying to pick up only one girl in a bikini and that's you." John Paul replied smiling as best he could under the circumstances.

Verona laughed with an infectious and alluring small curl to her smile.

"Well, John Paul, you are doing a good job consider me picked up. What do we do now stay here in the sun, or go someplace with shade where we can sit and talk and maybe get a glass of lemonade to drink?"

They agreed to leave the pool area and to go somewhere that provided protection from the afternoon sun. They showered and put on their street clothes then met near the pool entrance with their swimwear and towels tucked away in their athletic carry bags. Fully clothed, Verona was still a hot item, her body lotion gave the impression she had just emerged from a field of fresh flowers. An almost indescribable fragrance waffled on the air as John Paul walked toward her. His first feint whiff caused him to look around searching for the origin of the scent, he saw only Verona the obvious source of the arousing fragrance.

"You are beautiful, between you and that aroma, I am going wild."

"I don't want to drive you wild, but you can kiss me if you like," said Verona whose hormones were also humming along at a speed exceeding that of her brain. They embraced kissing for a long while before walking down the street hand in hand toward the Whataburger. Verona knew she really liked John Paul and was certain that he liked her as well. By mid-afternoon, they were committed to spending as much time together as possible. From the way John Paul's kisses affected her, Verona knew she had to discuss John Paul and the day's events with Clare before she did something totally stupid.

Verona explained how John Paul's kisses made her want to have sex with him to the point she could barely control herself and how she apparently affected him the same way. Although they had just met, she had been attracted to John Paul for some time and had, in fact, more or less schemed to make their meeting inevitable. She wanted him, she

74

was sexually attracted to John Paul, seeing his body in a bathing suit had aroused her in a maddening way as did kissing him. He had a beautiful masculine body which resembled that of a mythical male God who had come to fulfill her every desire. The real problem troubling her was, she wanted him.

None of this was lost on Clare it all sounded ever so familiar the difference between then and now was, she had made no effort to control her own desires until after she entered the Gentex program at twenty four. Verona was seventeen the same age Clare had become sexually creative and active. Clare's own mother had imparted only one bit of advice when it came to sex don't do it and don't do it. Clare found her mother's advice to be totally unacceptable in her own case and in Verona's case now. Clare decided to advise Verona the way she wished someone had done when she was seventeen and having her first experience with real sex.

"Verona, when I was your age I had the same feelings and the same desires you are having with John Paul, unlike you, I had no one to give me any useful advice. These urges and desires are only going to get stronger over the next ten to fifteen years, at some point, no matter how much a person resists, these feelings will conquer reason in the end. Knowing this, you must resist as long as you can, once you are convinced this is the time and the right guy, take all steps necessary to protect yourself. I'm not telling you to have sex with John Paul, even though I know you want to, I'm not telling you not to either. What I am telling you is that when you can no longer resist having sex take care of yourself use a contraceptive or start taking the pill. Verona, you are the only one who can make this decision no one can make it for you." Clare wished her mom had given her that same advice when she was Verona's age. She would have done some things differently.

Over the next few months, nothing more was mentioned concerning John Paul or Verona's unrelenting desire to have sex with him. One evening while the two of them were relaxing, Verona revealed that she and John Paul had sex several times and that she liked it. In spite of the pleasure she derived from sex with John Paul, something very important was missing, an essential part she had expected was not there, she liked John Paul a lot, but they were not in love she only liked him.

"I decided to end our relationship because I don't love John Paul what we have is a mutual physical attraction and nothing more. In the future there will be no more sex with John Paul or anyone else until I am sure I love the man. Sex without love is not for me."

Clare reminded herself. "Some things never change. I have high hopes for Verona's future happiness, she makes very good decisions. Much better than the ones I made at her age."

Verona's last year in high school turned into a fun time she dated casually and spent more time on her studies. She hung out with several of her girlfriends doing things as a group which she found to be both refreshing and a lot of fun. She discovered that she could have a good time without boys or sex some of the things girls did together were cool plus being great fun and fulfilling in a special way. Previously, she had not considered that being a girl with girls could be so rewarding she learned to appreciate that close friendships were important and being best friends with someone you really liked was an unusual and rewarding experience that rarely came about.

During the summer following her last year in high school, Verona and her best friend Joanna went to *Puerto Vallarta,* Mexico for a week before starting college in the fall. The trip was to be just the two of them hanging out together doing a little Scuba diving, sightseeing or whatever caught their fancy. They agreed in advance that there would be no romantic interludes with guys they might meet no matter how good looking and charming they might be. The two of them were lounging around the pool having frozen *margaritas* when a well-tanned young man approached.

"Ladies, if you would allow me. I would like to buy you another round of *margaritas.*"

"We appreciate your kindness, but this is an all girl's week. See you around." They both laughed as he put his hands in the air and turned away. They used the same technique several times to preserve their girls-only vacation each time eliciting a similar reaction from their potential suitors.

The Alpha-1 agents reported: "Verona and her friend are staying out of trouble and having a good time in Mexico. Wait until she starts to college in the fall things may change."

Chapter 4 Meeting at the Tmex

Well into her and Bruce's second year of living in the neighborhood, Peggy decided she should look for a part time job, preferably, in a large restaurant bar similar to Bobby's where she worked during her stay in Dallas. She found just what she wanted at the Tmex, a large luxury hotel serving the energy corridor, and which was located a short distance from her home. It was a watering place for local business men and transient hotel patrons alike, mostly men. They came to the bar after work and into the early evening hours to have a couple of drinks to break the tension that had been building during their workday. Almost instantly, Peggy became the favorite server at the Tmex bar, she joked with the patrons constantly often making them smile even when they didn't want to. Peggy felt at home in the bar she enjoyed the fun and laughter among the regulars and the ease with which she could interact with all of the patrons, who were mostly professionals about her age, or a little older. For her it was fun, therapeutic almost. As much as Peggy liked working at the bar, Bruce was her first concern she made sure they spent quality time together when she was not working. She lavished him with love and attention when they were together. Working at the Tmex, made it necessary for Peggy to hire a full time baby sitter to look after Bruce while she was working evenings during the week. Her work schedule allowed her spend all of the weekend and the week days with Bruce. Peggy enjoyed teaching him things, he was learning to walk and sometimes she could coax what she thought was a word from him. She was an excellent mother, but she needed a little time to be herself in surroundings that made her feel good apart and separate from nurturing little Bruce. The bar was such a place, she was happy and had fun there.

After a few months of working at the Tmex, Peggy noticed, among the patrons, a young, good looking man who was always dressed in a suit and tie. For some unknown reason, he showed up at the Tmex regularly in the third week of each month. Obviously, he was not known to the regulars because he never sat with them even though they sometimes exchanged nods with him, but they never interacted with him or included him in their conversations. He talked with Peggy like the regulars telling jokes and laughing at Peggy's responses sometimes commenting about how demanding his job had become over the past year and how he needed a little time to just be himself and to enjoy things. Peggy sort of recognized herself in his remarks understanding quite well how he could feel the need to get away from his job for a while. She, on the other hand, needed a job in the bar to be herself when she was not being a mom.

After a few extended exchanges with the stranger, Peggy asked, "Do you have a name, or do you want me to continue calling you, Sir?"

"I'm sorry, my name is Zane Kraft. And what shall I call you other than, Miss?"

"You can call me Peggy, if you like, that's what all of the regulars call me."

"From now on Peggy it will be, by the way, I think the name fits you very well. Short and sweet."

"Thank you, Zane. I have noticed that you come here often, but are not associated with the regulars who come almost every day."

"No, I am not a local my home base is El Paso, I'm in the import-export business and make trips to Houston on a regular schedule. I always stay here at the Tmex Hotel for one or more days each month."

When he was in town, Zane began coming to the bar later in the evening after most of the regulars had gone, so Peggy could spend more time with him. The number of customers in the bar dropped dramatically after seven, the regulars had gone home to their families and only a few transits and late night diners remained in the bar. Peggy and Zane became friends talking endlessly with less of the joking and more and more of I like your company conversation. After several months, Zane shocked Peggy by asking.

"Could we meet at another place for dinner and drinks, I mean have a real date?"

In her years at Bobby's and at the Tmex, none of the men had ever asked her for a date or indicated they were interested in her other than as a funny bar maid. She was aware Zane liked her, but it never occurred to her that a good looking guy like him might be romantically interested in her. Peggy heard herself saying to Zane.

"It will have to be on a weekend night, I work here nights Monday through Friday."

Peggy could hardly believe what she had said, she never intended to become romantically involved with Zane, he was good looking and interesting, but Peggy had never considered romance an option. One thing led to another and now she was overwhelmed by his attention and recklessly in love with him. Peggy was looking forward to their first date and more, her mind was racing as she considered the possibilities.

"I can't leave for Texas A&M next month, like I planned, it would ruin everything if I do. Zane and I will not be able to see each other and I don't want that to happen now that he has expressed a romantic interest."

She had never mentioned her goal of graduating from A&M in any of their long discussions, Zane was totally unaware of her circumstances other than she was single, here and as crazy about him as he was about her. She arranged for the nanny to spend Saturday night at her house in case she was late getting home from their date.

Their first date was a masterful success, Zane arrived at Peggy's home at seven o'clock sharp, driving a new black Mercedes. She greeted him at the door when Zane rang the doorbell, but did not invite him inside instead she stepped out closing the door behind her. Unfazed he rushed to open the door of the Mercedes for Peggy who thanked him profusely as she took her seat before he closed the door. Once inside, Zane took Peggy's hand then kissed her firmly. She returned his kiss hotly then they kissed again before he drove to the Top of the Mark, an expensive and exclusive restaurant, overlooking downtown Houston. Zane ordered a vintage wine to go with their dinner which consisted of a salad, filet of sole and dessert. After dessert, the orchestra played slow sweet music from the forties, to which Zane and Peggy danced as one when their bodies met for the first time. They felt each other in a way only lovers can. While dancing, they did not talk rather they let the rhythm of the music do the talking as they swept gracefully around the dance floor, Peggy's head was back and slightly to one side, her back was straight and their lower bodies flowed in perfect harmony, occasionally, she laughed quietly when they performed a complicated dance maneuver.

Following a fast and exhausting dance, Peggy insisted on returning to their table for a break, once seated she took a sip of her wine then began hesitantly.

"Zane, there is something I need to tell you, tonight, before the evening gets any older. I have a son named, Bruce who is about to have his second birthday. He and I are involved in a scientific program for which I volunteered, Bruce was conceived by artificial insemination using sperm from an unknown donor that I have never met and will never meet. In this program, Bruce and I receive a monthly stipend plus other benefits which I can't reveal. I hope you can forgive me for not telling you this earlier."

Zane did not hesitate he put his finger across her lips saying, "Peggy, you are the love of my life, nothing that you say or have done can change that, I will always be here for you." He removed his finger from her lips whispering in her ear, "I have reserved a room here for the night, shall we go?"

Peggy could hardly believe she and Zane were about to spend the night together. It was beyond her comprehension that Zane could be in love with her, yet she said nothing just nodded in assent as she picked up her purse from the chair beside her.

They were good together. Peggy had not anticipated Zane's loving attention, or his desire to insure her pleasure as well as his own. They fell asleep in each other's arms happy to know they were in love.

Peggy postponed her return to school indefinitely once she and Zane began meeting regularly in the third week of each month. Sometimes, they spent one night together, or on some happy occasions two, strangely he never came to her home other than to pick her up for dates. He did not see Bruce, or ask to meet him, or even ask questions about him which puzzled Peggy immensely. She did not dwell on Zane's lack of interest in Bruce rationalizing that should the time ever come for Bruce to know about him, Zane would bring it up.

They spent their nights together at a variety of hotels scattered across greater Houston each month they melded their minds and bodies into a rhapsody of love and fulfillment rarely experienced by most young lovers. They were consumed by their love for one another devoting their free time to being together. Zane was an attentive loving man, he brought her small gifts, made sure she enjoyed their time together as much as he did and he always made her feel as though she was the only woman in his world. He worshiped her, but he never really told her much about himself, or what he did in his job. Peggy was reluctant to push the issue, or ask questions which might be difficult for him to answer. She was so possessed by her love for Zane that nothing else mattered to her, except Bruce.

"When the time is right, Zane will ask about Bruce!"

Several months passed with the bond between Peggy and Zane growing stronger with each encounter when suddenly Zane had bad news which he chose to tell Peggy as they were preparing to leave the hotel following a fantastic night together. Speaking rapidly he said.

"Peggy, there has been a terrible change in my work schedule, which will prevent me from being here on the weekend, starting next month I will be in Houston only during the week. I can't do anything about my schedule, however, we must do something otherwise I will not be able to be with you at all, except at the bar which I find to be unacceptable."

Peggy did not panic rather she thought for a moment before answering.

"I don't want to lose you, Zane. We are so good for each other, we are meant be together and I don't want that to change. I'll do anything to keep us together. I love you Zane, there can never be anyone else for me."

After spending a sleepless night thinking about solutions to her and Zane's problem, Peggy came up with the perfect solution. She quit her job at the Tmex bar the next morning. The next day, she enrolled for the fall semester at the University of Houston. She would be free to see Zane when he returned to Houston and she would be earning credits toward her degree, which had been her original intent when she joined the Gentex program.

Abe received several cryptic messages from Alpha-3 in Houston concerning Peggy's new found lover. The first read.

"Peggy Wilkerson has been seriously involved for several months with a man named Zane Kraft, picture attached, whom we have been unable to reliably identify through our local sources. He may be working for an import-export company headquartered in El Paso, but this is unconfirmed. We keep coming up with nothing other than dead ends in our efforts to clarify the true identify of Zane Kraft. Please send aid and technical reinforcements."

Abe dispatched a sophisticated team of experts to Houston, assembled from within Imperial's foreign branch, the team consisted of five senior employees all specialists in investigations concerning hidden identities and hidden backgrounds. The team did not make direct contact with the

Alpha-3 surveillance team, by design the two Abe units remained independent of one another for the mutual security of the members of each group. A part of Abe's operating policy was to protect the identity of their agents from outsiders and confined them to the group in which they worked. It took most of a week for the team to get all of their electronic gear installed and running at their new quarters located in a non-descript one story building on North Shepherd Street.

The special team spent grueling days and nights searching data bases, their efforts produced nothing, Zane Kraft remained a complete mystery. Unsuccessful in their initial efforts, the team switched methods resorting to hacking data bases at the FBI, CIA and Bureau of Alcohol Tobacco and Firearms among others. None of these massive criminal data bases revealed anything about Zane Kraft. After a week of intense electronic search, he remained a total unknown. At Abe it became clear that Zane Kraft was not a regular citizen, he had no credit cards, had a Texas driver's license showing a fake address in El Paso and had no Social Security number or birth certificate.

"Zane Kraft is one crafty son of a bitch, it's going to take a lot of hard work for us to figure out just who in the hell he is. In my personal opinion, he is a damned criminal." Said the lead agent loud enough for all to hear.

His second in command replied.

"Well, he doesn't have a criminal record that we can find, so we have to do our own ground work. What a bummer. I'm off to El Paso tonight to check out the import-export business connection maybe I'll come up with something to help us."

It was a direct flight, yet the agent managed to have two scotches before landing in El Paso at ten thirty which made the flight less onerous than he anticipated when he boarded in Houston. The next morning, he met with the managers of three El Paso import-export companies. None of the companies were large, compared to those in Houston they were quite small, yet two of them relied on Mexican trucks to deliver goods from across the border which piqued the agent's interest. This could be an avenue for smuggling illegal drugs into the country possibly involving the elusive Mr. Zane Kraft in a criminal activity. At the first company on his schedule, the agent asked the manager.

"Do you know a fellow in the import-export business, named Zane Kraft?"

"I sure don't, never heard of him."

Holding out a large photograph of Zane taken by the surveillance crew, the agent asked. "Would you mind taking a look at this picture? Do you recognize this guy?"

"Nope, can't say that I do. Who is he?"

"That's the guy I'm asking about. He calls himself Zane Kraft."

"Well, I've never seen or heard of him. Look, you are free to ask all of our employees if they know this guy, so long as you don't take up too much time and don't interfere with our work schedule."

After making inquiries among the employees, the agent became convinced that none of them had heard of, or seen Zane, he was a stranger to all of them. The agent repeated the procedure at the other two import-export companies with similar results. He later, interviewed the Chief of Police who had no information regarding Zane Kraft either. Zane certainly did not work for any of these companies, if there was any connection to them or to El Paso it was not obvious. The following morning, back in his office, the agent commented to his coworkers.

"Zane Kraft is unknown in El Paso. He does not work for an import-export company located there. I did not find a single person who had ever heard of, or seen him. Who is this guy? Does he actually have a connection to El Paso? I am getting tired of chasing dead ends. We need to identify this slippery bastard and soon!"

A review of the information collected by the team indicated their best approach to determining who and what Zane Kraft might be, would probably be through his liaisons with Peggy. So far as Abe had been able to determine, she was his only known regular contact! He appeared to be invisible except for those brief periods he spent with her in Houston. They knew from the surveillance team that on most occasions Zane picked Peggy up at home and returned her one or two days later, until recently their liaisons were always on the weekend. On one such occasion the surveillance team traced Zane and Peggy to the Tmex Hotel where they spent the night. Since that encounter, the agents had been unable to follow them to their hotel on Zane's visits to

Houston, he always managed to give them the slip when they attempted to follow them.

Using Peggy to get to Zane presented a serious security problem for Abe, Zane Kraft was no novice at this game he seemed to be non-existent everywhere except in Houston. Should he suspect he was being followed, Abe might be inadvertently endangering both Peggy and Bruce, which had to be avoided under all circumstances. Protection of Peggy and Bruce was the paramount responsibility of Alpha-3. After much discussion at Abe, the agents developed a scheme to obtain finger prints and possibly a DNA sample from Zane on his next appearance in Houston.

Under their plan, Peggy and Bruce would not be directly involved and would remain out of harm's way, Peggy's PC and phones had previously been bugged by Abe and her every movement was being watched and videoed around the clock. Although Zane's previous contacts with Peggy had been by phone or in person, every possible means of communication between them was being monitored to alert the team to Zane's next trip in Houston. Success of their plan depended on following Peggy and Zane to their hotel and putting operatives in the public areas, such as the bar and the dining room, where they would attempt to obtain a wine glass or water glass with Zane's finger prints on it. If they were lucky the agents might get a sample of Zane's DNA from a glass or spoon.

Zane arrived punctually at seven in the evening to pick up Peggy, this trip he was not driving, for the first time he was in a black limousine with a uniformed driver who spoke only broken English. As the driver opened the back door, Peggy jumped in to embrace Zane who was impatient to hold her in his arms. They kissed a second time while the limousine quickly pulled up onto I-10 and sped away in the darkness. At Zane's direction the driver made several detours through busy side streets and off the normal route before arriving at the Airport Hotel where the driver was instructed to return the following day promptly at eight in the morning. Zane made it clear to the driver that he was not to come to the hotel, if for any reason he thought he was being followed, but should call Zane's cell phone instead. Zane gave him a burner phone and the number to his own burner phone which he had purchased for this one time use. If not used by the driver, the phone would be discarded the next morning. Following their usual practice, the lovers went directly to the bar in the observation room for a quiet drink. Later they dined and danced until midnight before retreating to the suite Zane had retained. There was no one in sight as they unlocked the door to enter, nor was there anyone in sight when Peggy left to meet the limousine the following morning. Surveillance reported the limousine's return and Peggy's arrival at home in the early morning hours. The special team was not as successful, they had been unable to follow the limousine to its destination because of the evasive measures taken by the driver. It would be another month before they could make another attempt to collect finger prints or DNA from Zane. In the meantime, their search for an identity by other avenues continued. Abe was unrelenting in its effort to unmask Zane, the agents resolved that nothing would keep them from their goal, the inevitable might be temporarily delayed, but not avoided. Frustrated, Frank began to devise his own plan to learn who Zane was and what he did when he was not in Houston!

The latest operation had not been a total loss, the limousine license plate was captured by the surveillance video when Peggy returned home the following morning. The team had another piece of information which might prove invaluable to their cause. A check of the State records subsequently showed the limousine belonged to Omar Shara, who had been in the country six years and in the limousine for hire business for five of those years. He was a political refugee from Teheran, a minority Christian among the Shiite Muslim majority who wanted to execute him for offending Mohammad by worshiping a false prophet. The Abe agents had little difficulty locating Omar Shara who was interrogated the following day. At first, he was reluctant to reveal any information at all, but after the lead agent handed him two thousand dollars in one hundred dollar bills he became a fountain of information, most of which proved to be worthless. In his broken English, Omar managed to say.

"The client called a day in advance to arrange for limousine service. I did not know the man, this was the first time he has called. It was strange though because he did not give me his name, but he did give the name of the company he represented, Cross Border I&E. When I picked him up, he paid in cash including a sizeable tip. He made no mention of hiring me again he just directed me to this house where we picked up a female before going to the hotel. For some reason this guy had me drive a weird route to the hotel, with a lot of turns and using a bunch of side streets."

At this point the agent became very interested in Mr. Omar Shara, he took his hand covering it with an additional five thousand dollars before asking.

"How would you like to earn this?"

"What would I have to do?"

"Nothing illegal or dangerous. I'm going to give you this money now, in exchange, you are going to call me immediately at the number on this card should this client ever call for your limousine service again. If that should happen, I will give you another five thousand dollars to allow me to put a GPS tracking device on your limousine. If this client never calls, you can keep the five thousand you have in your hand."

"Do we have a deal, Omar?"

"Yes, yes. We have a deal, I'll call you."

The agent added, "One more thing, do not discuss our arrangement with anyone, ever."

Omar could only hope his client would return the following month, with twelve thousand dollars he could pay off the remaining loan balance on his limousine and be debt free. "God, be praised," he uttered as he clutched the seven thousand dollars tightly in his hand. After the agents left he raced home to tell his wife of their good fortune.

Peggy was feeding Bruce when the phone rang interrupting his supper of Cheerios and fruit, Zane spoke softly the sound of his voice brought a big happy grin to Peggy's face.

"I will be in town for only a short while tomorrow, I have much business to attend to, but I need to see you, if possible. I can't pick you up at the house, as usual, so I will send the limousine to take you to the hotel. If that is OK with you?"

"Zane, you know that's OK with me. When will the limousine be here?"

"Seven sharp."

"I love you, Zane."

"Yes, I love you too."

This short cryptic conservation set in motion Abe's latest plan to identify Zane Kraft. No one involved could have foreseen the consequences related to this single phone call between two lovers. Surveillance forwarded the conversation to Abe immediately.

Omar called his Abe contact, as soon as he finished getting his instructions from Zane, setting up a meeting with the agent early the next morning. The GPS was installed and Omar received his additional five thousand dollars as agreed. He was jubilant, he would be out of debt at last!

Peggy stepped into the limousine promptly at seven and was whisked away to the Tower Hotel located a short distance from her home. She met Zane in the Upper Bar where they embraced then retreated to a table for two in a dark corner where they kissed before ordering drinks. Two Abe agents arrived in the bar while Peggy and Zane were having their drinks, they took a table nearby watching the lover's every move being very discreet not to arouse suspicion by their actions. The two agents, a well-dressed blond female and an equally well-dressed male, ordered drinks then kissed before the female giggled slightly while holding the males hand. They looked like another pair of lovers enjoying the hotel's ambiance before retiring to their room for the night.

Zane had Peggy's hand in his as he spoke.

"My lovely, Peggy, I will be unable to spend the night although we have a room in the hotel, my schedule requires me to leave here at midnight in order to make my flight. Shall we have an early dinner and go directly to the room?"

"I would like that very much, but I suggest we skip dinner and go to the room now," said Peggy with a slight smile breaking across her face as she picked up her purse and stood up.

Their unfinished drinks were left on the table remaining in full view of the Abe agents as Peggy and Zane walked to the elevator hand in hand oblivious to everyone and everything around them. Once Peggy and Zane were out of sight, the Abe agents swiftly switched their drink glasses with those left behind carefully placing them in plastic bags to preserve any finger prints or DNA which might have been left on them by the lovers. Step one of the plan had been executed perfectly. Their hotel room could not be checked until after Zane and Peggy left the hotel, presumably the next morning.

Zane and Peggy sat and talked at length before undressing, for the first time during their relationship, Zane mentioned Bruce.

"I know you love your son very much and that is as it should be. A mother who does not love her child, is no woman at all, and is undeserving of the love of a man. I love you more than anything in this world and want you to be with me from now on. I know that for this to be true, I must also love your son as I love you. I promise you that I will love both you and your son equally for all of eternity."

Peggy had never heard more reassuring words in her life, it had bothered her that Zane seemed to ignore Bruce as a part of their world, she was torn between her love for Bruce and loving Zane, but now to love one was to love them both. Her dilemma was solved. Peggy did not reply, instead she pulled Zane on to the bed kissing him as they lay in each other's arms. Zane was overwhelmed by Peggy's love and passion. Afterward, she fell asleep in his arms. Zane covered Peggy with a blanket then kissed her softly making sure not to awaken her. He quickly dressed then silently closed and locked the door on his way out. Shortly he was in a taxi on his way to the Houston International Airport to catch a late flight to the West Coast. The next morning Peggy called the limousine driver arranging for him to meet her in the lobby as Zane had instructed, without any conversation between them he delivered Peggy to her front door. Back in the limousine, the driver waved to Peggy and was smiling broadly as he eased the limousine out of the driveway.

The finger prints were well defined on both glasses and after processing were shown to be none other than Peggy Wilkerson and an unidentified male. DNA samples were obtained from both glasses and preserved for future use in identifying Zane if needed. Abe's contact in the FBI had no finger print records indicating the identity of the unknown male, as a favor he agreed to send the prints to Interpol for a check in the international criminal data base. Several weeks later, Abe received a copy of Interpol's reply.

"The finger prints from your unidentified male are those of Zane Kraft a thirty eight year old citizen of Costa Rica. He is believed to be involved with the South American cocaine trade as banker and financial advisor to the *Bastardos Locos* (Crazy Bastards) cartel. He travels extensively in the United States for the purpose of collecting the cartel's cash from the sale of cocaine and moving it through various international banks to safe haven accounts outside of the country. He is also their financial advisor who in recent years has built a solid ownership in legitimate companies worldwide for the Crazy Bastards. Their wealth, outside of the cocaine trade, makes them an economic force in the business world their investments are concentrated in Europe and South America, but they also have holdings throughout North America, Asia and Africa. Their legitimate business empire is growing swiftly and in time is expected to surpass their cocaine empire in value. Good luck, we have not been able to directly connect Mr. Kraft to any criminal act, but we believe he is involved as stated above."

"It looks like Zane is more slippery than we thought," remarked Abe's lead agent. Frank was quick to reply.

"We don't really give a damn what he is up to, except as it relates to the safety of Peggy and Bruce Wilkerson, so long as he does not put them in harm's way, or become a threat to them, we will take no action other than intensify our observation of him, Peggy and Bruce."

He continued, "We need to think about Zane in the context of our main objective. Do his activities pose a current or future threat to either Peggy or Bruce?"

A senior agent responded.

"We need to know exactly what Zane is doing, not rely on what Interpol believes he is doing, crap he may be putting both of them in danger as we speak. We need to chronicle his activities around the clock, he may already represent a serious risk for our wards. Our team's first objective is to protect Peggy and Bruce, so we need to determine the true nature of Mr. Kraft's business activities and his connection to the Crazy Bastards, if any. Only then, can we evaluate his potential danger to Peggy and Bruce. We may have to make a preemptive move to protect Peggy and Bruce."

"I agree with you completely. I have developed a plan to determine just that!"

Chapter 5 Caribbean Cruise

Darlene and Alan flourished in their new surroundings, by the time he was three, Alan had more than quadrupled in weight and grown into a robust, happy faced, vigorous, blond boy who was into everything. Alan was a quick learner, he walked early and began talking shortly thereafter. Darlene was also learning fast, she had not taken a job after Alan arrived instead she immersed herself in a self-devised improvement program. She concluded several months after his birth that her high school diploma qualified her for little more than the job she left in Joaquin when she joined the Gentex program. Now thanks to their financial support, she could afford to take care of Alan and go to school at the same time. Darlene had always been curious about faraway places she enjoyed learning more about the world and what went on in it. Everything fascinated her, but her underlying motive was to prepare herself to guide Alan to a way of life completely different from her own upbringing. Unlike the limited opportunity she had in Joaquin, she planned for Alan to have access to an advanced education and the freedom to succeed at whatever he chose, Darlene intended to expose Alan to many alternatives as he grew up, so that he would have a wide variety of opportunities to choose from. Darlene felt strongly that she needed to improve her scope of knowledge in order to make her dream for Alan become reality.

She checked out the educational institutions located in the general vicinity of her home then enrolled in the Dallas Baptist University College of Business which she thought was her best option to earn a degree in Business Administration. After four years of hard work she was awarded a BBA degree graduating the week before Alan's seventh birthday. Alan was already exhibiting an above average proficiency in science and mathematics plus a desire to learn all he could about everything. He was an outstanding student with an exceptionally high IQ. Following her graduation ceremony, Darlene told Alan.

"Alan, you and I are now ready to embark on the great experience called life and we are going to enjoy every day of it!"

Darlene had also worked hard to improve her image, she lost twenty pounds, tightened her waistline and worked off the flab on her arms through a long and rigorous exercise program. She had been very frugal with the money she received from Gentex, now she planned to put it to good use, she purchased a new wardrobe of stylish dresses complete with complementary accessories. She had her hair styled and learned to use makeup to highlight her best features. Almost overnight, she transformed into a well-dressed, attractive, slightly plump, short blond with the most brilliant green eyes imaginable.

For the first time in her life, she stood out from the crowd, were she to walk down Main Street in Joaquin, not a person would have recognized her as Darlene Strong who grew up nearby on the banks of the Sabine. Darlene had completed her preparation to take on the world and to educate her son Alan, she was ready to do those things she could only dream about a few years ago. Darlene was extremely grateful to Gentex for making it all possible, without them she would still be in Joaquin working at the Uptown Cafe and her beautiful blond son would not exist at all.

School was out for the summer prompting Darlene to book a ten day Caribbean cruise, on Carnival Cruise Lines, sailing out of Galveston. Alan was in awe as they boarded the ship, in his wildest imagination, he had not anticipated the size and grandeur of an ocean liner.

"When you said a ship, I had no idea how big it was going to be. This thing is humongous!"

After putting their luggage in the cabin and storing everything in its proper place, Alan could not wait to go about exploring the ship, he wanted to see it all now. Darlene allowed him to go look over the ship with certain reservations.

"Alan, it is OK for you to look around the ship for a while, but we will be sailing within an hour. You need to return to the cabin in forty five minutes, so the two of us can be on deck together when the ship sails. You will have plenty of time to explore the ship once we are at sea. Just think, you can take some pictures as we pull away from the dock and the ship moves out of the harbor into the Gulf of Mexico that will be exciting to watch."

Alan inspected the ship on his own returning to the cabin promptly and on time for the two of them to go to the upper deck where they stood at the shore side railing to have a view of the harbor before they sailed. Alan took several pictures of the ships in the harbor which included two drill ships at anchor which provided an unusual photographic scene for the ship's passengers. Alan and Darlene took pictures of each other standing at the rail. In order to get a picture of the two of them together, Darlene persuaded a young man standing nearby to take their picture using Alan's camera. The two of them were standing at the rail smiling with their arms around each other with the city of Galveston visible as a backdrop. The ship pulled anchor a few minutes before sunset, treating the passengers to a glorious reddish orange and blue display as the sun retreated below the horizon behind the city of Galveston. The ship's captain made an announcement over the P.A. system alerting the passengers and crew when the ship officially entered the Gulf of Mexico. Alan let out a loud cheer yelling, "We are in the Gulf, mom, we are in the Gulf!"

On most cruise ships, attire for the evening meal is usually formal or semiformal and the table and seating are fixed for the entire cruise. Alan and Darlene were seated at a table of ten which included two couples and their children. Among the children were a boy and a girl about Alan's age which made him happy because he had someone his own age to talk with during dinner. Once all the places at the table were filled, introductions were made around the table, luckily, the families were amenable and friendly, one family was from Kingsburg, Illinois and the other was from Warren, Indiana. Discussions among the adults, during dinner, exposed Alan to the mid-western brogue spoken by the group. He found it interesting that some Americans sounded different from others even though they were all speaking English. He had no difficulty understanding what they were saying it just sounded different from what he was used to. Alan and Darlene kept this seating arrangement in the dining room for the entire cruise although they seldom went there for breakfast or lunch preferring instead to eat topside around the pool where it was quicker and easier. Alan liked the fast service because it allowed more time for other things besides eating which he considered a necessary waste of time.

Upon returning to their cabin, Darlene read the cruise line literature searching for on board activities available for Alan and other children his age. Even though Carnival is known as the Party Line by the younger cruise patrons, Darlene was delighted to find there were many daytime activities designed for children like Alan. The next morning, she discussed the menu of activities with Alan who was gung ho to participate in several of the programs. She promptly signed him up for those he liked most since conflicts in scheduling made it impossible for him to take part in all of them. These on board activities provided an opportunity for Alan to interact on his own with children about his own age who were from different backgrounds and different geographical areas. He was excited as he started the first of the activities which involved a scavenger hunt designed to meet the conditions on board the ship.

Darlene went to the upper deck pool where she located an unoccupied table on the shaded side of the ship. She deposited her handbag and towel before removing her robe and entering the pool wearing her new bikini for the first time. Taking a good look around the deck as she walked to the pool's edge Darlene found it exciting the way the men looked at her, she had not experienced this kind of attention in her entire life. After a few laps around the pool Darlene returned to her table observing the approving smiles of the men around the pool as she did so. Her fair skin prohibited her staying in the sun for long without burning which had prompted her to select a table in the shade to relax and to enjoy the warm sea breeze blowing across the deck. It wasn't long before the fellow at the next table who had been watching Darlene for several minutes asked.

"Would it be possible for me to join you?"

Darlene nodded yes, inviting him to sit across from her.

"Where might you be from?" he asked. "I saw you and the boy at dinner last evening and needless to say the two of you were eye catching with that blond hair," he added before she could answer.

"Alan and I are from Dallas. Where do you call home?"

She smiled in her delightful soothing manner as she waited for his reply. Talking with men came easy to Darlene, ever since she started working at the Uptown Cafe, she found that men enjoyed her conservation. They felt at ease with her joking, soft laugh and great big smile. Darlene was an outgoing person who never met a stranger, she liked people and was not the least bit uneasy talking to a total stranger on a cruise ship in the middle of the Gulf of Mexico it seemed like the natural thing to do. People didn't go on cruses to be alone.

"I hail from the fair city of Waco where I am a professor of history at Baylor University."

"That is interesting and a little amusing. I just graduated from Dallas Baptist University last month and all the professors were much older than you and not nearly as handsome. Do you have a name professor?"

"Well, yes, my name is Randall Felton. I'm originally from Orange over near the Louisiana border. I thank you for the compliment, but I must tell you that I am much older than you think," he said hurriedly.

Her green eyes lit up as she responded.

"Professor, I make no secret of my age, I am a thirty-two-year-old single woman with a seven-year-old son whom I love dearly."

The professor did not blink, he countered.

"I am thirty seven, single and have never been married. I love your green eyes and with your permission would like very much to buy you a drink to enjoy while we continue this entertaining and delightful conversation."

"In that case, I will have whatever you are having I am an inexperienced drinker," she replied accompanied by a silky soft laugh.

Randall felt at ease with this green eyed blond stranger he had a strong desire to know more about her she was interesting and easy to talk with and attractive. They chatted about their backgrounds and the many features of the cruise until Darlene announced she had to pick up Alan at the Children's workshop. Before leaving the pool area, Randall and Darlene agreed to meet at nine thirty that evening in one of the lounges. Randall indicated he preferred one that had a band and a dance floor, they selected one that played old favorites rather than the loud modern music favored by the younger passengers.

Preparing to dress for the evening, Darlene looked through her limited selection of evening wear trying to decide which dress was the sexiest, yet moderate and tasteful. She selected a simple solid black dress which she thought would show off her best features to their greatest advantage, particularly, her golden blond hair and bright green eyes. On her way to the lounge, several women in the elevator commented on how attractive she was in her black dress and how it accentuated the beauty of her hair and eyes confirming her choice. Darlene entered the lounge alone where she stopped near the bandstand for a moment looking for Randall in the dimly lit area surrounding the dance floor. She smiled broadly when she located him at a table on the far side away from the band. Many of the patrons nudged their companions directing their attention to Darlene as she crossed the dance floor to Randall's table. When he saw her coming toward him, Randall stood in admiration before offering her his hand.

"Darlene you are absolutely stunning. I have never seen a more beautiful woman in my life."

Randall bowed slightly at the waist as he seated her at their table before kissing her lightly on the cheek. Those seated at the nearby tables were fascinated by the pretty blond they could not help commenting on the dazzling contrast between her golden hair and the black dress. Darlene became aware that she had been noticed by others in the lounge and that they were talking about her. All of this attention was welcome, but new to her she had never been treated as an attractive woman before, she had always been just a likeable blond with green eyes and a gift of gab.

She thought to herself.

"Apparently my efforts were worth the time and trouble. People keep staring at me like I am exceptional."

She could feel the difference in the way people looked at her and she liked being a person of interest. Randall ordered drinks which they sipped as they talked while waiting for the band to begin playing. To his delight, Randall found Darlene to be an excellent dancer who could follow his every move and turn in step to the beat of the music. Until a year ago, she had never danced at all. As a part of her upgrading effort, she had enrolled in a ballroom dancing class at a local studio to learn how to dance and to expand her social skills. After a few lessons, Darlene found she enjoyed dancing very much, after that she dedicated her efforts to becoming a good dancer rather than an adequate one. Drinking sparingly, they danced and talked to well past one in the morning. Darlene discovered that dancing with Randall was a thrill apart from displaying her dancing ability he was also an exciting guy. She liked the way he held her in his arms, forceful yet delicate. Randall was a tender loving person.

"I would like to meet your son, if I may, he sounds as interesting as his mother. Maybe the three of us can meet for lunch by the pool tomorrow," said Randall as they were parting to go to their separate rooms. Darlene enjoyed the evening immensely talking and dancing with Randall had been entertaining and maybe even exciting, she agreed to his proposal for the three of them to meet for lunch. Alan was fast asleep when Darlene opened the cabin door, she thought to herself.

"Alan will enjoy meeting the professor tomorrow, what a nice guy he turned out to be, I really liked him."

The three of them met by the pool for lunch the following day. After introducing Alan to the professor, each of them ordered a salad and sandwich with ice tea. Alan was intrigued by Randall, he had never met a college professor and wanted to find out what made a professor different from other people. Their discourse covered a variety of subjects with Alan expressing his views candidly and to the point on all the issues and subjects Randall mentioned. He spoke with the assurance of a well-educated adult, which came as a great surprise to Randall.

"Alan, what are your favorite subjects in school?"

"It's really hard for me to say which I like the most because I like everything, math, science, languages and history. I just like learning stuff. If I had to select just one, it would probably be science. I like science because it covers so many different kinds of things and is endless, it changes all the time due to new discoveries. I like that."

"How about sports, are you into sports?"

"I like most sports, I play shortstop on the Chiefs baseball team in the Junior League. I like football too, but mom won't allow me to play. She thinks it is too dangerous, which is probably right, since some of my friends got hurt playing this year. I run in junior track and participate in some field events, but I am not very good at it."

"Do you make good grades?"

"Yeah, I do OK."

Upon hearing Alan's answer, Darlene interrupted.

"Alan is in the accelerated learning class at his school. He is a straight A student even though most of his classmates are older than he is by a year or more."

"For some reason, I am not a bit surprised to learn he is an outstanding scholar!"

Hearing Randall's reply Alan stood up, excused himself then walked to the edge of the pool. He eased himself into the water then swam to the other end of the pool where he was greeted by group of kids. Darlene and Randall sat in the shade watching Alan interact with the other youngsters while they talked. The professor had been stimulated by Alan's responses to his questions and equally electrified with the questions Alan had asked. He leaned close to Darlene.

"Your son is an exceptional young man, he is knowledgeable beyond his years and he has a sharp mind. He is brilliant. Did he inherit this from you or his father?"

"That is a very difficult question for me to answer, since I never knew his father, but I doubt very much that it came from me I have never been considered what you would call smart."

She answered staring him straight in the face with her emerald green eyes sharply focused on his looking for a sign of reaction or rejection.

"So Alan Is adopted?"

"No, he is my child," she responded offering no further explanation.

The professor's mind was roiled by her reply he turned to her with a puzzled look on his face. Darlene paused before speaking to make certain her response was exactly as she had rehearsed, many times, in preparation for such a moment as this. She spoke slowly and precisely.

"Randall, I want very much for you to understand what I am about to tell you, it will be difficult because I can reveal only a limited amount of information. Alan was conceived by artificial insemination using sperm from an unidentified donor. This was part of a voluntary scientific project in which I was chosen to participate. In exchange for my participation, Alan and I receive certain benefits which I am prohibited from revealing to anyone. There you have it that's our story. Alan is every bit my child, whom I am free to raise as I see fit."

Stunned by Darlene's reply, Randall said nothing just frowned slightly, not because he objected to the project, but because in Darlene he had found a smart attractive woman with whom he felt a special empathy. She was exciting, enjoyable to be with and most of all they were attracted to each other. He could tell she liked being with him as much as he liked being with her by the way she smiled at him.

"That is an interesting situation which I would never have considered had you not told me. Do you know how many other women volunteered for the program?"

"I have no idea how many volunteered, I do know there were only four of us chosen for the program. I do not know any of the others we have never met and probably never will. I appreciate your interest, but I think we should change our conversation to another subject."

Randall obliged asking about her aspirations for Alan's future and was impressed by her plan to maximize his exposure to different fields of learning. The three of them met regularly for lunch with Darlene and Randall meeting for drinks and dancing throughout the remainder of the cruise. After a couple of days, Alan began calling Randall, "Professor." They became friends talking at length about anything that interested either of them. Alan, the Professor and Darlene took advantage of the many onshore tours available when they were in port almost always going ashore when the ship docked. The one exception being a rain filled day in Key West when they remained on board the ship to avoid the foul weather. When the ship was in port, but there were no interesting tours, they went ashore for shopping and sightseeing on foot. The professor always provided a commentary on the local history and items of interest which he liked to describe in detail. Alan soaked up all the information provided by the Professor and others they encountered on their trips ashore in the various ports of call making the cruise an education in itself for Alan.

Of all the tours they took, Alan's favorite was the underwater voyage they made in a miniature submarine. The submarine had large portholes by every seat allowing him and the other passengers to see the sandy bottom of the Caribbean and the fish and other aquatic animals in the crystal clear water. The sub cruised the shallows for the most part, but as an exciting finale the Capitan went to the edge of the drop off into the deep Caribbean Sea where the water depth suddenly changed from two hundred feet to two thousand feet. Over the edge of the drop off the water was suddenly dark and ominous, no matter how hard one looked, the bottom was hidden from sight it was exciting and scary looking into the dark unknown. The interior of the sub became eerie quiet until the submarine reversed its course. Alan and the other passengers were relieved when the submarine retreated to the shallow water where they could see the bottom again. The vertical drop off into the depths of the abyss had been unexpected and frightening to all of them, looking down and seeing only darkness frightened even the experienced adults onboard.

Darlene was delighted that Randall took such an interest in Alan. Since he had no male for guidance at home, she felt Alan needed a man in his life whom he respected, someone to show and teach him things from a male perspective as well as to exert male discipline, things which she could not do for him. The three of them stood together on the upper deck savoring their time at sea as they approached Galveston and the mainland. Alan was fascinated as he watched the power boat come along side to deliver the pilot on board the ship to guide it to the dock in Galveston. The whole operation was neat and dangerous, Alan respected the skill of the pilot in boarding the ship once the power boat put him in a position to scramble aboard. "It was probably a lot of fun too," surmised Alan

"Professor, will we be seeing you again once we're home?"

"I'm sure you will Alan, I'm sure you will."

Alan jumped high in the air waving his arms yelling, "Yeah, Yeah!"

The seasoned sailors disembarked in Galveston, loaded their luggage into the car and after waving goodbye to Randall headed up Interstate 45 toward Houston. Their cruise was over, but never to be forgotten.

Alpha-2 had checked Randall Felton's history and character in detail following his first meeting with Darlene onboard the cruise ship. The four Abe team members onboard kept tight surveillance on both Darlene and Alan. Even though they were essentially invisible and unknown to the ship's passengers, the Alpha-2 team members did an excellent job of protecting the pair. The second day aboard, it became apparent to the surveillance team that there were two con men onboard who specialized in befriending then duping unattached women passengers between the ages of thirty and sixty. The con men targeted Darlene early on, but were cleverly steered away before they could make contact. On one occasion a nice looking man attempted to start a conservation with Darlene, but he was in interrupted by a fellow passenger asking for directions to the Arivis Club. By the time she had finished answering the question, the good looking guy had moved on. A couple of days later the same man tried to talk with her again. This time another man, who she did not know, stepped between them forcing the man to turn away. Darlene was confused by both incidents not comprehending what was going on. She had no particular interest in talking with the man, so she did not dwell on the circumstances surrounding their being interrupted when he tried to talk with her. Darlene was not approached again, for some unknown reason, she did not see the guy during the rest of the cruise.

Her Abe protectors cornered the con man and his working partner while they were having a drink in the upper deck bar. One of the agents put his hand on the con man's shoulder then said to him and his friend.

"Ok guys, we are on to your game! The blond with the green eyes is off limits. Do you understand? Otherwise, you may find yourselves swimming in the ocean without a life jacket!"

The con man turned looking at the two Abe agents standing behind him.

"Gentlemen, she won't be seeing either of us the rest of the cruise. We don't want any trouble. We understand your message."

The shysters left their drinks unfinished hurrying out of the bar happy to get away unharmed, they did not look back before reaching the stairway and disappearing from view. Eventually the con men found other targets leaving Darlene to the Professor for the remainder of the cruise.

Most of the voyagers were ordinary tourist seeking ten days away from the routine of everyday life many were in their twenties or early thirties enjoying the nuances of an ocean cruise.

The Alpha-2 team noted, with amusement, the number of random romances they observed during the first days of the voyage. It was interesting to see how these young people paired off, at least for the remainder of the trip, causing the agents to wonder if they were such freelance lovers at home. The young couples danced and played into the wee hours of the night, every night. They're fun loving, carefree attitude affected everyone on board some of the older passengers also met someone of interest and started a relationship for the duration of the cruise and possibly longer. The older travelers were much more discrete making their romances less detectable to their untrained fellow passengers.

Over the following months, Randall became a regular visitor to Darlene's house on most weekends. He enjoyed Alan calling him Professor, even encouraged it, he felt it strengthened the bond between them. While Alan was away playing or spending the night with friends, Darlene and Randall came to know each other in an intimate way. Finally Randall, at Darlene's insistence, began to spend his weekends with Darlene and Alan. She told Randall with a smile.

"After all, Randall. Alan has already asked if we are having sex, to which I replied, yes. So there is no reason for you not to spend the night here."

Darlene and Randall married the following year in a simple wedding performed by a Justice of the Peace in Waco. Alan was the only family member in attendance he was as happy with their marriage as were his mother and the Professor. The Professor was now his dad.

After the wedding, Darlene and Alan moved into Randall's house in Waco where she enrolled Alan in school before the fall term began to make sure he got into one of the schools for advanced learning. At the same time, Darlene put her house up for sale at a price slightly under the market with the idea of making a quick sale. To her astonishment, she received several bids which were in excess of her asking price. A fact she never forgot after closing the sale for much more than she had originally asked.

Alan was in the fourth grade waiting to gobble up everything anyone would teach him. His mind had the qualities of a dry sponge, it soaked up everything it touched without regard to its suitability for a young mind. Alan was far more advanced than the other children in his class, so much so that after extensive testing the school selection committee placed him in the sixth grade where he would be challenged. This made little difference to Alan, he didn't know anyone in the school and had no established friends there, to him it represented a new place full of information for him learn. He liked being with the older kids rather than those his own age because they made more sense to him they thought more like he did. The school was co-ed, approximately half boys and half girls, the student body was made up of high achievers from schools all over the district and represented its brightest young minds. There were boys and girls of every background and racial division imaginable, including one American Indian boy whose father was a professor at Baylor like the Professor. He and Alan hit it off right away becoming best friends who shared common interests in mathematics, science and world geography. Alan developed a love of geography following their Caribbean cruise, he yearned to know more about the world as well as the people in it, there were places he wanted to see for himself. This was an interest he shared with his mother, who had envisioned seeing other parts of the world as a girl in Joaquin, she planned to do more travelling with Alan and Randall in the future.

Travel broadens one's view of the world and the people in it, for Alan, every trip would be a unique educational adventure.

Alan's new friend Jim was uncommon, Jim was his real name not a nickname. His mother and father were Osage Indians who had grown up near Pawhuska, Oklahoma. Their family name, Running Horse, was Jim's father's family name. His grandfather had kept their original Indian name rather than adopting a European one because it represented his family's history and traditions which he wanted to keep alive. Jim's parents were from two of the Osage families who had not squandered their oil fortunes and ranch lands during the oil boom which swept across Osage County in the 1920s and early 1930s. Instead their families adapted to modern business methods and saved their money from the oil royalties distributed by the Osage Tribe, who owned all the mineral rights in Osage County, while improving and expanding their ranching operations. Both ranches were still intact thanks to good management and emphasis on higher education by the elders in each family. Jim Running Horse, patriarch of Jim's family, was an exception in his time he believed the way to survive in the modern world was to become well educated and to work hard. When he was a young man getting started he had heard a saying from one of his white neighbors which he had never forgotten.

"If it's worth doing at all, it's worth doing right."

Although he did not know where this saying originated, it became a part of his mantra for the rest of his life. He proved to be correct, education and hard work together were hard to beat, his family not only survived it became prosperous. He started his son's education early to ensure he would be equipped to attend any school of higher learning that he chose. Both Jim's father and mother had earned advanced degrees from the University of Oklahoma, his father a PhD in physics and his mother a PhD in education. Both of them taught at Baylor University.

Over the next two years, Alan and Jim were together whenever they were not in school or involved in some family function, they built rockets, climbed hills and investigated the geology of Waco and the surrounding area. They became experts in the local surface geology surrounding the city, they came to know more about the subtle changes in the topography than did the County Agent who advised the local farmers. The two adventurers showed the Professor the notes and GPS readings they had taken during their study, impressed by their work, he became an ardent supporter encouraging them to expand their geological project with the idea of preparing a written report of their findings.

To aid in their project, the Professor obtained several copies of a base map showing their study area. These maps, which were on a scale of one inch equals two thousand actual feet, showed the survey boundaries along with their names and abstract numbers. The maps also showed the county, state and federal highways and roads and they had a feature critical to completion of their study, they had printed tick marks consisting of two straight lines crossing at right angles to each other with the latitude and longitude noted at the intersection. North, south, east and west were indicated by the four points of the cross. The maps were oriented with north pointing to the top of the map. By knowing the latitude and longitude of the tick marks, the boys could tie all of their GPS readings of latitude, longitude and elevation above sea level from their notes to corresponding points on the maps. They then contoured their topographic map by connecting the points of equal elevation above sea level presenting a visual picture of how the elevation varied over the study area. Using the same GPS information and their notes they were able to construct a map showing the composition of the surface soil at each GPS location on the maps. The boundaries of the different formations were contoured and labeled resulting in a map showing the composition of the surface and the proper geological name as established by the USGS for the outcropping formations.

The boys were finishing the final details of their report when Jim remarked.

"Doing this study has been great, it's like we are explorers, a modern Columbus or Marco Polo."

"Think about it Jim, we have done something that has never been done before. Now that is exciting!"

Alan's mind was soaring with the thrill of being first.

Jim raised his arms in the air as he shouted, "We are a couple of mad scientists on a quest to unravel the secrets of the universe. I like it don't you?"

"Yes, it's sort of like coming upon a wild animal in the woods, you know that funny feeling you get, it's exciting. You and I are going to be unstoppable, unstoppable do you hear? We are going to conquer the world, wait and see!"

Alan was already anticipating their next project.

"Alan, we need to show this to the Professor he may have some suggestions before we make the final copy."

"Yes, you're right. I think he is in the study, I'll go find him."

The Professor was astonished by the quality and organization of the material, the exhibits the boys had prepared were very professional and practical. He was beaming with admiration for these two young achievers. After what seemed an eternity, with the Professor carefully inspecting each page of the manuscript along with each exhibit, he finally broke the deadening silence.

"I am proud of you boys, you have done a wonderful job collecting and compiling the data as well as preparing and presenting your exhibits along with an excellent explanation of techniques and results. In as much as you now have a finished product, what do you plan to do with it?"

Alan and Jim looked at each other for a moment, but neither of them spoke. Sensing that the young scientists had not considered an end use for the material, the Professor suggested.

"Might we discuss among ourselves how, when and where this report might be of the most benefit to someone?"

"Well, other than just knowing the facts for fun, probably the best use of the material would be in farming or construction, we were not really thinking about a use for the data when we collected it, it was mostly done for ourselves this was something interesting that we wanted to know about."

"How about you Alan? Anything to add?"

Alan shrugged before answering.

"Not really, I just wanted to do the study for the fun of it I like discovering new things."

Alan regretted that they had not foreseen that the information might be useful to someone. The Professor again reiterated his praise for their study then said.

"Here is what I am going to do. I'm having four bound copies of this study printed, one for each of you, one for myself and one for whoever you decided might find it useful. How does that sound?"

The printed copies had red hard back covers with black lettering showing the title. On the inside page the names of the authors and the date of publication were also shown. When the Professor presented the boys with their copies, they were exuberant and so excited they skipped around holding their copies high in the air as if they were spoils of war.

"We have been published, we have been published," they repeated over and over again as they grasped the significance of the event.

The Professor smiled as he watched their celebration and thought to himself.

"There is no limit to what these two will accomplish provided they can be kept on course and out of harm's way."

He returned to the task at hand.

"Boys, have you decided who gets the fourth copy?"

"If you are in agreement, we are going to give it to the County Agent. Jim and I decided he could probably do the most good with the information."

"Alan and I plan to take it over to his office as soon as we can."

After waiting for a while on a hard bench in the Courthouse hall, the boys were led into the County Agent's office he was a large rotund man with a jolly face and good humor. The boys had not told him why they had asked to meet with him, but he was always glad to help any youngster he could. Jim pulled the book from his backpack thrusting it toward the agent.

"What's this?" He asked as he took the book from Jim.

The County Agent read the title, then looked inside, the amount of data contained plus the maps got his attention in a hurry he was amazed at the amount of detailed information it contained about the surface and soil around Waco.

"This is really something, I could use a book like this in my work, where did you get it?" asked the agent looking directly at the boys in anticipation of learning the source of such a detailed report.

"That is why we are here, Sir," said Jim who continued. "You see, we did this study as a fun project, but when we finished the Professor, Alan's dad, told us we needed to find someone who could put this information to good use. We want to give you this report in case you can use it in your work."

"Good golly, boys this will really be useful to me and the farmers around here. The only way I can accept it though is if both of you sign the cover page for me," replied the agent holding out a pen to Alan.

Walking home following their meeting with the County Agent, Jim and Alan discussed their latest experience, the County Agent had thanked them profusely for their gift, but most of all he had made the day special when he requested they autograph the report. That had been a great honor and left them with a good feeling about their accomplishment.

Alan commented as they walked along.

"You know, Jim it's funny how doing things for fun can turn out to be good for others too. I like doing both, don't you?"

Jim agreed he like both. They genuinely appreciated the County Agent accepting their gift. On their walk to Alan's house to report their experience to the Professor they switched their discussion to the merits of fishing and fishing techniques their young minds were already searching for another interesting quest.

Darlene opened a real estate agency designed to fill a specialty niche in the Waco market that of buying older homes in need of repair then either upgrading them for resale or replacing them with a new modern house or condominiums to be sold on the open market. This was a risky business with success dependent on the acumen of the person making the decisions. Darlene's approach was deliberate and well planned from the start she studied every purchase carefully with the end use determined before making an offer to purchase an existing home.

Her first purchase involved an older home, in a respectable neighborhood, which she remolded and upgraded for resale. This project turned out to be the landmark trade of her real estate career, she barely broke even, prompting her to analyze the entire project in order to produce better results in the future. After much detailed study, she concluded that she had either paid too much for the house, underestimated the cost to remodel, overestimated the sale price or some combination of the three. It didn't take a genius to realize that income had to exceed cost in order to make a profit. The problem was, how to make sure in advance that a profit would be the outcome. Darlene determined that by using sophisticated methods available in the industry she could reasonably control two of the factors in advance, but that the sales price could not be fixed without making a sales contract in advance of making a purchase. To fix the sales price in advance of starting a project appeared to be nearly an impossible task. She devised a business plan to reduce her risk by controlling the other two components. Her plan entailed making term option contracts to purchase properties at a fixed price and by working exclusively with contractors agreeable to providing time limited fixed cost turnkey contracts for both remodeling and new home construction she had only to determine if the current market price provided an acceptable profit margin. If her estimated current market price exceeded the cost she had fixed by term limited contracts, then the project was undertaken, otherwise, the purchase option and turnkey construction contracts were allowed to lapse at no cost to Darlene. Although Darlene's business plan was not fool proof, it forced her to become an expert in determining the market value of housing in the Waco area, a talent which made her business very profitable over time. She thrived as a business woman, yet she never allowed business to interfere with her devotion to Randall and Alan. She took appointments and phone calls at the office between 8:00 a.m. and 5:00 p.m. her home phone number was unlisted. Her time outside of these hours was reserved for her family, with no exceptions, a rarity in the real estate business.

Randall and Darlene had expected she would become pregnant, sooner or later, but it never happened even though they took no steps to prevent her conceiving. After the first two years without a pregnancy, they accepted the fact that they were destined to have a great love life, but were not going to have any children for themselves, Alan was all there was going to be for them. The Professor was dismayed initially, then realized he loved Alan as his own child and that he was needed to help Darlene mold Alan in to a man. He did not dwell on being childless himself instead he concentrated on guiding and teaching Alan to be a good human being while loving and admiring the exceptional blond with the green eyes who happened to be his wife and Alan's mother.

Alan entered high school at age twelve, he was considerably younger than most of his classmates who were one to two years older. Age made no difference to Alan he was blind to the physical differences between himself and the others his acceptance as a mental peer was what mattered to him.

On his first day in high school, a girl came up to Alan between classes, she told him her name was Betty and that she was fourteen. Smiling she asked, "Alan, how old are you?"

To which he immediately responded.

"I was twelve my last birthday. Why?"

"You are so good looking. I was thinking we might be dating this year, now I guess not," replied Betty somewhat disillusioned by his answer.

"Why would you say that?" Asked Alan who was totally confused by her reply.

"That you are good looking, or that we won't be dating?"

"That we won't be dating. Why won't we be dating?"

"Silly, you are too young for me. A fourteen-year-old girl can't date a twelve-year-old boy," said Betty as she turned to walk away.

"Who says so?" Shouted Alan unaware that their difference in age had anything to do with dating.

"If she thinks I am good looking, what difference does it make that I am twelve years old?"

Alan decided he needed to find out more about dating.

"Maybe I should ask mom and the Professor about dating and this age thing. Who cares, I may not like dating a girl, anyway."

Betty's father, who was President of Baylor University, was proud of her accomplishments he took time from his duties to oversee his daughter's education. Like Alan, she had excelled in advanced classes while in middle school, her intellect far exceeded her physical age. She had the knowledge of a college freshman coupled with the body of a fourteen-year-old girl. Betty's meeting with Alan was not a random thing, she had first noticed Alan when they were in eighth grade even then his blond hair and bright blue eyes captivated her imagination. She had been scheming to meet Alan since the last day of middle school and was determined to find him on the first day of high school to introduce herself. Following their brief meeting Betty, thought as she walked away.

"He is the best looking boy I have ever seen. I sure wish he was a little older. How can I date a twelve-year-old boy?"

During the ensuing days, Alan was constantly in her thoughts, she could not get him out of her mind even if he was only twelve years old. Desperate to maintain contact with him, she made sure they met as often as possible, so she could see him and talk with him. Betty had a strong desire to kiss Alan every time she saw him, unfortunately she didn't know how to make him want to be kissed. She decided to work on the problem as if it were a school project she made a detailed plan to get a kiss from Alan. Step one had been accomplished she had met Alan, he knew who she was, and he knew she thought he was good looking.

Alan and Jim had been computer literate most of their lives, lately the normal social networking had become boring causing them to look for more challenging and exciting things to do with their computer knowledge. After much deliberation, they decided to tackle encryption as a new project. At first they were writing secure programs to communicate between themselves on the internet, so that others could not read their messages. They soon advanced to the point they were able to detect the hidden security protection features contained in many of the commercial operating systems. In a short while, they were able to read other people's email. At first it was fun to see what their classmates were discussing on the internet although it proved to be boring after a while. As an experiment, they developed software to hack into each other's computers to see if they could take over operation of another person's computer without their knowing they had been hacked. Jim used the program first, he took over Alan's computer without Alan seeing any indication that his computer had been compromised. They celebrated their success by slapping each other's hand, their hacking program worked and was not obvious to the victim.

"Alan, we have done it!" said Jim extending his hand to Alan.

"Now, let's check to see what's on your computer, just for the heck of it, before we hack into mine."

They spent the next hour looking at all the programs, cookies, spyware etc. on Alan's computer before Alan remarked.

"There is something strange here that I don't understand. See this little icon it won't let me open it or shut it down. No matter what I do it does not respond to any commands."

"OK, let's get out of here and hack into my computer to see if it is there as well," said Jim.

Two hours later they established that the mysterious icon was not present on Jim's computer which added greatly to Alan's anxiety.

"I really didn't want to do this, but I think we need to hack Mom's and the Professor's computers to check for this undefined icon," said Alan concerned that someone might be spying on all of them.

"We will have to wait until tomorrow. I have homework tonight."

"Me too," responded Alan.

They cleared their laptops, folded them up and went home to do their homework. Tomorrow would be another day to work on their experiment.

The following day, Alan and Jim met under their favorite oak tree after school, working on their lap tops they managed to simultaneously hack into both the Professor's and Darlene's computers. Just as Alan suspected the pesky icon was on each of his parent's computers meaning every computer in his family's possession had been infected with the same potential malware.

"We have a mystery to solve, I don't know why anyone would want to spy on us, but we need to find out who is doing this and why. If we can get into this icon, maybe we can find out who put it there."

Alan was excited at the prospect of a new challenge, yet he was frightened by the implication of the icon being on all of his family's computers.

"Remember to use our encryption program when you send me emails, so they can't be read by anyone other than me," reminded Jim.

"Holly shit," shouted the computer operative at Alpha-2. "We have a security problem with the computers in Alan Strong's family unit, all three of them have been hacked."

Checking Abe's spy bug on their computers he said, "Our spy bug is still in place, but indications are that it could be in danger of being compromised or even worse being traced back to us."

One of the other agents asked.

"How in the hell could that happen? Don't we have the best of the best in spyware?"

"Yes, we do. For some reason we didn't update our old version on this project. I'm not sure what is going on here except Alan and his friend Jim started using an encryption program a couple of weeks ago when exchanging emails. It's a very sophisticated program which we have yet to decipher. We also know someone has been trying to remove our bug from Alan's computer and may be trying to capture it. I am erasing our old spy bug from all of these computers right away. I'll replace it with our new version which is completely embedded in the operating systems, it is virtually undetectable."

"Then you need to find out who hacked these computers in the first place, so we can keep them under surveillance and possibly put them out of business."

"I hate to think how hard it's going to be to keep up with Alan in the next few years, damn he is one smart kid," thought the supervising agent who suspected Alan and Jim might be involved in tracing their spyware.

"Guess what, Jim?" asked Alan when they met before school the following morning.

Jim jested, "You have a date with Betty."

"No, it's more exciting than that, the mystery icon disappeared from my computer. What do you make of that?"

"That's strange, have you checked your parent's computers?"

Alan grinned as he explained.

"Not yet, I'm reasonably sure someone is spying on my computer, so we need to use yours instead. If the icon is gone from the Professor's and mom's computers, I suspect they know we are on to their game, whatever it is. This is getting more mysterious and challenging every day."

"I'll meet you at the oak tree after school," said Jim before he walked away toward his first class.

Alan headed in the direction of his classroom, on his way he crossed paths with Betty who smiled when they met, but she did not speak. After they passed he wondered.

"Does she still think I'm good looking? The next time we meet I'll have to ask her."

He was preoccupied with his computer mystery and did not give Betty another thought the rest of the day. Jim and Alan found a shady place under their favorite tree, one of the many live oaks lining the campus where they sat down to hack into Alan's parent's computers using Jim's laptop.

"It's missing from the Professor's computer," exclaimed Jim.

"One down and one to go," remarked Alan as Jim started hacking into Darlene's office computer. Jim worked swiftly and a half hour later announced.

"It's gone here too."

"Let's analyze the information we have, maybe we missed something that will let us trace the icon to its source," said Alan with a bit of uncertainty.

Jim thought for a minute before he responded.

"You know, whoever is doing this probably knows more than we do about hacking and spying so we need to be doubly careful from here on. We don't want to endanger anyone. This is getting spooky."

"Why would anyone spy on us?" asked Alan as much to himself as to Jim.

They agreed to rethink the situation over night before deciding what to do next.

Crossing the campus after school, Betty saw Alan coming her way she altered her path to make certain they would meet face to face. When they were within a few feet she stopped greeting Alan in a sugary voice.

"Hi Alan, I haven't seen you in a couple of weeks. Where have you been hiding?"

"I haven't been hiding. I guess we just missed each other, I am really glad to see you though."

"Really, I am glad too. I've missed seeing you Alan. We need to get together once in a while, so we don't lose touch." Said Betty edging ever closer to Alan.

Alan was determined to ask even though he was somewhat embarrassed. He asked sheepishly.

"Betty do you still think I am good looking and why can't we date?"

Betty pounced like a young kitten replying.

"I do think you are good looking and I have been thinking maybe we should have a date after all."

She was touching Alan's arm by the time she finished answering, she then took his hand in hers and leaned forward kissing him softly on the mouth.

"Wow! I've never been kissed by a girl before it was nice."

"You know, if we had a date we could kiss more than once," replied Betty who enjoyed the kiss even more than she had imagined in her wildest fantasy about kissing Alan. Alan had unknowingly added to a torrid fire burning within Betty a fire which would soon become a raging torrent. She was determined to have a date with Alan as soon as she could arrange it.

"Could we go on a date to your house tomorrow after school?"

"Sure, there won't be anyone home, we can get a soft drink from the refrigerator and maybe watch TV or listen to some cool music."

"Good! OK, meet me here as soon as you get out of class tomorrow we will go to your house on our first date," exclaimed Betty her heart singing in anticipation, she was so excited she could hardly wait for tomorrow.

They met as planned at the end of their last class then walked holding hands to Alan's house, which was only three blocks away. Alan unlocked the front door then motioned for Betty to enter before him, just as Betty stepped inside, she felt a warm flush sweep over her entire body unlike anything she had ever experienced. Once the door had been closed, she put Alan's arms around her waist and began kissing him on the mouth. Her lips were warm and soft on his causing Alan to respond in kind he kissed her back feeling warm all over as he did. Although he had not given kissing much thought before, Alan liked kissing Betty this way he loved feeling her close to him. After a few minutes Alan stepped back asking.

"Would you like to have a soft drink, Betty?"

"No thanks. What I would like is go to your bedroom instead."

"Follow me," said Alan as he led her down the hall to his room.

They kissed several times before Betty asked.

"Can we undress?"

Somewhat dumbfounded Alan replied.

"Sure. Why not?"

Alan had never seen a naked girl other than his mother and that was only once or twice when she wasn't looking. Alan began removing his clothes all the while watching Betty with curiosity as she undressed, neither of them showed any embarrassment or uneasiness about being naked in front of the other.

Alan laid his socks on the chair beside his bed then looking at Betty, who was completely naked, he smiled saying.

"You have fine black hair on your front, can I touch it?"

"If you would like to."

Betty moved next to Alan to be more accessible she was trembling in anticipation of his touch.

"Put your hand here," she said guiding his hand to the top of her hair.

Alan loved the soft silky feel of her pubic hair rubbing it gently with his fingers he said, "I like the feel of it, so soft and fine."

"I like it too, now move your hand a little lower, I like that even more."

Betty indicating the exact spot she wanted Alan to touch. Several minutes passed before Betty laid back on the bed with her legs parted, she drew Alan on top of her so that their parts met. Alan, who was aroused by the touching and kissing, instinctively pushed to enter and began a quick bouncing movement with his erected organ which was throbbing with every heartbeat. Almost immediately Alan reached a climax before Betty was anywhere near a state of excitement necessary to achieve a climax. He stopped rolling beside Betty in ecstasy the first time he ever had sex. Betty pulled him against her kissing him hotly on the mouth while reaching for his penis. Once she grasped his still erected organ Betty kissed him on the neck then whispered.

"No, no, Alan you need to wait for me. Let me show you. Put your head here, now kiss my breast on the nipple. Yes, like that it feels so good, I really like it, but you have to do it gently. Put your hand here and caress me slowly see how much I like it when you do that. It feels so good Alan, don't stop. Oh, Alan, I love you. Keep doing it just like

114

that until I tell you am ready for you to put yours in and do it again. Remember, wait for me so we can finish together."

Alan was determined to make sure Betty got what she wanted. He followed her instructions perfectly, and they climaxed together. This time Alan did not stop until her wiggles subsided and she became still. They laughed and kissed afterward laying naked exploring each other's bodies while reveling in the marvel and afterglow of sex for the first time. Neither had experienced sex before, it was new and exciting, their sexual appetites had been awakened never to sleep again.

Alan spoke first.

"We've had our first date Betty, and I liked it more than anything you are so beautiful. We did it together. I really liked it, didn't you?"

"Alan you were wonderful, you made me feel good all over, I almost died when we finished together. I'll never want to date anyone other than you. Can we do it again next week?" Teased Betty who was absolutely serious.

Still feeling the after pleasure of sex Alan replied.

"We can do it whenever you want, next week or tomorrow. I promise to wait for you every time, I really like making you wiggle when we're doing it, but right now we better get dressed before someone shows up while we are naked." Replied Alan as he started putting on his clothes.

Betty dressed hastily then tenderly placed her hands on each side of his face before kissed him passionately her lips burning into his.

"I love you Alan." She whispered putting her arms around him and pulling him close.

Alan kissed her again wanting more of this new found pleasure. Taking her hand he volunteered.

"I'll walk you to the bus stop."

He waved goodbye as the bus pulled away from the curb, Betty was sitting next to the window and was smiling when she waved back at Alan thinking, "Oh, I love you Alan you make me happy."

"She is fantastic, I didn't know sex with a girl could make you feel that way. I really like Betty we make a good team."

Walking home all he could think about was Betty and their date. He promised himself to never forget what Betty had shown him about how to make her enjoy having sex with him.

"I'll always wait for her. It makes both of us feel good when I do!"

The following morning, Betty began searching for Alan the moment she arrived on campus eventually finding him just before their first class started. She touched him with her hand saying.

"Alan, Alan I've been looking all over for you. Can we meet after school today?"

Alan had been searching for Betty too, he wanted more than anything to be with her again, excited he replied.

"Let's meet at the same place."

They exchanged knowing smiles then rushed away to class. Alan had little problem concentrating in his classes he became absorbed in learning new things to the exclusion of thinking about Betty and the wonders of being with her. At the end of the last class his focus changed to Betty and their date, he rushed to their meeting place expecting to find Betty waiting for him. She was nowhere in sight he was the first to arrive. Ten minutes later, Betty still hadn't appeared causing Alan to fear she might have changed her mind. He was distraught at the thought of not having another date with Betty as they had planned. He was already excited just thinking about seeing her naked again and kissing her nipple like she had requested yesterday. Unknown to Alan, Betty was also upset because she was late getting to their meeting place she was afraid Alan might have left thinking she was not coming. She had been delayed by her teacher who wanted to compliment her on the great presentation Betty had made in class. The teacher kept talking and talking unaware she was keeping Betty from something very important. Betty was breathless when she arrived.

"Alan, I am so sorry I'm late, the teacher held me up. Can we go now?"

They walked toward Alan's house laughing, they were happy to be on another date, it was exciting they were both anticipating the thrill of having fantastic sex again.

A block from the house Alan said, "I can't wait."

"Me either." Replied Betty.

They ran the rest of the way. Both were breathing hard as Alan unlocked the door they kissed once inside then rushed to his room and began undressing. Alan finished first then watched as Betty removed her panties. Much to Betty's delight, Alan became the aggressor pulling her soft body firmly against his, kissing her hotly on the lips while gently feeling her butt with one hand. They were both panting, their hearts racing wildly as the kiss ended. Alan began kissing Betty on her nipple before he laid her on the bed where she parted her legs as he lay kissing her breasts, first one then the other, both were throbbing with excitement and pleasure. Alan began massaging her body with a soft gentle touch rubbing the exact spots Betty had directed him to touch the day before. He lay against her kissing her until her bottom began to twitch then wiggle with his every caress. The more she wiggled the more aroused Alan became he was near a climax as Betty began to squirm and wiggle more vigorously. Remembering Betty's request, Alan fought to wait for her even though it was becoming exceedingly difficult. The more Betty wiggled, the more excited Alan became, and the more intense was his body's urge to climax.

"Now, now Alan, do it now."

Whispered Betty as she spread her legs wide. Alan performed magnificently, slowly establishing a rhythm synchronized with Betty's increasing wiggles and squeals of joy. Although his parts were aching horribly, Alan maintained control, they climaxed in perfect unison as a feeling of intense pleasure engulfed their conciseness. Uncontrollably and together they let out moans while grasping each other's body to confirm their pleasure with one another.

"Don't move Alan, just stay there and kiss me."

Whispered Betty breathing hard and still shaking. He moved only slightly as he lay his upper body on top of her kissing her again and again. Their lips were burning hot, searing an unforgettable imprint into their minds. As he lay on top of Betty, Alan was relieved the pain in his groin had subsided before turning into intense body wrenching pleasure as the two of them finished together. The feeling was exhilarating an unforgettable experience for Alan. The overwhelming pleasure took over his body consuming his entire being, the thinking portion of his brain shut down completely overpowered by uncontrollable primordial pleasure.

Once her euphoria subsided Betty pushed Alan over on his back then lay close to him with his leg between hers and her arms around him, she whispered in his ear.

"Alan, I love you. You waited, and it was absolutely wonderful, I loved the way you did it. My pleasure was so intense I nearly passed out when we finished, thank you for waiting."

She pressed closer as Alan put his hand on her bottom and began kissing her nipple. Later while dressing they agreed the second time had been even better than the first.

"If it keeps getting better every time, I may not be able to stand it."

Said Betty playfully kissing Alan on the neck.

Alan kissed Betty on the mouth before replying.

"If there is anything better than this, I don't want to know about it. When can we do it again?"

"Soon I hope. We can't do it here every time, your neighbors will suspect something if I come to your house every afternoon. Maybe we could go to my house sometimes. You will like my room, Alan. I also have a surprise I want to show you when we go there."

"Ok, next time we go to your house."

The Alpha-2 members were in acute distress as they viewed the latest reports which included both the physical observations and the surveillance camera footage of Alan over the past few days.

"Do any of you see what I see here?" asked the agent in charge. He answered his own question.

"It looks to me like our twelve-year-old Alan is having sex with a fourteen-year-old female. How in the hell could this happen? He's not old enough to have an organism, why would he be having sex?"

One of the younger agents was quick to dispel any misconceptions about twelve-year-old boys and sex.

"First, Alan is a very advanced pre-teenager so far as smarts are concerned and secondly he may not be able to have an organism, but he can have an exciting and pleasurable climax just the same as you or anyone else. He is probably in the transition stage his body development is slightly behind that of his brain. Some twelve-year-olds are better developed biologically than others. In any case it will only be a short time before his body catches up then all hell may break loose because he could get her pregnant."

"They could be studying you know, instead of having sex," he added.

"Nah, they are not studying. There were no books involved, not only that who would run the last block home just to study?" commented the chief.

"Do we know who the girl is?" He asked looking around the room for an answer.

"Yes, we do, she in the daughter of the President of Baylor University and is a good looking advanced student in Alan's class," replied a female agent eager to demonstrate the detail and effectiveness of their observations.

"Well, I'm glad Alan is showing good taste," quipped the chief.

"We have a dual problem here, the girl thing plus Alan and his good friend Jim appear to be trying to hack into our computer even though we changed our spyware on Alan's and his parent's computers. I want you, computer people, to come up with a way to shut down their hacking program and to scare the shit out of them, so they don't try this sort of thing again. Are there any questions?"

The chief agent summed up with.

"Keep up the good work and let's get started on this hacking project right away and keep a close eye on Alan and Betty we can't have a twelve-year-old father on our hands."

Three weeks passed before Betty and Alan managed to go to her house for their third date. After their first two dates, Alan thought of her in a completely different way than he had before, he now saw Betty as a good looking brunette whom he cared for and wanted to kiss and please even when they were not on a date. He liked her even more than Jim, but in a different sort of way.

Once they reached Betty's house, they went directly to her room which was tastefully decorated with posters of popular entertainers hanging on brightly colored walls. Her bed had pink frills with a beautifully designed bedspread made using several matched colors blended into a unique design. The room smelled very much like a girl with a slight hint of perfume in the air. Alan was stimulated by the smell as well as his anticipation of kissing Betty. He kissed Betty several times then started to undress before Betty stopped him. "Not yet, there is something I want you to see first." Said Betty motioning toward her desk near the far window. She withdrew a paperback book from the top drawer holding it up so Alan could read the title. In bold red letters he saw: HOW TO ACHIEVE THE PERFECT SEXUAL EXPERIENCE. Turning to the last page, Betty asked Alan to read the last sentence.

Taking his cue, Alan read it aloud.

"It takes most men several years to learn the techniques presented in this book and unfortunately some men never learn to please a woman, if you find one that wants to please you, never let him go."

Alan closed the book then looked toward Betty somewhat bewildered. Betty kissed him before he could put the book down saying.

"Alan, you learned everything in this book on our first date, you made me so happy. I love you Alan, I always will."

They finished undressing before Alan replied.

"I love you too Betty, you are so beautiful. You make me feel good and I want more than anything to please you. I will wait for you no matter what."

Although Baylor University has always maintained a very conservative environment, Betty's mother a practical liberal, made sure Betty had access to and knew how to use birth control pills. Betty's mother remembered well what it was like when she was fourteen and had sex for the first time. She had worried for over a month that she might be pregnant which would have been a disaster for her and her family. She did not want Betty to go through the same agonizing experience if it could be avoided.

Alpha-2 enlisted the aid of their maximum security computer experts to decipher Jim and Alan's encryption program making it possible for them to read Jim and Alan's email correspondence. They learned the boys were making little progress in determining the source of the original spyware installed on Alan's and his family's computers, but now they were attempting to find new spyware which they believed had been installed after the old version had been removed. The chance of them being successful was remote, however, these two had developed their own brand of encryption and hacking software, so they could not be ignored. With the new information gleaned from their emails,

Alpha-2 decided to implement a new approach in dealing with these young experts, in the meanwhile they would continue to monitor their efforts to find the new spyware.

"Have we finalized a plan to handle this hacking problem?" asked the Alpha-2 manager. "Yes sir, we have a two pronged plan which should solve the current problem and prevent any future problems from this duo of young hackers," responded the computer expert. He went on to outline their plan in detail.

"Our plan is simple. First, we will simultaneously shut down and destroy their encryption and hacking software to alert them to the fact that we know what they are doing and that we can counter any actions they might take. Second, we have arranged for a federal agent to speak with them personally and off the record to discuss the severity and possible prison time associated with hacking. He has agreed to tell them our icons were part of a federal investigation. If they are as smart as we think, they will not want any further investigation of their activities by the feds and certainly will want to avoid facing criminal charges for hacking."

Jim called Alan on his cell phone, he was agitated and alarmed a bit frightened as he exclaimed excitedly.

"Alan, we have been found out! Someone has shut down our safe email program it doesn't work anymore."

"Uh Oh, what about the hacking software?"

"I haven't tried it yet, Alan. Let me see if I can get into your computer to see if it works. I'll call you back."

An hour later Jim was on the phone again, this time he was frightened.

"It doesn't work either, both programs have been destroyed. See if you can get into my computer."

Alan went to work trying furiously to determine the state of their hacking program he was upset and alarmed when he realized someone had destroyed several months of their work. He called Jim saying with urgency in his voice.

"Mine didn't work either! Let's meet at the oak tree to think this through before we do anything!"

Seated in the shade of their oak they proceeded to analyze the situation particularly with respect to the hacking program.

"So far the only thing we have done wrong is hacking into my parent's computers. Our hacking each other's computers was by mutual consent, so it probably doesn't count," said Alan as he retraced the events of the past month.

"It looks like whoever had the spyware on your family's computer found out about us and know that we were trying to locate them," added Jim alarmed at the thought of an unknown group destroying their work.

"No doubt about it, we have been found out," agreed Alan.

"What do we do next? They have disarmed us and ruined our work, I think this is a warning, don't you?"

"Yes, Jim they want us to stop and I'm sure we should. The thing is, we still don't know who they are or why they were spying on my family, do we?"

"No, but I think we should stop trying to find out. Don't you?" Replied Jim firmly.

"Yes, we need to shut it down, at least for now."

They agreed on a plan of no action of any kind for at least two months opting instead to play a waiting game to see what moves their advisories might make. They both agreed it would be difficult to defeat an enemy they could not find or identify maybe their adversaries would inadvertently show themselves if they did nothing. The two young scientist were setting under their oak tree a week later, discussing their next project when a large man approached them holding a badge in his hand. He held the badge in front of him at arm's length making sure the boys could easily read the FBI inscription before he spoke.

"Gentlemen, you are Alan Strong, and Jim Running Horse, are you not?"

"Yes sir." They answered simultaneously with a ting of fear in their voices.

The federal agent was pleased at the indication of fear, it meant he would succeed in his mission without having to resort to threats of retribution. He continued in a stern voice and with a grave scowl on his face.

"You know why I am here, we have found hacking software on both of your computers. Furthermore, we have records showing you used that software several times to hack into other people's computers as well as your own. Gentlemen, hacking is against federal law!"

"We only hacked into my parent's computers and then only to see if a strange icon we found on my computer was on theirs as well."

"We had reason to think it was spyware. When the icon disappeared from his family's computers, that's when we started trying to find out who had removed it." Stated Jim with a little less fear, still his voice did not have its normal crispiness and conviction.

"We meant no harm, Sir, we were only trying to protect my parents," added Alan.

"That reminds me, Alan, you have been seeing a lot of this girl, Betty. Is she involved in this plot?"

Alan replied immediately and with finesse befitting an adult.

"She's my girlfriend, she knows nothing about this she's a girl."

The agent had to hold back a smile as his interrogation continued.

"Did either of you ever attempt to take over someone's computer for personal gain?"

"No, we were only interested in protecting my parents from being spied on," insisted Alan.

"OK, I understand your motive, but it's still against the law! Do you understand that?"

He continued talking, but changed the tone of his voice becoming somewhat more consolatory and a lot less gruff.

"I want you to listen carefully because this time I am letting both of you off on the hacking issue, but there is something you don't know about. You have interfered with a federal investigation to shut down an international hacking organization. The icons you were so worried about are ours they were put there to detect attempted hacking and to trace the source. Any further attempt on your part to trace the source of our icon will constitute willful interference with a federal investigation and could result in jail time for both of you. Do you understand?"

The agent did not wait for a reply, he hurried to his car and drove away grinning, grateful that he could play a role in keeping two exceptionally bright boys out of trouble and on the path to possible greatness in the field of computer science.

Both Jim and Alan were frightened and worried it had never occurred to either of them that they could be interfering with a federal investigation. They were glad the federal agent did not officially charge them with anything and they were obliged to him for explaining the presence of the mystery icon, he didn't have to do that. They're hacking experience had been enlightening and exciting, but their hacking careers had come to a climactic end.

Jim turned to Alan as they were parting for the day.

"What is this business of Betty being your girlfriend?"

Alan did not answer instead he hurried away smiling to himself thinking about Betty, but he was perplexed by the federal agent's comment about Betty.

"How did the agent know Betty, and I had been seeing a lot of each other, am I under surveillance by the government?"

Alan dismissed the idea as being highly improbable, after all, he was only twelve years old. He rushed directly home approaching the Professor in his study.

"Professor, if you have time, there is something I need to discuss with you."

Alan spent the better part of the next two hours detailing his and Jim's foray into encryption and computer hacking as well as their findings and the resulting visit by the federal agent. The Professor was pleased Alan had chosen to confide in him thinking.

"I probably would never have told my father anything had I been in a similar situation."

Back at Abe's headquarters the chief agent read the latest report from Alpha-2 before telling those assigned to protect Alan.

"Gentlemen, the hacking thing has been solved, but the girl thing is in full bloom and will not be going away. Alan and this girl Betty are getting together on a regular basis which makes me ask, do we need to interfere?"

The answer was a resounding, no.

"No, she is not endangering him, just screwing him. Actually they are screwing each other it's a mutual thing."

"OK, but keep me informed,"

Darlene reacted like most mothers when she became aware of the details concerning Alan's and Jim's foray into computer hacking. She was relieved they had not been arrested or charged by the federal agent, nevertheless, she was pissed off at Alan for not using his head before the situation got out of hand. Still she was proud of him for trying to protect all of them from being hacked by unknown parties. Once she calmed down and thought the situation through, Darlene decided this would be a good time for Alan to spend a little time with his grandparents and uncle, away from computers, on the banks of the Sabine where she grew up.

She called her father arranging for Alan to stay with him and Gerta for the remaining three weeks of his summer break. She, Randall and Alan stopped for lunch at the Uptown Cafe in Joaquin, where Darlene was recognized by the owner who had been staring at her for several minutes before he spoke.

"Just look at you Darlene! Were it not for your blond hair and those beautiful green eyes, I wouldn't have known you. I'm so glad to see you, Darlene, you look great. We have all missed you around here!"

They discussed old times for a bit before Alan insisted on ordering lunch he was hungry after spending four and a half hours riding in the car. Afterward they drove directly to Darlene's parent's home where they were greeted by the entire Strong family, or what was left of it, the two older brothers were no longer living there.

Little had changed since Darlene last visited her parents, the house was still in disrepair, there was no electricity and her family looked the same just a little older. James and Sid the oldest of her brothers no longer lived in the area. James, the oldest, had taken a job as a roughneck on a drilling rig and then moved away with the rig when it moved to West Texas. Sid enlisted in the U.S. Marine Corps and had not been home for the last three years. He wrote once in a while though not regularly. Karl, the youngest brother, who was twenty-six, still lived with Jessie and Gerta their survival was dependent upon his help. Old age and acute arthritis made it difficult for Jessie to walk and impossible for him to provide for Gerta and himself without help. Karl wanted to leave, but he could not bring himself to abandon his parents, as the only son in the area, it was his duty to take care of them.

Alan and Karl hit it off immediately, Karl enjoyed listening to Alan explain the way things were in Waco and appreciated Alan's interest when he talked about life here near the river. Right away Karl sensed that Alan was a smart kid who knew about a lot of things, some of which Karl knew little or nothing. Alan considered Karl an intellectual equal, a person who knew interesting things he had never been exposed to or even heard of. During their ongoing conversations, Karl expressed a willingness to teach Alan how to live on the banks of the Sabine without the conveniences he had at home which appealed to Alan's inquisitive nature and inclination toward adventure. Although he was willing to live like Karl and his grandparents while staying with them, Alan insisted on keeping his cell phone which connected him with his mother, the Professor, Jim and most of all Betty who he talked with every night before going to sleep. Jessie agreed to recharge Alan's phone at the ranch house on his last round each day, he went there twice daily to check on the house and facilities and to recharge his own phone on the last trip. Alan appreciated Jessie performing this service it made it possible for him to make calls each evening before retiring and still have enough battery charge to last through most of the following day. Unlike Jessie, Alan used his cell-phone for things other than making and receiving calls, he routinely checked the news and weather forecast and took pictures of anything and everything that interested him. Some of his more compelling pictures he sent to Jim and Betty for their immediate enjoyment, he saved all of his pictures in a folder on his cell phone as a pictorial record of his experiences at his grandparent's home. After he returned home, Alan planned to download the folder to his computer as a permanent record, he then planned to make a slide show presentation of his pictures to his mom and the Professor. The photos would be a part of his account of his summer visit at the Strong Plantation as he liked to call his grandparent's place. He was also keeping a written account of his experiences which he planned to integrate with his pictures to produce a documentary which he titled: A Summer Stay at the Strong Plantation.

Gerta and Jessie were drawing Social Security checks each month, although they were receiving the minimum amounts payable under the law, they were thankful to have a supplement to the meager salary the Dalton's paid Jessie to look after the ranch house and lake. Darlene's

$500 per month contribution helped them maintain a reasonable standard of living, by their measure, but it did not provide much more than a comfort factor. Mostly they were happy to have Medicare, previously they had no medical insurance of any kind for themselves or for the family members. Fortunately, there had never been a medical problem in the family which required the attention of a doctor, they had minor illnesses from time to time, which were treated and cured with natural remedies using medicinal plants and herbs found in the woods and open areas along the Sabine. Knowledge of the healing ability and specific treatment qualities of local plants and herbs had been handed down from generation to generation in the Strong family this knowledge was considered a part of their heritage. Karl had insisted his parents apply for Social Security and helped them complete the necessary paperwork while pointing out other benefits for which they qualified. Jessie and Gerta refused to accept food stamps or any form of welfare from the local, state or federal agencies. In their view, to accept welfare would be degrading to the family name, the Strong family had always taken care of themselves, it was a matter of pride, and they had no intention of disgracing the family name. The Strong family would remain independent and self-sufficient they were not accepting welfare or a free handout from anyone.

After washing the dishes and cleaning the kitchen following supper, Karl and Alan were sitting on the front porch enjoying the twilight and discussing the next day's plans when Karl asked.

"How would you like to help me snare a wild pig tomorrow?"

"What kind of snare? I'm not sure I know what you are talking about," replied Alan more than willing to help Karl and to learn about snares.

"Well, there are several kinds of snares, but it takes a really strong one to hold a wild pig because you never know what pig you're going to catch. It could weigh from fifty pounds to three hundred fifty pounds, so the snare has to be able to hold a three hundred fifty pound pig."

"I want to help anyway I can. I've never seen a real snare. One time Jim and I made one out of string when we were trying to catch a rabbit, but it didn't work, so I guess it doesn't count. What are we going to do with the pig after we catch it?"

Karl felt it was important for Alan to understand the reason for catching a pig, other than showing him how it was done, he replied soberly.

"The reason we are going to snare a pig is for the meat, we need to catch and butcher a pig, so mom, dad and I can have pork to eat next month. Our supply will be running out soon. If we don't snare a hog, then we don't have pork to eat."

"Do we need to get up extra early in the morning?"

"Nah, we are going to set the snare in the afternoon wild hogs don't like to forage in the daylight they prefer the twilight hours and just before dawn. Don't get me wrong, these wild pigs will eat any time of the day if it suits them, but they mostly stay out of sight during the daylight hours. I'll tell you what, we will start getting everything together just after noon that way we can finish up by supper time. After we have everything we need, we have to find the best location to set our snare which may take us several hours. The conditions have to be just right or there is no chance of us catching a pig. I'll see you in the morning, Alan."

Karl did not wait for a response instead he walked off of the porch and disappeared into the woods.

Alan went directly to his room and called Betty.

"Hey, Betty, it's me. Can we talk?"

"Yes, my handsome man, there is no one here except me, so we can talk about whatever you like."

Alan had been at the Strong Plantation for over a week and Betty was aching to touch him and to feel his body next to hers. She missed him terribly, even more than she had expected when he told her he would be visiting his grandparents for three weeks. Being with Alan gave her great pleasure, touching him reinforced the love between the two of them, it was very satisfying to Betty to know that Alan loved her unequivocally. He made his love for her clear by his actions and devotion, he made her happy.

"My beautiful, Betty, I miss you like you cannot believe. Every night I keep thinking about kissing you and about you kissing me. I try not to think about being together with my arms around you, but I love you so much it is impossible not to."

"Alan, how much longer before you come home? I want to hug and kiss you. We need to be together, I can hardly bear our being apart like this."

"Me either. Just two more weeks, until we will be together again, then I will kiss you just the way you like, I promise."

Betty knew exactly what Alan meant, she was delighted and grateful that Alan remembered how much she liked being kissed.

"Alan, I hope you know how much you mean to me. I don't ever want to be without you."

He went to bed thinking about Betty after a while he fell asleep then dreamed about her most of the night.

The next morning Alan was up early ready to help Karl set the snare to catch a wild pig, or hog as the larger ones were called, he was excited to see how Karl made a snare and to be part of the process. He had all sorts of visions about how the snare was going to work and what it was going to look like. The only snare Alan had seen was one he and Jim has set to catch a rabbit and that one had not worked the way they planned the rabbit got away.

Just after their noon meal, Alan and Karl went to the storage shack out back of the house to retrieve the material needed for their set. First, Karl showed Alan a lightweight steel trap similar to those used on mid-sized animals except his trap had a very soft spring so that the trap would not crush a bone or hold onto the leg of an animal that tripped it. That was not the purpose of this steel trap it was intended to aid in the operation of the snare which would hold the hog once he or she tripped the snare.

The snare itself was made up of a long piece of strong steel cable capable of holding several hundred pounds, on one end was an adjustable noose and on the other a super strong clasp connected to a steel chain which could be used to anchor the snare to a large tree or other suitable immovable object. Steel cable was used to prevent the trapped hog from chewing himself free, these beasts are smart and will not give up trying to get free until they are totally exhausted or dead.

The heavier snare parts were loaded into a backpack which Karl strapped on before they left the pickup to enter the woods. He had a hatchet, a large knife and other tools attached to his hunting belt. Karl hefted a 30/30 semi-automatic rifle over his shoulder which he carried along with the backpack filled with the heavier supplies. Alan carried a fold-up military style shovel in one hand and a small backpack containing the lighter components of the snare. They walked into the woods amid the lush green of the trees and the tangled undergrowth which quickly engulfed them. It was quiet, nothing was moving except the tops of the trees which rustled slightly when the wind blew the shaded expanse below the green canopy was humid and hot it had a wild primordial feel and a raw smell which increased in intensity as the hunters trudged further from the pickup seeking signs of their prey. Alan was filled with a strange sense of adventure as the hunters ventured deeper into the woods, he felt the thrill of the hunt for the first time experiencing a slight rush when he realized it was a battle of wits between themselves and a wild animal to determine whether the animal would survive or be eaten. For the first time in his life, he was a part of a basic battle which had gone on since the beginning of time.

Karl kept up a continuous narrative of what they were doing, what they were looking for and why this information was important to their being successful in snaring a hog.

"We would like to find a good site to set our snare which is not too far from the pickup. Any hog we catch will have to be transported to the house to be butchered and stored. With just you and me to move it, we don't want it be too big or too far away from the pickup."

"Yeah, I understand. What do we do first?"

"The first thing we need to do is find a pig trail that has fresh tracks, so we know it is still in use. Look at these tracks here, Alan. These are pig tracks, see how the two front toes are split and make a deep print? This is what we are looking for, but they need to be fresh these are old prints. Fresh prints will have little bits of dirt around them and they will look wetter than these do. See how these are all dried out? That means they were made some time ago."

Alan looked carefully at the prints in the narrow trail and after making his own analysis asked.

"Does this mean that the more prints we see, the more pigs there are in the group? Or does it mean the pigs use the trail more frequently?"

"Yes, to both questions," replied Karl before he added.

"We also need to look for areas near the trail where the hogs have been rooting they dig up the ground to find roots they like to eat. If we can find a new rooting area and fresh tracks on one of the nearby trails, then we have a good place to set our snare with a high chance of catching a hog. I also like to look at the size of the prints too, I don't really want to catch a big hog. I'd rather have a medium sized one that you and I can handle without having to ask one of the neighbors for help. Not only that, they taste better."

Karl and Alan examined a half dozen potential sites before Karl decided they had found a promising place to set their snare.

"Alan, why is this a good place for us to set our snare?"

"Well, first of all, there are a lot of fresh medium sized hog tracks in the trail and second there are new rooted areas nearby. One on the up side of the site and one on the downside which means the hogs may be going both ways on the trail improving our chance of success. We are not far from the end of the clearing just south of the house, so we can handle the catch without help."

"All right! Alan, you are a born woodsman for sure. Now comes the critical part to be successful you have to understand that these hogs are not easily fooled. If we make one mistake like leaving our scent here, or leaving the snare visible our chance of catching one of them goes to near zero. From here on we have to be careful. You watch while I make the set."

Karl unloaded his backpack placing each item on the ground in the order he would need them. First, he scooped out a shallow hole slightly larger than the steel trap and deep enough so that when completed the set would be level with the surrounding part of the trail. He then set the steel trap in the hole with the trip facing upward. Next Karl carefully laid the snare loop around the perimeter of the steel trap making sure to pull it up snugly so that it could not fall away. Once convinced the snare would stay in place, he anchored it to a nearby tree with the chain. The snare, steel trap and nearby area were gingerly covered with light dirt and leaves to conceal the entire apparatus. Karl sharpened several short sticks on both ends with his hunting knife placing them in the ground at selected spots where Karl did not want the hogs to walk. The idea was to encourage any hog that came by to walk near the snare. As a final enticement for the hog to step where he wanted, Karl dug a shallow hole just off of the trail in which he buried fresh roots from the nearby area where the hogs had been eating. The hole was placed so that a hog on the trail would more than likely step into the snare should it attempt to eat the buried roots.

Alan watched with interest as Karl completed the set. Until watching Karl, he had no idea that setting a snare was so complicated and required such detailed knowledge of the habits of the query. Alan was stimulated by how scientific setting a snare turned out to be he had never thought about it before, nor had he appreciated the knowhow and knowledge required to do it right. Karl's final step was to mark the site with two pieces of red cloth that he hung from tree limbs on either side of the path. Anyone from the area would recognize them as a warning to be careful that a trap or snare was set nearby. These warnings were intended to prevent him or anyone else from accidentally stepping into the snare. The hunters returned to the pickup then drove to the house leaving the snare unattended while they waited for it to be activated by their query, or some other wild animal which happened to step in the wrong place. Alan and Karl checked the snare set the next morning, much to Alan's disappointment, it was empty they had not caught a hog. Karl looked about for several minutes finally remarking.

"This is encouraging, Alan, see there has been a lot of rooting activity around here which means the hogs are still feeding in this area and could stay here for several more days. We will check again in the morning maybe one of these critters will make a mistake before we come back. These wild hogs are really smart, you know. Even with all of our detailed planning there is no assurance we will not come up empty handed with this set."

As they approached the site on the second morning, Alan could hear the snarling of an angry wild boar he was making a horrendous noise and was obviously still capable of putting up a fight if approached. He was snared by his hind foot and no matter how hard he tried he could not get away or break the cable, yet he jumped stretching the chain to its limit and bit furiously at his captors all the while snarling and defiantly shaking his head from side to side. There was a lot of life and fight left in this hog!

Karl motion for Alan to stay back as he raised his rifle to his shoulder. He slowly squeezed the trigger hitting the hog squarely between the eyes dropping him to the ground. The hog jerked several times against the restraining cable before the snarling decreased in intensity and finally stopped altogether and the hog lay still. Satisfied the hog was dead, Karl removed the snare from his hind foot and the two of them dragged the lifeless body to a nearby tree at the edge of a clearing. Karl

132

retrieved a light rope and pulley system from his backpack which he rigged up on a sturdy branch then hoisted the hog off of the ground with the rope around his hind feet so that his head hung down. After tying off the rope, Karl, with one quick slash of his knife cut the hog's throat. Alan looked on horrified as the blood gushed from the animal's slashed throat and began to pool on the ground. He could smell the warm blood as it spread in the dirt it had a unique nauseating odor unlike anything his nose had ever encountered. The blood smell almost made him vomit as he stood there motionless. He walked away to avoid throwing up, he didn't want Karl to think he couldn't handle the situation he choked back his nausea and returned to the hanging hog to be whatever help he could.

"This is the first step in preparing the hog for butchering we need to let him bleed out before we haul him to the house. This way all the blood will soak in the ground and be left in the woods. It will make a terrible stench, if we did it at the house the foul odor would make us miserable for quite a while," said Karl as he wiped his knife clean before putting it back in his belt.

The pickup was parked in another clearing not far away, Karl directed Alan to stay with the hog while he tried to find a way to drive the pickup to the hanging tree, so they could avoid hauling the hog to the pickup. After what seemed like an eternity, Karl came crashing through the underbrush driving the beat up old pickup directly to the hanging tree, where he lined the floor of the pickup bed with used burlap bags before they lowered the hog into the pickup and closed the tailgate. Alan was amazed at how efficient Karl had been in the entire process of killing the hog and getting it into the pickup. The whole procedure had not been very hard observed Alan.

"Like most things, if you know what you are doing, they are not difficult at all."

Rumbling through the underbrush in the pickup Karl explained.

"Our next step in getting this hog ready to butcher will be scalding him. Do you remember the two big iron kettles next to the smoke house? We are going to fill them with water then build a big fire under both of them. When the water starts boiling, we are going to pour it in that open-ended fifty-five gallon oil drum sitting next to the lifting post. By that time, we will have the hog on the rope and pulleys with him hanging directly above the drum. When the drum is nearly filled with boiling water, we will lower him into the scalding water several times to make his hair soft so we can easily shaved it off. You have to be careful not to overdo the scalding or the hair will become hard and will be tough to remove. The scalding has to be done just right to be effective. We will save the skin and fat when we cut up the pig. By frying the skin and attached fat until it is crisp we get cracklins which make great snacks that is the reason we remove the hair so we can eat the skin. Some people remove the fat before frying the skin and call the resulting product pork rinds which is a little different from cracklins, but are still good." You can render the fat and later make soap or keep it for cooking.

"How do you know when the hog has been scalded enough?"

"Alan, it's something that comes with experience. After you have done it several times, you just know."

Alan pitched in when they reached the smokehouse, he helped carry water to fill the kettles, tended the fires and filled the drum once the water was boiling. After scalding the hog, Alan tried his hand at scraping, or shaving off the hair, but he was not very skilled at the task he took far too long in removing a small patch of hair from the hog's back. In the interest of saving time, he gave way to Karl and his grandfather who were experts at scraping hogs in no time the hog was ready to be skinned and cut up. At the end of the day, half of the hog had been salted and was hanging in the smoke house ready to be cured. Shortly a plume of hickory smoke rose from the smoke house and floated on the air moving downwind away from the Strong's place. The smoke was needed to keep the flies away from the meat while it cured that it imparted a flavor to the meat was a minor benefit which city people thought was the reason the meat was smoked in the first place. A generous coating of salt actually preserved the meat, whether it was smoked or not, the whole process was much the same as that used by early Americans during colonial days and up until refrigeration became the norm throughout the country. The other half of the hog had been fully butchered, carved into the various cuts used by the Strong family for generations. The intestines and other organs, unsuitable for human consumption, Karl saved to be used later as fish bait for his bank lines and trotlines which he regularly set in the Sabine. By the time the butchering was completed, it was late in the day, Alan was dead tired and could still smell the hog's blood it seemed to be permanently

134

lodged in his nasal passages. He had blown his nose hard several times in an attempt to get rid of it, but the odor would not go away no matter what he tried. It was a smell he would never forget.

Karl announced, "As soon as everyone gets cleaned up, we will be having barbequed pork for supper."

Alan was not sure he would be ready to eat the hog after spending the whole day killing and cutting him up. Still, he gathered clean clothes and headed to the makeshift outdoor shower which consisted of a barrel full of water attached to a beam below the roof of the storage shed. There was a hose attached to the bottom of the barrel with a shower head on the lower end which was also fitted with a valve to turn the water on or off. Water for the shower was supplied by rain runoff from the roof of the shed except during dry periods when it had to be supplemented by water drawn from their cistern which had to be added by hand. Alan stepped naked under the barrel standing on a slightly raised brick platform then turned the valve allowing the water to spray on his head first, surprisingly the water was relatively warm. With a little movement, on Alan's part, the water covered his entire body. He lathered with the homemade soap making sure to clean every part of his body he sucked water through his nose several times then rinsed off and toweled himself down before putting on his clean clothes. This refreshing ritual had been performed outside in the open for anyone to see since the shower was not enclosed. So far as Alan knew no one was watching, not that he cared anyway, all he wanted was to get the blood smell off of him and out of his nostrils once and for all.

The dirty clothes were collected then thrown into the boiling pots along with some homemade lye soap then left to soak overnight. The next morning the clothes were rinsed in clear water before being hung on the clothesline to dry. As he was walking back to the house, Alan could still smell the hog's blood it seemed to be permanent, no matter what he did it would not go away! It was sickening.

"I hope it goes away soon, I'll never forget this horrible smell as long as I live. Now I can imagine how the battlefield must have smelled when the battle ended back in medieval times, I'm glad I wasn't there!"

Over the following days, Karl taught Alan how to hunt and fish he became a good marksman with a keen eye and learned the art of catching fish using bank lines and trot lines. Alan appreciated that Karl never killed for fun, or for the sport of it, he only killed to put food on the table for himself and his parents. Sometimes, he gave away fish and other game to his neighbors when they had more than they could use. On some days he caught a lot of fish and other days he caught none it depended on the luck of the draw so to speak. As the last week of his stay was drawing to an end, there were several things Alan wanted to ask Karl about, yet he was hesitant he was not sure it was the right thing for him to do. Putting aside his misgivings he finally asked.

"Karl, I was wondering, do you have a girlfriend?"

"Sure, Alan, I have a really nice girlfriend. Frieda is her name, she lives just down the road a couple of miles from here. We've been friends since high school."

"Have you ever thought about getting married?" Asked Alan sensing that the door was open to further discussion on the subject.

"We have talked about it for several years and we want to get married. It's sort of complicated because I can't leave mom and dad here alone. They need me now more than ever, since James and Sid are gone," replied Karl without a hint of regret in his voice.

"Can't you live here after you marry?"

"No, we can't. You see, we agreed when we first started dating that when we marry, we will leave this area, we are going to make a better life for ourselves and our kids than is possible here. Look at what your mom has done. Both of us have been taking college correspondence courses, so we can finish our education before we marry. To live here is not in our future," replied Karl.

To change the subject Karl asked, "What about you, Alan do you have a girl friend?"

"Yes, I'm glad you asked because she is the nicest and best person I have ever met and we are a great pair we love each other very much."

"Don't you think you are a little young to be in love?"

"Not really, Betty and I like being together." Replied Alan not wanting to reveal anything more.
Alan asked quickly.

"Karl, what is your girlfriend like?"

"Well, I'll tell you what, I am going to meet her tonight, so I'll take you along and you can see for yourself. I'm sure you two will like each other, Frieda will be happy to meet you, since I have told her all about you."

Karl was amazed at Alan's ability to avoid further questioning about his relationship with Betty. After supper, the two of them drove in the battered pickup to Frieda's house. Alan was fascinated by Frieda from the moment they met, she was a redhead who dazzled him with her good looks and East Texas friendliness. As the evening progressed, she talked with Alan more than she did with Karl. Frieda asked a lot of questions and was very interested in Alan's description of Betty and the bond between them. Alan spoke much more freely with Frieda about himself and Betty than he had with Karl producing a huge smile on Karl's face. It was obvious that Alan liked and trusted Frieda because he open up about Betty. As the end of the evening drew near, Alan excused himself pleading exhaustion he knew Karl wanted some time alone with Frieda before the evening ended, so he returned to the pickup to wait for Karl. When Alan called Betty later that night he told her about Karl and Frieda and how much they were in love. He ended by saying.

"They are in love just like you and me, only they're older. Mom and the Professor are picking me up tomorrow. I will see you as soon as I can after we get home. I love you Betty."

"I'm counting the hours until we are together. I'll be waiting for you tomorrow," said Betty as she blew a kiss into the phone relieved that they were going to be together soon and she could actually touch Alan.

Alan's stay at the Strong Plantation, as he liked to call it, not only changed his perspective on those things which he considered important it also reinforced his understanding of love and duty as well as right and wrong. He admired Karl for his sense of duty to his parents and also for his intelligence. Alan perceived that lack of formal education does not mean a person is not smart, only that their exposure to an advanced education has been limited. A situation which can be remedied by determined individuals such as Karl and Frieda who were fighting to further their educations in order to make their lives better for themselves and their future children. He learned that life is not about you, it's about how you interact with those you love, your friends and family and most of all your children the most valuable and most cherished asset two people can ever create. He was impressed by

Karl's love for his parents and his dedication to them in their old age even though it infringed on his own life plans.

The last report to Alpha-2 concerning the Strong Plantation read in part.

"This has been an interesting assignment, camping out in the woods for three weeks while trying to keep track of Alan and Karl proved challenging we managed to do the job and gained some interesting knowledge not available in Houston. Be assured, we did not go undetected by Karl, he knew we were there all along, but fortunately he had no idea what we were doing on the banks of the Sabine. He checked us out on a daily basis to make sure we were not there to cause trouble or create some unwanted mischief. It doesn't appear Alan ever knew we were here."

During their senior year in high school, everyone knew Betty and Alan were a couple they went to all the school functions together as well as the outside social events. Alan was too young to have a car, so Betty, whose parents had given her a new Thunderbird, drove on their dates. Both of their parents were well aware they were going steady and approved. Betty's parents had met Alan several time and were fascinated by his intellect and clean cut, good looks, particularly Betty's mother who thought he was handsome and a perfect match for her Betty. Darlene and the Professor both liked Betty she was smart, good looking and an interesting person and although she was older than Alan, they made an extraordinary pair. Alan had grown tall and muscular in the last three years, he was six feet tall, blond and still growing.

Darlene suspected that Alan and Betty were having sex together, but unlike Alan when she and the Professor were dating, she did not ask. Alan and Betty were inseparable, during the summer following their graduation from high school. They spent as much time together as possible doing all sorts of things such as going on picnics, dancing and visiting nearby parks and game preserves, Alan was interested in everything. Neither looked forward to parting in the fall, but there were some things they could not control or avoid.

Chapter 6 Rachel's Project

Rachel continued her rapid advance in her career at Camex Petroleum, Inc. She was outstanding in her performance and excelled in making in presentations to upper management. Consequently, she was promoted to Senior Engineer over several coworkers who had been with the company much longer, but who did not possess her drive, or her ability to analyze projects and work with others. In her new position she was charged with handling all company matters related to partner operated properties. Her responsibilities required some travel to attend joint operating meetings which were normally scheduled in the home office of the company operating the properties. On rare occasions, it was necessary for Rachel to travel out of state for two to three days at a time. Such meetings with her contemporaries from other companies were focused on current and future operations of the jointly owned properties. Approval for most actions were defined in the applicable Joint Operating Agreement as was the voting percentage of ownership need for that approval. Rachel became exceptionally adept at conveying her ideas at these meetings. She did her homework beforehand, so she knew in detail the economics and engineering requirements of each project being considered by the company representatives. Rachel became an accomplished negotiator for her company in her dealings with other company representatives, her expertise applied equally to determining a project's feasibility and to formulating agreements governing proposed new projects.

The travel involved created a serious problem for Rachel forcing her to hire a full-time nanny to care for Martha in those instances when she was away overnight or for several days. She moved the nanny into the guest room over the garage, so she would be available to care for Martha when Rachel's travel schedule required her to be away overnight. This arrangement worked well, yet Rachel disliked being separated from Martha for any reason. She understood the demands of her job came first if she planned to advance into a management position she needed to be available whenever and wherever needed. She wanted to succeed as both a mother and a business person, so she needed to be away from Martha for short periods to attain her goals. Income from her Gentex stipend plus income from her job placed Rachel in the upper tier of the middle class. She and Martha were financially independent allowing Rachel to plan Martha's future without monetary constraints. They lived modestly, yet enjoyed the finer things in life. Martha took music and dancing lessons, which she loved, she became a gifted vocalist and a polished dancer while still in grade school.

Within five years, Rachel became Vice-President and Manager of Joint Operations for the company. In this position she supervised a staff of thirteen including eight engineers and technicians plus five administrative and secretarial people. Her department was responsible for all joint operations conducted by the company. As manager, Rachel was charged with maximizing Camex's profit from this segment of their business which accounted for one third of the company's gross income. Finding and evaluating new jointly owned projects for Camex to operate and negotiating favorable terms for the company became her exclusive domain. She and her staff also analyzed and negotiated terms for their participation in joint interest projects proposed and operated by other companies, but Rachel's focus was on new projects to be operated by Camex.

Martha had her seventh birthday the day after Rachel's promotion to Vice-President the two of them celebrated by having a birthday party for Martha. Rachel baked Martha's favorite cake, German chocolate with thick chocolate fudge icing. It was topped by seven pink candles. Several of Martha's friends and their parents came to her party to join in celebrating her birthday. They were her close friends, some of whom were the children of executives and managers at Camex Petroleum, Inc., while others were schoolmates or neighbors with whom she played and occasionally spent the night. Martha blew out all seven candles with one big breath before the festive group sang happy birthday! Martha beamed as she opened her presents they were great gifts befitting a seven year girl who loved music and dancing. Rachel kept her special present hidden until Martha finished unwrapping her other gifts from the boys and girls and their parents. When Rachel rolled the pink Tauki TM 16 inch bicycle into the room Martha squealed with delight.

"Mamma, it's just what I wanted, thank you!"

Martha thanked everyone for coming to her party she thanked each of them for their gift, naming each individual gift as she did, which impressed all the adults.

Rachel arranged for a clown, a retired Camex engineer, to entertain the children after the gifts had been opened. One of his acts included sleight of hand magic tricks he made things appear or disappear sometimes out of one of the children's nose or ear. He was hilarious making both the children and the adults laugh at his antics the party was a roaring success for both Rachel and Martha, but it was Martha who was almost bursting with joy, she was seven years old!

Camex Petroleum, Inc. discovered a giant natural gas field in the Gulf of Mexico offshore from Padre Island, the field was in State waters located thirty miles southeast of Corpus Christi. Production from the discovery and subsequent developmental wells was scheduled to come on stream upon the completion of a pipeline under construction by Camex Petroleum, Inc. and its partners. The pipeline, a joint venture between Camex and the other operators in the field, had been designed and was being constructed by Rachel and her staff. Through extensive reinterpretation of their seismic data Camex identified several other potentially productive geological structures near the new field making further drilling and development in the area highly probable. The initial production plan for the field entailed separating produced water from the gas and condensate on each offshore production platform then sending the gas and condensate to shore through the pipeline under construction where it would be separated at a central onshore facility. The gas was to be dehydrated and treated then delivered to one or more onshore gas pipelines with which operators had sales contracts. The operators had a choice of sending their condensate either to storage tanks or directly into a liquids pipeline. Camex owned a majority of the leases and wells in the new offshore field and owned leases covering most of the undrilled nearby geological structures. After a meeting with the exploration department in which they described the new prospects and their future potential, Rachel viewed the company's redefined position in the offshore area as an opportunity to create a low risk long term profit stream for Camex. She called her engineering staff together for a conference to present her ideas for evaluation and discussion by the group. She opened the meeting stating.

"You are aware all aware that we have a mammoth new gas discovery offshore of Padre Island and that it will be coming on line when our pipeline to shore is completed. Something has come up making me think we may be missing a great opportunity."

Her senior engineer who was several years older than she, inquired.

"How is that? Our onshore facility is designed to separate the gas and condensate and provides dehydration for the gas before it goes to sales. We provided for delivery of the condensate to either a pipeline or to storage tanks. What did we miss?"

"I'm not talking about the separation facility, it is well designed and meets the needs for which it was intended, but I believe there is a much larger opportunity here that is not quite so obvious."

"What do you have in mind?" He continued feeling a little more at ease since he had designed the separation facility using some of his own ideas.

"I think we need to take a look at Camex constructing an onshore gas processing plant to extract natural gas liquids from the gas before we deliver it to the sales pipelines. It could be a windfall for the company."

One of her younger and more astute engineers grasped the significance of Rachel's statement, replying.

"I see what you mean, we can incorporate the function of the separation facility into a gas processing plant design provided there are enough recoverable liquids to make a plant economical."

"That is precisely what I have in mind."

Speaking directly to her senior engineer Rachel said.

"Your assignment commencing today, is to determine whether a gas processing plant would be commercial, and if so, how much cash flow would be generated under current and future producing rates taking into account full development of the field and the other nearby potentially productive geological structures."

"We will get right on it. We already have an analysis of the gas produced from each of the platforms and the reservoir group can give us a production forecast over the life of the field. Our geological department and reservoir engineers will be consulted on potential reserves and producing rates for the unexplored structures."

"Use current gas and product prices with our normal sensitivity analysis in your economic projections. If the economics look good based on developed reserves, we can proceed with a plant design incorporating the ability to expand in the future to accommodate additional production from new reserves developed on the other structures."

The following week, the senior engineer came to Rachel's office with his report.

"Rachel, you are a genius. Our analysis shows that a standalone gas processing plant will be a big money maker considering only currently developed reserves after deducting the producer's share of extracted liquids under a standard processing agreement. Since our company is by far the largest owner and producer in the gas field, our profit will be much greater than shown in this analysis because our production department will receive its share of the plant products under a processing agreement."

He handed her a copy of the report and as he was leaving said.

"With your permission, we will be requesting bids on a cryogenic plant from three construction firms this week. Here is a copy of our specifications and bid sheet. Please note that one or more parallel processing trains can be installed later to double or even triple the plant capacity should production rates increase in the future."

Upon completion of their detailed study, using actual construction costs, Rachel and her senior engineer presented their proposal to the company president and his staff. All of those hearing Rachel and her Senior Engineer's presentation were pleased with the results of their evaluation and the depth of its investigation. Camex's President was instantly an ardent supporter of the idea and could not wait to pursue construction of the plant with Camex Petroleum, Inc. as the operator. He congratulated Rachel and her senior engineer on their presentation and the thoroughness of their evaluation.

"This is a go project. Rachel, I want you to commence negotiations immediately with the other producers for construction of our proposed gas processing plant, keep in mind that I am not opposed to our building the plant alone and charging the other operators a processing fee."

He then added.

"We have funds in our current budget to cover construction costs, so I do not have to get further approval we can proceed right away. This is the best project that has crossed my desk this year the stock holders will be happy and so am I. Rachel you and your staff have my congratulations for coming up with this well thought out project to increase our company's future income. Your contributions will not be overlooked."

The president's annual bonus and stock options were tied to the company's economic performance. Rachel's proposed gas processing plant would add substantially to the company's bottom line increasing the president's income for years to come he couldn't have been happier with Rachel and her group's proposal. Pleased with the quick approval of the new plant, Rachel returned to her office intent on briefing her staff on the outcome of the meeting and to congratulate them on their superb evaluation and design work. After taking care of her obligations to her employees, the first item on Rachel's agenda became compiling a list of her counterparts at those companies with operations in the offshore gas field, so that she could began negotiations for construction of the processing plant as soon as possible. During her search, she was surprised and a little pleased to learn her ex coworker, Phil Jensen, would be representing Martek Resources, Inc. located in Houston. He had left Camex Petroleum, Inc. four years earlier after Martek made him an unsolicited offer for his services at a salary he could not turn down. She missed working with Phil he was a nice guy who treated her with respect, he was smart and most of all he was not always trying to put the make her like the other guys. Rachel decided Phil should be her priority call, she wanted to talk with him before she made her proposal to the other company representatives. She respected his ability and knowledge, she thought it would be a good idea to hear his comments first.

Phil picked up his phone hearing what he thought was a familiar voice.

"Is this Phil Jensen?"

"Yes, may I ask who is calling?"

"This is your former coworker at Camex in Corpus Christi. Rachel Schuber, remember me?"

Phil was in a near state of paralysis when he finally recognized her voice he was dumbfounded momentarily. After a long pause he managed to regain his wits saying.

"Rachel, is that really you?"

"Yes, Phil, it's me. We have all missed you at Camex especially me! I kept thinking you might drop by sometime, but you never showed up."

"Rachel, I have missed you too. I haven't had time for much of anything except work, since I took this job. It's great to talk to you Rachel, what's going on with you?"

"Phil, I am in charge of joint operations for Camex and we are proposing to build a gas processing plant to handle the gas produced from our offshore Padre Island gas field in which your company has a substantial interest. I am polling the other operators to determine their interested in either participating in the plant as a partner or entering into a processing agreement for their produced gas."

"Rachel, my first inclination is that we will want to participate, but I need to see the details of your proposal before I can give you a definite answer. You can send me a written proposal, including cost and economic projections, or even better we can meet at a place of your choice to go over the details in person."

Not waiting for Rachel to answer Phil continued.

"Rachel, what have you been doing the past four years? I sort of lost track of you and Martha after I left Corpus Christi. Are you doing OK?"

"Thanks for asking, Phil, we are fine there is just the two of us. We manage to stay happy and involved most of the time. Martha loves school and is a good student she recently turned seven, so we had a big party for her. And yourself, how are you doing, Phil?"

"Well, I am still unattached, but married to the job so to speak. I haven't had time for much of anything except work we have been swamped with projects that demand most of my time and attention."

"I understand that feeling, sometimes I don't get to see Martha for days at a time when I am traveling."

"Speaking of Martha, I have a suggestion. Why don't we meet in your office next Monday? I can come to Corpus on Sunday and if you like, I will take you and Martha to dinner Sunday evening. We can get reacquainted and catch up on the past four years."

Rachel started to refuse the dinner invitation, but for some inexplicable reason put caution aside saying.

"We will be happy to join you for dinner on Sunday, Phil. Martha and I are looking forward to seeing you."

145

Martha was excited when Rachel told her they were going to dinner with Phil Sunday evening. Her first response was.

"Are we going on a date?"

Rachel did not answer Martha's question directly it was a business meeting and nothing more. She did like Phil though as men went, he was a nice guy.

"No, it's not a date, Martha. Phil and I worked together before he moved to Houston, the three of us are just having dinner together."

Phil had been counting the days until he would be seeing Rachel he was having a hard time believing that after all of this time he was actually going to dinner with Rachel. He had admired her from a distance since the first time they met at Camex. Driving along south of Houston his thoughts were all about Rachel, he had been attracted to her from the first time he saw her, yet he had never been able to approach her or to express his feelings for her.

"She never indicated any interest in me that I remember. Maybe she has changed her mind!"

For whatever reason they were going to spend an evening together which suited him just fine. He reminded himself.

"Well, together yes, but not alone Martha will be with us."

Phil became absorbed in his thoughts about dinner with Rachel and its possibilities. He automatically switched to US highway 77 south of Victoria and after passing the Tivoli turnoff he suddenly noticed he was speeding along at eighty five miles an hour on the straight stretch of road approaching Refugio. When the speed limit sign flashed, his brain shifted back to reality, and he automatically slowed to seventy miles per hour before putting his car on speed control for the remainder of the trip. Phil had booked a room at the Oasis Hotel for two nights, Sunday and Monday, although one night would have been sufficient for his ten o'clock meeting with Rachel on Monday. He envisioned persuading Rachel to have dinner with him again Monday evening if not he could always cancel the reservation and drive back to Houston Monday afternoon. Phil pulled into the hotel still thinking about Rachel.

"I'm sure she is still as beautiful and sexy as I remember. I can hardly wait to see her again."

Phil called Rachel immediately upon entering his hotel room it was four thirty five in the afternoon and he was anticipating hearing her voice again. When she answered the phone all, he could say was.

"Rachel, it's me Phil."

"I've been expecting your call, Phil. I hope you had a safe trip. Martha is excited about having dinner with you a little later. She thinks it is a date."

Phil tried to control his own excitement because in his view, it was a date.

"At least Martha and I know that even if Rachel doesn't." He mused to himself. Phil's mind returned to the real world before he said.

"Rachel, I can hardly wait to see the two of you. I have checked in at the Oasis, room 1010. They have a wonderful restaurant here on the top floor it looks out over the bay and it has superb food and great dance music. Would you and Martha consider dinner here tonight?"

"Tomorrow is a school day, so Martha and I can't be out too late. Why don't we have an early dinner? Say about seven so that she can be home at a reasonable hour."

"Seven it is, I will pick you up at six thirty. Oh by the way, what is your home address?"

Martha insisted on wearing her finest dress for the occasion her first evening out on a date. Not wanting Martha to look out of place, Rachel selected a little less ornate dress, yet one which displayed her exquisite figure in a sexy and provocative way. Rachel's black dress was low cut in front and tight across the rear she was a stunningly beautiful woman whose magnificence was enhanced by her long black hair which almost reached her waist. She normally kept her hair up, except for rare occasions outside of her professional career, uncharacteristically she let her hair down for their dinner meeting. At work she wore fashionable business suits which shielded her superb body from casual viewers and saved her considerable consternation in dealing with the opposite sex.

Phil rang the doorbell then stepped back a pace to greet Rachel when she stepped out of the door. Martha came out first smiling as she extended her hand to Phil.

"Hello, Mr. Phil, I'm Martha."

Rachel followed close behind, her dark brown eyes were large and round which accentuated her beautiful face and sensuous red lips. Phil was looking at a beautiful sexy woman, one even more desirable than he remembered, the image left him almost speechless, yet he managed to ask in a cheerful voice.

"Are we ready, ladies?"

To which Martha excitedly replied.

"Yes, yes, let's go to the Oasis."

Rachel stepped forward saying.

"It's so good to see you Phil. You'll have to excuse Martha she is excited about going to the Oasis for dinner."

Rachel locked the door then turned to Phil saying.

"I think we are ready, shall we go?"

Phil ushered Martha into the back seat then seated Rachel in the front for their drive to the hotel. Neither of them said much on the way because Martha kept up a constant stream of chatter from the back seat preventing either of them from starting a meaningful conversation.

Phil dropped them at the hotel entrance then left his car with the valet for parking before joining them in the lobby. After taking the elevator to the top floor they made their way to the restaurant. Upon entering, Martha gushed.

"Mommy, this place is beautiful and so large. Thank you, Mr. Phil, for bring us here."

"Martha, I'm happy we came here too. I'm glad you like it."

Rachel looked around before commenting.

"Phil it's beautiful. I haven't been here since they renovated the dining room several years ago."

The happy trio were escorted to their reserved table next to the windows where they had an excellent overlook of Corpus Christi Bay at night. The lights on the high bridge and those of Portland were visible across the bay adding to the gorgeous view of downtown Corpus Christi. Martha stood next to the window peering at the bay scene intently before proclaiming.

"It's beautiful, I've never seen the bay from this high up before. There sure are a lot of lights out there. Look there goes a big ship, I can see its lights moving away over there?"

Phil joined Martha at the window where she pointed out the ship's lights in the distance. He replied, "You have good perception, Martha. That is a large ship headed down the ship channel toward the Gulf of Mexico. In a few minutes we won't be able to see its lights at all."

During the meal, they talked about the food and how good it was and speculated as to where it came from and whether or not it was a local product. Phil was unable to ask Rachel any of the pressing questions he had on his mind, instead he had to settle for being in her presence making small talk while he admired her and her beauty. When the orchestra began playing, Martha immediately jumped up asking Phil.

"Are we dancing?"

"If you like. May I have this first dance, Martha?"

"Yes. Mr. Phil, I would be delighted to dance with you."

She and Phil took their positions then glided around the dance floor with Martha looking every bit the professional as they danced to the Merry Widow Waltz. They were greeted with loud applause from the other dinners when the dance ended and they returned to their table. Martha was smiling, she thanked Phil for the dance then did a curtsey before returning to her seat. Phil was amazed at the artistry of Martha's dancing he had expected a stilted beginner instead Martha danced better and with more skill than himself. Her talent had carried him throughout the waltz.

"That was beautiful, you made a nice dance team, my congratulations to both of you on your performance," said Rachel with a mischievous lilt in her voice. She then explained to Phil.

"Martha has been studying dance since she was three and is an accomplished ballroom dancer. She has won several local titles for her performances and loves to dance waltzes."

Rachel suggested she and Phil dance the next dance since she would need to leave soon in order to get Martha to bed on time. They were in luck the next dance was moderately slow, yet still fast enough to demonstrate one's dancing skills. Phil held Rachel close as they danced, it was something he had often fantasized about when they worked together she seemed to enjoy their bodies touching as they danced around the floor with grace and ease. The dance came to an end while they were on the far side of the floor away from their table, Phil held Rachel's hand after the music stopped and he continued to hold her hand in his. As Rachel was about to return to the table Phil implored.

"Please, one more dance before we go?"

Rachel loved dancing and Phil was an excellent partner, not only that, she was having a great time she liked Phil.

"OK, but just one more."

Phil put his arm around her waist pulling her close, he was in heaven dancing with Rachel her body so close to him. She was more beautiful than he remembered, being in her company made him feel alive and important, he coveted her conversation and company he did not want their evening together to end. Phil wanted Rachel, holding her near him made him love her more than ever. The dance ended as they neared their table, Phil made sure they were still holding hands as they left the floor. Martha was delighted their dancing together had been beautiful to watch. She could not help commenting.

"Mommy, you and Mr. Phil were beautiful dancing together. I watched you and I liked it very much."

Phil walked the two of them to the door and as Rachel opened the door Martha turned to Phil.

"Good night Mr. Phil. Thank you, it was a wonderful date."

She then disappeared inside.

Rachel also thanked Phil for the evening and was about to go when Phil took her hand in his.

"Rachel would you consider having dinner with me tomorrow night at the Oasis? Tonight was delightful, but it ended too soon. Don't answer now, tell me tomorrow after you have thought about it." He squeezed her hand slightly before letting go. Rachel looked back smiling as she closed the door behind her.

Phil was the happiest man in Texas as he drove back to the Oasis.

"Corpus Christi is a wonderful place to be alive because this is where Rachel lives. God, I love that woman, hopefully she will accept my invitation."

Phil arrived early the next morning showing up at Rachel's office twenty minutes before their scheduled meeting. Rachel's secretary informed him that Rachel was in conference and would not be available until a few minutes prior to his scheduled appointment. She offered him coffee, black or with cream and sugar. While he waited, he thought about the previous evening and how Rachel felt in his arms, it was heavenly he could still smell the scent of her perfume. After what seemed like an hour, Rachel's senior engineer came to the waiting room looking for Phil, following the customary introductory greetings, he escorted Phil to the conference room where Rachel and the other members of her staff were assembled. Rachel was standing when he entered, to his surprise, she was wearing a dark blue business suit and her hair was up. The person before him had only a vague resemblance to the bedeviling woman he had dinner with the previous evening. Phil convinced himself he loved both of them, Rachel could not hide herself from him no matter how hard she tried. It might work on other men, but not on him.

She was attractive even though the suit almost hid her remarkable body and the hair style detracted from her natural beauty. Rachel greeted Phil in an articulate formal business voice which did not surprised him at all.

"Good morning, Mr. Jensen, good to see you again."

She introduced him to each member of her staff before requesting they begin their individual presentations. Projections of exhibits and details of the proposal were presented with written copies of the studies and the proposal provided to Phil for future reference. A question and answer period followed each phase of the oral presentation allowing Phil to ask questions about each particular phase of the project, how it was developed and how it worked. Rachel moderated the overall presentation making small contributions while keeping the meeting flowing at a smooth pace without interfering or neglecting the details needed for a person first hearing of the project to understand its purpose and its economic advantages. Upon completion of the post presentation discussion, Rachel thanked her staff complementing each of them for their contribution before she asked Phil to come to her office for a further exchange of views on the project.

Phil was seated opposite Rachel who sat stately behind her large desk, she inquired.

"Phil, what do you think of our proposed processing plant now that you have heard the details?"

"Rachel, I was duly impressed with both the presentation and with the merits of the overall project. This is a great economic opportunity for the producers and should be an easy sell to their managements. I do have one question though. How many of the other producers are on board for the project right now?"

Rachel blushed slightly although there was no reason for her do so.

"Phil, you are the only company representative I have contacted so far, I wanted you to be the first person I talked to about this proposed project. I appreciate your business judgment and value your opinion. I also know that if you did not like the project, you would not hesitate to tell me. You were my friendly test so to speak."

"Your confidence is well noted, Rachel, take my word for it this project stands on its own merits. So much for business, let's get on to the important things," stated Phil with a half-smile. He then asked the question which had been burning in his mind all day.

"Rachel, are we going to dinner tonight, or are you going to send me home feeling rejected and deprived of your company?"

The corners of her lips curled up into a smile he had seldom seen. She had spent several hours thinking about a response to this question and had a ready answer.

"Yes, we are going to dinner tonight, Phil. Just you and I, the nanny will be looking after Martha this evening. I will be expecting you around seven."

As he was leaving, Phil took her hand squeezing it slightly while he thanked her for accepting his invitation. Rachel watched as he walked out of her office standing there transfixed for a few seconds before returning to work.

Martha was in her room doing homework when the doorbell rang, momentarily, she heard her mother talking to Phil outside causing her to peek through the window to see them walking to his car side by side. She giggled and repeated to herself several times.

"Mommy has a date, mommy has a date."

She raced across the room to look at herself in the mirror then started laughing and giggling happily as if she had uncovered a secret that only she knew.

"Phil is neat and good looking. He really likes mom and I think mom likes him."

After dinner Rachel and Phil danced and made small talk for a couple of hours before their conversation turned from old friends and coworkers to more personnel subjects. Phil was longing to know more about Rachel, the hidden person no one knew, he also didn't want to do anything to jeopardize seeing her again. His curiosity was fed by his love for Rachel, he wanted to know everything about the most desirable woman he had ever met, who was sitting just a few feet across the table from him. Phil was careful not to bring up subjects Rachel had always refused to discuss with anyone when they worked together at Camex. In spite of his forebodings Phil could constrain himself no longer.

"Rachel, Martha is such a beautiful child, may I ask where you met her father?"

For a moment, there was total silence as Rachel looked quizzically into Phil's eyes. To Phil, the moment seemed to last several minutes before she replied without emotion.

"I have never met Martha's father."

Rachel's response was a jolt to Phil's senses it was not remotely close to the answer he had expected. Confused he asked.

"How can that be, Rachel?"

"Martha is not a love child as everyone believed, she was conceived by artificial insemination, her father is unknown and unimportant to me. In a sense she is a love child, in that I had her because I wanted a baby of my own to love and to give my parent's name."

Phil was stunned, he was almost in shock, yet relieved at the same time. He could not believe what he was hearing Martha was not the result of an affair as he had always thought. Before he regained enough control to speak Rachel added.

"There is more, you may as well hear it all. I volunteered to have Martha as part of a genetic study program using sperm from an unknown donor. The program guarantees certain benefits including health care and a monthly income to me and Martha. There I have told you everything no one knows about Martha's origin other than you, me and my parents."

Phil was astonished by Rachel's revelation, at the same time, he was gratified to learn Martha was not the result of a love affair. Shocking as it was, the news did not affect Phil's feelings for Rachel he loved her more than ever. Overjoyed to hear Rachel had not been in love with another man Phil replied.

"I am happy for you and happy for Martha you are fortunate to have each other. I will never repeat what you have confided in me to anyone, ever, you have my word. You, Martha and your information are safe with me. I am happy you chose to tell me about Martha, it clears up a lot of confusion for me."

A sense of comfort swept over Rachel once she realized that at last she had told someone about Martha, yet she was unsure why she had told Phil. Their dinner date was intended to be her first evening alone with a man she liked and respected and nothing more. She had always loved dancing and having fun with men, in the past she only did so in a group, never with a special man and never alone. Last evening's dinner with Phil and Martha was as near as she had come to being with a man for a night out and she had enjoyed it very much. She accepted Phil's invitation because she liked and trusted him he was not always trying to have sex with her and he made it clear he cared for her as a person.

"By the way, I think Martha really likes you. She was as impressed with your dancing as am I," said Rachel deftly changing the subject.

Phil was somewhat bewildered, but reveled in the presence of this marvelous woman he could not get enough of her. Phil walked to the door with Rachel at the end of their fantastic dinner date they were about to part when he kissed her softly on the lips. Then asked.

"Rachel, will you marry me?"

She pushed him away gently saying in a warm compassionate voice.

"No, but I would like to see you again. Good night, Phil, I enjoyed the evening very much. Call me the next time you are going to be in town."

Martha giggled as she closed the curtain and jumped back into bed her mind was fast to process the information it had just received.

"Phil really likes mom he kissed her good night!"

Phil walked slowly to his car turning back to look at Rachel once more before leaving. "OK", he said as he waved goodbye.

Driving back to Houston the following morning, Phil reviewed the events of the previous evening over and over concluding he would be traveling to Corpus Christi as often as possible.

Almost a month passed without Phil being able get away to make a trip to Corpus Christi, he was becoming depressed because his work load prevented him from seeing Rachel and there was no end in sight. He considered calling her, but decided against it. Calling would be an inadequate substitute for seeing Rachel in person hearing her voice without seeing her would only make him feel worse. Phil was laboring over specifications for a gas fired turbine he was ordering for one of the company's projects when the phone rang. He expected to be greeted by one of the many sales representatives who called on him regularly, much to his delight it was Rachel.

"Hey, Phil this is Rachel. How are you today?"

Her voice was like the music of angels he replied cheerfully.

"Now that I hear your voice, I am fantastic. How are you?"

"Martha and I are doing great we have been busy with work and school, among other things, which is why I am calling. I will coming to Houston tomorrow to make a presentation to one of the offshore operators the following morning. Martha suggested that I take you to dinner tomorrow night. Would you be interested in joining me at the Tmex Hotel say around seven?"

"Rachel, nothing would please me more I will be counting the hours until I see you. Shall I meet you in the restaurant or in the bar?"

"In the bar if you don't mind, I'll see you there."

Phil may as well have left his office he accomplished little on the prime mover problem. After Rachel's invitation to dinner, his mind was so jumbled he couldn't tell a gas fired turbine from an internal combustion engine!

Phil left work early to make sure he was not late for their dinner date, he arrived at the Tmex bar a full half an hour before their scheduled meeting and was enjoying a drink when, a few minutes before seven, Rachel entered the Tmex Bar and was immediately noticed by one the regulars who putting his drink on the table nodded to the others saying in a loud voice.

"Jesus Christ, look at that! You don't want to miss this one boys she may be our only number ten of the year!"

They all turned their attention to Rachel then stood up in unison raising their drink glasses and clicking them together while facing in Rachel's direction they saluted.

"To you beautiful!"

Rachel smiled in their direction as she continued looking around the bar trying to locate Phil.

One of the regulars was so affected, he said to the others in awe.

"Oh, my God, where did she come from? She has never been here before?"

Rachel was wearing a red dress trimmed in black, her long black hair was falling loose which combined with the black trim on her dress accentuated her facial features while the black belt encircling her waist emphasized her sexy figure. She presented a dazzling image of the ultimate female figure which coupled with a beautiful face with delicate features rendered her absolutely gorgeous to those who saw her. No man or woman could fail to notice her in the crowded bar the regulars looked on in admiration as the hostess approached the beautiful stranger.

"Would you like a table or a seat at the bar?"

The blond hostess smiled then added.

"I hope you are not in pain, the guys are staring at you so hard it must hurt."

Rachel laughed at the remark then requested a table for two. Phil arose from his seat at the bar then walked directly toward her table, there was a hush while all eyes focused on them as Rachel greeted him politely holding out her hand which he kissed before sitting down. One of the regulars quipped.

"That guy must be exceptional or rich as hell to have a woman like her. They don't come along looking like her every day of the week!"

They were envious as they watched transfixed by her beauty. After the waitress delivered drinks to Phil and Rachel, one of the regulars motioned her to their table.

"Judy, who is that gorgeous woman?"

"I don't have clue, but she is even better looking up close. Sorry guys, I'm afraid I can't help you."

"In that case bring us another round, so we can either grieve at our loss or salute the guy with her."

Rachel and Phil had one drink each before moving to their table in the restaurant where they were not the focus of attention and much less conspicuous among the other patrons.

"I'm glad Martha thought of me, I'll always be in her debt for her suggestion. Please tell her I said so. Rachel you are ravishing, do you realize that you are the most beautiful woman in the world?"

Phil looked into her brown eyes as he spoke hoping to see a spark of love. There was something new, but he was not sure what it meant. Maybe it was only his imagination.

"Phil, I am happy you agreed to come to dinner with me. Since I hadn't heard from you, I was afraid Martha and I might never see you again. Neither of us would like that."

"I didn't intend for it to be so long, Rachel. Things just kept getting in the way making it impossible for me to get to Corpus Christi. I considered calling, but decided against it. I still don't know when my schedule will allow me to get to Corpus. Things are in a mess at the office preventing me from traveling out of town until I straighten everything out. I'm sorry Rachel, I thought it best not to call."

"I understand, Phil, I've been busy too."

"You are here now, so let's enjoy the rest of our evening. I promise to call at least once a week in the future," said Phil placing his hand on her forearm.

Rachel's first inclination was to remove his hand instead she placed her free hand on top of Phil's indicating it was alright for him to touch her. She liked Phil very much and felt at ease with him even though they were alone together. He made her laugh she was happy when she was with him. Rachel had avoided being alone with men all of her adult life she hated them touching her in an intimate way or having sexual interplay of any kind she did not trust them, but somehow Phil was different. She thought to herself as she felt the warmth of his hand.

"Something about Phil attracts me while other men do not, what is it?"

Over dinner they talked about various things of interest concerning their work and careers until Phil changed the subject saying to Rachel.

"The last time we were together, I asked you to marry me and you said no. If I were to ask that question again, would the answer be the same?"

Rachel thought for a moment before she replied.

"I know you meant it when you asked me to marry you and I think I might be in love with you, but for me to say yes would be unfair to you. This may sound weird, but if we were to marry, I could not have sex with you."

Rachel proceeded to recount the complete story of how her Uncle Hector had raped her and the odyssey that lead her to Orange Grove and eventually to Corpus Christi. She explained that the very thought of sex had been repulsive to her ever since her childhood experience with her uncle.

"I love you Rachel, nothing can change that not even your uncle."

She said calmly facing Phil so he could see her face.

"Knowing what I have just told you, would you ask again?"

Taking both of her hands in his, Phil said slowly emphasizing each word.

"Will you marry me, Rachel?"

"Yes, Phil I will."

The two of them were oblivious to the fact they were in a crowded upscale restaurant. Phil took her in his arms kissing her passionately he had never experienced such pleasure in his entire life, his brain was on fire with happiness. His heart was racing wildly the love of his life had said yes. Rachel savored the kiss, kissing him back with equal passion of a different kind, she loved this man. She had never allowed herself to be kissed this way she didn't think she would ever want to. Kissing Phil excited Rachel the pleasure was almost overcoming, yet it failed to produce any welling sexual desire. Rachel experienced a warmth spreading over her body a feeling of being loved by someone you loved in return it was comforting to know someone loved you just for yourself. Phil held her close and to her complete shock and surprise his next words made her love him even more. Phil whispered in her ear.

"I promise you that after we marry, we will never have sex until you want to and that I will always love you even if that time never comes. I love you as much as a man could love a woman."

Her response was even more surprising to both of them she spoke quietly and directly.

"Let's leave this place and go somewhere not quite so public like my room."

They left their dinner and drinks unfinished, Rachel held his hand tightly in hers as they made their way to the elevator and to her room. Once inside, Rachel closed and locked the door without turning on the lights, she put her arms around Phil's waist pulling him against her.

"Please kiss me again."

They kissed several times with ever increasing passion when suddenly Rachel turned the lights on and began undressing. Phil looked on in astonishment before Rachel asked.

"Aren't you going to undress?"

He had no trouble getting his clothes off although he was fumbling a bit because of his bewilderment, Phil was totally confused as to what was happening and why. They stood facing each other totally nude. Rachel had that bewitching little smile her mouth curled up in the corners making her look both mischievous and mysterious. She asked.

"Please come closer? I want to touch you."

Phil had been staring at her light cream colored body scanning her from head to toe she was even more beautiful undressed than he had imagined. In front of him stood the unflawed perfect female, and she had agreed to become his wife. He was aroused as he moved closer at Rachel's request she touched him then pulled his body next to hers putting her arms around him and kissing him on the lips then the neck. Phil was in a state of ecstasy. She led him to the bed sitting him down next to her. She whispered.

"I want you to make love to me have sex with me."

"Rachel, are you sure you want to do this?"

"Yes, I am certain. Please, have sex with me."

He could feel the softness of her body next to his as they sank to the bed the very smell of her made his blood pulsate sending wild signals to his brain. He began slowly, touching and kissing her body lovingly while caressing her, he showered her with loving attention and did not stop until they were together. They left the lights on.

When Phil awoke sunshine was peeking around the edges of the curtains which were partially open. He looked around for Rachel and was dismayed to find she was not next to him in bed. When he heard a low humming sound coming from the bathroom, he was certain that all was well. He crept to the bathroom door opening it silently there stood Rachel naked in front of the mirror putting up her hair. When she saw his reflection in the mirror, she turned letting her hair fall he pulled her close. They kissed several times before returning to bed. He pulled her down with him as her hands moved over his body. She began kissing him on the neck then his chest while she lay against him. She kissed him on the mouth again then they were together.

It had been a hectic twenty-four hours for the both of them Phil did not understand how this had happened or why things turned out the way they did. The one thing he did know was that he was the luckiest man in the world. Rachel loved him and they were going to be married.

Over breakfast, Phil cautiously asked, "I thought we could not have sex, what happened, what changed?"

"I did it for you, because I love you. I didn't think I could do it, but I forced myself for you. Once you started it was so different from what I expected that after a while I actually began to like what you were doing. In the end, I enjoyed it, I like what you did very much. Since I am a novice, you must promise to teach me how to enjoy sex to the fullest. I am not afraid of having sex so long as it is with you, my love. I am so glad I tried. We must do it again and soon I promise to be a star pupil for both of us!"

In the following weeks, Phil did not call Rachel once a week as he had promised, he called every day and made weekend trips to Corpus Christi whenever possible sometimes putting off critical decisions on his projects until the following Monday.

Rachel moved ahead rapidly with both of her projects, at work she enlisted all the offshore operators as partners in her proposed gas processing plant and was nearing finalization of the Joint Operating Agreement, at home she was learning that the pleasures of love and sex properly done with the right partner were boundless. Rachel was delighted with her progress on both projects, as was Phil, who still could not believe Rachel had picked him from all of her potential suitors. Martha liked having Phil around on weekends, he took her to the mall and sometimes took her to the beach she loved him, he was nice to her and fun to be around. Aside from all of that, she could tell he was madly in love with her mother.

Martha relished the thought of a wedding, she was anxious for them to set a date it was nearly impossible for her to tolerate the suspense, the excitement and the waiting. Phil was going to be her dad and live with them all the time which would not only make her happy it would make her mother happy too. Martha was extremely pleased their first date had turned out so well.

Rachel remembered what her mother, Martha, had told her was the secret to a happy life.

"Every day you spend being unhappy is a day of your life wasted."

She intended to live her life being happy and planned for Martha to do the same.

Alpha-4 reported to Abe.

"Not much to report here, Rachel is planning to marry one of her former coworkers sometime in the near future. Our investigations shows him to be a clean, hardworking petroleum engineer there is nothing out of the ordinary in his past. He is currently spending weekends with Rachel and Martha. All seems to be in order. His name is Phil Jensen, he lives in Houston and works for Martek Resources, Inc. You might want to do a more detailed background check on him in case we missed something."

Abe responded,

"We performed a detailed investigation of Phil Jensen when Rachel first showed up in Houston and spent the night with him. He meets all of our required standards. Keep us informed of any new developments."

Rachel and Phil were wed in a private ceremony with a few friends, Martha, Burt and little Martha as attendees. Both Martha and Burt were overjoyed when Rachel told them she was going to marry Phil. Her rejection of male attention in the past had led them to believe she would probably never marry because of her childhood experience with her uncle. They were happy for Rachel, apparently she had conquered her fear of men and was able to find someone she could love. It meant she had a chance at true happiness which excited both of them they cherished Rachel for her love and the fullness she had brought to their lives.

The newlyweds set up housekeeping in Rachel's Corpus Christi home which required Phil to commute weekly to his job in Houston where he spent most of the week taking care of business. This arrangement prevented his being home except on weekends which after a while became a bummer for all of them. Phil and Rachel were determined to be together most of the time they jointly decided on a plan to correct this troubling situation which was interfering with their life and love.

Phil resigned from his job with Martek Resources to open an engineering consulting firm in Corpus Christi. Rachel earned a moderately high salary at Camex and received generous annual stock options and bonus payments based on her department's performance which plus her monthly payments from Gentex provided more than enough income to sustain their standard of living indefinitely. With their many contacts throughout the oil and gas industry it was reasonable to expect Phil's consulting business to catch on and to prosper in a short time. Within a few months of setting up shop in Corpus Christi, Phil was earning nearly as much as he had in his old job. His special knowledge and experience was in great demand in the booming oil and gas business. Life, love and economic success were looking up for the Jensen's as was their future together. Martha was overjoyed having Phil at home every day he was a lot of fun and made her mother smile all the time. From Martha's point of view, life was perfect, they were all happy.

Alpha-4 was equally glad Phil moved to Corpus Christi it simplified their surveillance and protection of the extended family.

At seventeen, Martha became a junior in high school. A few months later, Rachel left her position as Vice-President at Camex to joined Phil in his engineering company. Together they started a new venture building natural gas gathering systems to transported gas from the wells to one or more intrastate pipelines or in some instances to a gas processing plant. Their new company, which they named Tex Con,

Inc., charged the well owners a fixed fee per MCF (thousand cubic feet) for transporting their produced gas. This technique created a steady cash flow stream for Tex Con, Inc. which was independent of the price of natural gas at the wellhead. Tex Con, Inc. constructed three gathering systems in quick succession over a four year period which provided a large sustainable cash flow stream for the company.

In Tex Con's ventures, Rachel negotiated the transportation contracts with the oil and gas companies while Phil handled all the design, construction and operation of the pipeline systems. They were a great business team each of them contributed their special talents to make the company a success. They were able to expand Tex Con rapidly without jeopardizing their long term objective to become a mid-stream company owning both pipeline systems and gas processing facilities. All corporate management decisions were made jointly no project was pursued without mutual agreement beforehand.

Phil and Rachel concluded the company needed an infusion of capital to support their planned accelerated growth program. They were considering two available options to raise additional cash, to go public and sell a limited amount of company stock, or to remain private and raise money through joint ventures with outside investors. The one thing they refused to do was over leverage the company with expensive bank loans.

The growth of Tex Con had not gone unnoticed by Abe and ADAM they had been watching intently since the company was first organized. As Jerry read the latest report from the security group regarding Rachel, Phil, Martha and Tex Con he was delighted with their progress.

"George would really be pleased, if he could see how well his surrogate mother and her husband are doing in business without any outside help. These people know what they are doing, they are natural born business people, at the same time they are teaching George's daughter Martha about what really matters in life as she grows up."

George Angleton had passed away the previous year leaving Jerry in control of his financial empire and ADAM. George's death came as a shock to all who knew him, following a business meeting in New York, he retired to his hotel room and was found dead in bed the next morning by the maid when she came to clean the room. The cause of death appeared to be a heart attack. A detailed investigation by the NYPD and the pathologist's report indicated George died in his sleep. He probably never woke up, when they found his body, he was laying serenely on his back in a bed that had hardly been disturbed. In death, George had not made near the fuss that he made when he entered this world.

Jerry called a meeting of the original founders of ADAM to review the status of Rachel, one of their protégés, her husband Phil and most of all George's daughter Martha. Included in the review was a detailed evaluation of Tex Con, Inc.'s business plan as well as its expected performance in the future. Specifically, Jerry wanted to know whether they might want to invest in the company as individuals or if Imperial Enterprises might want to invest for its own account. By consensus of the advisors it was agreed that Tex Con was too small for Imperial Enterprises to consider investing, but it might be just right for individual investors including themselves. One objection the advisors raised concerning Imperial's participation was that taking a direct position in Tex Con might in some way connect Imperial Resources and Rachel to ADAM thereby violating their secrecy mandate. Even though the risk was small, they decided to play it safe! If Tex Con was going to be successful, it would have to do it on its own without Imperial Enterprises.

Chapter 7 Buyout

Frank, was astonished as he read the report from his agents, in spite of all the time and effort they had expended, they still knew very little about Zane Kraft's activities except when he was with Peggy. He agreed with their conclusions and recommendations regarding Zane Kraft; it was imperative the true nature of Mr. Kraft's business be established with certainty before Abe could devise and implemented a comprehensive protection plan for Peggy and Bruce. Several thoughts came to mind as he poured over the details of the report.

"What exactly is the relationship between Zane and Peggy? Are they both truly in love, or are they just having an affair based on physical attraction and sex, a temporary liaison so to speak? What are their future plans together and where does Bruce fit in those plans? These questions have to be answered in order to assess the problem and to find a suitable solution. Remember, George wanted these women to be happy to marry if they choose and for the children to spend their early years in a middle class environment unaffected by drugs and criminal activity."

The last thought provoked another dilemma, so far as Zane Kraft was concerned, he certainly was not living a middle class life and appeared to be involved with some sort of illicit operation.

"But, that can change if they are really in love."

There was also the security aspect of Zane's involvement with a Gentex participant, does he pose a security risk for the program and ADAM as well? After careful consideration, Frank called Jerry who had been in charge of ADAM's security since its inception.

"Jerry, I think we should get together to discuss the Zane Kraft problem from both a protection and security perspective. Do you have a preference for a place to meet?"

"Normally the Tmex bar would be my choice, but this may be a tedious undertaking, so let's meet in my private office away from any distractions."

The two Imperial Enterprises executives met in Jerry's personal office which was on the top floor of the former Transco Tower located near the Galleria just outside Loop 610. When he entered, Frank marveled at the décor and size of Jerry's office. The view was magnificent, it was a clear day with unlimited visibility, he could see for miles to the west almost to the edge of Houston. Much to his surprise, Jerry closed the blinds before they sat down to talk. After exchanging pleasantries, Jerry explained that he wanted absolute seclusion with no distractions during their discussion. He and Frank got right to the heart of their mutual problem.

"Jerry, what did you think of our assessment of Zane Kraft?"

"I agree with Abe's recommendations whole heartily, unfortunately several other questions arose while I was reading the report. Whatever we do must comply with the principles George set forth for ADAM. This particular situation involves several of those principles which may work to oppose each other in the final analysis. I think we need to utilize all the assets of ADAM in our investigation of Mr. Kraft. I assume your people are already at work on this, however, I can make a significant contribution by enlisting our international intelligence arm at Imperial Enterprises to help you determine who Zane is and what he is doing."

"How can Imperial be of service to us?"

"One thing we can supply is inside information on the Crazy Bastards' operations and structure. The internal workings of the cartel's upper echelon is not readily available, but we have resources that can ferret out this type of information. If Zane Kraft is involved with the organization, we will learn everything there is to know about his position and exactly what he does for them. This will take some time even though I am activating a rush order for this intelligence."

Jerry summoned one of his staff on the intercom a giving him instructions which were inaudible to Frank. A few minutes later Jerry responded to a signal on his cell phone then announced.

"Our intelligence group have Mr. Zane Kraft centered in their sights, it won't be long before we know all there is to know about him and the Crazy Bastards."

Realizing the importance of Jerry's actions, Frank relaxed a bit, he had been tense and highly irritated because Abe had been unable to penetrate the Crazy Bastards organization. His agents had learned next to nothing about Zane's possible involvement with them. Frank could not help smiling at the unexpected turn of events.

"At Abe, we will concentrate our efforts on monitoring and recording all contact between Peggy and Mr. Kraft on a twenty-four-hour basis. This includes all modes of communication and physical contact. We have already established a group to follow Zane 24/7 they are on the job as we speak, monitoring and recording where he goes, who he meets, how he travels and where he stays. In other words we will be aware of his every move and know where he is and what he is doing at all times. Jerry, this has been the first serious protection issue we have encountered with the Gentex women. Based on her past history, I would never have expected Peggy to be involved in any of this. I'm glad George anticipated such things when we set up ADAM. Peggy doesn't know it, but she needs our help in the worst way."

"You are right, Frank," said Jerry as he poured two Scotch whiskeys from the secret bar hidden in the bookcase behind his desk. Offering one to Frank, he continued, "Peggy, we will protect you and Bruce from harm whether you know you need it or not." He then touched his glass to Frank's then in unison they raised their drinks in salute.

The following morning, Zane called Peggy to set up a two night date starting on Wednesday. He pleaded.

"Peggy, please say yes? I have missed you, I need be with you this coming week."

Her response was equally short and to the point.

"When will I see you my love?"

"Wednesday at seven, I'll pick you up."

The agents listening to these calls were always astounded at their brevity. One of the agents remarked to his coworkers.

"What kind of lovers talk to one another like this? They rarely spend more than half a minute talking on the phone even when they have not seen each other for over a month."

Their brief telephone conversations were no accident, Zane was cautious, he made sure his calls were untraceable by standard methods always making them short and brief. Wariness was a part of his strategy to prevent the Crazy Bastards from learning about Peggy and Bruce. His scheduling of different hotels for their engagements each month was a planned maneuver designed to avoid predictability and being followed. Once he fell in love with Peggy, Zane knew she had to remain hidden in order for her to be safe from the *Bastardos Locos*.

As their love affair heated up, and they became ardent lovers whose lives revolved around each other, Zane realized that the danger to Peggy was increasingly greater. He purposely never mentioned the Crazy Bastards and his connection to them for fear of frightening her, instead he began considering ways to disassociate himself from the cartel and its operation with the hope he and Peggy could live a normal life like other people. Zane was certain what would happen should he fall into disfavor, or become a liability to the Crazy Bastards they would not hesitate to kill him, and Peggy as well, if they knew about their love affair.

Zane had originally been recruited by the cartel as an investment advisor he did not discover until several years later that his employer, Cross Border I&E Company, was actually owned by the powerful *Bastardos Locos* cartel and was being used to launder drug money. By the time he discovered the source of funding for his investment activities on behalf of Cross Border I&E Company, it was too late. He was trapped.   As time passed, the value and revenue from his investments for the *Bastardos Locos'* grew enormously, as a result he became a trusted associate who not only invested their money he also collected cash from their distributors' sale of cocaine across the United States. In this capacity Zane came to know all the cartel's leaders, their master cocaine distributors and the bankers who helped them move money out of the country. Serving as investment advisor for the cartel, Zane with their approval, became a rich man in his own right with investments in the United States and throughout South and Central America, yet he more or less belonged to the Crazy Bastards. They ultimately controlled his life and his future. Before becoming involved with Peggy, this had not been a serious problem for Zane he liked being on the move never staying in one place very long and above all it was an exciting life. Before Peggy showed up in his life, Zane relished making money for himself and for the cartel he enjoyed his rich life style along with its many amenities. Zane's intimate knowledge of the cartel's money handling operations made him a key person in their organization one who could not just leave or disappear without undesirable and possibly fatal consequences. Finding a way to get away from them, without being harmed in the process, would not be easy all of his cunning and ingenuity plus a large helping of luck would be needed.   The cartel remained unaware of his involvement with Peggy, partly because they were not checking and partly because he continued to perform his duties for them flawlessly, but mainly because of his efforts to keep her hidden. None of his contacts in the United States had ever seen them together or knew about Peggy, Zane was thankful they were not looking either. Zane mulled over various plans to gain his freedom from the cartel. He considered asking them to allow him to retire, but realized he knew too much about their business for them to allow that to happen. Such a request would alert them to his desire to leave creating a trust issue with the cartel leaders. He could not mention Peggy and their love for each other it wouldn't make any difference to the cartel's thinking, but it would put her in great danger. If he disappeared without their approval, he would be a hunted man with a bounty on his head creating a serious danger to anyone close to him. Zane asked himself the key question!

"How can I vanish without leaving a trace?"

He answered his own question, concluded that the only safe solution to his dilemma would be for him to give up Peggy now.

"There is no way in hell I'm giving up Peggy, she means everything to me more than life itself. There has to be another way. I just need to find it!"

Zane was desperate to find a way out before the Crazy Bastards became aware of Peggy and Bruce. He continued with his normal money handling duties for the *Bastardos Locos* while secretly seeing Peggy when possible. Neither, Zane nor Peggy suspected Abe existed and had them under constant surveillance. Had they known, both would have been suspicious and questioned the purpose and intent of Abe's actions. Even though the surveillance was designed to assure Peggy's safety and to protect her from harm, it would be difficult to explain without creating a serious problem for Abe and ADAM.

The combined efforts of Abe and Imperial Enterprises produced a complete picture of Zane Kraft including a detailed chronicle of his movements over the past several months. He was followed night and day by Abe agents who managed to trace him from one coast to the other with stops in virtually every large city in the country. He had met with known drug distributors and bank executives, sometimes on the same day. So far as the agents could determine, Zane was unaware he was being followed or that his every move was being recorded by video and electronic devices. Abe had hacked into the airline's reservation system and was able to track Zane's daily flight schedule making their job somewhat easier. To avoid detection, Abe switched agents at every airport stop placing a different agent on the plane with Zane for the next leg of his flight. Should Zane change flights or destinations Abe had a provisional plan which allowed another of their agents to board the plane with him. Every Abe agent not specifically assigned to the permanent surveillance teams were activated for service in tracing Zane and recording his activities.

When travelling, Zane always paid close attention to his surroundings and the surrounding people, he would recognize anyone boarding the plane that had flown on the previous flight on his schedule. He regarded his fellow passengers with suspicion checking them out thoroughly both in the boarding area and in the cabin of the plane. Once the plane was in the air, Zane routinely made repeated trips to the lavatories to get a good look at the faces of all the other passengers. He did this as a check to insure there was no person or persons on board who might be following him. This procedure was part of his *Bastardos Locos* training, to be suspicious of everyone and pay attention to your surroundings at all times. Zane had traveled for several years without detecting anyone following or spying on him, he did not expect this flight to be any different he relaxed as the plane began its descent to Houston International Airport. The trip had been uneventful and in a few hours he would be with his beloved Peggy.

On the ground, Abe agents were in place to follow Zane's movements as they had done at all of his previous stops. This stopover in Houston was special because he would be meeting Peggy on Wednesday and it was critical to Abe's plan to learn where the meeting was to take place in order not to lose contact with Peggy and Zane. Zane had been difficult to track on his previous trips to Houston because of his unpredictability and evasive tactics to keep their *rendezvous* secret. This time Abe was better prepared, Omar had been paid an additional five thousand dollars for his services should he be contacted by Zane and special Abe agents were assigned to follow the limousine's GPS signals should it be commissioned. Other agents were on standby alert ready to be deployed once Zane and Peggy entered the limousine and were on their way to a hotel.

Omar's limousine arrived at Peggy's house at seven in the evening on Wednesday as planned. Peggy greeted Omar then stepped into the limousine as he held the door for her, within minutes of his arrival, she was on her way to meet Zane at the Downtown James Hotel. Abe's trackers were at their stations following the GPS signals emitted from Omar's limousine as it sped down I-10 on a direct course to the hotel. There were no evasive actions, which came as a surprise to the agents following the limousine, Zane had been able to elude them in the past by taking side streets and other evasive actions on the way to his destination. Omar's limousine arrived at the hotel in less than forty five minutes after picking up Peggy. She walked directly from the limousine into the hotel lobby where she took the elevator to the restaurant and bar on the top floor. Zane was waiting in the bar where he was having a gin and tonic when she entered the bar he greeted her with open arms they embraced before being seated at a table next to the wall. Peggy carried a small bag and a purse which she set on the floor next to her chair before kissing Zane. He was excited returning her kiss with love and anticipation. Within minutes, the hotel was swarming with Abe agents determined to find which room Zane had reserved. Time was of the essence, they intended to bug the room while the lovers were still in the bar. The lead agent walked briskly across the hotel lobby to the check in station waving his arms and speaking very loud to get the desk clerk's attention.

"What can I do for you, sir?"

"I need a bit of information from you concerning a guest, his room number to be exact."

"I can't provide that information, sir. It's against our management's policy unless you are with the police or another law enforcement agency."

"Can we speak privately somewhere? I have something here that you will find interesting."

"If you could step into my office, please."

The agent quickly closed the door behind him making sure no one was watching, he took five one thousand dollar bills from his wallet holding them toward the clerk saying.

"These are yours, if you can give me the number of the room rented by either Zane Kraft or Cross Border I&E Company. It will be for two nights starting with tonight. I promise you there will be no repercussions and no one will ever know this happened. What do you say?"

"Let me look at the registry. Yes, here it is. Cross Border I&E Company has room 11,005 for tonight and tomorrow night," he said nervously his hand shaking noticeably as he reached to take the bills before shoving them into his pocket.

"Will there be anything more?"

The agents posted in the bar reported Zane and Peggy were still there and probably would remain there for some time assuming they had dinner before retiring to their room, any unusual movements on their part would be reported immediately. The door clicked as the Abe agents inserted a pass card, in an instant, they were in room 11,005 with their electronic gear.

"This is going to be a special night for us, Peggy. I have made a couple of decisions which will affect us profoundly, but before we go to the room, I would like to have dinner and dance a while."

Peggy held her curiosity in check throughout dinner and the dancing which followed. On their way to their suite she found it difficult to restrain her curiosity, but not wanting to blemish a perfect evening with Zane she held his hand and kept quiet.

Zane closed the door kissing Peggy before he spoke.

"Let's sit here on the couch for a few minutes, I want to explain to you several decisions I have made and why I made them."

"I hope nothing has changed between us."

"No my love, but you must hear this."

He hesitated briefly then continued determined to lay out his past and his future plans to Peggy.

"About my work, it is not as it seems, I work for Cross Border I&E Company which purports to be in the import-export business, but that is not the true nature of the business. It actually is a two facetted endeavor involving money laundering and investing funds from that activity. It gets even worse, the company is owned by the *Bastardos Locos* drug cartel which specializes in cocaine distribution in the United States. I am their collection agent, I collect cash from their distributors all over the country which is why I travel all the time. I also am their investment advisor I make business investments for them worldwide."

Peggy attempted to say something, but Zane held his finger across her lips, so that she would not interrupt.

"To tell you this was my first decision. My second decision, which presents a dangerous challenge to both of us, is to find some way to separate myself from the cartel. That accomplished, we can safely marry, so that you, Bruce and I can happily live our lives together."

"If that is a proposal, I accept," said Peggy no longer able to keep quiet. "But only when you have put all of this behind you. I will not endanger Bruce to make myself happy. Do you understand? There can be no us if it puts Bruce in danger!"

She kissed him gently on the lips then allowed him to continue his explanation.

"I have been trying for months to find a safe way to be rid of the cartel without endangering you and Bruce in the process. So far, I have not found a way to escape without reprisals from the cartel for my actions, but I shall continue to search for a way out. At this time, the only safe thing for me to do is to give you up and disappear from your life before the cartel learns of your existence. If they find out about you and our relationship, you and possibly Bruce could be in grave danger, if something went wrong between me and the cartel."

Zane told Peggy how he became involved with the cartel revealing to her the life he led before he met her and how he had fallen in love with her almost the first time they talked. After a long and fitful conversation, they undressed and prepared themselves for bed. Every word spoken in the suite was transmitted and recorded by Abe's electronic gear over the next two days and their actions were viewed and recorded by the hidden cameras planted by the Abe agents. There was not a single nook or cranny in the suite which was not covered by these devices. The Abe agents watched and listened intently as the evening progressed. Zane and Peggy turned out all the lights before getting in bed disappointing all the Abe agents viewing the monitors in real time. They could only imagine the interaction between Peggy and Zane as they listened to the audio which functioned well in the dark. Both Frank and Jerry had access to the streaming data from the hotel, following the two day love-in between Zane and Peggy, they agreed to meet again to rehash the new information Zane had revealed and to determine their future course of action with regard to Zane. This time they met at the Tmex bar.

"There is no doubt these two are in love, they have a special relationship that is somewhat rare in today's world," said Jerry clasping his hands in his lap while he spoke.

"I must agree, based on what we have heard and seen, I would say they are as devoted a couple as I have encountered in my years of watching people."

"The thing that strikes me about this Zane is that he is smart, he has been uncannily successful in investing the cartel's money," added Jerry who now managed Imperial Enterprises and was constantly on the lookout for talented people to add to the organization. Before his death, George had purposely stepped aside from management of ADAM leaving Jerry in charge. Jerry continued with his analysis of the situation.

"I like the way Zane made it clear he would love Peggy and Bruce alike that is crucial to our coming up with a plan to help."

"I think he would give up his personal wealth to be with Peggy and Bruce and I also think he wants a regular life for the three of them, he is a caring man. Jerry, what do you think? Have I missed something?"

"It's obvious to me that he is searching for some way to get away from the *Bastardos Locos* without getting himself killed or endangering the two people he loves, Peggy and Bruce. That is admirable on his part and I respect him for it, but that will be virtually impossible to accomplish given the cartel's reputation in dealing with deserters. Frank, let's look at this realistically, either Zane makes a clean break with the cartel, or the safety of Peggy and Bruce will surely be compromised sometime in the future. The Status quo isn't an option, Zane knows this as well as we do, which is why he revealed his situation to Peggy. I don't think she comprehends exactly what this means for Zane, he is willing to try to get away because of his love for her even though it may be the end of him. He will not wait until the cartel knows about her even if it costs him his life. From our perspective, I see two choices, we can get rid of Zane now, or we can help him break clean from the cartel."

"Well, damn it, Jerry. I hate to see the cartel win. Zane actually appears to be a good man, I dislike the thought of seeing him killed without our trying to get him free of the cartel. What do you think?"

"I think you and I are in agreement on this, in fact, I would like to have him in the Imperial Enterprises organization if we can get him out. He is a whiz in the investment world."

With these words the resources of Abe, ADAM and Imperial Enterprises were committed to making an attempt to free Zane from the *Bastardos Locos be*fore they learned about his connection to Peggy and Bruce.

Through an intermediary, contact was made with the Crazy Bastards' requesting a secure and private meeting between their business manager, Joe, and a highly successful business man for the purpose of discussing a deal far removed from and totally unrelated to the cartel's normal operations. They met at a neutral site, a room in a small hotel located on the fringe of the downtown business district. Jerry was unrecognizable when he sat down with the cartel representative, although they had never met, Jerry took the precaution to come disguised just in case something went terribly wrong. He broke the uneasy silence.

"I am a business man with no interest in the drug trade, but your people have something I want and I am willing to pay a high price for it under certain conditions."

"You understand, I am only the messenger here and cannot give you a direct answer today. With that understanding, please continue." Said Joe in perfect American English.

"Your people own a small company which I would like to acquire including all of its assets and employees. I am willing to pay a premium price for both the company and its assets. Your people will profit handsomely from my proposed transaction with zero risk to themselves."

Warming to the passion of making a trade Jerry asked Joe.

"Do you think your people might be interested?"

"We are always interested in making money, my friend. Can you be more specific, what do you want from us?"

Upon hearing the cartel representative's answer, Jerry was certain they would agree to his terms making him much more forceful in his pursuit of a deal.

"My proposal is simple, I will purchase all of your organization's Cross Border I&E Company for $450,000,000, in cash, including all of its assets and the unrestricted services of its employees. This represents a 50% premium to its current value. My only condition is that all employees be released by your organization and that they will never be contacted or touched by your people in the future."

"Why do you think we would keep our word once this kind of deal is done?" asked Joe with an incredulous know it all grin spreading across his face.

"This is one of those deals that are too good to turn down, believe me when I tell you I have the power to change nations, if I chose to do so. That's how I know your people will be happy to make the trade and honor the terms of our agreement. My organization has the names of all of your money men and collectors in North America, but as I said we have no interest in these operatives so long as our new employees are left alone. Should they be threatened or harmed in any way we can make all of your operatives disappear overnight. Do we understand each other?"

Jerry clenched his right fist holding it in front of him shoulder high with his thumb facing upward much like a gladiator requesting permission from the crowd to complete his victory with a kill.

"The deal is open for two days only, after that we will pursue other alternatives and keep our money. Call me at this number before 10:00 a.m. day after tomorrow with your answer, so that we can arrange to transfer the funds to one of your accounts."

The Crazy Bastards representative was shaken and highly pissed off by Jerry's statement, particularly his comment about transferring the funds as though they had no choice other than to accept his proposal. Joe said to himself while he digested Jerry's words.

"This is one arrogant son of a bitch to think he can push the Crazy Bastards around. Wait until Number One hears this shit."

The two of them parted with a hand shake as Joe said, "*Adios amigos, you'll be hearing from me.*" Joe was not at all pleased with the way things had gone he was still highly pissed off with the way the deal had been presented to him and he was concerned about relaying the deal to Number One without getting on his shit list. This rich bastard had placed him in a dangerous position with Number One without as much as a thank you in the process.

"This soft assed business guy is crazy as hell to think he can threaten the Crazy Bastards and get away with it there is no telling what Number One and Number Two might decide to do after I tell them about this deal. Who in the hell does this guy think he is, anyway?"

Joe called ahead to be sure Number One would be available when he got to headquarters, but he gave no advanced indication of the subject of his discussion with Jerry. Putting his cell phone is his pocket, Joe shook his head from side to side muttering.

"Number One will decide how to handle this asshole."

Number One was waiting in his office surrounded by several of his underlings, when Joe showed up an hour later, they were sitting at a large table having a drink of expensive Irish whisky. After a few greetings in Spanish, Number One ordered Joe to tell them what the business guy had on his mind.

"No damned interruptions until he has had his say, OK?" Said Number One to the group not expecting an answer from anyone.

Joe gave a detailed description of what had gone down between him and the businessman he outlined the terms of the deal repeating everything Jerry had said emphasizing his statements about power and consequences.

"I don't know who this son of a bitch is, but he was damned sure of himself when he was talking to me. Apparently he thinks we can be bullied around without there being any reprisals."

Number One responded.

"Most people don't have the balls to talk to us like that, but right now I don't give a shit about that. We can always take care of smart asses later if necessary. What I want to know right now, is this a good deal for us?"

The accountant for the cartel, who had recently completed his quarterly review of operations, spoke up immediately.

"The assets of Cross Border I&E Company are worth nowhere near $450,000,000. Hell, it was barely worth $250,000,000 on the latest report. Zane Kraft manages the Cross Border I&E Company, which is a front for our investments, and he collects and launders our money from cocaine sales in the U.S. He has made us a lot of money by investing in clean businesses. Boss, there is no goddamn way Zane Kraft is worth $200,000,000 to us. He can be replaced."

"If it becomes a problem that he knows our contacts and dealers we can deal with that. If it never becomes a problem then what the shit do we care?" Said Number Two expressing his unbiased and unsolicited opinion.

"Do we know who is buying?" Asked Number One ignoring Number Two's comment.

"It has to be someone big, bigger than we are, to pay that kind of money we need to be careful not to get screwed if we do a deal," offered Number Two. This time Number One nodded to Number Two saying.

"You are right it makes sense. Joe, you stay here with me and Number Two the rest of you guys get out. We need to think straight, so no more whisky."

There was a scramble to clear the room the underlings knew better than to get on Number One's bad side by not getting out promptly. Number One waited until the room emptied and the door had been closed then declared in a loud voice.

"We're going for the money! What I want from you two is a plan to make sure there are no hitches or screw-ups in this deal. Let's do some serious thinking before we do something stupid then wind up losing our ass and killing a bunch of people. It's settled we are doing a deal. The question is how we can do it safe without getting fucked?"

Joe came up with an idea which caught Number One off guard, yet got his full attention.

"What they really want is Mr. Kraft, if I am reading the deal right, so let's give them Mr. Kraft in a way that guarantees they will not screw us. Why not have Mr. Kraft close the deal for us? If I am right, they wouldn't risk losing him and he knows how to make this thing happen without leaving a trail of any kind. It's perfect, and it all fits together."

"That's it," exclaimed Number One. "Joe, that's one hell of an idea," he added with a loud chuckle as if he had just heard an amusing joke.

"Joe, call that damned number he left. Tell that son of a bitch we accept the deal with one small change, Mr. Zane Kraft will be closing the deal for us. He will handle all the details including the transfer of funds to our account. Make sure he understands that we can play hard ball too, and this is the only way we make the deal."

Joe placed the call as instructed after a few minutes on the phone he announced loudly.

"The deal is on. Mr. Kraft will be our closer."

"Then get Zane's ass over here, so we can get started," ordered Number One.

Zane had not been summoned to a meeting with Number One in over a year he was apprehensive when he walked into the room. Characteristically, Number One insisted they have a drink of Irish whisky before they began. Zane sipped the dark whiskey slowly, speculating in his mind as to what was afoot with the *Bastardos Locos,* hoping against hope, it had nothing to do with Peggy and Bruce.

"Zane, we have an opportunity to sell Cross Border I&E Company for $450,000,000 including all of its assets and current management. I have decided to accept the offer which means you will go with the deal and will no longer be associated with us. We hate to lose you, but this deal is too good to turn down. There's just one catch, we insist that you handle the closing and transfer of funds to make sure everything is on the up and up in this deal, you have to make certain we don't get screwed some way or another. Do you understand?"

Relieved that Peggy and Bruce were not involved, Zane seized the opportunity to be free of the cartel even though he understood full well that failure to protect the cartel's interest in the closing implied certain death for himself. He quickly replied.

"The price is well above the current value of the company, from that point of view, I see why you want to make the deal $450,000,000 is a lot of money."

Zane's head was still reeling with the prospect of being traded as part of the deal when he added in earnest.

"Number One, I will be more than pleased to close the deal for you and I assure you that I will make certain nothing goes wrong with the transfer of funds. In addition, for your protection, I will transfer the funds to you in such a way that no one will ever be able to trace this transaction to you or your organization."

Zane knew he could make the deal work, he had to a serendipitous escape from the *Bastardos locos* had been presented out of the blue. It was a stroke of luck, which solved his problem of ending his association with them without the threat of reprisal. He would be free to marry Peggy upon a satisfactory completion of the deal. Thinking about how his circumstances had suddenly changed, Zane became convinced that for some unknown reason God had smiled on him from afar it couldn't just be luck. There was no other plausible explanation for his sudden change of fortune in the face of a near hopeless situation just the day before. Whatever the reason Zane was quietly jubilant, his dream was about to come true once he complete the transaction to Number One's satisfaction.

Zane's meeting with the buyer's representative proved to be fortuitous he did not recognize the man who appeared to be from one of the Islands offshore from Florida. Zane suspected his counterpart was probably a hired expert in clandestine business arrangements who had no direct connection to the eventual buyer of the company. This was very much to Zane's liking because the buyer's rep did not know him either and the chance their accidentally meeting again was near zero. Through tedious manipulation of secret accounts, the title to Cross Border I&E Company was transferred to an offshore company previously set up by Jerry to facilitate the purchase. The $450,000,000 payment was made by an untraceable bank transfer to a numbered offshore account belonging to a new company Zane had organized for the Crazy Bastards. Followed several more transfers to shadow companies the full payment eventually wound up in the hands of the cartel. The entire operation, although tedious and complicated, went smoothly and to all parties' satisfaction. Upon verification that the money had been cleanly transferred to the Crazy Bastards, Zane contacted Number One to inform and congratulate him on completion of the sale.

"You have my congratulations, Number One. Your money is in the bank and the buyer has its company there were no problems it went as smooth as silk. Everything has been done as you directed."

"Thanks, Zane you did well! *Adios*, we will not be seeing you again, forget everything you know about us."

Number One leaned back in his chair before pouring an Irish whisky for Number Two and, Joe, his new Number Three. He was smiling broadly.

"Welcome to Number Three, Joe. You earned it."

Jerry reviewed the reports tracing the ownership of Cross Border I&E Company from one offshore company to another checking carefully to be certain that the eventual owner, Offshore Enterprises, could not be connected with its purchase from the Crazy Bastards. Convinced they were in the clear Mr. Kevo Brandt, President of Offshore Enterprises, arranged a meeting with Zane. Cleared of his association with the cartel Zane had moved his office from its original location with the Crazy Bastards to leased space on the tenth floor of the newly completed New Oil Building located in the energy corridor. The new quarters consisted of a tastefully decorated reception area, Zane's office and a large conference room. Cross Border I&E Company employed only two people, Jane the secretary-receptionist and Zane. Kevo was cordially greeted by Zane, who did not know him personally, but knew who he was professionally.

"What might we do for Offshore Enterprises?" inquired Zane smiling as he did so.

"That depends," replied Kevo closing the door to Zane's office.

"We have been watching you for a good while and are very impressed with your success in making investments at Cross Border I&E Company. You are aware it is wholly owned by us through a shadow subsidiary, right?"

"Yes, I knew early on who was buying us, at the time I couldn't figure out why. Which is still my question why did you buy Cross Border I&E Company?"

"Quite candidly, we bought the company to get you away from the Crazy Bastards," said Kevo with no indication it was anything other than a business decision.

"You see, it's a very complicated and complex issue, simply put, we could not have you working for us if you were even remotely tied to the cocaine trade, so we bought you out."

Kevo made the whole thing sound like a routine business transaction something that happened every day in the normal course of things.

"I am flattered, how could I be of such value to you?"

"That is the purpose of my visit today to explain what we envision for both your future and ours. We plan to absorb Cross Border I&E Company's assets into Offshore Enterprises making it completely disappear. We want to make you one of our principal investment managers with the title of vice-president. We are offering a competitive pay package including incentive awards tied to your performance. You will have the freedom to make your own trades, deals and acquisitions without any input or oversight from us. If you like, you can stay in this office, or move to a larger one it's immaterial to us. We want you to operate independently although we will make all of our company research resources available for your use. At Offshore Enterprises we have earmarked two billion dollars for your first year's budget, you can take some time to think about our offer before you reach a decision." Said Kevo ending his sales pitch. Then he added.

"We are well aware of your personal investment accounts, which you can continue to manage while in our service."

"I don't need any time to think about it, I accept your offer. I am ready to go to work right now. Believe me, I will never forget your purchase of Cross Border I&E Company, so far, it is the high point of my business career and my life you have no idea what this means to me."

In all of his considerations on how to get away from the *Bastardos Locos* Zane never imagined such a turn of events could be possible. Whatever their reason Offshore Enterprises had freed him from the *Bastardos Locos*. Throughout the closing and transfer of funds, Zane had not mentioned what was going on to Peggy he was waiting for confirmation that he was free before breaking the news to her. Mr. Kevo Brandt had just confirmed his freedom from the Crazy Bastards he was a free man. He and Peggy could marry, she and Bruce would be safe and he would serve them well. As soon as Kevo left the office, Zane called Peggy telling her he had some great news he wanted to share with her.

"I'll meet you at your home right away. It's important."

Zane had never been happier he could feel his heart beating in his neck as he rang the doorbell he was so excited he was trembling by the time Peggy opened the door. Rushing inside, Zane kissed Peggy picking her up in his arms and swinging her around as if they were dancing. He sat her down on the couch then sat down next to her holding her hand. Before she could recover from his whirlwind entrance, Zane shouted.

"Let's get married."

Peggy couldn't believe what she was hearing she kissed Zane again before responding.

"You know the answer is yes, yes and yes. Zane, what has happened?"

Peggy knew before he answered that his situation must have changed because Zane knew she would never accept unless he was free of the *Bastardos Locos*.

"Everything has changed I am free of the *Bastardos Locos*. They sold me and Cross Border I&E Company to large American company. All of us you, me and Bruce are free of them. Do you understand what this means?"

He did not wait for an answer instead continued with his explanation.

"I know how this happened, I just don't know why it happened and probably never will, but I do know we are free of them. I suggest we celebrate our good fortune by getting married let's catch the next plane to Reno."

They were married two days later. Although modestly dressed for the occasion Peggy made a beautiful bride she and Zane embraced following the ceremony then turned and walked hand in hand from the chapel.

"We are married and Bruce is safe," she thought as they entered the limousine to return to their hotel. After enjoying a one night honeymoon, the newlyweds returned to Houston the following day. Four-year-old Bruce was happy to have Zane come to live with them there would be someone for him to play baseball with.

The operatives at Abe quietly congratulated themselves on a job well done, through their efforts and aid provided by ADAM and Imperial Enterprises Bruce, Peggy and Zane had been delivered from the dangerous *Bastardos Locos* safely and cleanly. A huge problem had been solved Peggy and Bruce were no longer in danger from the cartel.

"Gentlemen, I hope this proves to be the greatest challenge Abe and ADAM ever face. Little Bruce will be growing up, so don't relax yet there may be worse to come over the next twenty-six years." Said

Frank extolling their good work and preparing them for new tasks in the future.

Frank produced a bottle of Irish whisky from which he poured a round for the entire group to celebrate a job well done.

"This is the one good thing we learned from the *Bastardos Locos* during all of this. To your health gentlemen, keep up the good work."

Little did any of them realize the significance of their saving Zane from the *Bastardos Locos* or its future impact on Texas and national politics?

Chapter 8 Saved

Martha was tall with the body of a model sort of skinny, still beautiful to look at her skin was a golden light tan slightly lighter than her mother's. She was participating in many of the extracurricular activities at school and excelling in her class work. Voice and dance were her first love. She had dated off and on since she was sixteen and even though she was popular she did not have a regular boyfriend preferring to avoid going steady. Her mother insisted that Martha adhere to strict dating rules which included being home by 10:30 p.m. during the week and no later than 11:30 p.m. on weekends.

Every boy she dated was required to come into the house to meet her parents before leaving on a date, there were no exceptions. Her parents insisted on knowing who she was with and meeting the boy in person. Phil was a great judge of character, among young men, he would never allow Martha go out twice with someone he felt was untrustworthy or unsuitable. This happened only once, Carl an ignorant little twerp, who showed little respect for either Phil or Rachel while they were talking with him before a date, earned Phil's complete displeasure. Phil planned to discuss Carl and his manners with Martha when she returned home with the idea of dissuading her from accepting another date with him, but it proved to be unnecessary Martha thought he was a twerp too and had no interest is seeing him again. At the conclusion of the incident, Phil surmised Martha exercised good judgment as well as being a beautiful and outstanding young woman. She had a happy and bright future ahead of her.

Stephen and Martha met while on a beach trip to Padre Island with a group of friends during summer break. He was included in the group although he did not go to the same school as the rest of them; he attended a private Catholic high school in Corpus Christi and was a friend of a friend. After unloading their gear and ice chests from several cars and a pickup the mixed group of boys and girls assembled on the beach to set up the volleyball net and to choose teams. Two of the better male players served as captains they made the selections of their players after drawing straws for first pick. Purely by luck of the draw Martha and Stephen were picked on the same team and were initially assigned to play next to each other on the back line. During progression of the game, Martha and Stephen were often out of place interfering with each other and occasionally bumping together as they went for the ball. At the first break, Stephen introduced himself.

"My name is Stephen. Please, excuse me for repeatedly bumping in to you when I was out of position."

Martha looked down shyly then replied, "Stephen, it's not necessary to apologize its part of the game, anyway, I am the one who was out of position most of the time. My name is Martha."

After the match ended they sat together near their other teammates talking. A while later Stephen pointed toward the surf saying to Martha.

"If we are going for a swim in the surf, we better do it before it gets too late, otherwise we will never dry off once the sun starts going down."

"You're on Stephen," shouted Martha standing up to meet his challenge.

Stephen took her by the hand as they raced bare footed across the soft sand toward the surf which was some fifty yards away. Once in the water, they moved steadily out from the beach with the water coming above their knees after a few steps.

"Martha, I dare you to go out to the third bar with me. It's deep out there, but you will enjoy it, it's exciting."

"I accept your dare, but don't you let go of me."

Wading out to the second bar was not difficult since the water was only waist deep, however, in wading from the second to the third bar the water became increasingly deeper. Marsha found herself standing on her tip toes to keep her head above the surface midway across she could no longer reach bottom. Stephen took her in his arms carrying her until they reached the front of the third bar. After moving a little farther out from the beach, Stephen found the crest of the bar where she could stand on the bottom again the water was shoulder deep, but she was not frightened.

"Don't you find this exciting?"

"Yes, Stephen, very much."

Stephen took her in his arms pressing her body against his as he kissed her full on the mouth holding her tight all the while. She put her legs around his waist kissing him back they continued enjoying their bodies touching for several minutes before a huge wave crashed over them

186

submerging them for several seconds. Martha clung to Stephen with all of her might the entire time and did not relax until their heads were above water again. The waves were growing with the incoming tide becoming rollers as they reached the fourth bar and growing in height as they approached the third bar before collapsing in a loud roar once they reached the crest. Martha, who was still clinging to Stephen kissed him vigorously as a second wave crashed over them. Once their heads were above water again Martha whispered.

"We must go back it's becoming dangerous out here."

Stephen carried her in his arms all the way to the second bar which was long after she could stand up. From there they walked hand in hand back to the camp both of them were soaking wet and their hair was matted from being submerged by the last big wave. Before toweling down Martha's bikini stuck to her like a second skin leaving little to the imagination as to her bodily attributes. The minute details of her anatomy which had been partially hidden when she was dry became obvious. Stephen had been fascinated before they went into the surf, but after being with her in the water and seeing her in a wet bikini, there was no question that Martha was hot. It was also evident she was not afraid of anything. She had put her long dark hair in front of her right shoulder making her look even sexier Stephen was captivated by Martha's body and personality. He wanted to spend more time with her, he enjoyed her fun loving personality and she was beautiful.

The volleyball net had been taken down and loaded in the cars and pickup along with all the other equipment for the journey home. The group which was paired off boy and girl, sat on blankets around the camp fire eating and drinking the provisions they had brought in their coolers. Each couple was so engrossed in their own not so private activity that they paid little attention to what other people were doing around them. Martha and Stephen remained together following their swim and were sitting on the perimeter of the warmth provided by the bonfire when Stephen kissed her. Martha kissed him back caught up in the excitement of the moment. She kissed him again to make sure the good feeling sweeping over her was real.

Stephen lived on his parent's ranch, located several miles to the west of Corpus, which accounted for Martha not having met him before even though they were near the same age. He was over six feet tall and muscular as Martha noted that there was no fat on him, nor was there an excess of body hair. Martha had a distinct dislike of male bodies covered with hair, most of all she had a strong aversion to male bodies with hairy backs. To her, they seemed more like cavemen than someone she might be interested in touching. She thought Stephen's body was beautiful, just what she liked, he was handsome with thick curly black hair and unlike Martha had blue eyes. With twilight approaching, the beach party began breaking up with the various drivers gathering their passengers for the trip back to the mainland and home. Martha and Stephen kissed good bye promising to keep in touch and definitely to see each other again. On the drive home Martha could talk of nothing other than Stephen, she really liked him, he was her type of guy and he was hot.

The following week Martha told both her mother and Phil she had met a boy that she found really interesting. She went into great detail explaining how they had met who he was and how he was different from the other boys she had known. His name was Stephen Camp, whom she met on last weekend's beach outing, they had promised to keep in touch with the idea of dating. Her parents always knew some day she would see boys differently than she had as a little girl and that with time she would fall in love. Their plans for Martha included her remaining unattached until she had graduated from college. Rachel explained their position to Martha.

"We have no objection to your dating, even seriously, we would much prefer that you remain single until after you graduate from college. We strongly suggest you not become attached before you are very near completion of your college education."

Initially, Martha felt her parents were rejecting Stephen, but after he had been to their house several times, she found that they liked Stephen, thereafter, she concluded that by being reserved they were thinking of her not themselves. With her parent's approval, she and Stephen continued to date through her senior year in high school, but after graduation they went away to different universities. Martha entered the University of Texas College of Fine Arts in Austin to continue her study of dance and theater while Stephen enrolled at the University of Notre Dame in South Bend, Indiana.

Several of Martha's friends also enrolled at UT making the transition from high school to university life somewhat easier, they met frequently to talk about what they were doing at UT and what was happening back home. At the same time, they were making new friends in their classes and dorms as well as through participation in various school activities. Martha was the only one of the group in the Fine Arts school, she seldom encountered the others outside of their planned meetings, which with the passage of time became less frequent as their individual activities blended into those of their new friends and acquaintances.

Martha and Stephen kept in touch as friends, but as usually happens in long distance relationships they drifted apart after a while and quit calling one another on a regular schedule. After Stephen began dating a girl he met at Notre Dame, they quit corresponding altogether. Martha was not surprised or upset by this development she liked Stephen he was a really nice guy who would make someone else a good husband, she had never thought of him as a life mate although she had been attracted to him and enjoyed being with him a lot.

For the most part Martha concentrated on her classes she went out occasionally and then only with a group she had not met any guy who turned her on either physically or mentally. For the moment she was unattached and planned to remain that way for the immediate future. The chance of her encountering a person she might want as a lover and husband was remote among the males in her classes most of them were too effeminate, or more interested in each other than in the opposite sex. Although these guys were superb dancers and had beautiful bodies, they did not care for women not even those equally gifted in the Arts. Their only interest in Martha was in having her as a dancing partner because she made them look better than they actually were in the routines they danced before the professors for credit.

Half way through her sophomore year, Martha was invited to try out for an intramural ladies volleyball team sponsored by several dorms at UT. Her tall frame and willowy body coupled with her training as a dancer made Martha a natural, she could jump high in the air with ease. Following a workout witnessed by the team coach, she was chosen for the team over several others who were taller, but less agile. When Martha began practice with the Sirens, she found herself to be the shortest person on the team, yet she had the highest jump and was by far the quickest of all the players. The coach took an immediate liking to Martha and her athletic abilities. Although Martha had played volleyball extensively while growing up, she had not taken the game seriously until she joined the Sirens where, with the coach's help and dedication to perfecting her skills, Martha became a versatile player adept in all phases of the game. She was outstanding as an offensive player with her high jump and teeth jarring spikes of the ball and she was equally good at making digs and saving the ball for her teammates. On offense her quickness and deft handwork made her exceptionally good at keeping rallies alive often setting up her teammates for slams. She played both the front line and back line with equal finesse her passing and setting skills were unequalled in the league, much to the delight of her teammates, who scored often because of her expert saves and setups. The Sirens became a terror on the courts defeating much more experienced teams with ease due to their teamwork and ferocity of play. The Sirens were a sensation in intramural volleyball with fans drawn from the entire student body. Word spread like wildfire across the campus among the male students the Sirens were a great bunch of players, who had well developed bodies and were sexy to watch in their skimpy uniforms. Lady's volleyball was considered the best derriere watching arena on campus drawing large crowds of boisterous male fans.

The Sirens as a whole were tall and trim, none of them were overweight or had over sized boobs, they had long legs and firm derrieres all of their movements were graceful and well timed. Watching them perform was akin to watching a choreographed ballet with each player demonstrating their individual skills and grace. Martha's talent and beauty on the court could not be overlooked, her light golden skin stood out from the other players and her large liquid brown eyes and straight black hair enhanced her delicate classical facial features. She was beautiful and athletic, yet very feminine and super sexy. The male fans cheered when she leaned low to save a rally, or when she jumped high above the net to slam a spike into the opponent's court. She was their favorite and was fast becoming an object of adoration for some of her male fans. As the season progressed, Martha received a lot of attention off the courts from some of her more aggressive male admirers they bombarded her with proposals for dates and *rendezvous* at various nightclubs around Austin. She refused all of their offers, these male admirers hardly disguised that they were primarily interested in having sex with her. In Martha's mind, it was depressing to think sex was all guys really cared about. Following one of the more crass proposals Martha said to herself.

"Whatever happened to love and being friends?"

A few days later she was shopping off campus in one of the nearby boutique stores when, to her surprise, she was approached by a tall guy wearing shorts.

"Say, aren't you one of the Sirens?"

"Yes, I play on the team and who are you?"

"My name is Jimmy, I am an admirer of yours."

"What do you mean by that?"

"What I mean is, you are the best volleyball player I have ever seen and I admire your ability."

"In that case, my name is Martha. I'm pleased to meet you, Jimmy."

"I know your name, everyone who watches the matches knows who you are."

"Do you come to all the matches, Jimmy?"

"Only the ones the Sirens play, I am a fan of your team."

"And why is that?"

"Because I like to watch you play."

"Do you mean me or the team?"

"You in particular, but the team too."

"Why me, don't you watch the other players?"

"Because in addition to being a fantastic player, you are the most beautiful woman I have ever seen. You may not believe this, I have been wanting to meet you for a long time."

"So, now we have met."

"Martha, I would like very much to be your friend I would like get to know you. Will you allow me to buy you a cup of coffee or something?"

"OK, Jimmy, there is a place just down the street where we can sit outside and enjoy the solitude. There won't be many people sitting outside today because of the heat."

Martha abandoned her search for a new outfit, instead she walked down the sidewalk with Jimmy at her side when they arrived at the cafe they took an outside table which had an umbrella large enough to provide shade for both of them.

"Would you like coffee?" Asked Jimmy.

"No, Jimmy, it's too hot for coffee, I think I'll have lemonade, if you don't mind," replied Martha looking up at Jimmy who towered over her casting a long shadow across her face.

"A great idea, I think lemonade would be just right on a hot day like today," replied Jimmy before going inside to place their order. He returned with two tall glasses of lemonade and a small package of cookies.

"These go well with lemonade I always have some with mine. Please, try one you might like the combination like I do," offered Jimmy moving the package toward Martha while gesturing toward the open package.

"What are they, some special type of cookie they make here?"

"Nothing as fancy as that, they are just plain gingersnaps right off the display rack, try one they are really good."

Martha took a single cookie from the package holding it between her index finger and thumb she raised it to her mouth taking a small bite then arched her dark eyebrows before exclaiming.

"These are really good!"

Looking at Jimmy carefully, Martha asked.

"Do you buy these for all the girls you meet, or are they for special occasions?"

"Today, they are for a very special occasion, the day I met you."

"Thank you, I'll have another and we can celebrate together."

"I've watched all of your matches and I'm mesmerized by your superb athletic moves you must have been playing volleyball for a long time to be able to perform at the level you do," said Jimmy in an effort to demonstrate his interest in volleyball.

"I am sure it will surprise you to learn I never played the game seriously before making the Sirens team this year."

"No kidding. How could you be in such fantastic physical shape, do you play other sports?" asked Jimmy astounded at her answer.

In an effort to clear up any misconceptions Martha explained.

192

"Jimmy, I don't play any other sports I joined the Sirens to meet people outside my curriculum here at UT. I am a dancer and have been most of my life, which is why I am in such good physical shape. It takes a lot of hard physical conditioning to be a classical dancer."

"I should have guessed, the way you jump is a thing of beauty very graceful and powerful I might add."

Jimmy was marveling at Martha's beautiful face. He was a little uncertain on how to proceed because he wanted desperately to make a favorable impression, but so far he had not figured out the best way to engage her without unwittingly offending her in some way. Fortunately for him, Martha expanded the scope of their conversation.

"I have had crude proposals and propositions from a number of the guys cheering for the Sirens. Jimmy, I am pleased you were not one of them. These guys seem to be interested only in was getting me in bed. I turn down all of their offers, or just don't respond in some instances because I have no interest in any of them."

"I would expect you to refuse. Martha, you have made my day, I am the happiest guy in Austin to hear that you are unattached," responded Jimmy looking at Martha for some sign that the last part of his statement was true.

"I didn't say I am unattached, just that I refused all the crude offers."

"Then you do have someone special?"

"No, Jimmy, should I consider you special."

"Yes, thank you. Martha, does that mean we could meet again?"

"I think so, maybe a date this weekend."

Martha had left an opening for Jimmy to ask for a date, but before he could respond she asked.

"I assume you are a student at UT, is that right?"

"That is correct, I am in my third year studying business management. I am thinking of staying for a master's degree although that depends on the job situation after I get my BS degree."

"As I told you, I am in fine arts, dancing and theatre to be precise. I am a year behind you."

Martha found Jimmy to be interesting he was nice, fairly good looking, had a reasonable body and had a pleasing outgoing personality. He had expressed his interest in a way that made her think he cared about her not just her body. For Martha there were no clanging bells or rushes of sexual excitement, instead there was a strong feel-good sensation being with Jimmy. Martha liked him. She put her hand on his lightly.

"I really appreciate the lemonade and especially the cookies they were extra ordinarily delicious, but I need to be going."

He placed his other hand on top of Martha's exerting a slight pressure.

"What about our date this weekend, how about something simple like a movie or a drive around the lake?"

"Jimmy, why don't you decide what we should do on a first date? Just give me plenty of notice on your choice, I need to know what to wear and what time you are picking me up."

They exchanged phone numbers and address before heading to their respective destinations it was after five in the afternoon and there was tons of home work to be completed before tomorrow's classes. Their chance meeting and upcoming date seemed as though an unseen force had intervened on their behalf. Jimmy had been trying to get an introduction to Martha since the first match he had seen the Sirens play. None of his friends actually knew Martha, they were volleyball fans who knew her name, but none of them knew her personally. Jimmy had been unable to find a way to meet Martha even though he had made their meeting his top priority. It was totally by accident that they had been at the same place at the same time. Both Jimmy and Martha were pleased with the events of the afternoon each of them parted with a new hope for the future. Martha had not noticed Jimmy, or anyone else in the stands during matches, she was singularly focused on the game itself not who was watching. She had expected to meet someone of interest as a result of participating in volleyball, but she had not met a special guy until Jimmy happened along earlier in the day their random encounter improved her prospects considerably over what they had been the week before. She was pleased with herself, the conservation with Jimmy had been both pleasant and interesting, she felt he liked being with her for herself and he was very complimentary a trait of most kind men. She assured herself.

"He could be someone of interest."

Had Martha been more observant, she would have noticed Jimmy was not the only person who attended all the Sirens' matches there was a medium sized dark man with short kinky black hair who appeared whenever they played a match. He looked much too old to be a student, however, some of the foreign students were considerably older than their American counterparts. No one in the stands paid attention to him during the matches, they were too busy admiring the players and their skills.

Alpha-4 had reported Mohammed al Sultan's presence at the games early on because he had also been spotted by the surveillance team in the vicinity of the Fine Arts Center and near Martha's dorm. Although Mohammad's intentions were undetermined, and he had never directly approached Martha, Alpha-4 still treated him as a potential threat to Martha's wellbeing. Alarmed, Frank ordered a detailed check into his background and was attempting to put together a dossier with a history of his past and present relationships with the powerful tribes in his home country. The reason for his presence in the country and at UT was unknown as was when and how he arrived. These were among a host of unanswered questions Frank had concerning Mohammad al Sultan who appeared to be an avid volleyball fan.

Jimmy also showed up as a regular spectator in Alpha-4's surveillance of the games. Prompting a detailed investigation into his background during which they found him to be a well thought of business student from Wichita Falls. His family owned and operated one of the larger ranches in Texas he was beyond reproach, but he was possibly interested in Martha or one of the other Sirens. So far, he had not appeared on videos or been seen by the surveillance team anywhere near Martha other than at the games.

Jimmy eased his car into the dorm driveway in mid-afternoon on Saturday, since Martha left the choice to him, he had elected to drive around part of Lake Travis and later have dinner at one of the restaurants situated in the hills surrounding the lake. Martha was dressed in a frilly short skirt and a pullover top with a marginally low cut bust line, she was stunningly beautiful her hair was up exposing the symmetry of her neckline accentuating her classical facial features. Jimmy was clean shaven and was wearing a starched short sleeved shirt and a pair of pressed trousers, which fit him like a glove, tight all over. "Martha, you look fantastic. I'm so glad to see you." Said Jimmy as he took her hand.

"I'm so glad you decided on a drive around the lake, it is something I have not done before. I'm looking forward to a new adventure."

"If you are ready, so am I, let's get in the SUV and head out," said Jimmy as he opened the door for Martha. Jimmy drove north then west to reach the shoreline of the upper east bank of Lake Travis from there he drove on several farm to market roads to open access areas providing great overlooks of the lake. Martha had not viewed Lake Travis from such vantage points she was overwhelmed by the scenic beauty of the lake and surrounding hills. She was astounded by the majestic homes built high on the hilltops overlooking the lake and could only speculate on the dramatic view from their vantage points.

"Jimmy, it's absolutely beautiful out here, how did you know about all of these roads and scenic overlooks of the lake?"

"I Googled it on my computer then checked their on-line maps to determine which roads to use. After cross-checking the data, I came up with a planned route which provided the most overlook views on a convenient driving trip. Since you like it so much, I am naming it Martha's Lake Travis Overlook Route, in your honor," said Jimmy as he touched Martha's hand.

"How sweet Jimmy, I've not had anything named after me before," said Martha intending to kiss Jimmy on the cheek for his chivalrous act, instead she kissed him on the lips with a hint of passion before pulling back.

"I'm sorry, I should not have done that I was overcome by your thoughtfulness it won't happen again."

"Since you are sorry, I think the only way to get even would be for me to kiss you."

Jimmy put his arms around Martha's waist and pulling her close as he kissed her. His lips lingering long enough to let her know his kiss was more than just a reciprocal act of kindness. Martha was surprised, she felt a rush of excitement when Jimmy pulled her close and even more when he kissed her. She wanted to remain in his arms, but instead she pulled away saying.

"Now we are even."

Martha was flushed, her lips were slightly parted, and she was smiling, her brown eyes sparkled in the sunlight she looked wistfully into Jimmy's eyes as she stepped closer. He put his arms around her small waist pulling her firmly against him. Martha could not resist she put her arms around him pulling him even closer. Just as they kissed, a mocking bird began singing in the tree behind them their kiss continued until its solo was finished. When the bird's song ended Jimmy and Martha were breathless still standing with their arms around each other. Martha broke the ensuing silence as the mocking bird fluttered away.

"It looks like we are never going to be even again no matter how hard we try."

"If it means there will be no more kisses, I don't want to be even," replied Jimmy taking Martha's hand and walking back to the car. Once inside, Jimmy drove to The Oasis restaurant on Comanche Trail where they found a table in the shade outside on the deck which provided a magnificent view of the lake at sundown. Jimmy ordered two *Grande* frozen *margaritas* with *Anejo Patron tequila* with salt on the rim and two straws in each glass. Martha was enjoying the afternoon with Jimmy much more than she had anticipated his last kiss was still on her mind when she took the first sip of her *margarita*. It was slightly sweet and delicate somewhat like Jimmy's kiss.

"Jimmy is more than special, he is extra special just like this *margarita*. He is definitely a person of interest, someone I intend to spend a lot more time with in the future."

Sitting with Martha at The Oasis watching her sip her *margarita* with two straws made Jimmy catch his breath she was devastatingly beautiful and fun to be with he could not take his eyes off of her not even for a moment.

"Martha, you are the most beautiful woman I have ever seen, so delicate, yet so strong I could spend all day looking at you."

"I'm afraid we'll starve to death, unless we order soon, it's been a long time since breakfast," replied Martha jokingly.

Jimmy laughed then grinned as he responded.

"You are right, I am enjoying being with you so much that my stomach forgot to tell me it's time to eat, are you ready to order?"

"Not really, it was only a joke, let's have another *margarita* and talk for a while before we order. There is a lot more   I want to know about you."

Much to Jimmy's delight, they talked for over an hour before ordering dinner. Afterward they lingered talking well into the evening before deciding to call it a night. The second round of *margaritas* had lost most of their effect by the time Martha and Jimmy left the Oasis, yet they shared a rosy feeling about the events of the day. They arrived at Martha's dorm after midnight and even though it was late they sat in the car for several minutes talking. Martha suddenly raised herself so that she was facing Jimmy before she placed her hands on the back of his neck and head kissing him feverishly. Her lips were warm and moist staying on his for several moments before Jimmy took her in his arms kissing her passionately. By the time Jimmy released Martha, her heart was racing wildly, and she was short of breath from the extended kiss. She experienced a warm cozy feeling all over as she spoke.

"Jimmy, it was a wonderful day, I enjoyed every minute of our time together there is no place I would rather have been than with you. I thank you for making today happen, it was fun and enjoyable."

"It was special for me too, the world is an even more wonderful place when I'm with you. Martha, being with you makes me very happy. When can I see you again?"

Jimmy's heart was beating rapidly he could hear it pounding in his chest as Martha squeezed his hand while she was getting out of the car.

"Call me," she said waving as she closed the car door before walking toward the dorm. Jimmy watched every step bewitched by the provocative sway of her walk. He did not leave immediately, he stayed a minute or two after she went into the dorm still savoring Martha's parting kiss. He pinched himself to make sure he was not dreaming before driving away.

The following week, Jimmy called Martha every day, they managed to talk for several minutes each time usually about their time together and their daily routines. He couldn't resist calling, to hear her voice made his day more enjoyable. At the sound of Martha's voice he relived the kisses they had shared the past weekend they became real all over again stimulating his appetite for more. He had not anticipated a kiss on their first date the experience made him want another and another. He had to see her again she was the girl he had always dreamed of! Jimmy's mind was consumed by the thought of Martha and being with her again. Although he tried to set a time for another date with every call, he had been unsuccessful until Thursday night when Martha agreed to a date the following Saturday.

Between studies, practice and volleyball Martha had little free time during the week, so they decided to have a picnic lunch in the park on Saturday. Both wore shorts and tee shirts to take advantage of the warm weather. Jimmy pulled his car into a small parking area from which he and Martha walked together toward the park, Jimmy had on his backpack and carried a blanket under one arm and a large picnic basket in his free hand. They arrived at the park early with the idea of finding a shady spot near the river as a scenic venue for their second date. Walking along the river bank they came across the perfect setting, a shaded grassy spot nestled under the spreading branches of a huge oak tree situated within twenty feet of the water's edge. Jimmy laid his picnic provisions on the ground to concentrate on spreading his blanket on the grass. Once Martha arrange herself on the blanket, Jimmy retrieved a large thermos filled with lemonade from his backpack. He magically produced Styrofoam cups and a package of gingersnaps before pouring lemonade for the two of them. Jimmy held out the bag of gingersnaps toward Martha.

"Would you like one?"

"Of course, gingersnaps have become my favorite cookies."

"Tell me, Jimmy were you a cowboy back home?"

"Not really, I mostly worked in the business side of ranching. I rode horses and herded cattle once in a while and learned the workings of the ranch, but I was never a cowboy and never intend to be one. I'll probably end up managing the ranch in a few years, right now I am more interested in you."

Jimmy unpacked a small portable radio placing it near the blanket before tuning in a neo-classical station playing easy listening music. He kept the volume low to provide romantic background music for their picnic while trying to impress Martha with his selections to produce a relaxing atmosphere for the remainder of the afternoon. The music complimented the slight sound of the flowing water coming from the river creating a peaceful romantic atmosphere.

"Jimmy, how thoughtful, I love your music it is my favorite for a romantic setting."

"I'm glad you like it, it's my favorite kind of music too I'm not into country western."

"I brought smoked turkey and cheese sandwiches for the main course, let me know when you get hungry, until then why don't you join me?"

Jimmy was sprawled on the blanket laying on his side looking up at Martha. She said nothing, she slowly lowering herself on to the blanket laying on her back a few feet away. Jimmy loved looking at Marsha's profile her facial features were extraordinary, a straight nose, voluptuous red lips with a small chin and smooth neck line. Her firm breasts pointed skyward while her tummy was flat giving way to well-rounded hips and long beautiful legs. She was gorgeous from every perspective. He wanted her. She was awesome Jimmy could not look at her enough. After a while, his neck began to ache from being propped up on his arm while watching Martha, to relieve the pain, Jimmy moved nearer to Martha reclining on his back next to her. Grappling in Martha's vicinity without looking he found her hand taking it in his he squeezed it gently.

"Do you mind if I hold your hand it feels like it belongs in mine?"

"I don't mind at all I like the feel of it too," replied Martha as she squeezed his hand slightly in return. Jimmy's heart began pounding at the touch of her hand causing him to turn his head slightly to look at Martha. To his surprise, she was looking at him, her eyes were intense and she was smiling mischievously. Before either of them could speak, the radio station changed selections and began playing the Merry Widow Waltz. Jimmy turned the volume up slightly then turning back toward Martha said. "That is one of my favorite pieces of music I couldn't resist turning up the volume."

"That's strange, Jimmy. The Merry Widow Waltz is one of my favorites as well, dad and I danced to it on our first date."

"What do you mean, you and your dad danced to it on your first date? How could that be possible?"

"Phil is my dad, but he isn't my father! He took me on the first date he had with mom. I was about eight years old and he and I danced to the Merry Widow Waltz. Everyone cleared the dance floor while we were dancing and gave a huge cheer when we finished. I was thrilled it seemed they thought we were dancing stars."

"Then your mom was divorced before she married your dad?"

"No, Phil is the only dad I've ever had."

"You are confusing me, Martha, I don't understand."

"It is confusing, but allow me to explain. I am an experimental baby, part of an ongoing genetic research program funded by a company called Gentex. My mom volunteered for the program when she was single before she met Phil. I was conceived through artificial insemination using sperm from an unidentified donor. Every year until my eighteenth birthday they made a series of tests on me to chronicle my physical and mental development as part of the study. That is why my last name is Schuber rather than Jensen like mom and Phil. Schuber was mom's name before she married Phil. Does this make any sense?"

"Now, that you have explained it, I understand. I knew you were special the first time I saw you on the volleyball court with this added information I realize you are more special than I thought. You are super special!"

"It doesn't bother you that I don't know who my father is?"

"It doesn't bother me at all, Martha, it's you I care about!"

They lay talking for a long while before eating their sandwiches with more lemonade and gingersnaps for dessert. Jimmy and Martha were sitting facing each other with their legs crossed when Martha suddenly popped to a standing position.

"Would you mind doing me a favor?"

"You know I'd do anything for you, what do you want me to do?" replied Jimmy with a quizzical expression on his face.

"It's not a big thing. Please, stand up and remove your tee shirt for me."

Surprised, Jimmy jumped to his feet and slowly pulled his tee shirt over his head then standing at attention with the shirt dangling in one hand he asked.

"Like this?"

Martha did not say a word she slowly walked around him surveying his bare upper body carefully from every vantage point she then put her hand in the middle of his chest exclaiming.

"I knew it! You are just right."

Jimmy's chest and back were practically devoid of hair his body was smooth as a marble statue. Martha removed her hand before kissing him on the chest then she kissed him again on the back just over his left shoulder blade.

"What was that all about?"

Jimmy was totally confused by Martha's actions, yet he was excited by her kisses and did not want her to stop. Martha put her arms around his waist with her hands touching his back. She pulled him close then kissed him on the mouth her lips were hot and inviting. Jimmy kissed her back his passion growing in intensity whenever their bodies touched.

"You have a beautiful body and I love it. You can't possibly know how happy I am that you do not have a lot of body hair. I suspected as much because you hardly have any hair on your legs, I just wanted to see for myself that you have the nice smooth body that I thought you had."

"Then I passed the test?"

"You more than passed, you have a lovely body just the type I adore," replied Martha who still had her arms around Jimmy's waist.

"I don't suppose you would remove your tee shirt, if I asked?"

Martha smiled before she replied.

"No, not here."

Jimmy kissed her again.

"I didn't think so."

Much to their regret they were forced to end their picnic and return to their studies, but the events of the day cemented their relationship, it was clear to both of them that they were more than just friends. Thereafter, Jimmy and Martha grew closer and more intimate with every contact between them no matter whether they were having dinner, dancing or going to a movie together. Toward the end of her sophomore year, Martha became convinced she had found more than someone of interest. It was clear that Jimmy loved her and respected her he never pushed the sex issue although it was evident both of them were becoming aroused nearly to the point of no return. Extreme self-control was all that stood between them and wild uncontrolled sex. She loved Jimmy too, he was kind and funny, a really nice guy sort of like her dad. Jimmy turned her on, she loved touching his smooth muscular body, magically, it made her imagine being naked with him. They were having coffee at the cafe where they had their first lemonade together when Martha inquired.

"Are you planning anything special for the summer break, or are you going to summer school?"

"I have been meaning to tell you that my parents and I are making a trip to China this summer, so I won't be seeing you more than once or twice between the end of the spring semester and the beginning of the fall semester. I don't like it, but this trip has been in the planning stage for a while and was just confirmed two days ago. There had been some sort of hang up with the Chinese government, which apparently has been worked out."

"I was just thinking Jimmy, since we will be apart for the summer, maybe we should go on another picnic this Saturday. This time why don't we find a secluded spot with privacy rather than going to the park?"

"We can do that, in fact, I know just the place. A friend of mine owns an undeveloped section (six hundred and forty acres) west of town that has no buildings or ranching operations it's raw land with no improvements other than a couple of dirt roads. There are no houses for miles around, this place is so far out in the sticks it's almost isolated from the modern world. I'm sure I can get a key to the gate."

After half an hour of driving on a gravel road, Jimmy turned on to a dirt lane leading off into the mesquite brush. A few hundred yards farther they encountered a fence with a locked aluminum gate bearing a Private Property no Trespassing sign. The gate blocked the entrance to his friend's undeveloped section baring any type of ground vehicle from entering without the owner having a key to the lock. The only other way for a ground vehicle to enter was to knock down the fence and drive around the gate. Searching in his right-hand pocket Jimmy produced a key with which he unlocked the massive pad lock after removing the chain he swung the gate open then drove through before closing and locking the gate behind them. Martha was beaming when he reentered the vehicle.

"I love the scenery it's beautiful and certainly secluded."

"Like I said, this is private we are the only ones out here and the only entrance is locked behind us. Let's drive on to find a clearing with some grass near one of those large oak trees like that one over there."

Jimmy was pointing to a huge oak tree with large spreading branches which were nearly touching the ground. A few minutes later, he turned into a clearing in the brush several yards off of the dirt lane coming to stop near a huge oak tree, which shaded a large swath of grass covered open area. The native grass was thick and nearly six inches high making the clearing an ideal spot for a summer afternoon picnic. It was surrounded by mesquite trees and scrub brush, except to the west where were no obstructions of any kind, the view looked downhill presenting a diorama of the hills in the distance.

"How does this suite you, Martha?"

"It's splendid, Jimmy. Just what I had in mind."

The wind was barely blowing just enough to maintain a slight cooling effect to offset the summer heat. Martha was glowing as she climbed out of the car in the shade of the massive oak.

"It's perfect, Jimmy, look at the view of the valley it looks almost blue it's so far away, I love it."

Jimmy spread two blanket side by side overlapping them slightly to make a large pallet in the shade of the oak tree. Martha sat on the pallet with her legs crossed while Jimmy unloaded the cooler and picnic supplies from the car. Finishing up Jimmy placed the cooler just off of the pallet before sitting next to Martha. He made a dramatic show of serving lemonade and gingersnaps after kissing Martha lightly on the lips.

"Jimmy, it's so quite out here. Other than that bird singing in the distance, I don't hear anything. How refreshing!"

They had been lying side by side holding hands and talking for a short while when Martha suddenly stood up pulling her tee shirt over her head as Jimmy looked on in shocked awe. The sight of her beautifully shaped bare breasts created a wild uncontrollable reaction from Jimmy he jumped to his feet removing his shirt as he did. Neither spoke. They were standing facing each other as he kissed Martha on the lips when suddenly he grasped her bottom pulling her against him with both hands. Her hands were on his bare back pulling him forward gently massaging his chest against her breasts. Jimmy stepped back and began to remove his shorts. Martha quickly interrupted.

"No, Jimmy. Please, let me do it."

She moved forward then deftly stepped behind him, while kissing him on the back, she slowly lowered his shorts and then his underwear letting them drop to his ankles. When Jimmy deftly stepped out, he was totally naked except for his sandals which he quickly kicked off.

Turning to face Martha he was obviously excited.

"Now, it's my turn."

Martha threw her head back pulling her hair down, so that it was hanging over her shoulders black and straight. Jimmy kissed her on the mouth then on each breast as he removed her shorts leaving only her panties and sandals. He slipped his fingers into the back of her panties kissed each breast again then slowly bent at the knees as he slid her panties below her rear kissing her gently on her belly as he moved lower with both of his hands grasping her rear. Martha daintily stepped out her panties leaving them lying on the blanket she was totally naked. She stood frozen as, Jimmy continued kissing her body finally unable to restrain herself any longer, Martha pulled him to the blanket kissing him wildly. They caressed each other as they lay kissing naked in the seclusion of their own outdoor paradise. Hours later they were lying naked in each other's arms content to have their bodies touching intimately neither of them spoke. They were exhausted their bodies physically spent from their repeated episodes of wild love and sexual pleasure. Making love outside awakened their primal instincts urging them to abandon all restraints and to enjoy sex to the fullest their pleasure was intense and exhilarating they did not want it to end.

Lying on her back enjoying the afterglow of intoxicating sex Martha raised her arm pointing to the sky.

"What are those birds circling way up there? They look like specks they are so high."

At first, Jimmy could not see them at all he peered intently at the area Martha was pointing toward before spotting the circling birds high in the sky.

"I'm not sure, but from the number of them and the time of year I would guess they are Mississippi Kites, a small bird of prey that migrates to Central America for the winter months and returns to the Southern U.S. in the spring. Why do you ask?"

Martha smiled before answering.

"Do you suppose those birds could see us from way up there?"

Jimmy laughed before responding.

"Kites do have great eyesight that's probably why they keep circling above us to see what we are going to do next."

The birds continued to circle high above them for the remainder of the afternoon they were still there when Martha and Jimmy dressed and prepared to head back to Austin. Jimmy was driving toward the main road when Martha softly rubbed the inside of his leg saying in a low sultry voice.

"Jimmy, we have let the genie out of the bottle and we will never be able to put it back. We will never be the same after today. You were so good, I loved every minute of it. You made my whole body vibrate with unbelievable pleasure, I can still feel it. Oh, Jimmy, I love you so much!"

"When you removed your tee shirt I almost exploded, but that was nothing compared to the sensation which swept over me when I felt your bottom while I was pulling down your panties. I could not help myself my only thought was to ravish you with kisses all over your wonderful sexy body."

"Jimmy, I loved it and I love you for making me so happy. I hope you enjoyed our being together as much as I did."

"Believe me, Martha, I will remember this picnic forever. If I had enjoyed it any more, I would probably have died overcome with pleasure. I love you, Martha, you have me as your eternal slave. Spending the afternoon with you is the highlight of my life so far, the only thing I can think of that I would like more is for you to marry me."

"Jimmy, I will marry you, but we will have to wait until I graduate from college."

It was twilight when Jimmy and Martha reached the entrance to her dorm they were in each other's arms kissing good night when he slid his hands down her waist until they were on her bottom.

"Not here, Jimmy. Next time." Said Martha placing his hands firmly on her waist.

"I couldn't resist I love feeling of your rear, forgive me, next time. Martha, it's important we get together tomorrow say at the cafe around two. I want to buy you an engagement ring to make sure you don't change your mind and to let the other guys know you are taken."

"An engagement ring really isn't necessary I'm yours with or without one."

Reaching the dorm entrance, Jimmy let go of her hand saying.

"I'll be waiting for you at the café."

He kissed Martha again and while walking toward the car he turned and waved before reluctantly getting in his SUV and driving away.

Martha was preoccupied reliving the day of fantastic love and sex when the elevator arrived at the ground floor in the dorm lobby. She paid little attention to the short dark man who stepped into the elevator just as the door was closing. His dark eyes were riveted on Martha as she entered her floor number on the elevator menu, he studied her body in minute detail. Once the elevator began its ascent, he continued to stare at her intently. When the door opened, he said nothing just looked at her with his beady black eyes as he exited the elevator with Martha on the sixth floor. Unnoticed by Martha, the dark figure followed a few steps behind her until she stopped to unlock the door to her living quarters where he paused briefly before walking down the hallway. She closed the door locking it behind her which was her normal procedure. Not long afterward, the swarthy stranger returned, pausing at her door briefly, before returning to the elevator and leaving the building. Martha had hardly noticed the man she would not have recognized him the following day had she encountered him again.

The on duty Alpha-4 agent watching live video from their hidden cameras identified the short swarthy man in the elevator as Mohammad al Sultan whom Abe suspected might be stalking Martha. This was the first time he had been observed inside of Martha's dorm, although he had been seen in the general area several times earlier. The alarmed agent called his supervisor who issued a Red Alert.

"Our suspicions have been confirmed we just observed Mohammad al Sultan inside of Martha's dorm and on her floor. He appeared to be checking her room number before leaving the building."

Abe responded quickly.

"Do not let Martha out of your sight she may be in imminent danger double the number of active agents assigned to Martha immediately. In addition, we want 24/7 surveillance of Mohammad al Sultan and identification of anyone that he contacts or meets. Our special team will be there tonight to set up electronic surveillance of Mohammed and his friends including their computers, phones, bank accounts, everything. Keep us informed around the clock Martha may be in serious danger. We still do not have a complete dossier on Mohammad, but we expect it to be here in a few more days. Prevent Martha from being abducted using whatever means necessary, including extermination of obvious kidnappers!"

Meanwhile back at Abe, Frank called Jerry his counterpart at ADAM to discuss Mohammad al Sultan and the current situation with Martha. Frank was alarmed because Mohammad was obviously interested in Martha for some unknown reason. He appeared to be stalking her and had been able to enter her dorm unobstructed by those assigned to protect her. Even though they were not certain he meant her any harm, his intentions appeared to be ominous. If he had some sinister plan involving her, they needed to find out what it was immediately in order to strengthen their protection of Martha. Jerry was equally alarmed because his worldwide organization had been unable to uncover the information they had requested about Mohammad. He was still essentially unknown to them and his motives remained elusive and secretive. Jerry decided as a last resort to contact the President of Afghanistan to press him for some answers about his fellow countryman Mohammad al Sultan. Jerry had been instrumental in arranging financing for the revolution that brought the President to power and had helped him to remain in control of the country for the past ten years. The President owed him, yet he was hesitant to provide Jerry with any information regarding Mohammad al Sultan because he was an ally. The President did not want to anger a powerful warlord who was supporting him, but under intense pressure from Jerry, plus the promise of complete secrecy, the President reluctantly agreed to provide the requested information right away.

A complete dossier on Mohammad was in Jerry's hands the following day. In addition to being wealthy from control of the heroin supply to Europe he was a merciless ruler of his autonomous area in the northern part of the country. Mohammad was a known sexual pervert who maintained a harem of young women gathered from around the world. Most were kidnap victims from outside of the country, but some of the foreign girls had been sold to Mohammad by their families at an early age. All of them were subsequently transported to his palace to become his personal sex slaves. It had long been rumored that Mohammad personally selected each of his victims before they were added to his extensive harem. Once in captivity, these women and young girls were forced to watch erotic pornographic films for days on end as training to please their new master. They were systematically brain washed and beaten into submission until they accepted that refusal to perform on demand was not an option. Nothing was outside the realm of his personal desire for sexual pleasure. New girls who did not perform to his expectations were killed, as were those who fell from favor with time, he was a ruthless barbarian and an extremist Muslim. He considered women to be worthless except for giving pleasure to their master and having his children which were rumored to number a hundred or more. There was much more to the report including the alarming information that Mohammad was on an extended shopping trip in Austin, Texas to add to his selection of harem girls. The bulk of the dossier dealt with his money laundering operation and the organizational pipeline he used to supply heroin to his European buyers.

After reading the report, Jerry left immediately for Austin to set up a command post, he planned to make his substantial personal services available to Abe in their stepped up operation to maximize protection for Martha. His agents hacked into Mohammad's computers with ease quickly learning the identities of his friends and employees in the Austin area and were able to read past and current correspondence between all of them and Mohammad. All, except four, of the people found to be associated with Mohammad were eliminated from suspicion they were not close associates or involved in his operations. The other four were in Mohammad's pay and part of his staff they were committed to doing his bidding without question. The four were placed under 24/7 surveillance and at the same time security was further tightened round Martha. All agents assigned to Martha's safety were armed with automatic laser aimed hand guns and were well trained in stealth and hand-to-hand combat. Their standing orders were: should anyone attempt to kidnap Martha, they were to kill the abductors on the spot and discretely dispose of their bodies. Jerry learned through people in the CIA that Mohammad had scheduled a flight back to Afghanistan the following week meaning Mohammad's thugs would be making their move to abduct Martha sometime in the next few days. How and when they planned to get her out of the country and into Afghanistan without being detected remained a mystery making Martha's security all the more critical.

It was inconceivable that Mohammad would attempt to fly Martha to Kabul on his chartered plane because it would be subject to inspection before departing from the United States, still several Abe agents were assigned to watch the plane around the clock and to report any suspicious activity. Special attention was to be paid to any suspicious cargo loaded on to the plane. The agents were directed to covertly check everything on board before the plane was allowed to depart American soil. Mohammad was just crazy enough to try anything meaning every possibility had to be covered whether it seemed logical or not. Abe concentrated on the four men working for Mohammad in Austin he had left for Washington D.C. and was unlikely to return to Austin before leaving the country. From his Washington hotel, Mohammad sent an encrypted email to his top lieutenant in Afghanistan, after its interception it took several hours for the Abe agents to decipher the message which read.

"The Sirens are all young and beautiful women with sensual bodies made for my eternal sexual pleasure. I regret that I cannot take all of them at this time, but there will be other opportunities. My cargo will be arriving at Kabul airport three days following my return. Arrange the customary transportation to my palace."

Upon reading Mohammad's message, Frank and Jerry agreed the situation has reached a critical stage requiring deployment of all of their resources to prevent Mohammad or his associates from kidnapping Martha. Jerry explained to Frank.

"He may have targeted several other Sirens as potential victims in his depraved quest for young sex slaves for his harem. At best we have no more than ten days to squelch the planned kidnapping or kidnappings and to put an end to any future attempts by Mohammed's henchmen."

Little information was available other than Mohammad's scheduled return to Kabul and the projected arrival of the victim or victims three days later. It was reasonable to assume the physical kidnapping would take place in Austin by the four men Mohammad left behind. There had been no correspondence between Mohammad and the four, no phone calls, no emails and no intermediaries talking with them since he left Austin for Washington. Presumably they received their orders before his departure. Frank and Jerry discussed several alternative plans which could be used to save Martha and any of the other Sirens who might be in danger.

Agitated because they had so little information concerning the plot, Frank said flatly. "Our first line of defense should be to kill anyone who threatens Martha in any way. I don't give a damn whether it is one of Mohammed's men, or someone we don't know, if they appear to be a threat then we should kill them."

"Frank, the problem with that is we might kill a lot of innocent people it's up to our field agents to determine what is and is not a threat. Human error could result in devastating and unwanted results."

"Yeah, Jerry, I know you are right. I just don't want this son of a bitch to get Martha or anyone else for that matter."

"Frank, we have two problems, one we don't want Martha harmed and two we don't want this crap to come up again."

"Well, I'll tell you what, Jerry, I can handle problem number two, if you can handle problem number one!"

"I was hoping you would say that, Frank, because I have a plan to solve the first problem which is to prevent Martha from being kidnaped in the first place. My solution will not implicate any of us, problem one will just disappear."

"Then we are in agreement, I'll take care of Mohammad al Sultan our problem number two and I promise you that this shit won't ever come up again. Put one of your people in charge here, Jerry. You won't be hearing from me again for over a week. Good luck, Jerry," said Frank walking toward the door.

"Same to you Frank!"

Jerry selected a number on his cell phone then pushed the call button, shortly he was talking with Number Three at the *Bastardos Locos* headquarters. After introducing himself, Jerry said.

"It's good to talk with you, Joe. It's been a long time since we did the Cross Border I&E Company purchase. I understand you are now Number Three in the organization, you have me to thank for that."

Jerry paused waiting for a comment.

"What do you mean by that?"

"The reason you are Number Three is that I called your boss and told him the deal would have ended in failure except for your outstanding abilities to negotiate. He was very interested in my comments and assessment of your abilities. In fact, he told me, 'In that case I think he

211

is our new Number Three'. Look, don't take my word for it, ask him, he will tell you the same thing," added Jerry knowing full well the question would be asked.

"What can I do for you?"

Number Three did not want to discuss his ascendency to his current position further.

"Joe, we need to meet tonight if possible, say at the Tmex Hotel bar at around seven. I have a proposition I think you will like."

"OK, my friend, I'll see you there."

Frank boarded the company jet at Houston International Airport at one o'clock in the morning. Other than the crew of three there was no one else on board, upon clearance from the control tower, the pilot reeved up the jet engines before the plane roared down the runway and lifted off into the starlit sky. Frank could not help thinking of his time in the Marine Corps his service in Korea still held a special place in his heart. He served during the Korean Police Action as a Colonel in charge of a Marine Corps unit which fought a protracted delaying action retreat after the Red Chinese hordes poured across the border into northern Korea. His unit had been cut off from the other retreating Americans twice, but under his leadership they were able to fight themselves free to continue their harassing action against the advancing Chinese army. Eventually the unit reached safety with only minor losses while the pursuing Chinese suffered heavy casualties from the withering fire put up by his troops as they managed to command the high ground during their retreat. The jet leveled off at 30,000 feet flying a great circle route on the first leg of its journey to Kabul airport. Frank rested little during the flight instead he spent his time planning his upcoming operation in Afghanistan he had little time to prepare a foolproof and executable plan.

Number Three showed up at the Tmex Bar at exactly seven in the evening, Jerry was disguised the same as in their previous meetings when he saw Number Three he approached extending his hand as if greeting an old friend. Number Three took his hand smiling.

"You were right, I owe you one."

Jerry did not reply rather he motioned for Joe to sit at a table in the corner where both of their backs would be toward the wall. This strategic location allowed each of them a clear view of people entering and leaving the bar as well as those sitting in the bar. As a precaution several Abe agents were stationed at various locations in and around the bar their job was to protect Jerry should anything go astray. Jerry ordered two double Irish whiskeys on the rocks before speaking further with Number Three.

"Joe, I need a favor. I don't expect it to be free. I am willing to pay $500,000 now and an additional $500,000 upon completion of the favor. This is an area in which your organization has developed a unique talent over the years."

"For that kind of bucks, we can do a lot of things. What we can help you with?"

"I want four people to vanish from the face of this earth without anyone knowing they ever existed, no publicity, no police action, and no nothing. I want them to disappear without a trace. To vanish into thin air, so to speak."

"Not a problem, for $1,000,000 we can make five hundred people disappear, if necessary."

"There is one condition, this favor must be completed within a very short time frame, no later than five days from today the sooner the better."

"That is no problem if you can identify or point out the four individuals requiring your favor."

Jerry retrieved an aluminum case from under the table placing it on top with the snaps facing Number Three who smiled broadly as Jerry implored.

"My friend, please open it. Inside you will find five hundred one thousand dollar bills and the names and addresses of the four individuals requiring your favor. There are photographs and videos of each of them plus a schedule of their daily routines. Here are two burner phones, which are for the two of us to use in any future communications, they can't be traced and neither can we."

Number Three felt the bundle of one thousand dollar bills then offered his hand.

"My friend, we have a deal. It's always good to do business with you we always make a lot of money."

"Good, I came to you, Joe because we trust each other," replied Jerry as he shook Number Three's hand sealing the deal. He placed his burner phone in his pocket handing the other one to Joe.

"When the favor has been granted call me on your phone, so we can meet for delivery of the remainder of my gift, if the favor is not granted within five days do not call. No additional gift will be due. Joe, would you like another Irish before we leave?"

"No thanks, I need to arrange for a bodyguard before I deliver this case to headquarters. Number One will be pleased!"

"I will be leaving now, so you can get to work. Joe, I'm expecting to hear from you soon."

While waiting for the valet to deliver his car, Jerry called his second in command in Austin.

"Jerry here, I've arranged for the favor as we discussed. There is a time limit of five days have our team assembled for further instructions when I arrive in about three hours."

His transportation was waiting when Jerry landed in Austin. He made a precautionary visited the men's room in the terminal before they sped away to headquarters where he met with his handpicked special team. They were crucial to his backup strategy in case the favor was not granted in the time frame agreed upon. Jerry was leaving nothing to chance in preventing Mohammad's men from abducting Martha or any of the other Sirens.

An automobile pulled up next to the company jet when it came to a rest on the Kabul airport tarmac, the plane's lone passenger was inside the car and moving away toward the airport exit in less than a minute all the necessary bribes having been paid in advance. Frank was relieved the flight was over, although he was dog tired, there would be no time to rest until his mission had been accomplished. The car arrived at a nondescript building on the fringes of the city where Frank was met by Colonel Jim De Soto of the U.S. Marine Corps a onetime junior officer, who had served under Frank in Korea.

"Frank, it's great to see you," said Jim extending his hand to Frank who was all smiles. "You too, Jim. It's been a while," said Frank as they moved into the interior of the building. Jim's office was located in the center of the building to provide maximum security and protection from Al Qaeda attacks. Following a brief period of reminiscing, Frank got right to his mission. He explained in detail Mohammad al Sultan's plot to abduct Martha and possibly several of the Sirens to become his personal sex slaves. Jim knew the history of Mohammad al Sultan well, including his brutality toward women whom he considered less valuable than a goat

"How can I be of service, Frank?"

Jim was ready willing and able to help in any way he could, he despised Mohammad even though he was supposedly aligned with the government in their fight against Al Qaeda.

"Neither you nor your men can be directly involved in my mission, Jim. It must be totally clandestine and unrelated to America or any of its military people here in Afghanistan. What I need is to make contact with a trustworthy local or locals who can help accomplish my mission. Can you help me with this?"

"I think the best way I can aid you is for me to put you in touch with a close friend of mine who is in charge of the CIA cadre here. He knows everyone in the country who could be trusted to handle this type of project."

"My mission has a short fuse, can you arrange an introduction right away?"

Jim placed a call from his desk then looking up at Frank, who was still standing, said crisply. "It's taken care of. He will be awaiting your arrival. My driver will take you there right away. Frank, will I see you before you return to the U.S.?"

"It's not possible this time, Jim, I really appreciate your help thanks again."

Frank put on his hat and left with the driver Jim had provided they were on their way in a matter of minutes. The driver drove a zigzag route to the center of the city where, after making sure he had not been followed, he pulled up alongside another automobile parked at the curb. The back door opened and Frank quickly entered the parked car before it roared away toward an unknown destination.

To Frank's surprise, the CIA agent was of middle-eastern decent, possibly from Afghanistan, it made no difference so long as he could help him complete his mission here in Kabul. The agent was very sympathetic with Frank's plan, he agreed to take him to meet with a local who had access to the skills required, he was also a person who could be relied on to discretely carry out the assignment without detection. Frank was dazzled by the local's splendid credentials he had been educated in England, yet spoke the language with an American accent. There was no problem communicating his plan or the timing requirement. When it came to negotiating a price for his services, the local was adamant.

"For this type of service my fee is two hundred thousand American dollars in cash, payable up front."

Frank, somewhat astonished by the modest fee replied.

"I am prepared to pay considerably more because of the nature of the service required."

"I will not accept more, my price is fixed, I will accept no more or no less, I am a man of honor. This price is fair for both of us."

Frank produced two hundred one thousand dollar bills from the lining of his coat and methodically counted them out to the local.

The local was emphatic as he accepted Frank's payment.

"Sir, I assure you that our performance will meet with your complete satisfaction, have a safe and pleasant journey home. We shall not meet again."

Back in Austin Jerry was working diligently to protect Martha and the Sirens. As planned, he was conducting a follow up briefing with his special agents after returning from his meeting with, Joe in Houston.

"Gentlemen, I have Plan A in place, if it is successful our problem will be solved within five days starting today. I expect Plan A to work perfectly, but there is always the possibility that due to unforeseen circumstances it could fail. That's where you come in."

Jerry was addressing the special team he had assembled which was made up of sixteen people, four expert snipers and twelve seasoned combat members all of whom were ex-Navy Seals trained in covert operations.

"Under Plan B you will be deployed four days from now, with each four man squad assigned to a specific target. If the targets or one or more of them remain after the fifth day, they are to be removed as soon as possible, but no action is to be taken until after mid-night of the fifth day. Under no circumstances will you make contact with the targets before that time. Everyone is to keep their distance from these four individuals until I give the order to implement Plan B. Is that clear? I am the only person who can authorize putting Plan B into action. Starting tonight, all surveillance will be pulled as far away from the targets as feasible to prevent our agents from being detected by, or interfering with the people involved in Plan A. We still need to follow the targets movements in case they attempt to abduct Martha or any of the Sirens. Should this happen notify me! Plan A does not involve Martha directly, our security for her is to remain tight and no one that we do not know gets near her. Are there any questions? If there is anyone among you who doesn't clearly understand this assignment, then we need to go over the instructions again. We can't afford to have any screw ups."

On the morning of the third day, Jerry's surveillance agents reported they had lost contact with all four targets they had somehow disappeared. None of the teams had seen any movement, nor had there been any correspondence of any kind between the targets and any outsiders since early the previous night when the lights were turned off in their rooms. Just before noon, Jerry's burner phone rang its beautiful melody, when Jerry answered Joe said emphatically.

"My friend, your favor has been granted. I believe another gift is due, meet me at the Tmex bar this evening at seven and, Jerry, please, don't wear that dumb assed disguise again I know who you are."

Number Three hung up before Jerry could reply leaving him to speculate about how the mission had been accomplished. Jerry was satisfied upon hearing from Joe, he called all the agents together to give them the good news.

"Things are back to normal, Plan B is cancelled and all special agents are to return to their regular assignments."

The CIA agent kept Frank up to date on the timing of Mohammad al Sultan's projected arrival at the Kabul airport. Expected landing time would be at approximately 2:20 p.m. give or take a few minutes. Frank was on board the company plane sitting on the tarmac with its engines running when Mohammad's plane landed a few minutes ahead of the projected time of arrival. Upon touchdown, Mohammad's pilot quickly slowed the plane skillfully maneuvering it on to a marked debarking area not far from the company plane's position. A mobile stairway was rolled up to the door once the plane stopped and had been secured. The door opened, Mohammad al Sultan stepped out on to the top of the stairway and raised his hand to adjust his headwear before taking a first step. Suddenly, he slumped forward then tumbled down the steps ending up sprawled on the tarmac, a single gunshot wound could be seen in the middle of his forehead.

Frank's pilot moved the throttle forward steering the plane toward the runway for takeoff. Frank saluted Mohammad al Sultan as they passed his lifeless body crumpled near the bottom of the stairway. In disgust Frank said out loud. "Fuck you, you son of a bitch. Don't mess with Texas."

On his flight home Frank called Jerry to inform him that problem two had been solved to his satisfaction there would be no further attempts from Mohammad al Sultan to kidnap Martha or anyone else. Frank was extremely pleased to hear problem number one had also been solved during his absence. He was intrigued by the sudden and complete disappearance of Mohammad's four henchmen he could not help wondering how Jerry had arranged that.

"It's another piece of the puzzle we can discuss the details when I get back to Houston. Right now, I need to get some sleep."

Sitting in Jerry's spacious office sipping Irish whiskey from large glasses containing a small amount of ice, Frank and Jerry rehashed the Mohammad al Sultan affair and its dramatic ending. There had been no mention by the police or the press concerning the disappearance of Mohammad's four associates in Austin. Even their landlords denied that they had ever heard of them, it was as if they had never existed, they had vanished along with all traces of their being there. They had evaporated into the thin Austin air in the middle of the night. Jerry went on to explain his meeting with Number Three and soon to be Number Two in the hierarchy of the *Bastardos Locos*.

"Following Joe's elevation to Number Two, he will no doubt be susceptible to granting us another favor sometime he is fast becoming a valuable asset to ADAM and our operation."

Jerry was proud that his part of the operation had gone unnoticed by the press and the public because of Joe's favor. Before summing up Jerry smiled broadly.

"I am happy to tell you that all the Sirens are accounted for, including Martha of course, the team will play out their schedule completely oblivious to the danger they faced from Mohammad. The Sirens will never know, that because Martha was a part of the team, our efforts saved several of them from the clutches of a sexual maniac."

"Jerry, when I got the news I wondered how you managed to solve the problem with no publicity. I see what you mean about Number Three, or is it Number Two, being an asset to our operation. Hopefully, we won't need him again, but in this business who knows?"

Frank turned to his part in the operation. He detailed the tangled chain of events leading to his meeting with the local whom he admired for both his honor and the cleanness of Mohammad's extermination.

"Unlike you, we were unable to avoid publicity, by the very nature of our operation it was carried out in a very public place with many witnesses. There was a bit of irony in it all, Mohammad's triumphant return to Afghanistan ended with his body lying face up on the tarmac with a bullet hole in his head. His assassination was meant to be seen, he was hated by almost everyone who was not on his payroll or receiving bribes from him. Even though he appeared to support the government that was a ruse to cover his heroin operation in the northwest part of the country where he ruled with an iron fist through abhorrent cruelty. He killed anyone who displeased him."

"Is that the only reason for his public execution?"

"No, Jerry that was just a part of the plan, listen to my favorite account of the incident in this article published by the New York International and then you will understand."

He began reading aloud from the newspaper.

"Mohammad al Sultan, an ardent ally of Afghanistan's President and a strong supporter of western intervention in the country, was gunned down today as he stepped from his plane at Kabul airport. Our investigation indicates he was possibility assassinated by militant Islamists who may be members of Al Qaeda, a Wahhabis terror group opposed to western ideas. Al Qaeda and its supporters have just begun their spring offensive against supporters of the government and the assassination of Mohammad al Sultan appears to signal al Qaeda's quest to exterminate those local leaders who have sided with the west."

Jerry laughed out loud upon hearing the quote.

"Leave it to the International, other than the fact he was killed all the rest is pure bullshit. It's a good thing they weren't really involved he would still be walking around with a halo over his head."

"Think about it, Jerry, this time the International has worked in our favor, as usual, they have diverted public thinking away from the truth which was part of our plan. That's why Mohammad met his end in a public place we knew we could depend on the New York International to produce a piece short on facts and long on misleading suppositions."

Jerry replied sarcastically.

"I see what you mean, I'm glad they're good for something! But I still don't plan to subscribe to that left winged piece of shit. I can't stand the misleading bullshit they print on every important social issue."

Martha and the rest of the Sirens remained undefeated for the season claiming the volleyball championship without being seriously challenged. Jimmy loved watching Martha play, but he was glad the season was over so they could spend more time together before the summer break and his departure for China. He and Martha scheduled a trip to Corpus Christi the following weekend for the dual purpose of his meeting Rachel and Phil and announcing their engagement to be married. Jimmy wanted very much to meet his future in-laws after hearing Martha's description of their life together, still he was a little concerned about their possible reaction to Martha's engagement. She was sporting a beautiful two carat diamond ring on her left ring finger, a brilliant solitaire mounted on a smooth white gold band, which she and Jimmy had selected together the day after Jimmy's proposal. She could not refrain from extending her arm now and again to look at her ring, sometimes, embarrassing herself when other people saw her admiring it in public. She had not told any of her high school friends about her engagement preferring to wait until after she and Jimmy broke the news to her mom and Phil.

Jimmy parked his car in the driveway then hurriedly jumped out to hold the car door open for Martha who had already partially opened it in her rush to see her parents. She and Jimmy walked to the doorway side by side holding hands as Martha was about to insert her key Rachel opened the door from inside. Martha rushed to hug Rachel then turned toward Jimmy.

"Mom, this is my boyfriend Jimmy."

Jimmy stepped forward taking Rachel's hand.

"I'm very pleased to meet you. Martha didn't prepare me for this, you are even more beautiful than she described you."

"After that kind compliment, you can give me a hug.   Come on inside, so we can get acquainted. Phil will be late he is unavoidably detained with clients. I don't expect him to arrive anytime soon, but he should be here before dinner."

"Mom, you look fabulous, how do you do it and work all the time?"

Rachel didn't answer she responded with a question of her own.

"I see you are wearing a ring, does that signify anything I should know about?"

"Mom, Jimmy and I are engaged to be married, but not until after I graduate from college."

Rachel hardly missed a beat responding cheerfully.

"Congratulations to the both of you, I expect Jimmy to become a part of our family long before the wedding."

Jimmy did not hesitate either, he replied simply.

"Thank you mam for your confidence I love your daughter she is the most outstanding person I have ever known and above all I want to make her my wife and for us to be happy together."

Rachel was pleased with Jimmy's response, it was the answer she had wanted to hear, Martha's happiness was important to her and to him. She looked Jimmy over with a keen eye he was tall, clean cut and reasonably good looking with a nice body, not too muscular, not too skinny. Rachel was determined to like Jimmy and although they had just met, she had already formed a favorable opinion concerning his character. The three of them talked at length before Rachel asked. "Why don't you bring in your bags, Jimmy? Martha can have her old room and you can take the guest room." Jimmy was pleased with his first impression of Rachel. "Good so far," he thought as he opened the trunk to remove their bags. While Jimmy was outside, Rachel took the opportunity to speak with Martha while they were alone.

"Honey, I know you have made your choice and I wish the two of you as much happiness as Phil and I have experienced together."

"Mom, I know about you and Dad there is happiness around you all the time. I noticed that on our first date, remember?"

Jimmy finished bringing in the last piece of luggage a short time later Phil arrived. Phil parked beside Jimmy's car then hurried into the house he was eager to see Martha and to meet her friend Jimmy.

Martha held out both hands to Phil before hugging and kissing him lightly on the cheek. He responded by holding her hand up while admiring her ring.

"What is this, if I may ask?"

Martha took Jimmy's hand.

"Dad, I want you to meet, Jimmy, my intended. We are engaged to be married."

Phil, a master at handling unexpected situations, turned toward Jimmy extending his hand.

"Welcome, Jimmy. Martha is a special person around here."

"Sir, she is more than special, Martha is a singular, a one of a kind," replied Jimmy still gripping Phil's hand firmly.

"Well put, Jimmy, I could not have said it better myself she is definitely one of a kind. Shall we go to the den? It's a little more comfortable than standing here. I might even find some refreshments in the bar if anyone is interested."

They had been talking about how Martha and Jimmy met for several minutes when Phil glanced at his watch announcing.

"I think I will call the Oasis and make a dinner reservation for four, anyone have any objections?"

Martha and Rachel responded in concert.

"That's a great idea, Phil, let's do it!"

Since Jimmy had no input, the decision was unanimous they would go to the Oasis for dinner and dancing to celebrate the announcement of Martha's and Jimmy's engagement. Martha could not have been more pleased their first date at the Oasis was one of her favorite memories. She and Phil had danced the Merry Widow Waltz, and it was there that she suspected Phil was in love with her mother. She appreciated the significance of Phil's suggestion it was his tacit approval of Jimmy. She loved Phil for his thoughtfulness, but then she had always loved Phil for loving her mother and making both of them happy.

Dinner was a huge success Jimmy participated in the small talk as if he had known Rachel and Phil all of his life. He also handled some of the personal questions posed by Phil with great skill always providing a straight forward reply with no hesitation or indication of misleading

222

answers. Phil liked Jimmy right away, he was articulate, honest and a very bright young man who seemed to be able to handle any situation in a calm straightforward manner. Phil surmised. "He is the kind of person I would like for a Son-in-Law. Martha, you have my congratulations, you have chosen well."

The orchestra played all through dinner remaining in the background to complement the meal no one paid attention until the first three notes of the Merry Widow Waltz were played. Much to Martha's surprise, Phil took Rachel's hand stepping briskly toward the dance floor, Martha had expected Phil to have the dance with her as he did on their first date. Sensing Martha's disappointment, Jimmy took her hand leading her to the dance floor where he took her in his arms dancing into the sparse group on the floor. Looking over his shoulder Phil commented to Rachel.

"I know Martha expected me to have this dance with her, but I have an ulterior motive I want to see how she and Jimmy handle her favorite dance. It's important you know."

"Yes, my love I know, it's our love song. You and Martha introduced us to it right here on this dance floor."

Rachel and Phil danced around the floor one time before stepping aside to watch Martha and Jimmy as did several of the other dancers. Soon they were alone all the other dancers abandoned the dance floor to become spectators. Martha had her head tilted back slightly which magnified her poise and beauty as she and Jimmy treated the patrons to a professional rendition of the Merry Widow Waltz. Martha was the most amazed person in the ballroom, she and Jimmy had not danced together before, so she had no inkling of his dancing talent, in fact, he had never mentioned he liked dancing at all. At the end of the dance, amid the cheers and applause from the onlookers, Martha embraced Jimmy kissing him for a long moment then she raised his right arm as they walked slowly to their table. She was smiling and radiantly beautiful Jimmy was smiling too, after seating Martha, he bowed to the table then sat down.

"Jimmy, you were marvelous, I had no idea you could dance like that. Why didn't you tell me?"

"It wasn't me they were cheering, Martha, it was you."

Jimmy was still smiling relishing their first dance together, dancing with a polished professional had been thrilling, Martha would make anyone look good she was so smooth and elegant on the dance floor. Rachel and Phil were aware that Phil made a special request for the Merry Widow Waltz as a tribute to their first date and as a compliment to Martha. Watching Jimmy and Martha dance together, they were astounded by the pair's fantastic performance, neither of them had expected Jimmy to dance with such skill he complemented Martha's ability perfectly they danced as one during the entire waltz. Rachel was convinced Martha and Jimmy were a perfect pair who were very special on or off of the dance floor, they loved each other very much. Everyone praised Jimmy's dancing skills an unexpected and well appreciated surprise for all of them and particularly for Martha who loved his performance. The festive group enjoyed an evening of dancing and conservation with a few cocktails in between, shortly after midnight, they decided to return home for a good night's rest.

Phil and Rachel reviewed the pros and cons of Martha's and Jimmy's relationship for an hour after going to bed eventually concluding they were probably right for each other they both liked Jimmy and he had Phil's unqualified approval. Phil raised up on his elbow to kiss Rachel goodnight before laying back on his pillow she pulled him toward her placing his hand on her breast as she kissed him. Her lips were moist and hungry. Phil responded kissing her repeatedly before saying softly.

"Alright, but no screaming we have guests."

"Don't be silly, you're the one who yells."

By the time summer break arrived, Martha and Jimmy had visited her parents several times in Corpus Christi and they had met with them in Austin on more than one occasion. The couple had spent several weekends with Jimmy's parents at their ranch they liked Martha she was beautiful and she was smart capable of fitting into any social environment. She was adept at mingling with their friends at the many social events they attended. Jimmy's mother loved Martha from the first time they met she found Martha to be a down-to-earth person, yet one who was well versed in the arts and finer things in life. Jimmy's mother liked what she saw a compassionate and beautiful person who loved her son. She told her husband.

"Martha will make a great wife and a wonderful mother. She and Jimmy will have a rewarding and beautiful life together full of love and respect."

Martha fell in love with Jimmy's parents they accepted who she was as a person and gave their unqualified approval for her to become a member of their family. Martha was invited to share in their upcoming trip to China. Jimmy's parents offered to pay her expenses, so she and Jimmy could share in the experience and be together during the summer. Martha declined explaining.

"I appreciate your offer and would love to make the trip with all of you, except I will be going to summer school for the next two summers, so Jimmy and I can graduate together and get married a year earlier."

She had promised her parents she would graduate before getting married and that promise was not going to be broken. Jimmy understood the importance Martha and her parents placed on her graduating before they married he would not consider altering their order of priorities. In order to speed up their wedding date, Martha and Jimmy conceived the summer school plan together. Although Jimmy regretted that Martha would not go on the trip with him and his parents, he wanted to get married a year sooner even more. China could wait.

Martha had finished the first half of her summer session and was at home in Corpus Christi when she and Rachel heard on a national TV news broadcast that three Americans had been killed in a plane crash in a remote Chinese province. Martha was alarmed when she first heard of the plane crash, but after a week without further mention of it on the news her fear faded away. The day before the beginning of second half of the summer semester she received a call from one of Jimmy's cousins who had been searching for her for several days.

"Martha, it is my unpleasant task to inform you that my father received confirmation from the State Department that Jimmy, his mother and his father have been identified as the three Americans killed in a plane crash in China. I am very sorry to have to break the news of their deaths by phone, but I felt you would want to know as soon as possible. No bodies were recovered, consequently, there will be a memorial service a week from Saturday at 10:00 a.m. at the United Methodist Church in Wichita Falls. I am so sorry for your loss, Martha, Jimmy was my favorite cousin I will miss him very much."

Martha was so stunned by the news that she did not say a word or react until after the caller hung up. She crumpled to the floor cutting her hand on the coffee table as she landed on her side. She lay on her back for a moment with her bloody hand over her face before she began screaming uncontrollably. "No! God no! Oh, Jimmy. Jimmy this can't be true. How could this happen to us?" After several minutes her screaming subsided, but she continued to cry uncontrollably. Between her sobs and tears Martha managed to call Rachel at her office. Rachel picked up her phone and heard one short sentence before it went dead.

"Mama, help me. Jimmy is dead."

Rachel rushed home to find her daughter, who was still bleeding from her wound, almost incoherent as she laid on the floor sobbing uncontrollably. Rachel took Martha in her arms once she got her off of the floor, she hugged her tight an attempted to console her as best she could. Phil arrived shortly and the two of them cleaned Martha's wound then took her to the hospital for stitches. The doctor gave her a sedative recommending they keep her in bed for the night and the following day. Several days passed before Martha became capable of controlling her grief enough to function at all. The news of Jimmy's death devastated Martha she had no interest in going anywhere or doing anything her life had been destroyed she was nearing a state of total withdrawal, yet she, Phil and Rachel attended Jimmy's and his family's memorial service in Wichita Falls. The church was filled with friends of Jimmy and his family only a few of which even knew Martha existed. Some fellow UT students came to pay their last respects to a friend as well, but Martha and her family found themselves essentially alone in a sea of unknown mourners. After the service, Martha and her family left quietly and drove back to Corpus Christi. It was a miserable trip, no matter how hard Phil and Rachel tried they could not get Martha to talk with them she withdrew completely remaining silent the entire trip even refusing to eat when they suggested stopping for a meal.

Heartbroken and deeply depressed by Jimmy's death, Martha resisted returning to UT for the second summer session she had no interest in school, dancing or anything else her world had disappeared with Jimmy's death. After much prodding from Rachel, she eventually relented and return to UT even though she was still hurting and despondent. Once volleyball practice began, Martha regained some of her interest because of the team. She became more like herself again, but she could not keep from thinking about Jimmy and what they meant to each other. He was the love of her life, now he was gone. Alone in her room she wondered.

"Will I ever hear the mocking bird sing, or see the Mississippi kites soaring high in the sky again? Or is that lost forever too?"

Martha spurned all proposals to date during her last years at UT preferring to concentrate on her studies and one outside activity, volleyball. She graduated a year early just as she and Jimmy had planned, but as she reminded herself there would be no wedding after the graduation ceremony. Upon graduating from the Fine Arts School at UT, Martha received several offers from agents to become a professional entertainer, instead she elected to open her own dance and talent development company in Austin. With financial backing from Rachel and Phil, she leased and outfitted the second floor of a building located on a feeder road to US Hwy.183 in northwest Austin as her academy for talent development. Her business plan was simple, provide expert instruction in an atmosphere promoting superb talent development at a reasonable cost for those needing her help. Martha specialized in dance, which was her favorite of all the Arts at UT, but she became well diversified acquiring extensive training as a vocalist and actress. She had the ability to teach any or all of these disciplines as required by the individual. Her company, Talent Development, Inc., focused on refining and upgrading established talents possessed by students ranging from eight to thirty years of age. There would be no troupes of three-year-olds dancing in tutus for their parents and grandparents, TDI was a different type of talent development school. Applicants were required to audition before being considered for enrollment and only those with demonstrated talent would be accepted the others would be referred to another venue.

Her studio was designed to handle acting, singing, and dancing students as well as musicians or a combination of talents. The individual instruction areas were sound proofed and all of them had video recording and playback screens complete with high quality audio for replays to aid in teaching. The dance area was by far the largest single facility in the complex it was equipped with high definition video, audio and a large playback screen. All the electronic equipment in the various teaching areas was interconnected with a central computer which stored the audio-video sessions. Using a program designed to sort and store the information by discipline and by student, TDI was able to study and display each student's progress. For safety and security protection all digital information was also backed up on a remotely located external storage device. TDI had the most advanced technology available, no other studio in the greater Austin area was competitive so far as physical facilities were concerned. Satisfied with the studio setup, Martha set about hiring two assistants one to operate the computer and electronic equipment and another to help in instruction and scheduling.

TDI's Grand Opening was announced on the internet through ads placed on social networks, at the same time, TDI opened its own sophisticated website developed by Squidz Ink Design of Houston. TDI's website outlined their objective, disciplines, credentials, and schedule for the fall session along with contact information both by email and by phone. Unexpectedly, Martha's first responder was not from Austin, but from San Antonio. He was an experienced sixteen-year-old male, who expected to become an actor or TV personality, he explained that he was still in school and could only participate in classes on weekends. He was interested in enrolling provided TDI operated on Saturday and Sunday. Martha personally advised him that TDI would be open on the weekends, but he had to come in for an audition before he could be considered for admission. He passed the audition handily, exhibiting a wealth of talent, becoming TDI's first registered student. Seventeen others were accepted for training in the first session which meant Martha and part of her crew would be working most of the week, leaving little time for anything else. This arrangement did not bother Martha, but she feared it might be a problem for her coworkers, so she developed a schedule leaving Monday as an off day for everyone. She took little time off herself instead she worked most Mondays reviewing the past week's audios and videos to assess the progress of the individual students. This time consuming task became Martha's Monday chore. She took the rest of the day off when and if she completed grading the previous week's performances. Often she worked late, sometimes, well into the evening. Martha worked hard to enhance the talents of those receiving advanced training at TDI she was well aware there had to be talent to begin with, but she maintained that even in the presence of talent training was required to produce excellence which was her goal.

No set time was required for an attendee to graduate from TDI, when Martha and her assistant determined a person had reached their limit of perfection, or had reached a level of development required for a professional career they were presented a certificate of training showing they had mastered their craft. When she started TDI, Martha had the foresight to make arrangements with a number of contacts in the entertainment world allowing her to make referrals for those talented individuals who had completed their TDI training and were seeking employment. One of the great advantages to TDI graduates was Martha's ability to make direct referrals to those seeking to hire entertainers. She had the ability to send a video of each graduate to potential employers, so they could see and hear the performers before making contact with them. This technique saved the agents and employers a lot of time while providing exposure for the performers to a clientele not available to them on their own. Because of Martha's contacts their talents could be seen by hundreds of potential employers and agents and the service was free. Among Martha's younger participants, some were interested in limited exposure such as commercials, while most others desired to continue developing their talents while aspiring for a career as professional entertainers. There were some enrollees who had no interest in becoming professional entertainers they continued their education in other fields, intending to perform as talented amateurs throughout their careers as doctors, engineers or other professionals. Martha established a separate set of requirements for those enrollees desiring to remain talented amateurs.

The number of TDI students doubled in the second session requiring Martha to add to her staff. She found it necessary to engage a diction specialist since most of the aspiring performers at TDI were from Texas and spoke with a distinct accent. The diction expert loved to point out to her students that over the years there had been a multitude of Texans who became national TV news anchors, yet none of them had a Texas accent. In her words.

"To be in show business or politics you have to learn to speak accent free American English."

Diction training was critical to the careers of those seeking to become actors or TV performers while dancers could get by without it unless they were required to speak in their rolls. Martha made diction a requirement for all of TDI's attendees, training to speak American

English became necessary to obtain a certificate of training regardless of the discipline of the attendee.

Following entrance of the second group of graduates into the entertainment mix, TDI became known throughout the entertainment world for the quality of its products. They possessed excellent talent, and they spoke the universal American English required throughout the industry they did not have to be retrained to speak before making their professional debuts. Among agents, talent scouts and producers TDI became the buzz word for excellence. The following session was filled to capacity in the first week with applicants coming from as far away as New York and Chicago. There were even a few from Hollywood. Carryover students from the previous session were given preference over incoming applicants to insure the continuity of their training until they were certified by TDI which became an important consideration by new applicants.

Martha was happy with the results of their training, TDI was producing top notch entertainers of all kinds and the company was a resounding economic success. She was immersed in work she enjoyed immensely. The largest problem Martha faced at TDI was whether to enlarge the facility to handle more students, or to continue to concentrate on quality rather than quantity. As TDI occupied more and more of her time, Martha thought of Jimmy only on rare occasions, mostly when she could not sleep at night. His memory hadn't gone away it just didn't pop up as often as it had in the past.

Chapter 9 A Lesson Learned

A short time after Zane and Peggy married, Peggy realized she and Zane were rich they could live however they wanted and wherever they wanted, but they were interested in a normal mundane lifestyle away from the bright lights and publicity. Their greatest desire was for Bruce to grow up as part of the great American middle class. New innovations, new businesses and most career opportunities originate from this group as do most of the outstanding American heroes. Zane and Peggy planned for their children to have the opportunity to participate in the joy and excitement of creating their own lives and to achieve their objectives through dedication and hard work. They chose to stay in Peggy's house in a middle class neighborhood and to live an upper middle class lifestyle quietly and with dignity to provide an environment they felt conducive to building a happy and productive life for their children. Bruce entered high school the year Peggy finished her degree at Texas A&M. He was proud of his mother for completing her degree it demonstrated her tenacity as well as her dedication to obtain an advanced education. While Peggy was working on her degree program, she and Zane had a daughter, Katy, who was six years old when the family went to College Station to witness Peggy's walk across the stage to receive her diploma.

By the time he entered high school, Bruce had grown tall and was a handsome young man with an athletic body which the girls found irresistible. During his second year at Stratford High, the hero worshiping girls were swarming around him; he had become an athlete of some stature making the varsity team in both football and baseball he also excelled academically consistently placing in the upper ten percent of his class. Almost all the students liked him, Bruce, had an outgoing personality and the ability to interact with everyone he met whether they were athletes, school favorites or ordinary students. Bruce considered all of them equals treating each of them as individuals who possessed their own unique qualities. He liked to think, "We are all just people."

As a youth in Costa Rica, Zane had been a blue-chip baseball player in the minor leagues and had an exceptional understanding of the game. Rather than pursuing a career as a professional ball player, Zane chose to earn an advanced degree in Business Management with the idea of making a career in investment management. After he and Peggy married Zane spent much of his free time teaching Bruce how to play the game. Bruce first experienced baseball as a six-year-old when he and two friends, who lived on his street, signed up for the T-ball league. Since there are no pitchers in T-ball, Zane concentrated on teaching Bruce to field the ball, later after Bruce moved on from T-ball, he began teaching Bruce to hit a pitched ball using eye-hand coordination techniques he had learned as a boy. They spent endless hours in the back yard with Zane whirling a baseball, attached to the end of a thin rope, around his head so he could change the path of the ball up and down as it passed Bruce over a plastic baseball plate. The objective of this technique was to enable Bruce to hit the ball irrespective of its position as it passed over the plate. Using the ball on a rope and batting cage practice at the commercial practice arenas, Bruce became a sensational hitter by the time he moved up to Pony League. Like all kids, Bruce wanted to be a pitcher which required Zane to become a pitching instructor as well as a catcher. Bruce had superb control of his pitches from the beginning, Zane's challenge was to improve the speed of his fastball and to help Bruce develop a second off-speed pitch to keep the batters off balance. To protect Bruce's arm from injury, Zane limited his pitches to the fastball which was his primary pitch, and a slider which was his change-up pitch used to fool the opposing batters. Curve balls and other exotic pitches were permanently banned from his repertoire of pitches. With Bruce's unerring accuracy the game plan reduced to forcing the batter to hit the ball then trusting the fielders to get them out. Bruce commanded a good fastball and slider making it no easy task for the opposing players to hit his pitches at all, many of them struck out without swinging. He excelled as a pitcher on the local league teams before becoming a starting pitcher for the Stratford High School team. He came to love the game almost to the exclusion of other sports, but he could not give up his position as tight end on the varsity football team because he loved catching the football in traffic then dodging tackles as he ran down the field toward the end zone. It was an immense thrill when he got away from the defenders and scored a touchdown for his team.

Bruce first became aware of Cathy at a school dance following a football game in which he starred scoring two touchdowns for the Spartans. He was acclaimed hero of the game by his fellow students as well as his teammates. They had won the game 14 to 0. Cathy liked being in or near the center of attention when there was excitement in the air, she connived to share in Bruce's spotlight even though she hardly knew him. A group of Spartan football players were huddled near the dance floor when she suddenly appeared next to Bruce taking his hand she looked up smiling as she said in sultry and suggestive voice.

"Please, come dance with me? I don't have a partner."

Bruce looked at the breathtaking blond with the sexy body and on closer inspection surmised she would make an interesting dance partner.

"Sure, I'll be more than happy to dance with you. What's your name?"

"My name is Cathy. Please, hold me tight while we dance, so I don't look bad. I am a little unsteady on my feet right now."

Cathy made certain their bodies touched as much as possible, she managed to get his leg between hers on several turns making it touch near her forbidden area. This maneuver did not go unnoticed, Bruce made as many turns as possible the upper portion of his right thigh still felt the warm velvety touch of Cathy after the dance ended. Bruce thanked her, but did not return to the huddle instead he held Cathy's hand saying.

"Cathy that was remarkable, thank you for asking me. Would you be interested in having the next dance too?"

She was sure as they took each other's hand and returned to the dance floor that he would be hers by the end of the dance. Her head was on his shoulder their bodies pressed tightly together her ample boobs rubbing against his heaving chest as they danced. She began her systemic seduction ritual, the more they danced the more she could feel his rapid heartbeat against her chest. She put her hand on his butt just before the dance ended pulling their lower parts against each other. Feeling Bruce hard against her, she was sure the capture had been made. Cathy kissed him lightly on the cheek whispering in his ear.

"That was the best dance of my life, thank you. Maybe we can do it again sometime."

She rushed away to join her girlfriends who had been watching with great anticipation and interest. Before she reached her seat, they were all clamoring impatiently.

"How was he?"

"Exceptional, keep your hands off, he's mine," replied Cathy mimicking a choke hold with her hands.

"What about your boyfriend, David?" asked Ruth her closest friend.

"David who?" replied Cathy who no longer had any use for David since he had been unable to attend the dance due to family commitments.

"Man that was some dance," said Bruce as he returned to the huddle.

"That Cathy is one wild bitch. You should stay away from her, Bruce. She's nothing but trouble," said Tom, the starting quarterback.

"What do you mean trouble?"

"Let me tell you about her, she is one good looking gal and sexy as they come, but she is a dangerous bitch who will do anything. She is nothing, but trouble in CAPITAL LETTERS! A group of us went to her house for a party one time, when her parents were out of town, she served drinks from the bar and doctored brownies for those who wanted them. By midnight the place smelled like burning rope, everyone was either drunk or stoned out of their gourd that's when she suggested we all go skinny dipping in the pool. She turned the outside lights off to keep from embarrassing anyone then after we had splashed around naked for a half an hour or so she turned on the floodlights and music. She and several of the others started dancing together naked around the pool it was embarrassing to see how fucked up they were. Half of them didn't even know where they were or what they were doing. I put on my clothes and split. I don't know what happened after that, but she and that bunch she runs with are all bitches. Stay away from them they are crazy as hell and will cause you a lot of grief!"

"Yeah," echoed one of the other teammates adding.

"Stay away from Cathy and her bitches, she's the ringleader, you know."

Bruce was surprised to hear that Cathy could be involved with such idiocy she seemed to be so nice while they were dancing. He found her to be very exciting.

Bruce did not see Cathy for several days not until she suddenly approached him in the school parking lot after school saying in her sweetest voice. "Bruce, have you been dancing lately?"

"No, but I haven't forgotten the last time we danced together. It was great."

"Neither have I, Bruce. Why don't you come by my house on your way home? We can dance on the patio to some really neat music that I have collected."

Bruce remembered his friends' warning, but he accepted her invitation, anyway.

"I can only stay a while because I have several things to take of when I get home."

Cathy waited anxiously for Bruce to arrive, as part of her preconceived plan, she greeted him at the door with a light kiss on the mouth, but once he was inside, she kissed him firmly with her arms around him so that they were touching intimately. Cathy had changed from her school clothes into tights, a short skirt and a halter that barely covered her ample breasts. She was as near naked as a teenaged girl could be without actually showing more than would be acceptable in public. Bruce kept his head, remembering the warning from his buddies. He had a glass of punch with Cathy before they turned on the music and started dancing. Once in her arms it was great fun, Bruce and Cathy made a good dance team their movements complemented each other and Cathy anticipated his every step as they pressed their bodies together. While moving to the rhythm of the music, Cathy massaged him with her whole body in a way Bruce had never imagined or thought possible. He was lost in paradise with Cathy pressing against him all he could think about was how great her warm body felt against his. He refused to believe this heavenly creature could be trouble she felt soft and warm in his arms he enjoyed their touching. They danced one dance after another their bodies caressing one another in a sexually explicit way. Cathy changed the music affording Bruce an opportunity to glance at his watch, to his utter dismay, he had stayed far too long he should have been home an hour ago. His mother and Zane had strict rules about coming straight home after school. Cathy restarted the music, Bruce held her in his arms with her body pressed against his and although he wanted very much to stay, he whispered.

"I'm sorry, I am already late I have to go."

She kissed him passionately grasping his buns and pulling him close so that she could feel the bulge in his trousers against her.

"I'm sorry too, if you stay we can have some real fun, but if you have to go I understand. We will do it again won't we? Next time maybe you can stay for the real excitement!"

Bruce rushed home to take care of his chores, much to his relief no one was at home when he arrived there, Peggy had gone to the grocery store and Zane had not arrived home from work, he had lucked out. Bruce changed clothes quickly and began mowing the lawn as he was supposed to have done an hour earlier.

The Alpha-3 chief agent called their weekly meeting to order then asked for a summary of the week's surveillance. Jane, one of the visual agents assigned to Bruce reported first.

"We all knew that one of these days Bruce was going to grow up and become a problem for us. Well he has, and he is. Let me explain, Bruce met this girl, Cathy, who is a classmate at Stratford and he seems to be attracted to her sexually. They have met several times after school, but there has been no sex even though she's been rubbing it all over him every time they're together. I don't think he will be able to resist much longer this girl knows exactly how to turn a guy on. There is more, we have made a routine check on this, Cathy, and believe me, she is one devious little bitch she's had sex with a half dozen or more guys and is into marijuana and maybe more. There is strong evidence that she uses ecstasy, the date rape drug, on herself and her friends at some of her parties. It's only a matter of time until she puts some in Bruce's lemonade if he doesn't put something in her pretty soon. She seems to be in heat all the time and won't wait forever for Bruce to make a move on his own. Being around her, there is a high risk of Bruce being exposed to a combination of illicit sex and drugs. You know what a mess that can lead to. Bruce even showed up an hour late getting home a couple of weeks ago, something he has never done before, just because he was dancing with her on her patio. In my opinion, we have to get rid of this little trollop before she causes some real harm. Bruce is enthralled with her right now and what teen aged boy wouldn't be with her good looks and her signals that it is available, come and get it."

One of the male agents commented.

"I don't see anything wrong with a little heat in his life. He needs to get accustomed to it. It's only going to get hotter from here on."

Exasperated, Jane replied.

"We all know what happens when young men get sexed up their brains turn off completely. Bruce isn't any different we need to do something about Cathy before she gets him in trouble we can't fix."

"Well, we can't kill her, but if she is taking ecstasy along with other drugs she may kill herself," replied the chief agent.

"Somehow, we must discredit this Cathy in Bruce's mind and do it in such a way that Bruce makes it his choice to cast her aside. Based on the crazy antics you have described, there has to be videos, emails or online postings and possibly photographs that will do the trick. Let's start looking, find her friends and their friends, find out everything there is to know about her. Check all of their computers and make discreet inquiries around Stratford about the whole bunch. I have a feeling we are looking at a pack of wild kittens who have gone terribly wrong. Let me know if you need additional help like checking the police records or hacking into a few computers."

The Cathy *coup de grace* was under way at Abe, meanwhile Bruce and Cathy continued to dance on her patio as the investigation proceeded. To his credit, Bruce was never late getting home again in spite of his longing to keep dancing with Cathy. Putting his hand on her rear while they were dancing excited Bruce he was thinking about having sex with her and his desire was growing stronger each time she pressed against him. His rampant sexual urge was beginning to overcome good judgment, he was teetering on the brink, about to succumb to his natural instincts and Cathy's magic.

It took little time for the Alpha-3 team to put together a series of compromising pictures not only of Cathy, but also of many of her girlfriends and their male companions. There were party videos featuring drugs and alcohol along with rampant sex among the participants many of whom were minors. In addition, there were emails from Cathy to her friends setting up parties at remote sites open to anyone who wanted to come. The most damning email of all was one Cathy sent to her girlfriends a few days earlier.

"It's almost time for Bruce to become my next conquest. I'm going to seduce him and screw his brains out within the next two weeks. Eat your hearts out girls, I'll keep in touch and send photos."

Once all the information concerning Cathy's activities had been collected, sorted and reviewed there were thirty three individuals identified among her party people who were doing drugs and participating in sex. Frank ordered Alpha-3 to package copies of the videos showing the activities of the thirty three individuals and discreetly deliver them to each of their parent's homes with an anonymous note which read.

"Your child needs help before he or she winds up dead. For your information, we will be watching to see what happens next!"

The information was also forwarded to Abe's headquarters for future reference, if needed. Bruce completed his homework before checking his email, unaccountably strange collections of photos showing Cathy having sex with several boys popped up along with an email from Cathy to her friends. The photographs and the email did not appear on any computer other than Bruce's. Alpha-3 had been computer specific when sending the photographs and email from Cathy to her friends which they had found on her computer. Bruce was sickened by the photos and email, yet he was even more disgusted with himself for ignoring his buddy's warnings about Cathy. He asked himself as he shook his head loathing his association with Cathy.

"How could I be so stupid? I'm damned lucky to get out of this shit before it became too late. What would Zane and mom think if they saw me in one of those pictures? Goodbye, Cathy you are a great dancer, but a horrible person. We will never be together again. Good riddance."

Bruce refused to speak with Cathy when they met at school, he offered no explanation, yet made it clear that he had no interest in her. Weeks later, Bruce heard through the huddle that Cathy's parents had withdrawn her from school. Later on, he learned she had been placed in a private rehab center for drug addiction. Bruce hoped she could save herself she could have been someone he wanted to be with if she had stayed away from drugs and sex.

Abe sent a message to Alpha-3 declaring.

"A job well done, keep up the good work. We will be following the other thirty two individuals from here. If further intervention is required to save these kids, it will come from us. Bruce is still your primary responsibility."

Bruce began dancing when he was in junior high it was one of his favorite ways to interact with girls, but after his involvement with Cathy he became very careful in selecting partners. He kept reminding himself not to become an idiot just because he liked dancing with a particular girl. He made sure he would not lose his head again, at least not until he knew the girl was OK, someone who would meet Peggy's and Zane's approval. He talked with Zane about the kind of girl he should be dating and was not at all surprised when Zane replied emphatically.

"One exactly like your mother, she is so special you may have to settle for one almost like her because there is no other woman on this planet like her, she is one of a kind."

Bruce appreciated Zane's comment very much he began looking for a girl who was fun and funny, who laughed a lot and could dance, someone who enjoyed being around people, someone like his mother, Peggy. He did not find a girl like his mother at Stratford although he dated sporadically the remainder of the year. He danced with a number of his classmates without becoming romantically involved with any of them they remained dance partners and nothing more.

Bruce had little difficulty making good grades he was an honor student who excelled with a minimum of home study or extra effort. Peggy enrolled him in a private school for his final two years of high school to better prepare him to be accepted in medical school when he went to college. He gave up both baseball and football to concentrate on his studies, but he refused to give up dancing it was a great way to relax and have fun even when things were not going according to plan.

Without any further distractions, Bruce graduated at the top of his class receiving many scholarship offers from prestigious universities that were looking for bright new students. After reviewing the options available, he elected to enroll at the University of Texas where he had already been accepted in their premed program. His first two weeks at UT were spent getting to know the campus and the classroom routine which he found to be much different from that he had been accustomed to in high school. The classwork required a lot more study time than he was accustomed to it took up most of his evenings and out of class time. After a week of nothing but studying, Bruce felt he deserved a little relaxation. He decided to explore one of the hot student hangouts everyone kept talking about, he headed downtown to 6th Street where he expected to dance a little and relax for a while before taking on his homework for the following day. The place was jammed full of young people there was standing room only with virtually no space available around the perimeter of the dance floor. He squeezed into a spot not far from a group of young ladies who appeared to be unattached. Bruce managed to dance with several girls in the short time he had allotted for entertainment before returning to his dorm to do his homework. None of the girls proved to be particularly good dancers they were adequate, but just barely. Bruce promised himself to find a capable dancing partner in the near future so that he could enjoy what little time he had off from his studies.

Verona had applied to several Texas colleges for the fall semester eventually enrolling at the University of Texas although she had not yet decided on a major or a career when she arrived on campus in Austin she was ready to start college and to determine what she wanted to do with the rest of her life. Clare and Ned insisted Verona live in a dorm near the campus rather than commute from home they reasoned that she should enjoy campus life and be on her own for the first time.

Estelle Winger, Verona's assigned roommate, came from Junction located in the hill country between Sonora and Kerrville it was a small town far removed from the city life in which Verona had grown up. Estelle's home town of Junction was originally named Denman, which like many early Texas towns, had been named after the surveyor who laid out the city. Located at the intersection of the North Llano and South Llano rivers its name changed several times before becoming simply Junction. Its population hovered at around 2,500 people over the last several decades, with little fluctuation from year to year, there was no compelling reason for people to move to Junction. The entire area has long been dominated by ranching, unlike much of Texas, Kimble Country and its county seat Junction, have remained outside of the oil and gas producing part of Texas. Because of its geology, the area has not experienced growth from the influx of capital for new investments or new residents related to oil and gas exploration and production as did most Texas communities. Junction accidentally became a place of interest due its association with the 1954 Texas A&M football team coached by Bear Bryant who brought his team to Junction for some of his extreme physical programs designed to separate the men from the boys. Later the program was referred to as ten days of living hell by sports writers and the participants themselves.

Those who survive the camp became known as the "Junction Boys," only about half of those starting the camp finished the remainder dropped out of football, or slipped away in the dark of night. The following season, Texas A&M fielded one of its better teams in modern times with several of the survivors becoming stars who later played professional football. At least one of the survivors became a successful professional football coach during his long career in football.

Estelle's family owned and operated a large cattle ranch near the town. Much of their ranch land was originally acquired by, Ben Winger, who came to Texas in 1870 to seek his fortune on the frontier. He was among the last group of ranchers to fight the Comanche, Apache and other Indians who raided the area for horses and food. The Indians mounted their last raid in the area in 1878 before being pushed west by the army aided by the armed ranchers and cowboys. Over the years, through many economic ups and downs, the Winger family managed to scrape out a living on their ranch often adding to their holdings when their neighbors were forced to give up ranching and move away. Estelle, a tall blond, was wiry as a cowboy during roundup, she looked and sounded like a teenager just off of the ranch. Following their first meeting, Verona could not help thinking.

"She's different, but friendly. I think I'm going to like her a lot."

The two had been roommates for almost a week when Verona inquired during one of their casual conversations.

"Estelle, do you have a boyfriend?"

"No, Verona, I don't. I dated some back home except I never met anyone I considered good breeding stock. Believe me, I will be assessing the herd for a suitable mate once we get settled in and I have a chance to see what's available. I don't plan to be an old maid."

Somewhat startled by Estelle's straight forward reply, Verona replied with similar frankness.

"I had a boyfriend back in high school, after we started having sex together I decided we were not in love, so I stopped seeing him. I think sex and love go together. How about you?"

"We're not like the mares and cows back on the ranch they don't care who gets them pregnant they just have babies. Me, I'm looking for someone to love and spend a lifetime with, love and sex go together and both had better be good. No half measures for me."

241

"You know, Estelle, I think it's time we started culling the herd. If you see anyone that excites you, let me know if I can help. Should I see someone who interests me, you can do the same. It's still early, why don't we get dressed and go look around for a while to see what's out there."

Verona was amazed when Estelle emerged from her room, she was strikingly good looking and attractive with makeup, she had changed into a sexy short skirt which emphasized her long legs and pert behind. The image Estelle presented was not at all what Verona had expected from the blue jean clad ranch girl she had been talking with a short while ago.

"Estelle, how can they resist?" commented Verona as they walked across campus toward the Union Building.

Verona and Estelle were an alluring pair, one with black hair, the other a blond, both good looking and both possessing outstanding figures which were advantageously displayed to attract attention. There were many long gazes and whispers as they made a tour of the Union Building before sitting on a burnt orange couch which provided them a view of all who entered and left the building. They sat talking and evaluating the passing herd looking for someone who might interest either of them. There were short ones and tall ones and some that were pudgy or skinny, unfortunately there were none that met either of their requirements for a person of interest.

"Well, I haven't seen much to choose from here, shall we go someplace with a little more action maybe one of those wild student hangouts on 6th Street where they have dancing?"

"I'll drive," volunteered Verona who had her Mustang at school.

The place was packed when they arrived, people were standing for lack of a place to sit and the music was loud drowning out all except the loudest conversations. The place was poorly lighted, yet there was a resounding WHOOOOO from the males crowded around the dance floor as the two of them pushed through searching for a little space of their own. Neither of them knew exactly what was going on some couples were dancing and everyone in the place had a beer in their hand. Estelle, talking above the roar of the crowd, said to Verona.

"I am not much of a drinker, how about sharing a beer?"

"Sure," replied Verona who turned to the guy standing next to her.

"How do we get a beer in this place?"

"What do you want, beautiful?"

"A Michelob Ultra, if they have it, otherwise any lite beer will do."

"I'll get it for you, in fact, I'll get two because it takes some time to get over there and back. Stay put, treat's on me, I'll be back."

He quickly disappearing into the crowd after taking a few steps he could not be seen at all. Sure enough several minutes later he found his way back with three cold beers. Verona handed one Ultra to Estelle keeping the other for herself. She turned to Estelle saying.

"I hope this is OK with you, it's the best I could do."

Verona thanked the stranger who was taking a swig of his Lone Star then asked.

"Do you come here often?"

"Yeah, it's one of the hottest places in town, it's mostly students blowing off steam we need a little relaxation once in a while. How about you, beautiful? I haven't seen you here before."

"It's our first time, want to dance?"

Verona took him by the arm before they made their way to the dance floor leaving Estelle alone holding all three beers since there was no place to set them down. Estelle was nearly immobile standing alone holding the beers, two in one hand one in the other, it was awkward, yet she managed to look over the dance floor to see what was going on. After watching the dancers for a while, her eyes focused on a good looking guy with black curly hair and possibly blue eyes the lighting was so dim she couldn't really tell. One thing she could tell for sure he was a beautiful dancer. The more she watched the more excited Estelle became saying to herself.

"God help me, that's the guy I've been looking for all of my life."

Estelle watched him move about the floor with one girl after another, all the while thinking.

"Come back Verona, come back now, I need help."

Suddenly he disappeared from sight becoming lost in the crowd, searching frantically, Estelle could not find him again no matter how hard she tried. She was in a near state of panic when Verona showed up with her dancing partner before either of them could say a word Estelle gushed.

"Verona, I think I just saw him!"

"You just saw who?"

"The one I told you about, I think he's here and I want to meet him. Help me Verona?"

"Then point him out to me and I'll see what I can do to help," answered Verona sensing desperation Estelle's voice.

"I don't see him anywhere I was watching him dance and turned my head for a moment when I looked back he was gone. He is tall and has black curly hair, a good physique, he is as good looking as they come and he is a marvelous dancer."

Estelle experienced a small sense of relief knowing Verona was there to help her find him again. Verona turned to their beer benefactor.

"Please excuse us, something has come up so we need to go. Thanks for the beer and dance maybe we will see each other again sometime."

She and Estelle elbowed their way around the dance floor looking for Estelle's dream man sadly he was nowhere to be found. Out of desperation, Verona and Estelle resorted to asking those standing near the dance floor if any of them had seen the guy with black curly hair. After several inquiries, one of the girls volunteered.

"We just danced, he told me he was leaving. I think he had unfinished homework to take care of before tomorrow."

Excited with the news Estelle interrupted.

"Do you know his name?"

"No, but he did say he was a freshman. He was very nice and a super dancer."

They continued making inquiries for another half-hour without adding to the meager information they had gleaned earlier. An hour passed before they gave up their quest for Estelle's dream man and returned to the dorm. Estelle was forlorn and upset that she had not been able to meet her dream man after seeing him on the dance floor.

"At least I know what he looks like and he is handsome."

She was determined to find him again and was looking to Verona for help. Verona thought for several minutes before offering a comment.

"We are all freshmen, so it is likely that one of us will run into him sooner or later. In the meanwhile, I suggest we put out a request on the internet for help in finding him. We can also ask our classmates whether they or their friends know a freshman who meets your description of your dream man."

"You know what? I haven't mentioned to you that I am a pretty good artist. I am going to do a sketch of him for our internet posting and then print some WANTED posters to put up near the campus. I sure hope he is not taken when we find him."

Verona considered the idea for a moment chuckling to herself.

"While all of this is going on, maybe we should also be looking for a Mr. Right for me as well. Seriously, depending on how this turns out, we might want to set up a website offering a service to the unattached students designed to help them find their dream mate while they are here at UT."

Estelle's WANTED poster featured an accurate likeness of Bruce along with the words: "If you know the person shown in this sketch, or someone who looks like him please, send his name and location to the following address. P.O. Box 3711 Austin, Texas."

In order to keep her identity secret, Estelle rented a box at the local Post Office to avoid releasing her own address. She and Verona established assumed internet identities specifically dedicated to their online search for Estelle's dream man. They were determined to remain anonymous in their search efforts to avoid becoming subjects of ridicule and jokes perpetuated by the other students. Two weeks of intensive searching turned up nothing until Verona showed the sketch to one of the female students in her English class. She looked at the sketch briefly then commented.

"Yeah, I know this guy. His name is, Bruce Wilkerson, he's in my social science class which meets in this building at nine on Tuesdays and Thursdays. Is he in some kind of trouble?"

Verona responded cheerfully.

"No, well maybe, my roommate wants to meet him, so he could be in a lot of trouble if you know what I mean."

They shared a laugh before the girl offered.

"Bring her around, I'll introduce them. I think it will be fun to see what happens. Don't you?"

Verona agreed, thanked her for her help then dashed to her next class which was all the way across campus. Estelle was all smiles when she heard Verona had found Mr. wonderful and that an introduction was in the making.

"Verona, I was so excited I almost peed in my pants when you called me! When can you arrange an introduction? I'll put on my sexiest dress and be on my best behavior I promise not to embarrass you."

"How about next Tuesday? Can you get to the English building a few minutes before nine?"

"You bet I can even if I have to skip class!" Exclaimed Estelle who was still fantasizing over meeting her potential dream man.

After the introductions were made on Tuesday by Verona's go between Estelle spoke directly to Bruce.

"Bruce, I've been wanting to meet you everyone says you are a great dancer. I love to dance myself. Should you ever need a dancing partner give me a call at this number?"

She handed him a card showing her name, phone number and address. Bruce looked at the card then smiled at Estelle as he put the card in his shirt pocket. Looking at Estelle his blue eyes lit up before he replied.

"Maybe I will, Estelle. Your art work is impressive the sketch looks just like me, I'm going to frame a copy of your WANTED poster and hang it on my wall. It's been great meeting you, I hope to see you again. In the meantime, happy dancing."

Bruce, excused himself before heading to class. Estelle was hyper excited asking Verona once he was out of hearing range.

"What do you think?"

"He is certainly handsome I see why you wanted to meet him. He has probably turned many a female eye with that curly black hair and that athletic build."

"That's not what I meant! Do you think he liked me?"

"Of course he liked you, didn't you see his smile when you handed him your card he was already thinking about dancing with you. Take my word for it he will be calling. By the way, I liked the way you played the dance theme it really got his attention. You planted an anchor thought in his mind, from now on, every time he thinks about dancing he is going to think about you. Intentional or not, Estelle, you were masterful."

Estelle grinned before she responded.

"Well, I did want him to know I like to dance. I didn't say it, but I would sure like to snuggle up next to him on the dance floor and maybe somewhere else."

Bruce was planning to check out a western dance hall he had heard about located on the south side of town. Even before he made up his mind to go there, he thought of Estelle Winger the tall good looking blond from Junction. A little voice in his head kept urging him to call her maybe she would like to join him.

"She said she likes dancing, but first I need to find her card."

He found Estelle's card stashed in the top drawer of his dresser where he kept his valuables. Estelle's cell phone rang and rang before it automatically rolled over to the missed calls feature. Bruce waited a while and was about to call back to leave a message when his cell phone rang.

"Hello, this is Estelle Winger. Did you just call me?"

"Estelle, this is Bruce Wilkerson we met last week. Remember?"

"Sure, I remember, it was at the English building. Kay introduced us?"

Bruce responded quickly with a bit of urgency in his voice.

"Yes, that's it. I am thinking of going to a western dance Saturday night and I was wondering, if you are not busy, would you consider going with me?"

He did not wait for an answer rather continued.

"If it's agreeable with you, we can have an early dinner before the dance to get better acquainted. I'd like very much to see you again I know you like to dance because you told me so when we met. Does that sound like something you would be interested in doing Saturday?"

Estelle's head was swimming she took a deep breath before answering.

"I will be delighted to accompany you on Saturday night and I will be glad to see you again. It sounds like a lot of fun. What time shall I expect you?"

"The dance doesn't start until eight how about me picking you up at six, so we can get an early start?"

A ripple of excitement ran though his head, he hadn't expected talking to Estelle would affect him this way. Talking with a female had not aroused such feelings since his dancing encounters with Cathy and he and Estelle weren't even on the dance floor yet.

Returning to the dorm after her last class, Verona found Estelle in their common room dancing and waving her arms about wildly shouting, "Oh, Oh, Oh!" Verona thought Estelle might be drunk, or high on something she was flitting around as if half out of her mind. Worried about her roommate she shouted.

"Estelle, are you all right?"

Estelle stopped dancing and sat down, once she recovered her breath, she responded enthusiastically.

"I'm fine, it's just that Bruce called like you said he would. We have a date this Saturday to go dining and dancing! I'm so excited I can't wait until Saturday gets here."

"Apparently you made a good impression on him, or he wouldn't have called. Congratulations, now I am anticipating our talk on Sunday morning, you can tell me all about it," said Verona with a touch of envy.

Bruce reserved a table for two at an elegant restaurant located on a small bluff overlooking Town Lake. The dress code was informal, which is normal in Austin, even though the food and services were extremely expensive. Estelle had on a foxy short skirt and a matching tight top that showed her boobs and cleavage to be real and provocative. Bruce wore cool trousers freshly pressed with a starched and ironed long sleeved shirt. In laid back Austin, they were a well-dressed young couple dining out on a Saturday night. Bruce ordered a bottle of red wine before dinner he approvingly tasted the wine before the waiter half-filled each of their glasses, first hers and then his. Estelle raised her glass to her lips while Bruce watched, his eyes focused on hers as she tasted the first tiny sip. She smiled indicating her approval before he inquired.

"Estelle, where do you live away from school?"

"My parents are ranchers they live near Junction," she said. She looked at Bruce thinking of something completely different, but managed to ask.

"Where are you from, Bruce? I don't think you mentioned home before."

"I am from big H, Houston. My mom and dad live there with my younger sister, Katy. Dad is in the investment business and mom is a housewife even though she has a degree from A&M. Basically we are just a regular family doing our thing." Bruce was unaware that his parents were actually very rich among the wealthiest families in Texas.

Bruce and Estelle hit it off during dinner they were feeling very comfortable with one and other by the time they reached the dance hall. Bruce found a table for two near the dance floor, yet far enough away from the band that they could talk without having to raise their voices. The hall had a spacious dance floor large enough to allow free movement for the dancers without their continually nudging each other or having to curtail their normal dancing styles.

The first time Bruce took Estelle in his arms to dance, she was lost he was everything she wanted, strong, good looking, an excellent dancer, he made her laugh, and most of all he made her feel warm all over when he held her close. Bruce was also enthralled, he discovered Estelle was not just a good dancer she was a well-disciplined dancing machine who could follow unerringly and never missed a step she was a perfect dancing partner. She also turned him on when they were dancing. During the evening, Bruce became aware how easy it was for Estelle to laugh and enjoy herself. She had that special gift she made everyone around her laugh and feel good about themselves. Although they had danced close several times, as the end of the evening came near, Bruce pulled Estelle closer until their bodies were touching intimately while they danced. Estelle could not help herself she whispered.

"Oh, I like that."

Bruce whispered back.

"I wish we didn't have to stop. You are overwhelming me with your dancing skills."

They finished the few remaining dances in breathless concert enjoying their closeness immensely. When the music stopped, they gathered their belongings and walked to the car hand in hand. Bruce drove directly to the dorm with no stops in between they chatted constantly during the drive and upon reaching Estelle's dorm Bruce pressed Estelle's hand saying.

"I think we should do this again."

"Me too," replied Estelle.

Before saying good night Estelle turned, so that she was facing Bruce, she wanted to make certain he could see her eyes clearly in the dim light. Watching Bruce's eyes closely, Estelle said emphatically.

"Thank you, Bruce. I had a great time you are a beautiful dancer and a great partner. I enjoyed the dinner and dancing very much."

Estelle was pleased to see his eyes brighten as she spoke obviously her words had registered with Bruce and had produced the effect she intended. The next morning, Estelle was glowing when she greeted Verona at the breakfast table.

"It was a wonderful evening. He was everything I had imagined he would be, charming and a lot of fun we danced until they closed the place. I felt so good in his arms, especially when he pulled me close to his body, I'm sure he could feel my racing heart. We laughed, talked and danced the whole evening I know he was having a good time too, I could see it on his face when he laughed."

"I understand you really had a great time. Did he ask you for another date or is it going to be a onetime thing?" asked Verona who was concerned Estelle might be over reacting she intended to protect Estelle should Bruce fail to call again. "As we were saying good night, he mentioned that he thought we should do it again, and I agreed that's the way we left it," said Estelle looking a bit innocent as she made a big grin.

"Did he kiss you good night?" inquired Verona still looking for a sign that Bruce was the genuine article for Estelle.

"There was no kissing. Verona, I would never kiss anyone on the first date not even the man of my dreams. We country girls do not give away our kisses that freely they have to be earned," recited Estelle as if reading from a printed manual on dating. Continuing with her thoughts Estelle added.

"It's the same with love. Even though I find Bruce attractive and really like him if he wants my love he will have to earn it. It's not something I am willing to give away."

Verona did not respond, she thought a while about Estelle's comments then decided Estelle probably could take care of herself without any outside help. Verona had not thought of love in the context Estelle had just laid out. She was learning a lot from this so called, country girl, she decided to adopt Estelle's guidelines as her own in future dealings with men.

Bruce thought about Estelle frequently in between classes and homework. The more he thought about her the more he wanted to see her again, much to his dismay, he was finding it difficult to keep up with the demands of his curriculum and still have time for other activities. Mid-week following their date he was desperate to see Estelle even if it were for only a brief interval. Her cell-phone rang several times before she could retrieve it from the bedroom.

"Estelle, here."

The response made her smile.

"This Bruce, can we talk for a while?"

"Sure, it's good to hear from you, Bruce. Where are you?"

"I'm in the dorm studying, I didn't want to let another day go by without talking to you. I am so covered up with homework it's hard to get out even for a few hours."

"I know about that, I haven't had much free time either. I'm ready for a break though," said Estelle hoping Bruce might suggest something.

"I was thinking. If you are agreeable, I can come by your place for an hour or so and we can go for a walk or just talk."

She held her breath for a moment before answering.

"If you are leaving now, I'll meet you at the door with my walking shoes on I'll be waiting for you Bruce."

His heart began pounding as he answered, "I'm on my way see you in twenty minutes, bye."

Estelle was waiting outside of the dorm when he arrived out of breath he had walked at a fast pace to save precious time which he could spend with her. They exchanged greetings before Bruce took her hand in his asking.

"Which will it be walking and talking, or just talking?"

Estelle responded by walking toward the park, she was delighted Bruce had taken the time to call, she had been longing to see him again and had considered making a call herself. They walked at a relaxed pace talking as they went. Bruce checked his watch periodically and at the half hour declared.

"We have to turn back my allotted time will be up by the time we get back to your dorm."

Estelle squeezed his hand exclaiming, "Yes, I know how studying goes, it takes up a lot of time."

They walked at a slightly faster pace on the return path, still they talked every step of the way with no letup by either of them. They enjoyed being with each other even if it were only for a short time. Each of them savored every moment they spent together it was the highlight of their day.

"I would like to see you more often, Estelle, is there some place we could meet for a while during the week?"

"There must be some place. Let me check with Verona, she'll know. I'll give you a call after I talk with her."

Bruce held the door open for Estelle to enter she turned slowly kissing him on the cheek before closing the door behind her. The kiss was unexpected although well received. Walking back to his dorm Bruce reflected on the refreshing hour he had spent with Estelle he was amazed at how easily they laughed together she was a happy person who made people around her happy too. He didn't feel the need to be doing something special all the time the way he had with Cathy.

"Estelle is a beautiful, warm and loveable blond that I really enjoyed being with. She is also sexy, even more so than Cathy, in her own refreshing way."

He was perplexed he had to find some way to see her more often. In the following weeks, Bruce often delayed doing his homework until late at night in order to spend time with Estelle. They went dancing several times on the weekends and regularly took walks together in the park they were fast becoming an attached couple. At Verona's suggestion, they sometimes met for coffee between classes when their schedules allowed, which did not happen very often because of their differing curriculums.

Alpha-3 reported to Abe.

"Bruce has met a girl at UT it may not come to anything, but they have become close friends and possibly more. Her name is, Estelle Winger, she is from a ranching family in the Junction area. A routine check shows her and the family to be normal people they are considered an outstanding family in the community. Her roommate is, Verona Cook, from Austin she is also from a normal family. Bruce met Estelle at her dorm today and they went for a short walk. Our operative reported what he thought might be another person watching Estelle's dorm. It does not appear to affect Bruce in any way, but it seems rather odd that Estelle's dorm would be under surveillance. Should we take action to identify this person?"

Abe's reply was short and to the point.

"Do not approach any person or persons who appear to be watching Estelle, but keep close to Bruce and report any irregularities you might observe."

Everything worked out well for Estelle, her date with Bruce turned into an ongoing romantic liaison which was becoming more intense with every passing day, while Verona still had not met anyone who interested her in a romantic way. Verona had learned a lot from Estelle in their first months as roommates, Verona had mistakenly thought she would be teaching Estelle about dating and love, but as it turned out one of Estelle's comments had profoundly changed Verona's outlook on love and dating. Several weeks prior, while discussing Bruce, Estelle had said.

"If he wants my love, then he will have to earn it. It's not something I am willing to give away."

Estelle's statement had stuck in Verona's memory and kept surfacing from time to time. On one of her weekends at home, Verona and Clare were discussing socializing at UT, when much to Clare's bewilderment, Verona asked.

"How did you know you and Ned were such a great match?"

"The first time I saw Ned I knew right away he had that something other men didn't have just looking at him made me tremble. I really didn't know we were a perfect match emotionally and physically until much later. To be truthful, we both thought we were right for each other for a long time, but we knew for sure we were a perfect match the first time we went to bed together. It was not the sex itself so much as the way we pleased each other and the consideration displayed for one other."

Although caught off guard, Clare was glad Verona asked the question. She summed up her explanation.

"It's strange about love and sex, they go together and to be a perfect match they both have to be good."

"That's what Estelle said!"

"What do you mean, what did Estelle say exactly?"

"That love and sex go together and they both had better be good."

Verona was amazed that her mother had not understood her without further clarification, her statement seemed clear to her.

Clare welcomed the opportunity that had been opened to inquire about Verona's thoughts on the subject of love and sex.

"And what do you think, Verona?"

"I agree with both of you, that's why I quit having sex with John Paul back in high school, I didn't love him. Love and sex do go together, one without the other is no good for me. Estelle said something else that I have come to appreciate, in talking about her boyfriend she said. If he wants my love, then he will have to earn it. It's not something I'm willing to give away."

"I'm proud of both you and your friend Estelle, I think you both will find your perfect match in time and will enjoy much happiness in your lives. Estelle sounds like an interesting person maybe you should bring her home some weekend. I would like to meet her," said Clare as she hugged Verona putting her head on her shoulder.

To Abe from the Alpha-1 team covering Verona.

"Verona is enrolled and attending classes at UT. At her parent's insistence she is living in a dorm rather than at home. Her roommate is Estelle Winger, from Junction, she is from a prominent ranching family. Not much going on here except Verona and Estelle conducted a fairly sophisticated campaign to arrange an introduction between Estelle and a guy from Houston named Bruce Wilkerson. It was harmless although very effective and entertaining to watch. Yesterday, Bruce and Estelle met at her and Verona's dorm then went for a walk. Our surveillance man was certain Bruce was being followed by an unknown professional who used the same surveillance techniques we employ. This does not affect Verona directly. It is strange though that

Estelle's friend Bruce is being followed much like we follow Verona. Do we know Him? Do we need to take any action on this matter?"

At Abe, Frank and his staff reviewed the latest reports from Alpha-1, assigned to Verona Cook and Alpha-3, assigned to Bruce Wilkerson with some consternation. Frank, was the only person in the organization who knew the true relationship between Bruce and Verona all the other agents and supervisors believed they were being protected as part of a long term genetic study being conducted by Gentex. Frank called for his entire staff to assemble in Abe's planning room where Frank stated the problems facing Abe with regard to Verona and Bruce.

"Our job to protect these two has been complicated dramatically by their attending UT at the same time. Verona and Bruce have met and know each other by name. This came about because Bruce is dating Verona's roommate Estelle. Their knowing each other casually is not a problem, on the other hand, should they become close friends our entire project could be inadvertently compromised and our entire program endangered. Gentlemen that is not going to happen. Before we leave today, there will be a plan in place to separate Verona and Bruce it's an absolute necessity that must be performed discreetly and with great care."

Frank did not single out anyone in particular instead he looked above the seated staff members as he continued with his assessment of the situation.

"In reading this morning's reports I'm sure you all noticed that each of our surveillance teams detected the other in the course of observing Bruce and Verona. I find it commendable that their training allowed them to do so, but it points out a severe flaw in our surveillance methods. I want our agents to be invisible and that means to everyone even our own people. If we can see them so can others. I want our techniques upgraded immediately. If we need new technology, get it. If our agents need retraining, do it. If we need more people, get them. Cost is not an issue, so let's get it done now."

A complete revision of the techniques and technology employed by Abe was under way. Frank would not rest until the surveillance methods had been updated to meet his standards. In his view, ADAM would be in jeopardy until that happened.

Chapter 10 Scholarship

Abe's staff felt a new urgency following Frank's remarks they divided into two teams to address the problems separately. One team was designated to devise a plan to separate Verona and Bruce while the other team's objective was to address the internal problem pointed out by Frank. Neither assignment was expected to be easy, but with unlimited funding and smart people nothing was deemed to be impossible. Sam, leader of the team devoted to Verona, addressed his colleagues.

"Obviously we need to remove either Verona or Bruce from the UT campus and put as much distance between the two of them as possible. Anyone have any ideas?"

"Both Verona and Bruce are excellent scholars. Bruce is premed and Verona is undecided, so there might be an opportunity in the form of a grant or a scholarship at another prestigious university," replied the young associate specifically assigned to analyze all information received at Abe concerning Verona.

"Great idea, it would definitely solve our problem if we can pull it off. You look into it Kevin."

The leader then asked for other ideas from the team, but none were forthcoming.

A detailed analysis of the relationship between Verona and Bruce led the assistant to conclude that the most logical solution to the problem would be to move Verona to another university. If she stayed at UT and Bruce left, she would still be in close contact with Estelle and indirectly involved with Bruce. Under these conditions Bruce and Verona would have a high chance of meeting repeatedly. Conversely, if Verona was removed from UT, their chance of meeting would be greatly reduced Verona would have to visit Estelle on campus for her to meet Bruce even casually. Young people make new friends in new environments and over time their new friends take on more importance than those far away and seldom seen. Removed from direct contact, Verona's friendship with Estelle could fade to insignificance since they had only known each other for a short time.

Frank and Sam reviewed all the scenarios presented for separating Verona and Bruce eventually embracing the idea of removing Verona from the UT campus and relocating her as far away as possible.

"Kevin, you devise a plan to entice Verona to move to another university. Once the plan is approved, its implementation will be your next assignment since you came up with the idea originally." Said Frank to his young handpicked subordinate. Frank motioned for Keven to follow him into his office closing the door behind them once they were inside.

"Kevin, I want you to know that Verona is very special to me. I expect you to look after her best interest in performing your assignment and to make her your primary concern throughout the entire process."

Like all the other agents and employees at Abe, Kevin was unaware that the subjects of their attention were the children of George Angleton the agents only knew that their wards were part of a genetic study conducted by Gentex and it was their assignment to protect them. The immense size and advanced techniques employed by Abe plus Abe's unlimited funding made it obvious to all of them that their subjects were special. Verona was well known to Kevin even though they had never met. He had seen photographs and videos of her constantly over the past two years and was intimately familiar with her daily activities and escapades. He admired her. Whatever the final outcome of Abe's mission, Kevin was committed to Verona, his aim was to make sure she was unchanged and free to be herself in the end. He felt it was the least he could do for such a beautiful person whom he secretly adored. He devised a plan with the objective of persuading Verona to voluntarily leave UT. Kevin was aware that she loved math, science and the arts. To facilitate his plan, he needed to determine which of these interests could be used to entice her to move to another university at mid-term.

The following day, Verona's student counselor requested a meeting in the afternoon to discuss her career program and her intended major at UT. The meeting had been instigated by Abe through ADAM using the influence of one of their UT alumni who regularly made large cash contributions to the university. Verona was amazed by the counselor's knowledge of her personal background he seemed to know a lot about her scholastic accomplishments as well as those subjects which fascinated her. She sensed the interview had been a good idea it demonstrated UT's strong interest in matching her interests and talents with a career program at the school. Verona thanked the counselor for taking time to talk with her. She left no doubt in the counselor's mind about her preference of a career she was determined to major in math and science. This information was reported to the UT alumni and consequently to Abe the following morning.

Verona had been Kevin Goodall's assignment from the moment he joined Abe two years earlier he received and analyzed all information pertaining to Verona's activities, both before and after his employment, consequently he knew her personality and habits well. He learned minute details about her such as the type of dresses she preferred and the brand of underwear she wore. He had viewed past and present videos of her over and overlooking for some hidden danger. Each time he reviewed new information about her, he was reminded she was an extraordinarily smart and a beautiful woman with a mind of her own. He could not imagine anyone wanting to harm her, yet Kevin took his assignment seriously analyzing the data carefully to make certain Verona was safe and protected from harm. Protecting Verona was his job, becoming attracted to her, just happened. It was his private secret which he mentioned to none of his fellow workers at Abe.

With the new information provided by the counselor, Kevin developed a strategy to entice Verona to transfer to Stanford University at midterm. Abe, with the help of several wealthy graduates, established a special scholarship in mathematics and science at Stanford University. The scholarship was set up to pay the tuition, and all associated costs to obtain a BS degree and it would also the pay the cost of living for a period up to and including earning a PhD. As an added incentive, the recipient of the scholarship would be provided a private apartment complete with a study room equipped with a state of the art computer and peripheral equipment. Abe's cover story alleged the scholarship was being awarded to a person meeting Stanford's enrollment standards and selected by the scholarship's founder. The scholarship awardee's education at Stanford would be totally cost free an opportunity no one could turn down.

Abe dispatched its scholarship manager, agent Sarah Wu, to Austin for a conference with Verona and her parents. She explained the purpose of her call in detail with the idea of making the scholarship so desirable Verona could not refuse to accept it.

"An anonymous sponsor, in conjunction with Stanford University, has reviewed Verona's academic achievements. In a joint effort to enroll outstanding students in the fields of mathematics and science in Stanford's program, Verona has been awarded their special scholarship. People talented in these fields are scarce, so the sponsor and Stanford feel special consideration is required to maintain an adequate number of outstanding students. The sponsor has selected Verona for this award over several other qualified candidates."

Ned was away on business, so Ms. Wu made her presentation to Clare and Verona who listened to the description of the scholarship carefully asking questions now and again as Ms. Wu detailed the many outstanding benefits of the scholarship and how it functioned. She made it crystal clear there was not another scholarship in the country which could compete with the benefits being offered to Verona.

"It is the best of the best with no close competitors."

Stated Ms. Wu who in closing turned to Verona adding.

"We do not need your answer today, but the position needs to be filled by mid-term, so we do need your response within the week. My phone number is on my card I would appreciate your giving me a call once you have made your decision."

She handed Verona her card, with her name and telephone number on the face-up side, so that Verona could not miss seeing her phone number. Verona smiled as she accepted the card, then replied.

"I am honored and appreciate being selected for your scholarship, but at this time I'm not sure I want to leave UT."

Ms. Wu glanced toward Verona incredulous at her words.

"Think it over and let me know what you decide as soon as possible. Timing is critical in filling our scholarship by the mid-term deadline."

Ms. Wu smiled as she bade her farewell, once she was gone, Verona and Clare discussed the scholarship at length reviewing its many benefits. In the end Verona asked Clare what she thought she should do.

"I think you should do what your heart tells you to do it's your life and your decision. You should do whatever you think best fits your own ambitions and aspirations. I do think you should give them your decision promptly, so they can close their scholarship before mid-term.

After all, they went to great lengths to make you the offer, so you should facilitate their filling the position."

"Thanks mom. I'll think about it overnight and give them my decision in the morning."

She gathered the scholarship material the lady had left, excused herself then went to her room to decide for herself. Clare was sure Verona would make the right decision, just as she had in the past, she was a smart girl who knew what she wanted. At breakfast the following morning, Verona announced to Clare and Angel that she had decided not to accept the scholarship to Stanford University.

"I just don't think it is right for me."

"I'm sure you thought it over carefully before making your decision, I must say I'm happy you will be nearby so we can visit often," said Clare as she kissed Verona on the cheek. Clare was pleased Verona had made this decision on her own it showed a strong tendency toward independence and self-reliance.

"It's settled then. Why don't you call the lady and give her your answer right away?"

Verona entered the number on the card into her cell phone, when another person answered, she requested to speak with the manager.

"Sarah Wu, here, to whom am I speaking?"

"This is Verona Cook, we talked about your Stanford scholarship yesterday. I'm flattered and appreciate your fantastic offer. After much consideration, I must decline, it does not fit my educational plan."

"Are you sure? Is there anything we could do to persuade you to accept?"

Ms. Wu was unprepared for a rejection and dumbfounded that anyone in their right mind would refuse to accept such an outstanding scholarship.

"I'm sorry, my decision is final, I cannot accept your scholarship offer," replied Verona.

Ms. Wu responded crisply.

"OK, Verona, I appreciate your call."

It was over, Verona would be staying at UT. Within minutes an urgent message arrived at Abe.

"Verona has unequivocally rejected our Stanford scholarship she will be staying at UT. Sorry, Sarah Wu."

Kevin read the message with dismay, his plan for transferring Verona to Stanford had failed miserably, yet he admired her for doing what she wanted. He had to fall back on and alternate plan designed to get Bruce Wilkerson to make the change. Arrangements were made immediately to switch the math and science scholarship to one at the school of medicine. This was not a problem because of the powerful people involved, Stanford was agreeable to the sudden change and was delighted the scholarship would be at their school of medicine. Ms. Wu contacted Bruce and his parents to announce Bruce has been selected to receive their medical scholarship. She made an appointment with Bruce, Peggy and Zane to discuss a special medical scholarship at Stanford which had been awarded to Bruce by the university and her patron. The many benefits and advantages provided by the scholarship as well as the outstanding medical degrees available at the university were discussed in detail. The diversity of medical degrees available intrigued Bruce as did the fact that all of them were available at Stanford without having to switch to another school for an advanced degree.

"I'm definitely interested," Bruce said following the initial presentation. Peggy and Zane participated in the discussions which followed. Peggy addressed the scholarship advocate first.

"Ms. Wu, I have a question. Will Bruce be able to transfer his first semester credits from UT to Stanford?"

"Certainly, he will receive full credit for all courses completed that is not a problem."

"I have another question too, what about housing? Will it be near the campus, so Bruce can walk to class?"

Peggy's was concern because she had heard of the nightmare housing conditions surrounding some of the larger universities. She was happy to learn the provided apartment would be adjacent to the campus within walking distance of his classes. Ms. Wu left a copy of the scholarship plan along with her card with Peggy. Ms. Wu had changed her attitude since her conference with Verona, she understood that acceptance was not a certainty. She explained to Bruce and his parents.

"He does not have to decide today, but we need an answer shortly because of the mid-term deadline. Please, call me as soon as possible."

They did not discuss the monetary ramification of the scholarship while Bruce was present, he still thought they were an upper middle class family and Peggy and Zane wanted it to remain that way for the time being. They did make it clear to Bruce that it would be his decision whether or not to accept the scholarship. Both agreed it would be good for Bruce to be more on his own and to make decisions concerning his future without overly relying on their opinions. Distance could enhance his decision making skills which made Zane and Peggy favor Bruce's accepting the scholarship. Neither of them knew Estelle existed, Bruce had never mentioned her in any of their past conversations. Bruce was excited by his good fortune, he rushed to his room so he could privately call Estelle to tell her the good news.

"Estelle, I have been awarded a full scholarship in the school of medicine at Stanford University starting at mid-term."

Bruce was expecting a positive response to his good fortune. There was a long silence before Estelle said anything.

"Then you will be leaving UT at mid-term?"

"That's one of the requirements, but I have not accepted yet. That's why I am calling, I'll be in Austin by five I'm not giving them an answer until after we talk. Can I pick you up when I get there?"

"Sure, call when you get close. See you."

Estelle was downcast at the prospect of Bruce moving to Stanford. It was an unexpected turn of events which could have a dramatic influence on her future. She had not considered the possibility that she and Bruce could be separated.

"Estelle must know how I feel about her, she is important in a much different way than other girls have been. I love Estelle and don't ever want to be without her. Maybe I should have said something earlier."

Bruce felt a chill as he turned off I-10 onto Hwy. 71, in his rush to get to Austin he had almost missed his turn preoccupied with thoughts about Estelle.

"What if Estelle doesn't feel the same way about me? I'm sure she does. I can tell by the way she likes touching me."

Convinced Estelle loved him, Bruce pressed on the accelerator to shorten the time before he could be with her. Nearing the campus, Bruce called on his cell phone arranging to pick up Estelle in ten minutes. When Bruce drove up Estelle was outside waiting for him at the curb near the dorm entrance. She was wearing shorts and a tight elastic halter. Her hair was up in a ponytail, she was the most beautiful woman Bruce had ever seen. He did not wait for her to reach the car, he jumped out rushing to meet her once face to face he put his arms around her kissing her passionately as she embraced him. She did not resist instead she kissed him back. Without speaking they quickly got into the car. Once inside, Estelle asked.

"What was that all about?"

"That was about, I love you,"

Estelle turned his face toward hers and kissed him repeatedly whispering.

"I love you too, I love you too. Where can we go to be alone, some place where no one will bother us?"

Estelle's hand was lightly touching Bruce's forearm which made him feel a little better than he did before he arrived in Austin.

"I don't know, let's drive out in the hills and look for a place. There has to be some secluded spot where we can talk without being disturbed."

Bruce started the engine, and they roared off looking for a place to be alone and undisturbed. They headed northwest and drove for half an hour until Austin was miles behind. Bruce found a cleared area on the side of a high hill far removed from a well-traveled road. It was several yards off an abandoned ranch road which had not been used in years. The air was still and even although the sun was slowly sliding below a hill to the west, it was still hot they rolled down the windows to take advantage of the slight breeze outside. The only sound to be heard was a mocking bird sitting in a mesquite tree several hundred feet away. Bruce broke the silence.

"You know, I've been in love with you from the first time we met. The better I know you the more I love you. You are beautiful and a beautiful person, Estelle, you are the most important person in the world to me."

"I am in love with you too, Bruce. You cannot imagine how much it means to me to hear you say you love me. I've wanted you since the first time I saw you down on 6th Street that's why we put out the

WANTED posters, I wanted to meet you," replied Estelle inching closer to Bruce with every word. Bruce kissed her again.

"Now that we understand each other, let's talk about this scholarship I've been offered at Stanford. I would like to accept because it would be a great opportunity for me. Stanford has an excellent medical school which offers special fields not found at other universities. I could receive the best training available in the medical profession, but there is one big problem! I'm not going without you! It's as simple as that!"

"Bruce, please, don't turn down that scholarship because of me there must be another way."

Bruce did not buy into the idea of being separated from Estelle at all.

"The way I see it, we have three choices: You can transfer to Stanford with me at mid-term, or we can get married and move to Stanford, or I can decline and we stay here. There is no way I'm going anywhere without you!"

"Did I just hear a proposal, or was that my imagination?"

"Yes you did. What I meant was, will you marry me?"

"The answer is yes I will marry you, but not now. My parents expect me to graduate before I marry anyone they insist on seeing Estelle Winger on my diploma. Let me talk to them, I think they would be OK with my transferring to Stanford at mid-term, if they don't agree, I'll tell them we are getting married. Now where were we?"

Estelle removed her halter then placed Bruce's hand on the inside of her thigh just above the knee. Bruce was sweating profusely as he removed his shirt, he began kissing Estelle enthusiastically as he moved his hand up the inside of her leg. Once he reached her shorts, they moved to the back seat leaving the doors open. In a frenzy of excitement they were soon naked, their kisses were hot as their hands moved slowly to find each other at last they were together.

It was well after midnight when they reached Estelle's dorm, walking hand in hand to the door, they kissed several times before saying good night. On his drive to his dorm Bruce felt as though a huge burden had been removed, he could still feel the warmth of her naked body against his he was elated, Estelle had said yes, they had incredible sex and they were going to Stanford together. It was a wonderful time to be alive!

Estelle's parents were in agreement with her desire to transfer to Stanford at mid-term, particularly her mother, with whom she had confided her real reason for making the change. As soon as Estelle told him her parents approved of her transferring, Bruce notified Ms. Wu that he was happy to accept the scholarship and would be making the mid-term move to Stanford.

Sarah happily reported to Abe that Bruce had accepted the scholarship. Kevin was content and very much relieved when Alpha-3 also reported Estelle had elected to transfer to Stanford at mid-term. His alternate plan had worked better than expected, they bagged a two for one both Bruce and Estelle were leaving UT meaning there would be little chance of Verona and Bruce stumbling into each other's secrets. A challenge to the program's security had probably been erased. Kevin did not celebrate until he knew Verona and Bruce had not compared notes on the Stanford scholarships. It would be a waiting game from here on, there was nothing more he could do without raising undue suspicion. He was happy that Verona remained free to pursue her own agenda without interference from Abe.

Estelle broke the news of Bruce's proposal to Verona the following morning.

"It came as a total surprise. He had called earlier in the day saying he was on his way to Austin and had something important to discuss with me. When he showed up, he kissed me and told me he loved me, then we went for a drive in the country. We were discussing an offer Bruce had received to go to another medical school at mid-term when suddenly he asked me to marry him sort of in the middle of the whole thing. As you know, I wasn't about to say no, I said yes, but only after I graduate."

"I am so happy for you Estelle. It looks like your WANTED poster did its job."

"At mid-term we are both transferring to Stanford, he wouldn't go unless I went with him. Verona, I really love this guy, he is everything I ever wanted in a man."

Estelle knew little about the scholarship, so she didn't discuss it with Verona she was more interested in talking about Bruce and how happy he had made her. He loved her.

"Then I take it you and Bruce will be leaving for good, which means I am going to have to break in a new roommate next semester. I am happy for you and Bruce. I know you will be happy together."

"Yes we will, Verona, thanks to your help."

"Honestly, Estelle I'll never find another roommate like you. It has been a pleasure and a learning experience for me no one could replace you. I love you both and wish you happiness in your new adventure I'm pleased to have played a small part in getting you two together. You said that, love and sex go together and that they both had better be good, how do you know about the sex part?"

Estelle blushed slightly then laughed.

"After he proposed, I seduced him in the back seat of his car. It was great even under those conditions with a little training he's going to be fantastic."

Estelle laughed again before becoming more serious.

"Verona, my only regret is that we have not found Mr. Right for you. I know it will happen, some day you will get the same feeling I did when I saw Bruce. It was love at first sight, so to speak, now that I know him he is what I always wanted. We belong together."

"Please give Bruce my congratulations and warmest regards, you know how I feel about both of you."

Estelle and Verona had enjoyed each other very much they had developed a special relationship during their short, but close friendship. Leaving Verona was the one thing Estelle hated about her impending move to Stanford, but her happiness with Bruce overshadowed everything else. She and Verona were determined to stay in touch no matter what happened they planned to remain lifelong friends.

Chapter 11 a Love Affair at the Tmex

Alan accepted a full scholarship at Rice University in the field of Computational and Applied Mathematics at the George R. Brown School of Engineering. Even though the scholarship was for only four years, he had his sights set on earning a PhD in his chosen field. Betty elected to attend Baylor Law School concentrating on Business Litigation she had been awarded a full scholarship which persuaded her to remain in Waco rather than seeking a law degree in Houston or Austin.

The night before Alan was scheduled to leave for Houston, he and Betty dated for the last time before their separation, they made love in a local motel most of the evening ending with both of them near tears as they dressed to leave.

"I don't know how I am going to get along without you, Alan, you are my life. I love you so much I don't want to be without you ever," said Betty kissing him passionately.

"I love you too, Betty. We were predestined to be together eternally. I hate having to leave, but we can still be together. I will come home as often as I can and you can come to Houston when you get a chance. We can still be together even though we are apart."

"I'm so glad you said that Alan, I'm already planning our next date."

She took him in her arms kissing him tenderly as she held him tight she wanted to keep him with her tomorrow and forever.

Alan and Jim had met earlier in the day under their favorite oak tree the site where most of their collaborations in mischief and science exploration had originated. They were both enthusiastic about moving on to college with great scholarships at outstanding universities, yet they disliked having to go their separate ways to take advantage of the scholarships they had been granted. Jim had accepted a full scholarship at Harvard meaning they would not be together other than during the holidays and summer break. In the meanwhile each of them would be following their dream preparing for a career and a life of achievement in the field of science.

"You know, Alan, we probably could learn just as much, staying here and doing our thing, as we will studying at a university unfortunately we can't give each other degrees. I've been thinking about all the studies and projects we devised and completed on our own."

"I think you're right, Jim. The one project that I remember the most, outside of the hacking incident, is when we did the geological study and presented a copy of our report to the County Agent. Remember, he insisted we sign it. That was a great feeling we had accidentally done something useful without thinking about it before we conducted the study. It made me want to have a purpose, other than just learning something new, in doing projects later on."

"I have to agree there has to be a purpose other than learning, knowledge unused, is not of much benefit to anyone is it?"

They vowed to call one another at least once a week in order to keep up with what the other one was doing and thinking. "See you at Christmas," they said together as they left their oak tree and headed for home. It was their last face-to-face meeting before Christmas break four months later. The two of them stayed in touch through emails and conversations on their cell phones, but it was not like sitting and talking under their favorite oak tree.

Alan and Betty discovered that attending different schools was not nearly as bad as they had anticipated they were able to get together several times before the Thanksgiving break. One of Alan's friends regularly made trips home to Waco on the weekends which proved to be fortunate for Alan he arranged to ride with him the day before Thanksgiving. He and Betty spent most of the weekend with their parents and to their utter dismay were unable to arrange any quality time to themselves. Much to Betty's distress, Alan was forced to return to Rice without their anticipated date being fulfilled she was downcast following his departure. Seeing how distraught and upset Betty became without having some time alone with Alan, Betty's mother came to her room that evening to comfort and console her.

"My dear, Betty, I know how much you were planning on having some free time to be with Alan this weekend and I know how upset you must be that it didn't happen. I tried very hard, but things just didn't work out that way as much as I tried. So, my love, here is what we are going to do. Next weekend, I am arranging for you to stay at the Tmex Hotel in Houston, so you and Alan can have some private time together. You can drive down on Friday after class and return Sunday afternoon. How does that sound to you?"

"Oh, momma would you do that for me? I will love you forever if you do."

"Dear one, I know how you feel about Alan and I know you need to be with him, I've not always been an old woman you know." Replied her mother who understood Betty's strong desires and feelings having been there herself more than once. Betty couldn't wait, she called Alan as soon as her mother left the room.

"Alan, I will be coming to Houston next Friday after my last class and will be staying at the Tmex Hotel until Sunday. We can have our date then."

Betty was disappointed she and Alan had not been able to get together alone while he was at home, but she would wait forever to be with Alan. They met at the Tmex the following Friday and did not leave the hotel room, other than to eat, until Sunday morning. Driving home Sunday afternoon Betty was extremely happy she hummed her favorite song all the way back to Waco. Betty's mother, who was a bit anxious to see her daughter, met her as she opened the door from the garage to the kitchen they hugged before Betty said modestly.

"Thank you, mamma thank you."

"I'm glad I could help, love," replied her mother as they smiled knowingly to each other before proceeding to Betty's room to unpack her suitcase. Betty's mother insisted that it would be appropriate for Betty and Alan to meet at the Tmex every other weekend provided neither was unavoidably committed elsewhere. Alan was overjoyed when Betty told him what her mother was doing, he had always liked her, but now he loved her for making their dates possible. On their third date at the Tmex, they found time to leave the hotel, Alan proudly showed Betty around Houston and Rice University. No one had ever experienced happiness more than Betty and Alan during their stays at the Tmex on these dates they lived in their own world being together was a natural consequence of being in love.

Alan and Betty became well known to the Tmex staff who had noticed them on their first stay at the hotel by the time they reached their senior years at college they were treated like family by everyone at the hotel including the management. Often times, they were awarded the bridal suite at regular rates, when it was not booked for the weekend, a reward from the Tmex management for their continued patronage and their

269

obvious love for each other. Alan and Betty became a fixture at the Tmex impressing all of those who came in contact with them. They treated everyone there as friends, they never complained and regularly stopped to chat with the employees. It was common knowledge among those at the Tmex that Alan and Betty planned to marry upon graduation in the spring and intended to make their home in Houston at least temporarily. When discussing Betty and Alan's relationship among themselves those working at the Tmex coined the phrase, "a love affair at the Tmex." Some of the hotel's regular clients were also aware of Alan and Betty and they too used the phrase when referring to them. They marveled at the young couple's devotion, charm and happiness and often talked in the bar about how happy Alan and Betty were during their weekend sojourns.

The agents at Alpha-2, who followed Betty's and Alan's romance from its inception, were fascinated that a love and sexual experimentation between two kids had not only survived it had grown in intensity and scope as time passed. What had started as an eighth grade infatuation was now an adult love affair on the doorstep of marriage. Alpha-2 had also adopted "a love affair at the Tmex" as their code name when reporting Alan's and Betty's weekend movements to their superiors at Abe. At first it was a joke which, with the passage of time, came to mean a dynamic lasting love affair of gigantic proportions. Everyone at Abe embraced the code name linking it to a true life love story for the ages.

Frank, the head of Abe, and Jerry, the leader of ADAM, were scheduled to meet informally to evaluate the overall progress of the Gentex program. Since Jerry called the meeting, he proposed one of his favorite places as the meeting site, which happen to be the bar at the Tmex Hotel. They met in the hotel lobby then proceeded to a secluded table in the corner of the bar before ordering drinks. Frank indicated Jerry should order for both of them since he seemed to be well known to the bartender. Jerry ordered two glass of Irish whiskey specifying his favorite brand which had a distinct robust taste that he preferred over other brands. Jerry had acquired a taste for the drink following his negotiations with the Crazy Bastards. Even though he met only one person in the organization, Joe their chief negotiator, Jerry became aware that the Crazy Bastard's, Number One, favored good Irish whiskey prompting him to try some himself. As a result he found Irish whisky to be a superb beverage which suited his taste, he had been drinking it ever since.

They raised their glasses in a toast.

"Here is to George Angleton, who made it all possible."

They discussed George at length before taking up the subject of progress in the Gentex program. Frank ordered another round of drinks then turned to Jerry as their drinks arrived.

"Jerry, there is something else we should be toasting tonight, here is to twenty one successful years of ADAM without a single breach of secrecy or security."

Jerry raised his glass replying.

"Aye, Aye. Do you realize why I chose the Tmex as our meeting place?"

"No, I just thought you liked the place. Does it have some special significance?"

"Think about it Frank, this place has played a prominent role in our most outstanding successes. Rachel and Phil spent their first night together here, Zane and Peggy's love affair started here, his escape from the Crazy Bastards was conceived here, a key part of our saving Martha from Mohammad al Sultan originated here and now we have Alan and Betty known by all of us as, a love affair at the Tmex. I don't know what there is about this place, but it obviously has some uncanny attraction for those people involved in the Gentex program. It is amazing that we have not lost any of our key players, the Gentex mothers have done well, none of George's children have strayed far from the path of personal independence and they all have a high regard for hard work and achievement in their chosen fields. George would be pleased if he could see the results of his program to date."

After the first year of their love affair at the Tmex, Alan and Betty spent more and more time away from the hotel, as their meetings became routine, they went to the theater and attended social events with Alan's classmates at Rice. On several occasions Betty agreed to attend football games at Rice Stadium with Alan although she was an ardent Baylor Bears fan who had little interest in the Rice football program. Nearing the end of their senior years in college, they were having dinner at the Tmex discussing their plans after graduation.

"You know, Alan, after we are married and I get my law license you can finish your PhD. Then we will have to decide where we want to live, here or somewhere else."

"I've already thought about that a little. What do you think about living in Austin? It's a beautiful place with lots of tech opportunities it's not too big and there will be some excellent public schools for our children."

Betty leaned forward kissing Alan on the cheek.

"That shows how well we are together, love. Austin would have been my first choice too."

Lifting her water glass she toasted.

"Here's to Austin, Betty and Alan."

Alan laughed raising his glass to touch hers.

"Here's to Austin and us."

They were still laughing when Alan squeezed her hand gently.

"Then it's agreed. Austin get ready, here we come."

Betty appreciated Alan's comment about the public schools she planned to start a family right away once they were married. She perceived that their children would be brilliant, with Alan as their father, it just couldn't be any other way. Good schools are essential for properly developing their children's intellect and the Austin area provided many outstanding opportunities.

Betty received her diploma from Baylor with Alan scheduled to graduate from Rice the following week after that they planned to marry in a quiet family ceremony in Waco. In the interim period, Alan had been looking at available apartments in the vicinity of the Rice campus while Betty remained in Waco with her family. She and Alan, along with their families, had finalized plans for the wedding which would take place in two weeks, thereafter they would be united permanently as husband and wife.

Alan found a suitable apartment near the Rice campus, one they could afford that had room for him to have a study area. He was in the process of paying the first and last month's rent before signing a lease when he received an urgent call on his cell phone from Darlene.

"Alan, come home as quick as possible, something terrible has happened."

"Mother, calm down, what happened."

"Betty has been in a horrible car accident her condition is critical."

"What hospital, what hospital mom?"

"Hillcrest Baptist Medical Center, hurry son."

When his cell-phone went quiet, the pen fell from Alan's fingers, he left his two month's deposit laying on the desk as he rushed to his car. He filled up with gasoline at the nearest station and once clear of the Houston freeway congestion he drove at top speed nonstop to the hospital in Waco. The nurse at the visitor's desk provided him with Betty's floor and room number in the intensive care unit. Alan ran into the elevator and entered the third floor on the menu, when the elevator door opened, he rushed into the hallway looking around frantically for someone to direct him. Alan was trembling with fear as he approached the nurse's desk. Upon hearing his name, the head nurse took Allan directly to Betty's room where he was met by her mother and father.

Betty's mother hugged Alan and between tears uttered.

"Alan, I always knew you two were perfect for each other, I was looking forward to being a grandmother, but now."

She paused then said, "Alfred and I will be in the waiting area, you need some time alone with Betty."

She and her husband stepped outside of the room and walked solemnly to the waiting area, their dreams shattered. Betty was gasping for air as Alan sat down on the edge of her bed he began stroking her hair slowly. She suddenly opened her eyes then whispered, "Alan, kiss me." He kissed her gently on the lips, then barely audible she said.

"Alan, I waited for you this time, promise me you will find happiness without me."

The moment the words passed her lips her body went limp, she passed from this world to another and was gone. Alan was shaken, yet had the presence of mind to call the nurse who quickly returned with Betty's parents. They found Alan holding Betty in his arms sobbing.

"No, no, no."

Betty's mother, who was also crying, persuaded Allan to release Betty on to the hospital bed she then turned him away from Betty's lifeless body hugging him.

"Allan she loved you so much, even now, she would want you to find happiness without her in your life. We both loved you Alan. I feel the same way, you must find happiness for all three of us."

Darlene and the Professor arrived only minutes after Betty died, just in time to comfort Alan, who was still sobbing quietly standing outside of Betty's hospital room. An overwhelming feeling of dejection and grief engulfed his entire being he was devastated by Betty's death the love of his life had slipped away for all time and there was nothing he could do about it.

Alan did not learn the details about the accident until after the funeral. A young mother of two was driving in the opposing lane of a two way street and while approaching Betty, she pulled across the center line into Betty's lane. Betty swerved to avoid smashing head on into the oncoming car, in the process, she hit an abutment before she could regain control of her automobile. The resulting crash left her and her car mangled she had suffered multiple internal injuries with no chance of survival. The young mother, responsible for the accident, had been texting a friend using her cell phone, neither she, nor her two children who were buckled in the back seat were harmed. The police gave the mother a ticket for reckless driving citing her as the cause of the accident. Alan was grief stricken over Betty's untimely death and after hearing the details of the accident remarked.

"I'm glad no one else was killed, one stupid mistake has taken Betty away from me! Our future together has been destroyed. How could a mother be so unthinking with her kids in the car? Betty did a brave unselfish thing, she saved them. Horribly, she did not survive to see the results of her actions. I'll never forget her and I hope that young mother never forgets what Betty did for her and her kids."

That was Alan's only comment about the accident he refused to discuss it again. After the funeral, Alan returned to Houston his plans for the future in complete disarray. He decided to complete the pending lease on the apartment partly because he didn't want to return Waco and partly because he needed a place to be alone to reconsider his future in a life without Betty. He graduated from Rice as originally planned, but decided not to pursue an advanced degree starting in the fall.

After spending a brief time searching, Alan landed a job with a tech start-up company located not far from Rice University. SeiRes, a seismic research company, funded by several large oil and gas companies was unusual, the company was free to develop any program or product it pleased so long as it related to the general field of obtaining, processing and interpreting seismic data. Terms of the development and funding agreement required SeiRes to offer exclusive and free use of any product, program or other development from its efforts to the sponsors for a period of one year before licensing or selling it to their competitors. SeiRes retained a 50% ownership in all products developed which was a strong incentive for the company and its owners. Future licensing had the potential to produce an enormous income for the company once the one year exclusive use period ended.

Alpha-2 reported to Abe following Alan's return to Houston.

"With a heavy heart we report the death of, Betty, who was killed in a car accident in Waco. This is the end of her, but not their love story. A love affair at the Tmex has come to a sad and tragic climax, but no end. It will live on in the memory of all of us who witnessed the incredible love story between Alan and Betty. Alan seems to be holding up reasonably well under the circumstances. He stayed in Houston after her death, but dropped out of Rice after getting his BS degree. He has taken a job with SeiRes, a local seismic research company, located near the Rice campus. We have intensified our surveillance of Alan, since Betty's death, just in case. What do we know about SeiRes?"

Alan had worked at SeiRes for slightly under a year when he received an urgent phone call from his longtime friend, Jim Running Horse.

Chapter 12 Mr. Right

Verona had a new roommate, Amanda Clark, who was a short slightly plump blond girl from Oklahoma. Her father, a rich and highly successful businessman, had earned a master's degree in Business Management from UT. Once his fortune had been established in the manufacturing and sale of horizontal drilling equipment, he purchased a home in the exclusive Nichols Hills section of Oklahoma City. But being a loyal Longhorn, he insisted that his only child attend his *alma mater* as well. According to Amanda's father there was no University on earth that compared favorably with UT. Amanda Clark, a direct opposite of Estelle, was quiet, soft-spoken and seldom discussed her personal feelings. She avoided mentioning love, sex, or men they seemed to be foreign to her world and missing from her vocabulary. In the beginning, Verona did not know what to make of Amanda they were so different it seemed they had nothing in common other than being female students in their first year at UT.

Little by little Amanda began to reveal some of her background to Verona. At home her father controlled everything about her life including what she did and what she was allowed to think. She didn't have the option to express her own opinions, or to do things on her own while she lived at home. She felt she had been in her father's shadow for so long she might not know how to manage her life now that the shadow had suddenly been lifted. Amanda was having difficulty grasping her current circumstances, she was free to make her own decisions and to say what she thought there was no one telling her what to do or think. After being roommates with Verona for a couple of weeks, Amanda came to admire Verona's ability to organize her time and to make her own decisions. Impressed with Verona's abilities, Amanda began discussing the details of her problems with Verona ultimately enlisting her help in changing things to the way she wanted them to be. Verona proved to be a good listener, after hearing about Amanda's life at home, she understood the anguish Amanda's father's actions had caused. She also was aware that cloaked by her demure outer appearance Amanda had a strong will to be her own person. With Verona's encouragement, things began to change, Amanda blossomed into a beautiful and determined individual. She confided in Verona telling her things she had never dared mention to anyone before. She wanted desperately for Verona to understand what she really wanted to be. During one of their many evening dialogues, Verona inquired.

"Amanda, have you ever had a boyfriend?"

"Good heavens no, Verona, I've never even had a date."

"Really, why not? Don't you like guys?"

"Well, Yes, but that is not the problem."

Verona was appalled that Amanda had never had a date she was slightly plump, yet not unattractive. Amanda did not hold back she felt it was necessary for Verona to understand her circumstances completely if she was going to be able to help her.

"In the first place, no one ever asked me for a date, I did not seem to be attractive to the boys I knew. They hardly talked to me outside of the classroom. It was sort of like I wasn't there, they ignored me completely and it was the same way with the girls none of them wanted to be close friends with me either. I've always been the invisible person, if you know what I mean."

"Is that what you want to be, invisible?" asked Verona still wondering how this could have happened to a nice person like Amanda.

"No, I hate being invisible, I like people and I'm determined to be myself from now on. I am going to step out of the shadows into the sunlight and I'm going to count. That's what I want, I'm tired of being ignored."

Verona was sure that Amanda meant every word she said, she could see determination in her eyes and hear conviction in her voice, all she needed was a little guidance to reach her goal. To Verona, it was amazing how this young woman, who would barely engage in a conversation a few weeks earlier, had come out of her shell fiercely determined to change whatever necessary to become who she wanted to be. Verona dedicated herself and her abilities to helping Amanda in any way she could, with her help and Amanda's tenacity, Amanda was going to become whoever or whatever she decided to be.

"I can see why the guys like you, Verona, you are so beautiful and have a great body which I'm sure they all like. Me, I'm just a plain Jane that no one notices."

"That's the first thing we are going to work on Amanda. With your approval, we are going to make your natural beauty apparent to

277

everyone, starting tonight, you are going on a low carbohydrate diet to lose a little weight. That doesn't mean you have to starve, just don't eat any white carbohydrates, such as bread or pasta and give up sugary foods. You can eat all you want and still lose weight."

"Thank you, Verona. I'm ready to get started. What else do I need to do?"

"Let's enroll you in a physical fitness program to assist in losing weight and firm up your body it will also enhance your figure. Starting tomorrow, we are getting you a new hair style designed to highlight your special features, such as your big brown eyes, you don't realize how attractive you really are tomorrow you can see for yourself."

Amanda was delighted Verona volunteered to help in her makeover, she was in agreement with all of Verona's suggestions, without them, she didn't know where to begin. Amanda's last words before retiring to her room were.

"You will see that I'm dead serious about becoming me. Verona, you will not be disappointed. See you in the morning I am ready to get started."

Verona was ready to begin too, helping Amanda had become her first priority outside of her school work she was committed to helping Amanda become herself which was going to be an interesting challenge. Verona had never had a problem being who or what she wanted to be, her parents were kind and approving and had encouraged her to be her own person since early childhood. She was expected to make her own decisions from an early age. Not so with her new friend Amanda whether intentionally or unintentionally her father had overwhelmed her with his oppressive attitude and personality.

The next afternoon at the beauty salon, Amanda took a deep breath when she looked in the mirror, she could not believe the person looking back was really her. Her stringy long blond hair was gone in its place she saw beautiful silky blond hair cut just below her ear lobes and pulled behind her ear on both sides to accentuate her brown eyes and facial features. She had on makeup, modest red lipstick eyeliner and a tinge of blue eye shadow she was attractive and tantalizingly interesting nothing at all like the Amanda who walked into the salon earlier in the day. The change had been remarkable and dramatic catching Amanda completely by surprise.

"Verona, can that really be me?"

"What do you think, are you beautiful or what?" asked Verona very pleased with the two hour transformation that had taken place at the salon.

"Oh, Verona, I never dreamed I could look like this. Is it really me?"

"It's you, if you want it to be. If not, we can try something else there are a lot of options."

"Thank you so much, Verona, and yes it's what I want to be that's the real me," said Amanda turning her head from side to side to get a better view in the mirror. On the ride back to the dorm, Amanda displayed a newly invigorated personality she talked on and on about how the makeup made her eyes stand out and how it made her look sexy a word she had not mentioned before in any of their previous conversations.

"Do you want to look sexy?"

"Yes, what girl doesn't? It's the new me, I never thought I could be sexy. Being unsexy was never what I wanted it was just how I looked to other people."

"With the workout program and your new diet you will be one of the sexiest and most attractive young women on campus within a couple of months or so. Since you are going to be super sexy, I need to ask. What do you know about sex?"

"Not much, I've never had sex or even considered it. My knowledge on the subject is limited to what I have read, what my mother taught me and a few tidbits I overheard in high school."

"Then you have a lot of catching up to do before the boys start calling. Love and sex go together and they had better both be good, according to my mother and my former roommate. I feel the same way and from experience, I strongly suggest you remember what I am about to say the first time you have an overwhelming desire to jump in bed with some guy. Fix this thought in your mind it is vitally important for your future. Love and sex go together and one without the other is not a good idea."

Verona expanded on the sex topic.

"Ask me any questions you like about sex, if I know the answer, I will be happy to tell you. If all else fails we can always call my mother."

Verona had been appalled at Amanda's previous statement that she knew nothing at all about having sex. They were going to start an accelerated program to catch Amanda up in preparation for her upcoming popularity with the guys. Under Verona's watchful eye and strict adherence to the diet and workout program, Amanda lost weight and her body began showing promise of things to come. She was getting second looks from some of the male students in her classes they noticed her new hair style as they did her body in progress. Interestingly, her rear was getting a lot of attention it no longer wobbled when she walked, instead it had a slight perky side to side up and down motion which was very disturbing and stimulating to her male classmates.

Amazingly, Verona noticed Amanda interacting with all sorts of new acquaintances, earlier she had been reluctant to talk to anyone she didn't know, now she was engaging strangers in her conversations. Amanda began participating in group and one-on-one conversations with confidence expressing her opinions freely, and more often than not, becoming the center of attention as other people became engrossed in her ideas. People listened to what Amanda had to say and enjoyed being with her she had developed a sense of humor and laughed a lot. Verona found Amanda's joking and laughter to be exhilarating a sure sign her true personality had taken over. Amanda's resurrection was complete, the shy reclusive girl Verona had met weeks earlier no longer existed. Verona was happy with her small contribution toward Amanda's remarkable reappearance in spite of her years of suppression. It was obvious to Verona that Amanda was going to find her own happiness at last and she was not going to allow anyone to alter her course regardless of the consequences. Verona took great pride in Amanda's progress, but in reviewing her own situation she realized she was no nearer to meeting her own Mr. Right than she was when Estelle moved to California. She was still looking, but there was no one in sight.

Alpha-1 reported to Abe.

"All is well with Verona she has been spending most of her free time working with her roommate Amanda, who has completely redone her looks, lost fifteen pounds and is well on her way to becoming a glamorous little blond."

The message had been received by Albert Gross, Kevin Goodhall's replacement, who had been assigned to review all things involving Verona. Upon the successful completion of Kevin's plan to separate Verona and Bruce, he had suddenly and without provocation, resigned his position at Abe. Kevin's resignation came as a complete surprise to Abe's managers and to Frank in particular, who considered him one of the best young agents at Abe one destined to move up rapidly in the organization. Before Kevin's departure, Frank made a point of the vow of secrecy he had made when he accepted his employment with Abe and the consequences should that vow be broken. Kevin thanked Frank for the opportunity he had been provided at Abe adding.

"I assure you that my vow of secrecy will go to my death bed unbroken. I am also well aware of the repercussions. I would never be able to work again or have a career of any kind should I break the secrecy covenant."

Frank liked the young man and his attitude he wished him well as they parted.

"Kevin, I am sure you will do well in your new endeavor whatever it is. Keep in touch. Should you ever need my assistance you know where to reach me."

Frank was confident Kevin Goodhall would succeed in whatever he undertook in life, but for now his plan for Kevin would have be put on hold until it could be revised to meet the challenge of the new unexpected circumstances presented by his resignation. Frank had no intention of allowing Kevin's departure to alter his overall plan.

The following month, Kevin and Verona met accidentally during the rush between classes at UT, Kevin bumped into her spilling her papers and notebook all over the sidewalk. He gathered her material into a neat stack before handing it to her while apologizing profusely.

"I'm so sorry, it's all my fault. I wasn't paying attention. If I had been, I definitely would have noticed you. My name is Kevin Goodhall, I'm a graduate student working on my PhD. I am new on campus, I came in at mid-term."

"Thank you, my name is Verona. What shall I call you, Mister Goodhall?"

"Please call me Kevin, I wouldn't answer to Mister I'm too young for that. Look, it's too late to make my next class. Why don't you allow me to buy you a cup of coffee to make amends for spilling your homework and books?"

Verona liked the ease with which Kevin talked to her, even though they were total strangers, she also liked his looks he wasn't handsome, yet he was good looking and several inches taller than her which Verona considered essential for a man to be a person of interest.

"Sure, Kevin. I would be delighted to have coffee with you."

They chatted about their studies at UT while they walked to the coffee house which was located up the street a short distance away. After waiting a few minutes for a table, they seated themselves near a window looking out onto the sidewalk in front of the coffee shop, from this vantage point they could watch the people passing by outside.

"What would you like, Verona?"

"I'm having whatever you are, Kevin. Surprise me."

Verona watched as he walked toward the counter he had a decisive step and a measured tempo to his stride creating an interesting view from the rear. In a few minutes, Kevin returned with two cups of special cappuccino one of which he placed directly in front of Verona with a flourish. She looked at Kevin, astonished at his selection, her eyes opened wide when she spoke.

"You are amazing, Kevin. Their special cappuccino is my favorite, thank you for ordering it."

Verona touched him lightly on the back of his hand not consciously knowing she had done so.

"How did you know it was my favorite?"

"I didn't, it just seemed to be a good idea. I like their special cappuccino myself."

They sat sipping their coffee and enjoying each's company for several minutes before Verona pointed to the window.

"See all of those people walking past? They all have dreams and aspirations, they all want to do something, to be something, yet we'll never know about them because we will never get to know those people or their dreams. Odd isn't it? To think of all the dreams passing by out there."

"What do you want to be Verona, is there something special that interests you?"

"I like math and science, I originally planned to make a career in those fields, but strange as it may sound several things have happened recently that make me wonder. Somehow, I seem to have a knack for helping other people to realize their dreams by giving them a helping hand it is a talent that has caused me to be a bit confused about what I really want to do at this point."

"Do whatever makes you happy is what my dad always said. His favorite paraphrase was: Every day a person spends being unhappy is a day of their life wasted."

"Your dad had some good ideas. What do you want to be Kevin?"

"What I want most of all is to marry the woman I love and for us to love each other and enjoy our life while we raise our family together."

"What about a career, how does that fit in?"

"A career is important in only a small way, loving the right person is happiness itself, without that a career is insignificant. A life without love is also insignificant, love trumps all."

"An interesting observation, you sound like my mother who is a very special person and I might add an expert on achieving happiness. Do you have a steady girlfriend? I mean, have you met the woman you just spoke of?"

"I am working on it," replied Kevin his blue eyes flashing as he looked at Verona.

They finished their coffee agreeing to meet at the coffee house the next day following Verona's last class. Outside they stood face to face looking into each other's eyes briefly, the moment vanished before either spoke and they parted after saying their goodbyes. Kevin took a few steps before he turned and waved to Verona then continued on his way. He whistled as he walked across campus toward the parking lot all the while in his mind he was analyzing his meeting with Verona.

"Objective accomplished. Contact has been made and Verona obviously enjoyed my company. As Frank would say, a job well done, Kevin."

When Amanda returned to their dorm, Verona could hardly wait to tell her about her chance meeting with Kevin it had been an interesting day exciting in a way much different from every day before.

"He didn't make me tingle all over, nor did he particularly attract me at first. Amanda, the longer we talked the better I felt. It's hard to explain, I couldn't make myself stop touching him on the hand or arm nothing sexual you understand. Well maybe, I almost kissed him as we were leaving the coffee house. It was probably just an impulse he was such a nice guy I thought he deserved it."

"It sounds to me like you felt more for him than you are telling me. Could this be Mr. Right?"

"Thinking about it, Amanda, this is the first guy I've been around in a long time that has interested me. I did almost kiss him, now I wish I had, it might have really turned me on. We are meeting for coffee again tomorrow maybe things will be different, who knows what may happen."

Verona changed the subject inquiring about Amanda's day. Not unexpected on Verona's part, Amanda had noticed a growing interest from some of the guys in her classes, none of them had asked for a date yet even though they were making it a point to stand next to her in line, so they could talk with her. One guy even asked whether she liked western music. Amanda was about to go shopping for a new wardrobe, with the weight loss she had achieved, her clothes no longer fit properly and they didn't match her new life style.

"Verona, I really need your advice before selecting a motif for a new wardrobe. Since I am so small, should I go girly, or should I try to look a little older maybe buy mixed? One thing for sure, I need to be bold and sexy without being an exhibitionist. I would like something to match my new me, something to set me apart from the other girls I know."

"Let's see what we can come up with, tomorrow we will go shopping to select clothes to fit your new body and new persona."

The two of them went on a shopping spree with Amanda's credit cards making purchases at several of the upscale shops near the UT campus. One of Amanda's favorite purchases came from the girly collection the outfit matched her new personality perfectly. It featured a short white, blue and pink skirt with a white ruffle along the bottom in combination with a light pink top which showed modest cleavage accentuating her bosoms, which were large for such a petite figure. When she walked the vision was maddening from both the front and the rear. Wearing her new combo, she was sure to ignite the imagination of males, especially young males. Amanda's special purchase was not meant to be worn to school rather it was meant for special occasions when the objective was to attract the opposite sex. Amanda was devastatingly sexy wearing her new attire her figure had become a thing of beauty rivalling the finest on campus and matched her new clothes perfectly. Her face had thinned slightly making her big brown eyes even more attractive, seemingly overnight, she had become an attractive and alluring little blond who had many admirers among her fellow students.

Methodically looking her over from top to bottom, Verona felt Amanda was about to make her debut on the stage of romance, she needed to prepare Amanda for the next big step. Her greatest concern was Amanda's unpreparedness to handle her upcoming popularity with boys. After all, she had never had a date, she might go crazy wild with all of the sudden attention that would surely be coming her way. Verona invited Amanda to spend the weekend with her family, so she could benefit from the best counsel in the world her mom, Clare.

Amanda enjoyed the weekend with Verona and her family she was astounded by how supportive they were of one another and how open their conversations were, it was completely different from the way her family operated. She learned a lot about how to handle popularity and sex in her discussions with Clare and Verona. One of Clare's comments got Amanda's attention, although she had never given the subject any thought it made sense.

"Popularity should be used as a selection tool, if there are many guys available then you have the option of selecting the one that best suits you."

Verona and Clare discussed the sex issue at length with Amanda stressing the need for self-control and good decision making. Clare emphasized that there were requisites for handling sex in an appropriate way.

"No matter how compelling your desire to have sex with some guy, you must think about the consequences. If there is no love involved, then you probably shouldn't do it. The rules are simple, the decision is up to you. Remember, you have to maintain total control in these situations because guys do not always think clearly once they are sexually aroused!"

Following their discussions, Amanda felt a lot more confident about her ability to handle any future challenges involving men, sex and love.

Alpha-1 had earlier reported to Abe.

"Today, Verona had coffee with a new fellow named Kevin Goodhall who registered at UT during the mid-term. He is a graduate student in math and science working toward a PhD. They accidentally met and seem to have become friends, maybe more."

Frank read the message twice then thought to himself.

"In a pig's ass, they met by accident. Kevin has always been clever and bright he purposely staged that meeting. He knows more about Verona than any living person, now it's apparent to me that he is attracted to her. That's why he quit, he wanted to be near her. Hell, I don't know, he may be in love with her. One thing for sure, he's got balls. He knows damn well we are watching her every move and will be watching everything they do together. We'll see, I always thought he was a perfect match for Verona. I never thought about him making this move on his own even though it was obvious he liked Verona. He had better treat her right or I will go to Austin and kick his ass myself, but he already knows that. If nothing else it's going to be intriguing. My plan is working out after all, but it seems Kevin also has a plan of his own."

Frank leaned back in his chair, looked at the ceiling and chuckled to himself saying out loud.

"What plan?"

He then returned to his regular routine systematically checking the latest messages from the other Alpha groups. Frank checked the reports in detail looking for some buried bit of information that might be significant to Abe's operation.

Just as Verona entered their dorm, Amanda grasped her by the hand frantically exclaiming.

"Something fantastic happened today! One of my favorite classmates asked me for a date this Saturday he wants to take me to a roadhouse for dinner and dancing."

"Really? What was your answer?"

"I told him I would go on one condition that we made it a double date."

"Did he agree?"

"Yes, and that's where you come in, I will not go unless you and Kevin join us. I need you along to sort of chaperone. What is a roadhouse anyway?"

"I appreciate where you are coming from, Amanda, support is reassuring, but Kevin and I are not dating we just meet for coffee sometimes. We are merely friends he has never even hinted he would like to go out on a date. Besides, I don't know whether he has an interest in dancing or not. What do you want me to do? Ask him for a date to go a roadhouse for dinner and dancing on Saturday?"

"Please, Verona I need you to be there!"

Verona was a little frustrated at first, but after thinking about Amanda's dilemma and her own relationship with Kevin, she decided this was a good opportunity to determine the extent of Kevin's interest. She called Kevin straight away using her cell phone.

"Kevin, this is Verona. Something has come up for this Saturday. My roommate has accepted a date to go dining and dancing at a roadhouse on the condition that I go with them and bring along a date. Would you be interested? If not, I will have to find someone else."

"No, no, please, don't do that. I will be happy to be your date. Who knows, I may sweep you off your feet. Seriously, Verona, I am honored you thought of me, nothing would make me happier than a date with you. I'm looking forward to Saturday."

Turning to Amanda, Verona smiled then winked her eye.

"Call your date, Kevin has agreed to go with us Saturday, the double date is on."

Verona was thrilled with Kevin's response he had made his feelings clear he did not want her to find another date his choice of words in accepting caused a sudden and unexpected rush Verona had not expected. She was visibly flushed to the point Amanda asked.

"Are you feeling ill or something?"

"I have never been better, I think Saturday is going to be a very exciting and telling evening for both of us."

Robert, Amanda's date, drove the four of them to the renown Western Roadhouse located some twenty miles northwest of downtown Austin. They arrived in time for an early dinner of steak and French fries in the dining room before the band showed up. Each of them sipped a frozen *margarita* during dinner before moving to their reserved table in the dance hall proper. The Western band started playing exactly on time shortly after Amanda's group were seated at their table. Nearly all the tables around the dance floor were occupied by young people from UT and the surrounding area who favored the Western band and its music. They played every kind of Texas music including some of the local German and Hispanic dances which were favorites among those patrons who grew up in central and south Texas. Verona and Kevin were the first to take the floor dancing to a slow Texas two-step, Kevin was careful to hold Verona at arm's length with his left hand held high as they eased around the edge of the dance floor. When the music ended, they returned to the table to check on Amanda and Robert.

"Aren't you dancing?" asked Kevin looking first at Robert and then directly at Amanda. Neither responded causing Verona to act quickly she took Robert by the hand leading him to the center of the dance floor where they stood stiffly until the music began. She put her head on his shoulder while they danced to a bit of western swing, Robert proved to be a good dancer who led easily anticipating her response to the music. As they were nearing their table after the dance ended Verona whispered.

"I think you should ask Amanda to have the next dance, don't you?"

Robert followed Verona's suggestion holding his hand out to Amanda for the next dance as they neared their table. Kevin and Verona watched Amanda and Robert as they approached one another before commencing their first dance together soon they looked like all the rest of the young people on the dance floor.

"Aren't they beautiful, Kevin? I think this is the first time Amanda has ever danced with a boy on a date."

"Yes, they are beautiful and they dance well together, but you are even more beautiful. Would you please, honor me with this dance?"

During their second dance Kevin made certain their bodies touched he held Verona close to him with his arm firmly around her waist and her head resting on his shoulder. The fragrance of her perfume was maddening, which combined with their bodies touching, made Kevin's pulse race wildly. He could feel the warmth of Verona's body against him exciting him even more as the danced ended. Verona started toward the table, but Kevin did not let go of her hand instead he implored.

"Let's not stop, let's keep dancing."

"An excellent idea. Did you notice that Amanda and Robert didn't return to the table either?"

"No, for some reason I was preoccupied and didn't notice."

Verona found herself in Kevin's arms with their bodies against one another more and more as the evening passed she did not object to the body contact much to her surprise she was enjoying it very much. Kevin's strong hand on her back was hot where it touched her she felt warm all over and was both mentally and physically excited she was almost breathless when the music stopped. Kevin held on to her with one arm around her waist he nodded to his right toward Robert and Amanda, who were standing in the middle of the floor.

"Look they are kissing."

"Another excellent idea," said Verona pulling his head down so she could kiss him. Kevin reacted by putting both hands around her waist pulling her closer while their lips fused in a furry of passion, neither wanted to stop or let go, they stood there embracing until it became apparent the band was taking a break and they were alone on the dance floor.

"Well, I see you are enjoying the evening Verona," remarked Amanda when Verona and Kevin returned to their seats.

"Kevin is a remarkable dancer, you should have the next dance with him it will be a treat. You and Robert appear to be having a good time as well."

Robert spoke up in the hope of impressing Amanda with his reply.

"Amanda is a great dancer, she is so good I sometimes don't realize she is there until our bodies touch, I can't recall having this much fun at a dance. Thanks to Amanda this is a night to remember!"

Robert put his hand on Amanda's as she added.

"I am having a wonderful time. Robert, I can't thank you enough for asking me to come here I've never been to a roadhouse before. It's great fun."

Robert took Verona's hand and headed for the dance floor as the band returned playing a slow waltz for their first number after their break. Kevin looked at Amanda smiling.

"Come on let's dance, we can't let them have all the fun."

She barely reached his shoulder, facing each other, she put her hand on his shoulder then they waltzed away to the one, two, three beat of a German waltz. The dance floor was crowded by this time everyone had finished their dinner and those who came just for dancing had claimed the few unreserved tables. For the others it was standing room only. Beer consumption reached its peak during intermission as the patrons quelled their thirst after a vigorous hour and a half of non-stop dancing. While they were dancing Robert kept telling Verona how much he liked Amanda.

"She is the best looking girl I have ever met, I've been trying to get up enough nerve to ask her out for weeks. She has always been friendly in class and we talk a lot, but for some reason she never showed much interest in me other than being friends. Do you think she likes me as more than a friend? I really like her, you know."

"Robert, I doubt that Amanda would kiss someone she didn't care about, think about it," said Verona thinking to herself that Amanda had not kissed a boy since she was eight years old and here she was kissing Robert on her first date. "Does that mean you think she might be interested in our becoming a couple," asked Robert excitedly.

"Maybe, you should tell her how you feel then ask her for another date."

"Thanks, that is just what I am going to do," said Robert as the dance ended. Reassured by Verona's reply he was determined to ask Amanda for another date. Amanda and Robert were alone at the table sipping the beers he had ordered from the roaming bar maid. The beer relaxed him a little more than he expected and at the same time added to his aggressiveness.

"Are you sure you are having a good time, Amanda?"

She smiled widely showing her dimples. Her brown eyes twinkled as she replied.

"Robert, I've not had this much fun in my entire life, I love it. Do you think we might do it again sometime?"

Hearing Amanda's question, Robert heaved a sigh of relief as the tenseness in his chest subsided. Amanda's words encouraged him to express his feelings for her.

"Amanda, I enjoy being with you very much, in fact, I have been dreaming of our being on a date together, but until this week I couldn't muster the courage to ask you out even though I've been attracted to you for a long time. We can come here again next Saturday and every Saturday after that If you like."

"Robert, I can't tell you how much I like being with you. Our dancing together thrills me beyond belief, you are a good dancer and feeling your body next to mine excites me. So does the kissing."

Amanda could hardly believing she had actually said those words out loud. She had spent most of her life keeping her feelings to herself and here she was telling Robert their bodies touching excited her. Verona and Kevin returned to find Amanda and Robert sharing a kiss the intensity of which lasted well after their lips parted. "Are we having fun," quipped Kevin. Neither answered, they grinned as Robert raised their clasped hands high in the air.

The car came to a halt outside the dorm, both Verona and Amanda kissed their respective dates goodnight before telling them what a great time they had with each announcing they would like to do it again. On the way to the parking lot where Kevin had left his car, Kevin inquired.

"What do you think of Amanda?"

"She was a lot of fun, I was somewhat apprehensive at first, but after she let me kiss her, I felt a lot better. Then when she told me she liked being with me, I almost died, you see I have been trying to date her for a good while. How about Verona, do you have a thing for her?"

"Well, this was our first date too. I must admit, Verona is a very interesting woman. I really enjoyed the dining and dancing and holding her close was an immeasurable pleasure. What really got me though was the kiss, I can't put it out of my mind. Yes, you might say I have a thing for her."

Kevin could still feel the warmth of Verona's lips on his. The thought of her was driving him crazy. On the way to his apartment, Kevin thought.

"I'll always be in Amanda's debt for tonight she put Verona in my arms where she belongs she solved a big problem for me by insisting on a double date."

Kevin tossed and turned all night sleeping very little, each time he awoke, he had been dreaming of kissing Verona while holding her in his arms, but she wasn't there he was in bed alone.

The next morning, Alpha-1 reported to Abe.

"Verona and Kevin went to the Western Roadhouse last night with another young couple for dinner and dancing. Kevin and Verona were very compatible throughout the evening, they danced together most of the night and were observed in what appeared to be a passionate kiss on the dance floor when the band took a break. The entire group appeared to have a good time dancing and laughing the whole evening. Verona and Amanda were returned to the dorm at 12:30 a.m. This is the first time Kevin and Verona have been on a date expect to see more of this in the future."

The following morning Amanda and Verona were both anxious to compare notes on their experiences from the night before.

"I had a wonderful time last night, I can't believe what I have been missing. Robert was such a good dancer he held me close most of the time, which I must say, I enjoyed very much. When he kissed me, I almost fainted my heart was beating so fast and this indescribable feeling permeated my whole body. I was numb all over and when he kissed me again, I almost lost control. I felt good in places I never suspected could be affected by a kiss. A totally new experience for me."

"That, Amanda, is what is commonly referred to as sexual arousal it is something that happens when you are stimulated by someone you are attracted to. This is going to happen to you again and again, so you have to learn how to handle it or you will be having sex with every guy that attracts you. We'll talk about his later. I was glad to see how happy you were being with Robert he's a really nice guy. Remember, you are good looking and sexy, all the guys will want to get in your pants sooner or later, so you have to get your priorities in order beforehand to prevent a disaster."

"What about you and Kevin? I saw that protracted kiss on the dance floor, did it affect you the same way?"

"It's interesting that you ask because that kiss did something for me it awoke a desire I have not had in a long time. Kevin has this knack of turning me on even when that doesn't seem to be his intent. I must admit that for a moment, all I could think about was making love with him, I wanted him to kiss me all over. Amanda, I was on fire with desire. I am very much attracted to Kevin this was our first date and control, control, and more control was necessary. It's strange about love and sex, they go together and to be a perfect match they had both better be good. I will not be having sex with Kevin or anyone else unless I know for sure we love each other. Until then my sexual desires will be kept under wraps. This is the best possible advice I can give you, Amanda, in the end it is your decision to make."

The foursome became regulars at the Western Roadhouse over the following weeks having dinner and dancing to the Western band on Saturday nights. Later on, they chose to go their separate ways because Amanda was confident she could handle herself in any situation and Verona wanted more time alone with Kevin. She and Kevin had become more than friends they met almost daily for coffee and spent much of their weekends together. After dating Kevin for six weeks, Verona decided it was time to introduce him to her parents, whom she had not informed of their puritanical liaison. She called Clare asking permission for the two of them to spend the upcoming weekend with the family. Clare was ecstatic to hear about Kevin.

"What's his name again? Kevin what?"

"Mom, his name is Kevin Goodhall he's a graduate student here at UT. We'll see you about noon tomorrow, OK? Love you."

Clare and the rest of the family were assembled in the den when Verona and Kevin arrived. Following introductions, Ned served drinks while pointing out that he would be cooking outside on the patio and that anyone wanting to share in the operation was welcome to join him, although participation was not mandatory. The temperature outside was extremely hot and there was only a slight breeze blowing from the west. The others, including Kevin, opted to enjoy the air conditioning inside and to leave the cooking to Ned. During the introductions, Kevin noticed Ned's last name was Stanley while Verona's was Cook, but he already knew this. His better judgment told him to inquire about the difference in names sometime during their visit to make sure he did not appear to know more about Verona than he should. Verona had never mentioned to him that she had a different last name than the rest of her family.

Verona's mom was very interested in talking with Kevin she wanted to know what kind of person he was and what he valued in life. It was obvious that Verona cared for him otherwise she would not have wanted to bring him home to meet the family. She asked in a crisp, but pleasant voice.

"What is you greatest ambition Kevin? To head a great corporation?"

"This may surprise you as it does many of my contemporaries. My greatest desire is to marry the woman I love and to live with her joyfully while we raise our family together."

"What about a career?"

"I'd like a career, but to me a life without love is insignificant, love conquers all."

A smile spread across Clare's face upon hearing Kevin's response he could not have said anything which would have pleased her more. He had clearly and concisely stated she and Ned's exact blueprint for happiness, Kevin had crossed the bridge to her heart with that simple statement and endeared himself with Clare.

Seizing the opportunity, Kevin opted to pose the necessary question.

"I was wondering why Verona's last name is different from the rest of the family, she never mentioned this to me."

"It's a question that comes up from time to time, although it's not simple to explain, here's how it came about. Before Ned and I met and while I was still young and single, I volunteered to become part of a genetic study. As a participant in the study I had a child through artificial insemination, Verona was that child, therefore she has my maiden name while the rest of us have Ned's last name. Ned wanted to give Verona his name after we married, but I resisted because I wanted her to know she is special. If you want to know more of the details, then you'll have to ask Verona, I'm surprised she hasn't mentioned it to you."

"Interesting, so Verona has been special from the beginning. One thing for certain, Verona is very special to me and everyone who knows her, you are right she is special!"

At that moment Clare perceived Kevin was irrevocably in love with Verona she could tell from his remarks and the pleasure he derived in mentioning her name. Her mind was racing ahead of the conversation thinking to herself.

"Assuming Verona has the same passion for Kevin as he does for her, they will make a wonderful couple."

Later in the evening Clare, Verona and Angel were enjoying the cool breeze on the patio while Kevin and Ned watched college football on TV in the den. Clare in her usual candidness asked Verona.

"Are you and Kevin in love or are you just good friends?"

"We are much more than just good friends, but we are not lovers in the sense that we are having sex. As you can very well tell, I really care for Kevin, he has this thing about him that I find hard to resist. He says the right things, does the right things and I can tell he loves me. When we kiss it's heavenly, I begin to sweat it's like I am on fire with passion for him."

Angel interjected.

"What do you mean you are on fire with passion? Do you mean you are getting clammy, or that you want to have sex with him?"

"I must admit, sex with Kevin has crossed my mind, but the feeling is different from being clammy, Angel. It's a lot more intense than getting a little warm and sweaty."

"What about Kevin?" Asked Clare diverting the conversation away from Verona's feelings to prevent Angel from asking too many explicit questions.

"When we kiss, I can feel his chest pounding his heart races and he really gets excited feeling me next to him he is always very tender and does not push for sex even though he is about to explode with desire."

"Where in the world did you find him in the first place?"

"I didn't find him exactly, he more or less fell out of the sky into my lap. We literally bumped into each other on campus and after apologizing for spilling my things all over the sidewalk he invited me for a cup of coffee. I think you will find what happened next uncanny to say the least. He asked what kind of coffee I would like and I replied that I would have whatever he was having. When he returned he had two cups of special cappuccino, your favorite and mine. At the time, I thought it was an odd coincidence, but after dating Kevin for several months I sometimes think he can read my thoughts he seems to know what I am thinking."

Clare smiled as she recalled her first cup of coffee with Ned at Starbucks.

"The special cappuccino may be a good omen, it certainly was for Ned and I we have been in love ever since."

"Yes, mom, I know. That's what I want, what you and Ned have."

Verona hugged Clare as she continued her narration about her romance with Kevin.

"Kevin and I had been meeting for coffee for quite a while before we had an actual date and that also happened sort of by accident," said Verona before describing the circumstances surrounding their double date and their subsequent dates involving Amanda and Robert.

"Kevin has made it clear that he finds me irresistible and is madly in love with me. I feel the same way about him, so we have become inseparable we are devoted to one another. I want you to know, I love Kevin very much and sometime in the future we may become permanently joined which is why I wanted you to meet him this weekend."

"Has Kevin proposed?"

"Not yet, mom, but he will. You do remember your and Estelle's rules about love and sex, don't you?"

"Yes, dear and they are as important today as they were the first time you heard them, I want nothing more for you than a life filled with love and happiness. As Kevin said earlier, love conquers all."

During halftime of the televised Longhorn game Kevin brought up the circumstances of Ned and Clare's meeting.

"Ned, how did you and Clare meet in the first place, was it an accident or on purpose?"

"Originally, Clare thought we first saw each other in her office after I came to work at MyTeeTech, but actually the first time I saw Clare was considerably earlier. I had come to Austin for my first interview with MyTeeTech and while I was waiting in the reception room for my appointment, I had a sudden urge to go to the men's room which was down the hall. As I passed the office of the head of research, I happened to glance through the glass door and there was Clare sitting behind her desk. She was unbelievably attractive, as much as I wanted to continue gazing upon the beautiful woman before me, in my condition I couldn't linger, I had to go. On my way back to the reception room, I purposely stopped to look again and there was Clare who without glancing in my direction got up and walked across the room to straighten out some magazines on the coffee table. She did not notice me outside the door as she straightened up and walked back to her desk, she was absolutely the most exciting woman I had ever seen. On my return flight home, I could think of nothing other than the gorgeous female I happened to see at MyTeeTech. I kept seeing her image in my mind over and over again. A week before my second interview, I was still thinking about her, I couldn't stop. I persuaded an old friend who worked at MyTeeTech, to check her name and marital status for me before I arrived for my second and final interview. My attraction to Clare was so strong that after my friend reported she was single and unattached, I accepted the job at MyTeeTech even though I had several better offers at the time. Once on the payroll, I introduced myself and the rest is a love story for the ages. I didn't tell her the whole tale until after we were married by then we were so much in love she only smiled at my admission. By the way, I still cannot get her out of my mind even after all of this time."

In spite of his better judgment, Kevin could not keep himself from saying.

"Just think, if you hadn't needed to pee, you might never have met the love of your life."

Ned doubled over with laughter then shook Kevin's hand before replying cheerfully.

"Like they say, a good pee never hurt anybody."

They were still laughing when Clare and the others came in from the patio wanting to know what was so funny. Neither elaborated.

Upon Verona's return to the dorm, she was greeted by Amanda who was excited, yet a little disturbed, her father had called inviting both she and Verona to dinner at the Driskill Hotel Sunday evening. He was coming to Austin for a business meeting Monday morning then flying to Dallas later in the afternoon for another meeting. She was looking forward to meeting with her father for reasons he could not have anticipated, Amanda was thankful he had been gracious enough to invited Verona to join them. Verona's presence would provide support for her to confront her father with her new self which he had no idea existed. Verona called Kevin to let him know that circumstances would prohibit their having dinner together Sunday evening. She explained the need for her to accompany Verona before saying.

"I am so sorry, Kevin I feel compelled to go, Amanda needs for me to be there."

"I understand, Verona. Remember, I love you. See you for coffee tomorrow. Tell Amanda, I wish her luck and for her to try to have a good time tonight."

Amanda accepted Kevin's good wishes then declared to Verona in a small soft voice.

"This is going to be really interesting, I've not sent any pictures home since my makeover, nor have I mentioned anything about the real me to either of my parents. Dad has no idea of the changes that have taken place in the last few months, is he going to be surprised!"

"How do you think he will react? I know he will be shocked when he sees you so slim, trim and attractive, but what about the rest?"

"He will no doubt be pleased with my looks, but I'm not so sure about how he will accept the real me. One thing for sure, I am going to be myself whether he likes it or not, I will never go back to being a submissive person, not for him or anyone else. Tonight, I will say what I think no matter what happens!"

"Remember, I will be there for support if you need me. Amanda, I feel certain that you can handle the situation on your own, you have come a long way since the real you came out of the closet."

Verona was pleased to hear Amanda's adamant declaration of independence and her determination to defend her real self. They were restless and a bit jittery when the cab Amanda's father hired arrived to whisk them away to the Driskill Hotel. Both of them were wearing modest semiformal dresses, which displayed their bodies brilliantly, not too much, not too little, just a slight amount of skin showing in the right places. Amanda's dress was a dark red while Verona's was bright blue. The two striking young ladies stepped out of the elevator and proceeded to the dining room where they asked the maître d for their table. While being escorted across the dining room, they noticed that every person there was watching as they halted at Amanda's father's table. His mouth was agape as he arose to greet them. Taking Amanda's hand in his he said in a barely audible voice.

"Amanda, what a pleasant surprise!"

He turned her around for a better look before hugging her while kissing her cheek then saying much louder.

"You are devastatingly beautiful, my dear."

He then turned his attention to Verona who was still standing. Holding out his arms he said. "If I may?" before hugging Verona.

"You are Verona and I must say as beautiful as your roommate described you to us."

He could not conceal his approval and admiration of Amanda. Talking directly to her he said with obvious pride.

"You have accomplished so much is such a short while, I am exceedingly proud of you and your mother will be too when she sees what you've done."

"I'm glad you like the changes, father, without Verona's help and encouragement it would not have been possible."

Amanda nodded in Verona's direction, but she did not stop there she charged ahead with her agenda for the occasion.

"There are a few other changes you need to be aware of dad, I have decided to be me! If that confuses you, let me put it this way, I now say what I think and do what I want. I do not allow others to speak for me or tell me what I should think, I speak for myself and express my own ideas. I plan to live the rest of my life the way I see fit."

Amanda watched her father's face intently while making her declaration. Much to her delight and surprise her father had a huge smile on his face.

"Amanda, you are my daughter and believe it or not, I would not have it any other way, I have always thought that sooner or later the true you would surface. Maybe it's being on your own, or it's Verona's influence, or a combination of both whatever the reason you have my full support and admiration. I am pleased with what you have done on your own without my or your mother's help or interference. You have become your own woman and I am proud of you."

Amanda jumped to her feet threw her arms around her father kissing him on the cheek, she then smiled before saying.

"Thank you father, you will always be in my heart."

The three of them enjoyed their dinner while discussing a variety subjects with each freely expressing their opinions on topics ranging from economics to welfare to international issues. Amanda's father ordered an expensive bottle of imported wine to celebrate Amanda's declaration of independence. After pouring the wine he offered a toast.

"Here is to Amanda's, Amanda. She shall reign supreme forever!"

They raised their glasses to commemorate the independence of Amanda and although unspoken the reconciliation of a father and daughter. Toward the end of the evening, Verona casually mentioned to Amanda's father.

"She has become quite popular among her classmates, both the males and females enjoy spending time with her, they appreciate her personality, ideas and conversation."

"That raises an important question I have completely overlooked until now, Amanda, are you dating?" asked her father embarrassed because he had not thought to ask sooner.

"I'm glad you asked, dad. I have a steady boyfriend named Robert, we go dancing and out for movies like the other kids at UT. You needn't worry about us though, we're being good."

"Well, ladies the evening is drawing to a close much sooner than I would like, unfortunately I have to be up early in the morning. I can't recall the last time I enjoyed an evening as much as this one, I thank both of you for joining me, and I shall not soon forget your beauty and grace. Before we go, Amanda, there is a special favor I want to ask of you. When I call your mother tonight, I am not going to mention any of your fantastic accomplishments, only that the three of us had a very enjoyable dinner together. I would appreciate it very much, if you would call your mother tomorrow and tell her you are coming home for the weekend, you will be a beautiful surprise and will make her extremely happy."

"I wouldn't call that a favor, but a pleasure instead. I will call the first thing in the morning to let her know I am coming next week. Thanks dad, for a wonderful and enjoyable evening."

He escorted them to the cab waiting outside the hotel where he and Amanda embraced again before she and Verona got into the cab for the drive back to their dorm.

"What I feared might be a nasty confrontation turned out to be a very enjoyable evening with my father it was not the reaction I expected from him at all. I wonder what changed."

"I don't really know what happened. Did you see the look on your dad's face when he realized the sexy young blond in red was you? He was in denial at first then a look of shock spread over his face before turning to complete adoration. I think he had a hard time comprehending what he was seeing. At any rate, you managed everything admirably and to your credit reunited with your dad. He appreciated your attitude very much, Amanda, it was a great thing you did for him, no recriminations, no rehash of the past, just love in the present. It was an evening he will never forget. Amanda, he was proud of you and so am I. And you should be too."

Conferring with Kevin over two cups of special cappuccino, Verona rehashed the past evening's dinner with Amanda and her father before Kevin mentioned his conversation with Ned on Saturday.

"Did your mom ever tell you that Ned was attracted to her long before she even knew he existed?"

"No, what makes you ask? The story I remember was they met at work shortly after he joined MyTeeTech and they went for coffee."

"He told me this funny story about seeing Clare through the glass door of her office on his way to the restroom during his first interview. She did not see him at all, but after watching her he became so infatuated he accepted the job at MyTeeTech so he could be near her."

"I'll have to ask mom about that sometime. Is it important?"

"No, I just thought it was a beautiful beginning to magnificent love story. Don't you agree?"

"However it began, their love affair should be a model for the entire world. I don't think there is a happier couple alive."

"We could be even happier."

Verona heard Kevin clearly, yet she said nothing. Instead she kissed him softly on the mouth explaining, "We need to go or I'll miss my class."

They gathered their belongings and were about to leave when Verona took Kevin's hand saying in a low mysterious voice.

"Kevin, I'll call you after your last class, I think we need to do something different tonight."

They walked their separate paths to class each thinking about what the other had just said. Verona wondered.

"Did he tell me about Ned and mom as a skillful lead-in for proposing or was there something I missed in the story? Either way, I love you Mr. Goodhall you have made me very happy with your sly proposal."

Kevin was preoccupied by Verona's last remarks.

"I'm sure she understood my proposal, yet she said nothing. Don't be upset Verona, you are the love of my life, you are my life. Different? What did she mean by different, different from what? We'll see."

Kevin's cell-phone rang immediately after he stepped outside of the classroom. Verona's voice had an unusual urgency.

"I love you Kevin."

"I love you too, Verona. What's on your mind?"

"It's not really that important Kevin, but it occurred to me that you have never invited me to see your apartment. Could you give you me a grand tour this evening?"

"Verona, I think that is possible. In fact, I will come directly from the parking lot to your dorm to save time. I'll call you when I get there. We can have an early dinner on the way to my place then I can bring you back afterward."

Verona was enthusiastic in her response.

"Hurry Kevin, my heart doesn't want to wait, love you."

Driving away from the UT campus, Kevin pointed out to Verona that he did not have an apartment, but rather he owned a townhouse which he had purchased as an investment when he enrolled at mid-term. When they arrived, Verona viewed the townhouse from the driveway. The building was imposing, and it was new, a light blue in color with white trim and it had three stories. A double garage occupied the front part of the ground floor while the living area made up the two upper floors. The back half of the ground floor was a utility and storage room which had a washer and dryer and a work bench with storage space for hand and power tools. There was an outside entrance to the townhouse, but they walked up the internal stairway after entering through the garage. Verona asked.

"Why didn't you tell me you owned a townhouse?"

"Actually, I wanted to surprise you a little later, but now my secret has been exposed!"

When they reached the second floor Kevin waived for Verona to enter first while he held the door open. Once inside, Kevin turned on the lights revealing a spacious living area, to one side there was a small kitchen and an enclosed bar with several tall bar stools. The entire floor was tiled in the living and dining areas, but was partially covered by two large Oriental rugs which gave the place an appearance of opulence. The furnishings and shear draperies with vertical venetian blinds for light control were in beautiful harmony with the rich décor of the entire living area. Three large oil paintings were strategically placed to enhance the balance and charm of the overall design adding a touch of artistry to the entire layout. Several built in book cases graced the windowless back wall where Kevin's desk and computer work area were located. Kevin had designed the TV mounting in such a fashion that the TV folded into the wall when not in use leaving an almost undetectable break in the paneling restoring the room to its original uncluttered design.

"Kevin, it's beautiful! Did you select all of this yourself?"

"I had a little help from the sales people they like spending other people's money, you know."

"Kevin, you are a genius," said Verona throwing her arms around him kissing him lavishly.

"Can I see the bedrooms now?"

"Sure follow me the stairs are over here."

Kevin pointed to a closed folding door behind the bar which when opened, exposed the stairway to the upper floor. The two bedrooms were moderate in size, yet large enough to accommodate king sized beds, each bedroom was furnished and decorated in a style consistent with the rest of the interior design. The beds were neatly made and had beautiful multi-colored bed spreads on both of them the bedrooms were neat and clean with everything in its place. There were no socks or shoes lying about Kevin's clothes were hanging neatly in one of two large walk-in closets adjacent to the bathroom. The bathroom itself was huge it had white counter tops, and a mounted mirror reaching from the counter to the ceiling and stretching from the shower to the Jacuzzi. There were two sunken sinks in the counter with a vanity nook between them. On either side of the vanity nook there were storage spaces with twin doors that opened either separately or together and pull-out drawers located above and to either side. The large custom built shower had a frosted glass door with gold colored metal trim and a frosted glass panel on one side with identical trim. Inside, the shower was spacious it had a non-slip floor and was equipped with a large programmable shower head capable of switching the water flow from a solid stream, to a mist, to a pulsating stream designed to massage the entire body.

"Kevin, how do you keep this place so neat and clean? It's spotless!"

"It's not hard at all, I have a maid who comes in once every two weeks. She cleans the place from top to bottom and she does my laundry for me. I just keep things picked up, stored and put my dirty clothes in the hamper she does the rest. What do you think now that you have seen the place?"

"I love it, you have done a wonderful job decorating. Do you have any other hidden talents I don't know about?"

They took the stairs back to the living area where they were standing next to one another enjoying the view from the large picture window. Suddenly Kevin took Verona in his arms.

"Thank you Verona, I'm glad you like it. I was saving it for a surprise."

He kissed her softly, his lips lingering hesitantly on hers, then he kissed her boldly his lips searing on hers which sent a wave of excitement sweeping over Verona's entire body she was quivering with pleasure when the kiss ended.

"Verona, now that the tour is finished, what would you like to do?"

"I would like very much to try your shower," said Verona still clinging to Kevin with her arms around him her heavy breathing becoming more pronounced. Kevin was unprepared for her answer, but he moved swiftly once he understood hoisting Verona in his arms kissing her hot soft lips as he carried her up the stairs. He interrupted his kissing briefly.

"Do you want a hot or a cold shower?"

Verona bit him on the neck replying.

"The hotter the better."

Kevin eased her to the floor looking into her large moist eyes he asked.

"Verona, are you sure you want to do this?"

"Yes, Kevin I want very much to do this. I love you."

They raced to undress, Verona stepped into the shower where Kevin was waiting momentarily they were facing each other with warm water pouring off of their heads their naked bodies against one another. Neither spoke, they stood there kissing their bodies entwined with their arms around each other. Verona was the first to awake up, it was early morning, and the sun was about to come up as she rolled over looking at Kevin who lay naked and uncovered next to her. He was still asleep with his eyes closed, yet he was smiling. She wanted to touch him and kiss him, but that would awaken him unnecessarily so she saved his reward for later. As she gazed at Kevin, Verona quietly thought about Estelle's remarks about love.

"Love and sex go together and they both need to be good for a perfect match. You my love were fantastic I'm sure Estelle would approve."

Kevin awoke a few minutes later slowly inching his body against Verona kissing her before either of them spoke he continued kissing and caressing her for several minutes before he felt her body respond. Several hours later they were in the shower together this time they were not in a rush and had time to talk.

"Verona, you are superb even more loving and exciting than I ever dreamed, I love you."

"Kevin, when you touch me it's heavenly you excite me to the point I have a hard time controlling myself after a while all I want is for you make love to me."

"Does this mean you accept my proposal?"

"Yes, Kevin that is exactly what this means, we are a match made in heaven and meant for each other," replied Verona putting her head against his wet chest pulling him firmly against her.

Estelle was happy to see Verona's cell number when she checked her messages she returned the call at the first opportunity.

"Verona, it's so nice to hear from you it's been awhile since we talked. What is going on in Austin?"

"Estelle, it has happened without my putting out a WANTED poster, I've found my Mr. Right!"

"Really, is he someone I know?"

"I don't think so, Estelle, I didn't meet him until after you and Bruce had left UT. It didn't happen anything like you and Bruce, I met him purely by accident. There was no tingling or burning desire at first then after being around him for a while we started dating and that's when things changed."

"Are you sure he's the right guy, Verona? Remember the rules?"

"That's why I haven't mentioned Kevin before, Estelle. We spent the night together last night and believe me the love and sex are not only good they are beyond belief."

"Are you getting married anytime soon?"

"I don't think so, he would like to marry me tomorrow, but at the moment I would rather wait a while longer until I decide what to do for a degree. How are you and Bruce doing? Have you become Californians?"

"We are having a blast out here everything is so different from back in Texas. It's hard to tell what is real from what is pure BS because there are so many political factions on campus and in the State. For instance, the standard oil field term for hydraulic fracturing, or sand fracing as it has been called for over sixty years in the industry, has been perverted from fracing to fracking by the liberal press. They added the k purposely to leave a negative impression on readers because the new spelling looks so much like the vulgarity fucking. It's just another part of the mind game played by the liberal environmentalist who run California they want everyone to be turned off with fracing which is nothing new. If the oil companies are fracking wells then it follows that they are fucking the environment and the American people, see what I mean?"

After a long pause to allow Verona to grasp her meaning, Estelle continued.

"Bruce and I are more in love than ever, he lives off campus, so I spend a lot of time at his place on the weekends. His training period didn't take long he is a fast learner and quickly became an ideal and innovative partner he pleases me very much."

Other parts of their educational programs were developing as expected, Bruce was engrossed in his medical studies and liked his professors it was evident his move to Stanford had broaden his opportunities and would be good for his career. She also liked school, her classes were interesting, and she was making new friends although they were a little weird.

"Verona, you will be interested to know that I have enrolled in an advanced art class devoted to painting using the Golden Mean to design paintings and place the major subjects on the canvas. I really enjoy the class as a result I think I am becoming an accomplished artist. I've decided to get my minor in art it's something I really enjoy and I have a natural talent for it."

Due to his study load, Bruce planned to attend school year around providing little time to visit home or Austin, but Estelle was following a normal degree plan and expected to spend two weeks at home during the summer visiting with her parents and friends.

"If you have some free time while you are home, I will introduce you to Kevin I'm sure you will like him. Estelle, he is that special man I always dreamed of being my husband and father of my children."

Estelle thought to herself.

"Knowing your rules makes meeting Kevin a must."

Bruce was happy to learn Verona had met someone, based on their short acquaintance at UT, he admired and respected her. He hoped she and her Mr. Right proved be as happy as he and Estelle. Had it not been for Verona's help he and Estelle might not have met in the first place.

A few weeks later Verona was spending a rare weekend without Kevin when her cell phone chimed, it was Estelle.

"Estelle, where are you, Texas, California or somewhere in between?"

"I'm at home in Junction visiting with my parents I'll be here for a couple of weeks. I'm hoping to see you and meet Kevin while I'm here. When can we get together?"

"How about Tuesday? I have a light schedule maybe the three of us can go to dinner. Oh, there is someone else I would like for you to meet while you are here my new roommate, Amanda. You'll find her very interesting as well."

The conversation between Verona and Estelle lasted for almost a quarter of an hour, during which they discussed the details of their recent activities before turning to their relationships with Bruce and Kevin. Estelle agreed to meet Verona and Amanda at their dorm following Verona's last class on Tuesday. Verona arranged for Kevin to pick them up later for dinner.

Verona was alone when Estelle arrived at the dorm Amanda was tied up and would not arrive for a couple of hours because of her schedule.

"You look great Estelle, I'm so glad to see you," said Verona as they embraced.

"You look fabulous yourself, your Mr. Right must be making you happy."

"Tell me, how are you and Bruce doing, is he as devoted as ever?"

"Bruce has been everything I expected and more, we are not living together, but almost. I spend the weekends with him and we are fantastic together, we love each other more every day I've never been happier, Verona."

"Kevin and I aren't living together either although we have agreed to get married. We often spend the night in his townhouse and it is wonderful! I don't know how much longer I can resist getting married. Estelle, I'm not sure I can stand not being with him all the time I love him so much."

"You still remember the rule, don't you?"

"Yes, Kevin and I love each other and sex together is fantastic we are a perfect match."

"I can hardly wait to meet your Kevin, he must be exceptional. By the way, I have exposed several of my California girlfriends to the rule."

"Great, that is one reason I want you to meet Amanda, she has also been exposed to the rule and to my mother as well."

Meeting Amanda was a different kind of experience for Estelle she was unlike anyone Estelle had ever known. Her first impression of Amanda was that she was forceful and adamant in expressing her ideas, which Estelle considered a good quality, yet a bit unusual for a soft spoken petite young woman. She was strong willed and determined, still somewhat naïve about some aspects of romance, love and happiness. Overall, Estelle could not decide what to make of Amanda, but once Amanda began recounting the changes she and Verona had made in her life style Estelle began to appreciate Amanda more and more. Her accomplishments in such a short time were amazing, she was indeed a remarkable person who had forged her own future through self-determination and guts. Estelle was well aware of Verona's talent for helping others to fulfill their dreams, she had been instrumental in her and Bruce getting together and now she had helped Amanda to become the person she wanted to be. Verona was a beautiful gifted person who was her best friend.

"Verona, did it ever occur to you that you have a natural gift for helping people?"

"I never thought of it as being a gift it's something I enjoy doing," replied Verona.

"In fact, I have been thinking of changing my major to include social science. I like helping people it's very pleasing to be of service to those wanting to improve their lives."

"Verona, look at what you did for me I'll never forget your help in getting Bruce and I together. You could do the same for others you're very good at it. It would be a waste not to use your talents to help people achieve happiness."

Estelle's first assessment of Kevin came as he opened the car door for Verona and then for her. She noted he was tall, sturdy and reasonably good looking, but the characteristic which commanded her attention was his smile it was spontaneous and natural. She also liked his manner of speaking, casual and evenly balanced with no emotional ups or downs just a steady stream of good English softly spoken. He could get by in most situations, including working with ranch hands, politicians, bankers and investors he was a natural conversationalist exuding honestly and trustworthiness. During dinner, Estelle found herself hanging on to Kevin's every word he spoke of Verona in such glowing terms it was obvious he adored her. The way he touched Verona made Estelle think.

"There is no doubt he loves her, Bruce does the same thing with me."

Before making her final evaluation of Kevin's suitability for Verona, Estelle posed her critical question.

"Kevin, if I could be so bold to ask, what is your greatest desire in life?"

"What I would like most is to marry Verona, the woman I love, and for us to live in happiness as we raise our children."

His answer clenched her assessment that Kevin was indeed Mr. Right.

"You and Verona will surely be happy together you are an ideal couple."

"Thank you Estelle, Verona's happiness means everything to me. I'm glad you think we are a perfect match, so do I."

They spent the remainder of the evening discussing Bruce's difficult courses and demanding study requirements which interfered with him and Estelle spending time together. Following dinner, Estelle called Bruce on her cell phone to give him the good news.

"Hi love, its true Verona has found her Mr. Right. You should see them together they are a great match just like us. I am so happy for both of them."

She and Bruce talked for only a minute before Estelle ended the conversation.

"Bruce, I will call you with all the details when I get back to Junction until then I love you and I miss you."

She rolled her Mustang out on to the freeway and headed toward Junction.

"What did you think, Kevin? Isn't Estelle one of a kind, a beautiful person?"

"I liked her, she is a down-to-earth person and beautiful I might add. Do you know Bruce well?"

"I met him a few times, he is a really nice guy and an excellent match for Estelle he complements her personality and most of all he makes her happy."

"Then you and Bruce are not close friends?"

"If Estelle had not spotted him down on 6th Street, I doubt we would ever have met. Why?"

"Just curious, it's nothing."

That Bruce and Verona were products of the Gentex long term genetic study was well known to Kevin, even though he was no longer a part of Abe, he understood their desire to keep them apart. He had mixed emotions concerning Verona's and Estelle's continuing friendship, but was loath to interfere in any way. There was no doubt in Kevin's mind that Abe knew about Estelle's recent visit and they also knew about his and Verona's relationship from Alpha-1's reports. He had to be extremely careful it was a perilous time for him and for Verona he could not make any mistakes.

Alpha-1 reported to Abe.

"Verona and this guy Kevin Goodhall spent the weekend in his townhouse, they have also visited with Verona's family in their home. This appears to be an ongoing love affair which has a high probability of ending in marriage between Verona and Kevin. We now have the townhouse under constant electronic surveillance in addition to our coverage of Verona. Verona's former roommate, Estelle Winger, also showed up for a visit. Estelle is engaged to Bruce Wilkerson who is going to college in California. We are awaiting your further instructions."

Frank read the report with anguish.

"God damn it Verona, you are screwing up all of our good work to keep you and Bruce apart. Kevin knows what is going on here, but he is in no position to do anything about it. Why in the hell did you and Estelle have to become such good friends? It could jeopardize our entire operation including ADAM. Something needs to be done, but I don't know what. I need to make a plan!"

The report was forwarded to ADAM resulting in a personal meeting between Frank and Jerry. Jerry poured two large glasses of Irish whiskey as had become their custom when they met.

"Here's to Verona and her future."

After having a sip of his drink, Jerry set it on the table exclaiming!

"In view of recent developments, we may need to rethink some of the rules laid out for ADAM!"

"What would we change, Jerry?"

Frank was somewhat surprised that Jerry was considering any changes in the fundamentals established while George was still alive.

"In our secrecy mandate we are charged with preventing anyone from discovering George is the father of his four children and also with preventing discovery of any connection between Gentex, Abe and

311

ADAM. Further, Imperial Enterprises shall never be publically linked with any of these organizations. Think about this, should Bruce and Verona or any of the others become friends and discuss their origins they could eventually discover they had Gentex in common and that their mothers participated in the genetic program. This would in no way indicate they had a common father, or that they were related, only that they were a result of the Gentex program. As you can see this could raise many questions in both the mother's and the children's minds. If required to do so, Gentex can extinguish any fears the mothers might develop concerning who are the fathers of their children. An inspection of the official records would indicate they have separate fathers. There are only three of us remaining alive who know George's secret you, me and Aaron no one associated with the Gentex program, other than Aaron, ever knew about George. With this safeguard in place, I think we should relax a little in our efforts to keep the children from knowing each other."

Frank thought carefully before he said anything.

"You are probably right, I don't see how there could be a breach of secrecy about their identities even if they became close friends. There would be no reason for them to suspect they were related. The only way to screw things up would be for them to compare DNA which is highly unlikely."

Following an exchange of ideas, Frank and Jerry refilled their glasses and saluted their decision.

"To friendly relations between the children, may they all share George's noble contribution without ever knowing he is their father?"

The next morning new instructions were sent to all the Abe agents concerning the Gentex children, starting immediately, any interaction between them was to be ignored unless there were specific orders from the director of Abe to the contrary. After all the time and effort they had expended to keep Verona and Bruce apart, the agents were relieved by the change, it had been nearly impossible to prevent any contact between the two. Their jobs would be much simpler in the future.

Frank placed a call to his former employee Kevin Goodhall requesting a meeting between the two of them in Pflugerville the following day. Kevin was surprised by the request, he was a bit anxious about Frank's possible reaction to his and Verona's relationship. He purposely did not mention his pending meeting with Frank to Verona it would create a problem which he wanted to avoid until he found out why Frank called. There was the possibility that it could pose a serious problem for him and Verona.

"It's good to see you Kevin, I see you and Verona have met and are seeing each other regularly."

Frank held out his hand in greeting. Having no idea why Frank had asked for a meeting, Kevin was a bit anxious he feared it could be bad news related to his love for Verona. He returned Frank's greeting with a hand shake, but did not respond to Frank's comment right away.

"Good to see you Frank, I know you are spying on us, so yes, I am seeing Verona. In fact, I recently asked her to marry me and she said yes."

"That's great, I'm glad she accepted. As you know, I have always thought highly of you and your work. I could not have picked a better husband for Verona."

Not knowing what to make of Frank's remark, Kevin sighed in relief when he realized it was Frank's tacit approval of their pending marriage which caused him to reconsider the nature of Frank's visit. Frank still had given no indication of his reason for being there. Kevin thought to himself.

"What the hell is going on here? If this is not about Verona why is Frank here?"

He knew from previous experience that Frank did not drive all this way to congratulate him on being in love with Verona. There had to more to it than that.

"Don't over react Kevin, you have just solved a problem for me. I came here to request a personal favor, that you and Verona marry as soon as possible," said Frank smiling slyly as if harboring a deep secret of some kind that was not obvious to Kcvin.

"Why would you want that, Frank?" Asked Kevin still in doubt as to what was really going on.

"I have my reasons, Kevin. Believe me, it is in both of your best interests. Do I have your word you will speed up the process? It will make Verona and I both happy?"

"Frank, I would do anything if it makes Verona happy, you know that. I'm glad our getting married pleases you too. I appreciate you approval, Frank, it means a lot to me although I don't understand the need to hurry." Answered Kevin who was still somewhat suspicious of Frank's motives. Frank replied sincerely.

"Keep up the good work, Kevin. I predict a long and happy future for you and Verona. Goodbye, I may not see you again."

With those words, Frank put on his hat and was gone leaving Kevin to try to figure out what had happened and why.

Kevin's plea for an early marriage came as somewhat of a surprise to Verona who could scarcely believe her ears. He did not make a detailed explanation of why he wanted to get married right away, just that he thought it was a great idea, which Verona embraced wholeheartedly. She had been ready to get married for several months. They were quietly wed in San Antonio by a Justice of the Peace the following Friday. Kevin booked the bridal suite at the Hotel Valencia Riverwalk for their two day honeymoon. It was not until Sunday that Verona called Clare to break the news.

"Good morning mom, this is Verona. I'm calling to share the wonderful news with you, Kevin and I were married Friday. We are spending our honeymoon in San Antonio."

"We've been expecting it for some time, Verona. I am so happy, dear. Ned and I think both of you have made a great choice. You two are made for each other! May you continue to bring joy and happiness to yourselves and those around you, tell Kevin we send our congratulations and best wishes. Enjoy the rest of your honeymoon we can talk about this later when things get back to normal."

Clare's response was evident to Kevin by Verona's big smile as she put down her smart phone. Hugging, Kevin Verona kissed him before saying.

"Mom and Ned send their congratulations and mom said to enjoy the rest of our honeymoon. She and Ned were very happy to hear we are married. All is well."

Kevin and Verona were back in class at UT on Monday morning it was business as usual with a full schedule of classes.

Frank was exuberant when he read Alpha-1's latest report which reflected the results of his handiwork in Pflugerville.

"Verona and Kevin were married in San Antonio on Friday and are back in class today. Other than the wedding there is nothing out of the ordinary to report."

Frank sat thinking for a few minutes before saying to himself.

"You two have no idea how happy you have made an old man."

From the inception of the birth of George's children, Verona had been Frank's favorite, he was thinking of her when he hired Kevin to come to work at Abe. Frank had personally selected Kevin to look after Verona and was in the process of arranging an accidental meeting between the two of them when Kevin suddenly resigned thwarting his introduction and throwing his plan into complete disarray. When Kevin managed to meet Verona on his own, Frank realized his selection of Kevin had been guided by a higher authority, Verona was in good hands.

"At this point, I think my work is almost finished."

Amanda was dismayed when she realized Verona would be moving in with Kevin, still she was extremely excited and pleased Verona and Kevin had married. Verona was her favorite person in the whole world nothing could please her more than seeing her happily married to Kevin whom Amanda had come to like and admire. Both of them had made a huge difference in her life especially Verona. She was a person Amanda planned to have as her lifelong friend she congratulated Verona on her marriage.

"Don't worry about me, Verona, thanks to you I can take care of myself. I just hope I can find another roommate for the fall semester who has some of your qualities."

"Just because I am married and living off campus, doesn't mean we can't still be friends I expect to remain in contact, remember we have cell phones and I will still be on campus."

The spring semester was ending as she moved her clothes, books and other belongings into their townhouse, Verona and Kevin had the entire summer to themselves without the interruption of attending classes. Kevin had taken the summer off it was a good time, except for the high water bills, they spent an inordinate amount of time in the shower. Verona and Amanda talked together regularly over the following two years and met on campus as time permitted. Amanda had her third roommate, a freshman from El Paso, who was a small person like herself. Her new roommate was from a wealthy Hispanic family, her father was a businessman like Amanda's and Yvette was having problems with her father and mother. Amanda explained Yvette's situation to Verona.

"Yvette's problem is somewhat similar to the problem I had with my father and family, except she is dealing with male dominance in all aspects of marriage, a cultural tradition that Yvette hates. Her mother has been subservient to her father all of their married life. Yvette is determined she will not allow the same thing to happen to her, she plans to share her life with someone she loves, a man who will treat her as an equal."

"Amanda, Yvette has a problem that is not unique to the Hispanic community we see the same thing in a lot of non-Hispanic families in Texas."

"Verona, do you think there might be some way we can help Yvette?" Asked Amanda, who was desperate to find a suitable solution to Yvette's problem.

"Well, there might be, you do realize a break with Hispanic tradition could result in a serious split with her family. Let me think about it for a while we can get back together next week."

Verona was unsure that an acceptable solution could be reached. She considered several possible alternatives to help solve Yvette's problem, but in the end she rationalized the first step in any case should be a meeting with Yvette herself. When the three of them got together in the dorm the following week, Yvette stated her case exquisitely.

"I love both of my parents very much, but I cannot live my life like my mother totally obedient to her husband's wishes."

Verona understood Yvette's situation very well, she considered over and over what she would do, if she were in Yvette's position.

"One of the greatest things for me growing up was that my mom was always available to discuss anything that was bothering me she gave good advice without being dictatorial. May I ask? Have you discussed this with your mother?"

"We never talk about this sort of thing, I doubt she would answer if I were to ask, she is very reserved," replied Yvette somewhat repulsed by the idea of discussing anything personal with her mother.

"Have you ever talked with your mother about what you think about things in general?" Queried Amanda.

"We talk freely about music, theatre, religion that sort of thing never about love and certainly not about sex or how to choose a husband."

"Well, that was one of the problems I had too, my mother never discussed love, sex or marriage with me either when I was growing up, she does now though because I asked her to," stated Amanda in support of a dialog between Yvette and her mother. Verona quickly outlined a basic plan for Yvette.

"I am sure your mother loves you, Yvette. Just as much as you love her, in which case, she will do almost anything to keep from losing your love. Before you do anything else, tell your mother how you feel and ask for her advice, you may be surprised at what happens, if nothing else, she will know that you are determined not to be a servant to your husband."

Yvette agreed in principle that she needed to inform her mother of her strong feelings on the subject of domination without being confrontational. She was reluctant to force the issue she feared her mother might be offended should she come out with a dogmatic statement concerning her disdain for male domination in marriage. Together the three of them devised a plan in which Yvette would arrange to meet with her mother in private, somewhere outside of the home. Yvette called her mother to implement their plan, she and her mother shared a few minutes of small talk before Yvette made an urgent request.

"Mother, I need for you to come to Austin alone this weekend, there is something very important that you and I need to discuss! Can you come?"

"Yvette, can't we talk about this on the phone?"

"No, we can't discuss it by phone, mom. It is important, we need to talk in person."

"In that case, I will be at the hotel tomorrow."

"You'll be at the Driskill? OK, call me when you arrive."

"I love you, Yvette."

"Yes, mom, I love you too."

Yvette became more and more nervous as her meeting with her mother approached, but Amanda's words of encouragement and assurance reinforced her resolve to explain her concerns to her mother. She was calm when the phone rang shortly after noon.

"Hi, mom, how was the trip? No, I haven't eaten yet. Ok, I'll be there shortly, love you."

"Amanda, that was, mom she is at the hotel waiting for me. I'll call you later."

Yvette was dressed and had not eaten in anticipation of her mother's arrival at the Driskill. She was a bit jittery, yet confident as she drove to meet her mother. After embracing, Yvette and her mother went directly to the dining room where they enjoyed a short lunch together with neither of them mentioning the reason for their urgent meeting. After dessert, they adjourned to the privacy of Yvette's mother's suite away from strangers and listening ears before either mentioned the reason for their untimely confab.

"Your father and I love you dearly we want only the best for you, Yvette. What is troubling you?"

"I love both of you too, there is something important I need to talk with you about, I need your advice on how to handle an awkward situation," replied Yvette.

"You are not pregnant are you?" Asked her mother with abject alarm in her voice.

"No mom, I'm not pregnant, I've never had sex with anyone!" Exclaimed Yvette shocked at the question it was out of character coming from her mother.

"I'm glad to hear that."

Slightly irritated by her mother's response, Yvette countered.

"That I'm not pregnant or that I have never had sex with anyone?"

"Well both, mostly that you are not pregnant, if you were that would present a serious problem for both of us."

Relieved of her worst fear, Evette's mother proceeded calmly.

"Now that we have settled that. What situation are you referring to?"

"This may surprise you mother, but there is no way I can live my life being subservient to a man like you are to dad. I hate the thought of it."

Yvette felt at peace with herself, she had said it at last, her feelings on the subject were no longer shrouded in secrecy her mother knew what she thought. Her mother hugged her rubbing the back of her neck.

"My beloved, Yvette, things are not always what they seem to be, let me explain. I have never been subservient to your father we have always been equals in all things even though it may appear otherwise. We agreed early on in our marriage that I would remain in the background publicly, for business reasons, while privately sharing equally in all decisions including business ones. You know how male Latinos want to think that it's exclusively a man's world. Well, it's not true! Behind the scenes, we women control much more than is universally believed by most Latinos. They all know it, but are too *macho* to admit it. That's just how it is in our society."

"Momma, I had no idea about you and dad. Is that how it really is in the Latino world?"

"There is one aspect of my relationship with your father that you need to understand, we are lovers and always have been, we love each other very much. Next to you, our love is the thing we cherish most in this world, we are devoted to one another and to you."

"How could you not have told me this before, mother?" Implored Yvette raising her voice a bit in anger.

"You needed be old enough to understand and discreet enough to keep quiet about things others needn't know. Today you proved you're old enough and wise enough to know how things really are in our world your father and I are proud of you. Your father and I married for love, not for convenience as is often the case, believe me, we want nothing less for you our daughter."

Yvette was inundated with an outpouring of love, she had never imagined how easily she could interconnect with her mother. For them an open discussion of importance subjects in a candid exchange of ideas was foreign to Yvette. Today's exchange with her mother extinguished the feeling of hostility that had been festering within her for the past two years. By the time their visit ended, Yvette understood she could talk freely with her mother in the future about subjects she had always considered forbidden without causing an uproar in the family. She had a new appreciation for her mother's wisdom.

"Amanda, it went so well I really never had a problem. I can't thank you and Verona enough for guiding me to such a wonderful resolution. I'll tell you all about it tomorrow, I'm spending the night with mom!"

Upon hearing the good news, Amanda promptly called Verona to tell her all was well between Yvette and her mother the problem had been amicably resolved and Yvette was happy.

Verona finished her degree program at UT and following graduation accepted a position with a marketing research firm while Kevin continued his studies at UT working toward his PhD. She and Kevin were living in their townhouse engulfed in married bliss happier together than either could have imagined in their most bizarre pre-marital dreams. As prearranged, Verona was visiting Amanda at her dorm on Saturday morning when the attorney rang the doorbell to the townhouse he had made an appointment earlier in the week to speak privately with Kevin to discuss an urgent legal matter.

Chapter 13 Land of California

Bruce arrive at Stanford several days before the beginning of the mid-term semester to become familiar with the Medical School and to acclimatize himself to his new surroundings. Shortly after moving into his apartment he began surveying the Stanford facility checking out the size of the campus, its architecture and the layout of the Medical School he found them all to be monumental in grandeur and scope. The grounds were well done and manicured to perfection Stanford appeared to be an ideal place to continue his medical education and once Estelle joined him the conditions would be perfect. His apartment had many unusual amenities and advanced high-tech innovations far superior to those he had enjoyed at UT. There was a complete computer room filled with the latest most up-to-date equipment available. He had both cable and wireless service allowing him to operate the apartment's electronic devices remotely using his cell phone which proved to be efficient when he forgot to turn on the burglar alarm or program the thermostat before leaving for class. Many special medical-specific programs had been downloaded on his computer allowing him to search the entire Stanford medical library plus medical libraries at several other top universities in the country all of which could be accomplished without leaving the comfort of his apartment.

Nearing the Stanford campus on the last leg of her long drive from Texas, Estelle called on her cell phone using the Bluetooth feature provided in her Mustang.

"Bruce, I'm here, all of my belongings are stuffed in my car. Where can I meet you?"

"Where are you Estelle? Your voice is coming in loud and clear like you are right next to me. I love it you are exciting me."

She gave him her location which was only a few blocks away prompting Bruce to direct her to the apartment entrance where he was waiting when she turned into the parking lot. As soon as she stepped out of the Mustang, Bruce lifted her off of her feet smothering her with kisses as he held her in his arms.

"I missed you Estelle, I don't want us to be apart ever again, I love you."

Estelle kissed Bruce with her hands pressing on his cheeks her lips were eager to find his as they embraced for a second time.

"I missed you too, Bruce, I love you. Can I come in?"

"Come on, I'll race you to the door!" Exclaimed Bruce holding her hand as he walked briskly toward the apartment. Opening the door to his apartment with one hand Bruce asked.

"What do you want to see first the study room or the living area?"

"Neither, let's go to the bedroom. I missed you Bruce."

They stripped dropping their clothes in two heaps on the floor. Bruce put his arms around Estelle pulling her against him while kissing her on the neck, his hands moved slowly down her back until they enfolded her soft buns Bruce pulled her tightly against him. Estelle's lips were on his, hungry to satisfy the passion building within her. Her skin was alive where Bruce touched her sending a steadily building sensation of pleasure throughout her body. Bruce responded by lifting her in his arms then laying her face up on the bed where he began caressing her bit by bit until their lips and bodies locked in an electrifying frenzy of passion. After the sexual tension subsided, and she began to relax Estelle remarked coyly.

"I guess, I need to find my dorm and unload my stuff before it gets too late."

"There is no need to do that you can spend the night here with me, I'll unload everything for you tomorrow. Tonight we celebrate being together in each other's arms again. By the way have you eaten?"

"I was in such a rush to get here that I sort of forgot to eat. I had other things on my mind!"

"You must be hungry then, let's go eat before we do any more celebrating. There is a good restaurant just down the street. Say you will stay all night, Estelle?"

"You have talked me into it. Unless you are really hungry, I suggest we not spend too much time eating because I feel like a long slow celebration after I get a snack to tide me over."

With less urgency to jump into bed when they returned from dinner, Estelle surveyed the room while slowly undressing. Her eyes fixed on the WANTED poster hanging on the bedroom wall she could not help being amused by the implication of its hanging just above the bed. They did not get out of bed until almost noon the following day they were relaxed and famished from a night of torrid love and sex. They dressed and then went out for lunch. Despite their late start, Estelle and all of her belongings were moved into her dorm by early afternoon. She and Bruce were worn out following the move in and from their previous activities causing them to spend the night in their separate beds to insure a good night's sleep. They agreed there would be plenty of time later for more celebrating.

Over the next few months, Bruce and Estelle settled into a fixed routine, during the week she spent her nights in the dorm while reserving the weekends for sleepovers at Bruce's apartment. Bruce's study requirements left little time for recreational sex during the week and much to their disappointment, sometimes, not even on the weekend. Bruce and Estelle each provided what the other needed they were devoted lovers each intent on satisfying the other in an atmosphere of love and passion. They were perfect for each other and madly in love.

Estelle had much more time than Bruce for activities outside of the classroom she soon knew most of the women in her dorm by name and became friends with several of them. One of the things Estelle noticed most, about her new friends and acquaintances, was that Californians were different. Their perception of many important aspects of life was contrary to that of most Texans. Estelle was self-sufficient and proud of it, whereas, her Californian counterparts seemed to expect others to make decisions for them and, for the most part, were followers rather than leaders. Estelle became well aware of this difference in thinking during conversations regarding social programs run by the State and Federal governments they were viewed as entitlements or rights of the citizens by Californians. This whole socialistic culture was opposite to Estelle's upbringing in Junction, Texas where these benefits were thought of as welfare, available to the needy, rather than a right of every citizen. Estelle learned early on not to discuss politics, the environment, or social programs with her fellow students. On these subjects she became an interested observer, but never an outspoken commentator. Estelle decided to get her minor in art which she had always enjoyed. She enrolled in a special oil painting class dedicated to using the Golden Mean for designing and placing the major subject on the canvas. She was interested in realistic paintings, yet appreciated the use of abstract design in producing eye pleasing pictures. Her art professors were also professional painters who sold the majority of their works at local exhibitions. Some also accepted commissions when the price was right, but they preferred to select their own subjects.

Estelle excelled as an oil painter quickly embracing the medium as her means of self- expression in the world of art. During those periods she and Bruce were apart, Estelle turned to her painting as a diversion for her loneliness.

Medical school and study consumed most of Bruce's existence, except for the time spent with Estelle, he had few outside activities. Sporadically, he would go a full week without seeing Estelle fortunately she was understanding and supportive. When they did get together their love for one another was intense and all-consuming they proved as a couple that love and sex do indeed go together just as Estelle had always thought. During these weekend interludes, Bruce loved to sneak up behind Estelle kiss her on the side of the neck then put his arms around her whispering.

"I love you."

Estelle enjoyed Bruce's devious little trick, she usually turned in his arms saying, "I love you too." Before kissing him back. They discussed their plans for the future as well as what was happening in their day-to-day routines at Stanford. Both were anticipating Estelle's graduation, so they could marry with her parents blessing. It could not happen soon enough to suit them, living apart was not nearly as delightful as spending their nights together.

Bruce decided to work toward an MD in neurology upon completing his BS degree in the spring. He had worked hard to reach this point as had Estelle, they and their parents were anticipating their upcoming wedding in Junction following Estelle's graduation in the spring. Bruce and Estelle found it difficult to believe the date was only two months away it had seemed so distant when they first came to California to pursue their dream of a life together. They were almost four years older with a definite plan for the next few years. Upon returning to California following the wedding, Estelle planned to find a job and Bruce was to complete his MD. After that they would go wherever Bruce's internship required before settling permanently somewhere in south central Texas.

With their diplomas in hand the happy graduates and their parents gathered for a celebratory dinner in a local restaurant and bistro noted for its Italian food and fine wine. Addressing the group while holding his wine glass high Bruce stated.

"Just think, in four or five more years Estelle and I will be able to establish a permanent residence somewhere."

All raised their glasses and saluted.

"Cheers."

The parents of the bride and groom were not strangers they had been together on several previous occasions and although they were not close friends, they liked each other and were congenial. Both sets of parents were in agreement that their counterparts would make good in-laws and great grandparents. Estelle's father expressed his preference for their ultimate location saying to Bruce and Estelle.

"I sure hope you settle within easy reach of Junction, Estelle is an only child and will someday inherit the Winger Ranch."

"Daddy, Bruce and I have not forgotten our family responsibilities, no matter what, we will take care of the ranch. Anyway, that will be a long time in the future."

"Thank you Estelle, I already feel better knowing you and Bruce have talked about the ranch."

Peggy and Estelle's mother addressed the next week's wedding, all the arrangements had been made, and the invitations had been sent weeks ago, Estelle's gown had been fitted and completed. Her mother was beside herself as the wedding date approached.

"Estelle's gown is absolutely the most beautiful wedding dress I have ever seen. She looks so beautiful in it, she will be the most beautiful bride Junction has seen in a long time, maybe ever."

The party broke up around eleven, Bruce and his parents returned to their hotel while Estelle went with her parents to their hotel. The next morning each family boarded their separate flights home encountering a minimum of difficulty and commotion. Even though they left at different times and at different gates, they arrived in Texas at about the same time safe and sound back in God's country. The wedding of Estelle Winger and Bruce Wilkerson became the most highly attended and acclaimed social event of the year in Junction. Everyone living in and around Junction knew the Wingers, and they all came to celebrate the marriage of their daughter, Estelle. Ranchers and their families for miles around came to the wedding which was held at the First United Methodist Church of Junction. The church was overflowing during and after the ceremony the ranchers along with the Winger's many friends from town came to the reception at the nearby Winger Ranch. Verona happily served as Estelle's Matron of Honor while Kevin was one of the many other wedding guests in the congregation he had no official function to perform. Together, they later managed to congratulate the bride and groom personally during the reception which was hectic due to the massive crowd. During the few private minutes they had together Verona, Estelle, Bruce and Kevin talked briefly about old times and their plans going forward. Kevin found these conversations to be extremely difficult, he had to be careful in what he said. It was imperative that he not inadvertently reveal facts about any of them that he should not know. He had to keep what he had learned through his work at Abe separate from what he knew in his real life. Kevin was genuinely happy to see Bruce and Estelle married it was another successful culmination of a beautiful love story for Abe and Gentex. He and Verona had been the first. Unknown to Kevin at the time, the other two love stories involving Abe's wards had ended in tragedy.

Bruce and Estelle spent their two week honeymoon in *Ocho Rios*, Jamaica before returning to sunny California. Shortly thereafter, Estelle took a job at a stock brokering firm as assistant to their top performing broker where she worked for the next two years while Bruce earned his MD. They were happy living in the land of California even though they felt out of place sort of like foreigners. There were things both Estelle and Bruce liked about California its mild weather and beautiful scenery were outstanding as were some of its smaller cities and towns. On one memorial occasion Bruce threw caution to the wind he took a full weekend off from school so he and Estelle could make a Napa Valley wine tasting trip. The following day they drove to the coast encountering Hwy. 1 for an exhilarating drive along the Pacific Ocean its beauty was breathtaking unsurpassed by any of the beaches they had seen Texas and the Caribbean Sea.

Estelle joined a private art class which met one evening a week in the teacher's studio which was located about a mile from their apartment. The teacher greeted each of the students as they entered checking them off of his list. When all ten students had arrived, he announced to the group.

"My name is Jason Bard this is a new class, so we will all be starting at the same place. Would each of you please stand and say your names so we can all get to know each other?"

Most of the students were women, but there were two men in the class. Kim Hurst who was about thirty and Sam Smith who was gray headed and approaching sixty. For the most part the women were about Estelle's age or younger. Estelle was by far the most attractive, but several of the others were also well built with sexy bodies although they did not possess Estelle's beauty.

"Now that we have made our introductions, everyone put your work away while I explain how the class is going to be conducted. As you have probably noticed there are easels available for each of you. The first hour of each class will be devoted to exercises designed to enhance your understanding of oil painting. Everyone is required to participate in these exercises, there will be no exceptions. If you do not participate in the exercises, you cannot attend my class. Tonight we are going to learn about shading and its importance to oil painting and art in general. I will be passing out the material for this exercise shortly. Once we have completed tonight's exercise you can work on whatever you please. I will be available for consultation and advice, however, I will not, let me emphasize this, I will not paint on your picture."

Estelle found the exercise to be enjoyable and enlightening it explained shading in a way none of her professors had mentioned. Although he was a bit gruff, Estelle liked the teacher he offered detailed advice on her in progress painting without being critical. The three hour class had been enjoyable and educational, she was looking forward to next week's class.

Over the next few months Estelle came to know the people in her art class fairly well, she appreciated their diverse talents and distinct painting techniques. They all worked, some were college educated professionals while the others were technicians and small business owners one of the ladies was a surgical nurse. They discussed all sorts of topics apart from painting during their classes which led Estelle to realize that not all Californians were alike these people thought a lot like Texans they were independent and had their own ideas about government and happiness. Sometimes several of them met after class for a drink at the nearby hotel bar. Estelle and her three lady friends had selected a table and were about to be seated when Kim Hurst suddenly showed up insisting on joining them. No one objected Kim was a likeable guy who took part the discussions in class. He was friendly, young and good looking. "Kim what prompted you to join us this evening," asked Susan who was near his age.

"I don't know, I just thought it was a good idea. Do you ladies come here after all the classes?"

"No, just now and again it's not a regular thing. Why?"

"I was thinking I had been missing out on a good thing not joining you before tonight. What are you drinking? The first round is on me."

"What a pleasant surprise, thank you Kim."

Kim looked directly at Estelle his eyes were focused on her beautiful face, he was looking at her intently when he said.

"Estelle what do you do when you are not in art class? Do you ever have any fun?"

"Oh yes, Kin I have a lot of fun doing my thing."

"That is very interesting, I'm glad to hear you are into fun."

They were on their second drink when the band began playing following their break. Kim asked Estelle to dance, but she refused. Her companions began urging her to dance just one dance, it couldn't hurt anything. After much cajoling Estelle finally relented agreeing to have one dance with Kim. When they started toward the dance floor Kim took Estelle's hand in his. Once on the dance floor he held her close he was a superb dancer making all the right moves. When the music stopped Kim whispered in her ear.

"Estelle you are so beautiful, why don't we go to my place and have some real fun?"

"I appreciate your compliment and interest, but I am a one man woman and I found my one and only man several years ago."

Kim returned to the table long enough to say good night to the other women before he left. Susan asked, "Why did he leave in such a rush?"

"I don't know, maybe he didn't like my dancing."

They finished their drinks then picked up their purses to leave when Estelle said emphatically.

"This was a lot of fun ladies, we should do it again sometime."

She laughed on her way to the apartment.

"I'm sure going to enjoy hugging Bruce when I get home!

Chapter 14 Reunion

When Alan answered it was a familiar voice on the phone and a welcome one to his ears.

"Hey, Alan. It's me Jim. How are you this fine morning?"

"Good to hear your voice, Jim. I'm doing OK. I've been on a downer ever since I lost Betty, but things are beginning to look up. My job at SeiRes is really working out great, the work is interesting, and we have come up with some new innovations which may make all of us rich sometime."

"I am glad you are doing well, Alan. Tell me more about SeiRes."

"I really like it here, we are free to work on any new ideas we have in our field then once an idea is selected for development we all work on the development phase. It's fun and rewarding. What are you up to?"

"Alan, the strangest thing happened to me last Friday. Have you ever heard of Imperial Enterprises?"

"No, I can't say that I have. Who are they?"

"Alan, they are one of the largest and most successful investment companies in the world. Friday one of their representatives contacted me by phone with an unusual proposal. Now listen to this carefully, Alan, they have made an offer to fund a startup technology company to be owned and operated by you and me."

"What kind of technological company?"

"He was very specific, under the terms of their proposal the two of us are to be joint and equal owners in the company, which can be located anywhere we chose so long as it is in Texas. Furthermore, we can work on any ideas that interest us with no restrictions of any kind."

"Jim that sounds too good to be true. Are you sure this is not a scam of some sort? He didn't ask for money did he?"

"No, he didn't ask for any money. Alan, I spent the better part of the weekend checking out Imperial Enterprises before I called you. I am convinced the offer is on the up and up, there is no scam involved here. My question is, are you interested in pursuing Imperial's offer?"

The prospect of reuniting with Jim as a partner appealed to Alan. Growing up they had collaborated on several of their own scientific projects which were successful and they had a great time working together. Not only that Jim, was brilliant and his best friend. His short tenure at SeiRes demonstrated to Alan the potential economic benefits of owning a successful technology company. Working with Jim in their own company was very appealing to him, they could develop new ideas, which was what they always liked to do and they could become rich in the process.

"Jim, I am definitely interested. When can we get the specifics of their proposal?"

"I don't know, let me make a call and I will get back with you."

Within twenty minutes, Jim called back. He was thrilled to report.

"Alan, the Imperial Enterprises representative would like to conference with us at the Tmex Hotel in Houston next Saturday afternoon at two, his name is Alex. He will meet us in the bar. Is that OK?"

Alan hesitated momentarily then replied.

"Yes that's OK with me, Jim. I have been avoiding the Tmex for a while, but it's OK. Jim are you bringing your girlfriend or coming alone? The Tmex would be a wonderful place for the two of you to spend some time away from New York."

"Yoko, will not be coming she has a family obligation this weekend maybe next time. I would sure like for you to meet her."

"I'm anxious to meet the girl who turned Jim Running Horse's head, she must be brilliant or a raving beauty or maybe both. At any rate, I'll see you at the Tmex bar on Saturday. I'm looking forward to seeing you Jim, thanks for telling me about the offer."

A little before two in the afternoon, Alan entered the Tmex lobby, looked around anxiously then proceeded to the bar which was empty. He checked his watch which showed 1:50 p.m. before speaking to the bartender.

"Hi John, it's been a while."

John peaked his head from below the counter where he had been adjusting the carbonation unit for the draft beer dispenser. He was astonished to see Alan, who had not appeared at the Tmex since Betty's untimely death.

"Mister Alan, I'm so glad to see you! We have missed you around here. How are you doing?"

Alan shook the bartender's hand saying.

"It's good to see you John. Betty would have been glad to see you too. You were one of her favorites here at the Tmex."

Alan deftly changed the subject.

"John, has a guy named, Alex, been in the bar today?"

"No, Mr. Alan. Look there is someone coming this way now."

He pointed to a figure in the center of the lobby making his way in their direction. Alan recognized Jim moving through the crowd, he rushed to greet him before he reached the bar.

"Jim, I'm so glad you made it, how was the trip?"

Waving his hands in front of him, Jim replied in abject disgust.

"Tiring. Nothing went right, first the plane was delayed on takeoff then we were diverted because of bad weather as a result I've just checked in. Have you made contact with Alex?"

"Not yet, he hasn't showed so far, let's have a seat at that table over there," said Alan pointing to the corner table.

"Your usual Mr. Alan?" asked the bartender.

"Yes, thank you, John. What would you like Jim?"

"I'll have the same, you know I rarely drink I wouldn't know one drink from the other."

The two of them were each sipping their Irish whiskey when Alex approached their table.

"Mr. Running Horse and Mr. Strong, I am Alex," said the stranger extending his hand as they rose to greet him.

"Would you like a drink?" asked Alan before Alex sat down.

"I see you have made an excellent choice. I'll have one of the same."

"I am sure you gentlemen are wondering what in the hell is going on. We at Imperial Enterprises seek out exceptionally talented people in a number of fields of endeavor, primarily young individuals with inquiring minds such as you two. Those who meet our strict code of honesty and who have a demonstrated capability for innovation and performance are offered positions with one of our subsidiary companies, or sometimes with the parent itself. In a few exceptional cases, such as yours, we fund startup companies to develop unique ideas which we can either license or produce for sale. Our program is unmatched in the business world in that we find the talent first, we then fund the startup whereas most startups must find their own funding which puts them at a great disadvantage should they become successful. Gentlemen, before I outline the specifics of our proposal, I want you to understand you were not selected at random. We know everything there is to be known about both of you. We probably know more about you than your own mothers."

Alan and Jim glanced at each other following Alex's comment. It was unexpected, but revealing indicating Imperial Enterprises had done an extensive investigation into both of their backgrounds

"Are there any questions to this point?"

In the absence of a reply from either Jim or Alan, he continued his explanation of the process.

"At the end of our session, I will provide each of you with a written contract which contains all the terms for our funding a company to be owned jointly and equally by the two of you. We strongly suggest you have a lawyer analyze the contract and then go over it with you paragraph by paragraph, it is very important that you understand all the terms and conditions contained in the contract. Today, I am presenting a brief summary of the primary terms so that you can decide whether or not to proceed."

Alex began listing the primary requirements of the contract.

"The startup company must be a regular corporation registered in the State of Texas. The outstanding stock must be owned equally by each of you. Imperial Enterprises will contribute all funding for the corporation with the first year's budget fixed at ten million dollars. Thereafter, the company's annual budget may be more, but never less than the first year budget. The joint owners shall have the exclusive right to select ideas and areas of interest for study to create projects for development by the company. At the end of three years, Imperial Enterprises, at its sole option, may elect to cease funding of the company. Imperial Enterprises shall have the exclusive right to any and all products produced at the company whether intellectual or physical in nature. Ownership of the company products shall be, Imperial Enterprises seventy five percent (75%) and the company twenty five percent (25%). At the end of ten years the company may, at its sole option, terminate its contract with Imperial Enterprises. Gentlemen, I assure you that terms comparable to those we are proposing for financing a startup company cannot be found anywhere else in the business world."

Upon completion of his presentation, Alex looked at each of them for acknowledgment of his last statement before inquiring.

"Gentlemen, what do you think?"

Alan was intrigued by the proposal and impatient to move forward, he spoke first.

"I am definitely interested, if Jim is."

Jim responded immediately before Alex could ask another question.

"We are interested in your proposal, what is the next step?"

Alex handed each of them an information packet including a written contract between Imperial Enterprises and the two of them.

"Once you and your lawyers have reviewed the documents and are satisfied with the contract, call me. We will then schedule a formal execution date to finalize the deal. It has been a pleasure meeting the two of you in person, I'm sure we will be closing the deal in the near future."

He shook their hands and hurried away leaving the two friends to discuss and analyze what he had said and what it meant for their future. Alan was delighted as was Jim, they would be united in a business that could not fail. They would be able to investigate any of their ideas with no restrictions. It was a miracle, how things happened, they would be doing what they had always wanted.

"Jim, I'm going to talk with the Professor about our offer from Imperial Enterprises I'm sure he can help us with the legal work. He and the head of the Baylor School of Law are close friends, I'm sure he can get him to help us for free. Is that OK with you?"

"Sure, where else could we find a better lawyer? And I like the free part. See if the Professor can arrange for his friend to advise us, meanwhile I have to return to New York to explain to Yoko that we will be moving to Texas. Keep me in the loop with your legal advisor's evaluation of Imperial's contract."

Jim was anxious to get back to the airport because of the tight flight schedule he had booked for the trip. Without further discussion, he rushed to catch the shuttle bus at the hotel entrance leaving Alan alone to decide their next move. Still sitting in the Tmex bar having a second Irish whiskey, Alan called the Professor giving him a general description of the situation at hand before telling him that he would be arriving in Waco early the following morning to review the information and contract with him. The Professor was both pleased and amused that Alan and Jim were to be working together again. He was delighted they had elected to seek his aid in their upcoming venture. The Professor had missed mentoring Alan and Jim since they had gone away to college and became involved in other personal affairs removed from their scientific wanderings. He was elated they had thought to include him in their future plans. Darlene was equally enthusiastic to learn Alan and Jim were planning to join forces in a startup venture. For the past year, she had been concerned the loss of Betty would have a lasting adverse effect on Alan and his future life.

"Reuniting with Jim will be a stabilizing force in Alan's life and could provide an incentive for Alan to reconstruct his personal life. I know Alan will be happy working with Jim on exploration of their ideas it was what he had always liked the best aside from Betty. It seems like God has intervened here. They're working together was meant to be."

The Professor and Alan poured over the information packet and the contract all day Sunday they separately analyzed each paragraph of the contract and then compared notes to reconcile any differences in interpretation between them. In the end, they both agreed the proposal, and the contract were very favorable toward Jim and Alan. It was obvious Imperial Enterprises expected them to produce important new scientific breakthroughs which would have significant economic value now and in the future. In exchange, Imperial Enterprises was willing to fund their development and to share fairly in the profits with the originators. There would be no cost or risk to Jim and Alan. It was a deal that was too good to be true! Alan wanted to call Jim, but the Professor urged him to wait until his colleague had studied and approved the contract.

"It looks great to us Alan, but we are not lawyers. Let my friend study the contract, for however long it takes, before you talk with Jim or contact Imperial Enterprises."

Wednesday of the following week, the Professor sent Alan an email which included the lawyer's analysis of the Imperial Enterprises contract. He had never seen a more friendly agreement in his long legal career, from a technical point of view, the contract was ideal for its intended purpose and afforded Alan and Jim every possible protection under Texas Law. He recommended execution of the contract as is, with no changes. Following a review of the legal opinion by both Jim and Alan, they agreed to meet Alex in Houston the following Saturday to execute the contract which would formally launch Cyber Research, Inc. as their legal vehicle for future operations.

Within a month, the company had been funded allowing it to lease space in a new building located in northwest Austin and their newly organized company, Cyber Research, Inc. had been registered to do business in Texas. Alan resigned his position at SeiRes and leased a condo near their new place of business in Austin so that he could officially open Cyber Research, Inc.'s new office. He was joined a week later by Jim who had cut his ties with his employer in New York. At Yoko's parent's insistence, Jim and Yoko married before leaving New York. Her parents refused to allow her to move to Austin with Jim without being married first, cohabitation was unacceptable in their culture. Once Jim and Yoko found suitable living quarters, the boyhood friends entered their new office space together as joint owners of Cyber Research, Inc. Jim unlocked the door before motioning Alan to enter with a small bow. Once inside Alan could no longer contain his joy.

"Who would ever have thought that the two of us would be owners of a research company?"

"Not me, particularly, after we went our separate ways to college and work."

"Jim, we can't do anything until we get this place furnished and buy the necessary computer equipment. Let's start with a list of computer equipment we need."

Alan took notes as Jim began calling out the names of specific equipment they needed to get started, a process which took up most of the day. They rechecked the list before leaving for the day. They would began ordering equipment in the morning

Alpha-2 reported to Abe.

"Alan and Jim Running Horse are now co-owners of a company called Cyber Research, Inc. They have opened an office in Austin and are about to commence doing business their sponsor is Imperial Enterprises of Houston. We have established the usual surveillance for Alan and the new office. Are there any special instructions so far as Jim Running Horse is concerned?"

Headquarters sent a prompt reply.

"No, he does not require surveillance other than when he is with Alan."

A month later, Jim and Alan had their computers and other equipment installed and operating they were ready to embark on their first project although it had yet to be determined exactly what they would consider first. After much discussion between them, the partners agreed they would each spend a week in their respective offices thinking of projects they might want to consider. The following week they would compare lists and jointly select their first project. While reviewing Jim's list, Alan exclaimed!

"Jim, I think you have come up with a gem of an idea the world needs a way which will allow remote monitoring, collection and transmission of massive amounts of data wirelessly while maintaining the integrity of the data and protecting it from theft! If you agree, your idea is my choice for our first project."

"Alan, we are like the team of old that is my selection as well. Let's get started."

A week of checking manufacturer's online listings, of in stock equipment needed to construct components for their project, indicated that for some applications there was no existing equipment suitable for their needs. They would have to design and assemble their own. They assigned their first project the code name JUMBO and went to work. After a few weeks of work on JUMBO it began to take shape as a viable multi-faceted project causing them to divided it into two parts, remote with commercial electric power and remote without existing electric power the two situations required different equipment to accomplish their objective. Jim and Alan worked at a fast pace to develop electronic devices and equipment needed to make JUMBO a reality. They worked twelve hour days most of the time, but Jim insisted he needed the weekends off to please Yoko. As work on the project progressed it became evident, they should first develop a basic system which met all of their original requirements, it could then be customized to perform specific tasks covering a wide range of diverse applications.

"Look, Alan you can't stay here working well into the morning every night, you need to get a life outside of Cyber Research," said Jim as he put on his backpack to leave for the day.

"Yoko and I do other things in the evening like going to the theatre or to dinner. We both believe you should find a female companion, someone who is interesting and fun. It would be good for you, Alan. Working these long hours dulls your brain and hinders it from producing at its highest level."

Alan set at his desk for a few minutes after Jim left the building rationalizing.

"Yes, Jim I know, but how can I forget Betty?"

The more he thought the more he realized Jim was right, he convinced himself to leave right away and treat himself to a night out something he had not done in the last year. Alan left his townhouse undecided on a specific destination, but he did not want to go far. Driving toward downtown Austin he inexplicitly stopped at the New Place Hotel which was just off of the highway to the right. He had always favored hotel bars because they were spacious and sometimes had local performers for entertainment. He had no motive or reason to stop at this particular place it was just a sudden impulse. He had never been in the New Place Hotel and wasn't positive they even had a bar. Alan looked around the lobby until he found the entrance to the bar which was dimly lit and tucked in the far corner of the lobby. When he entered, he was disappointed to see only two other patrons both of whom were older men sitting alone at the bar. Alan waited until his eyes became accustomed to the dim lighting then selected a table which would give him access to the dance floor and provide a good spot for listening to the band or watching individual performers if there were any. He had barely sat down when a striking young lady appeared out of nowhere she walked directly to the table he had selected. She stood on the dance floor just in front of him surveying the various tables available before turning to Alan.

"Do you have someone joining you?"

Alan was somewhat shocked by the question, but replied in a friendly tone.

"No, I am alone. Would you care to join me?"

"Thank you, if you don't mind I think I will. My name is Martha, I'm working, and this table is perfect for what I do."

Alan was mystified, but intrigued by the young lady she was beautiful.

"I don't know what is going on here, she is beautiful and certainly interesting. Working? Working at what?"

Intrigued, he continued.

"Welcome, my name is Alan, I am pleased to meet you, Martha. Could I buy you a drink while we get acquainted?"

"Normally I don't drink while I'm working, but since you have been so kind to share your table with me I'll make an exception this time. I'll have a frozen *margarita* with salt, please."

Alan ordered an Irish whiskey for himself and a large frozen *margarita* for Martha he then leaned back to savor the beauty of this fascinating person sitting next to him.

"Martha, what kind of work brings you to a hotel bar on a Friday night alone?"

The waiter delivered their drinks as Martha began her reply.

"I operate a talent development company, here in Austin, called TDI, which is located a few miles to the northwest of here. We train all kinds of talented people to become professional entertainers. One of my students is making his public debut here tonight. I am here to evaluate his performance, so that we can help him to improve in the future. I came early to get a table with the best vantage point to do my job, only to find that you had beat me to it."

Alan was pleased to hear Martha was not in another kind of business as he had first feared. This beautiful woman was more than interesting, she was bewitching and appeared to be fearless.

"Enough about me, what is a nice looking guy like you doing in a hotel bar alone on Friday night?"

"It's rather strange that I am here, my good friend and business partner advised me to get a life outside of our business, after a little thought I decided to have a night out for the first time in over a year. For some reason I wound up here. Maybe an unknown force deemed we were meant to meet!"

Martha smiled, she was having similar thoughts.

"How do you occupy your time when you are not talking to young ladies in hotel bars?" asked Martha who was attracted to the fair skinned blond man sitting next to her. Alan explained in detail how he and Jim Running Horse came to be partners and equal owners in Cyber Research, Inc. By the time he finished the bar was beginning to fill with patrons. At that time, Alan understood why Martha had asked to join him, what he didn't understand was how they seemed to think alike and to appreciate each other's ideas.

"Is it possible we have met somewhere in the past? It's like we have had this conversation before," said Alan marveling at Martha's huge brown eyes and alluring smile.

"I don't think we have never met before even though I feel like I have known you for a long time. I would have remembered you if we had met before because I don't know any other blond men."

Martha was surprised that this could be happening with a total stranger she had known for less than an hour. She felt very comfortable and at ease sitting next to Alan he seemed to belong there. In a way it was upsetting, yet Martha was enjoying herself in a strange way, she had a warm feeling when she looked at him.

"Alan, do you have a last name?"

"Of course, forgive me for not mentioning my last name, it's Strong. I'm Alan Strong. My mother and dad live in Waco where he is a professor at Baylor and she is in the real estate business. How about you?"

"My name is Martha Schuber and I am from Corpus Christi. My mom is Rachel Jensen and my dad is Phil Jensen they are petroleum engineers and own a thriving mid-stream company operating in South Texas."

"I take it that Phil is not your real father, since you have different last names."

"Mom had me before she met Phil, so I have her maiden name as my last name, Phil is still my dad just not my father."

"My God! You are going to find this hard to believe. Strong is my mother's maiden name, she had me long before she and dad met. In fact, we met him on a Caribbean cruise ship when I was about eight years old they stayed in touch and later married. Like you and Phil, the Professor is my dad, but not my father. What an odd coincidence that you and I are sitting here together. I could have just as easily gone to another hotel bar."

Martha put her hand on his replying.

"It seems we are kindred spirits Mr. Alan Strong. I am very pleased you decided to come here, if not, I probably would never have met you which would have been unfortunate."

"That would have been horrible, Martha, you are one of the most fascinating and interesting people I have ever met. Do you realize how beautiful you are? I can't take my eyes off of you!"

"Let's enjoy the entertainment the band will be playing shortly and Mike will play the guitar during their first break. We can dance if you like while we wait for Mike to perform, I guarantee you will like him."

Martha's hand felt hot on his and Alan liked the feeling he made no effort to move his hand away from hers. They did not dance when the band first began playing, rather they continued to talk about the uniqueness of their encounter at the New Place bar and the many things they had in common.

"Alan, are we dancing the next number or are we going to just listen to the music?"

Martha was on her feet before the number commenced holding her hands out to Alan who had not answered her question.

"I'm sorry, I was so engaged in our discussion I forgot to ask," said Alan as he approached Martha.

The instant they touched Alan's mind began to race, once on the dance floor their bodies touching he was completely captivated. They made one turn around the small dance floor before either spoke.

"Are you fond of dancing Alan?"

"Well, yes. Why do you ask?"

"You seem a bit reluctant, relax and enjoy the music."

"I'm sorry, dancing with such a beautiful woman distracts me, I promise to relax."

"I appreciate the complement, Alan. I find you to be extremely attractive as well."

Alan put his arms around her waist then lifted her off of the floor so their lips were almost touching. He kissed her lightly before lowering her until her feet were back on the floor. She looked up at him smiling.

"That was very nice Alan. Clever too I might add."

She pulled him closer putting her head on his shoulder as they continued dancing. Alan held her close reveling in feeling her next to him the warmth of her body awakened feelings in him he thought were no longer alive. When the dance ended, they returned to their table for a short break, they were both satisfied and intrigued by the effects of Alan's importuned kiss while they were on the dance floor. A wave of good feeling and ecstasy had swept over Martha, she had been a little shocked at Alan's boldness, yet she felt fulfilled that he had kissed her. She didn't really know why, it just seemed right, it was something that should have happened. Alan thrilled her. For his part, Alan was glad he had the restraint to kiss Martha lightly rather than full on the lips as he had wanted. She excited him, being near her made him feel vigorous and alive his adrenaline was rushing and his hormones were working overtime he was revved up. They danced several more times before the band took a break, each of them were excited by the other aside from the sensual excitement of their bodies touching. There was a spark of sexual excitement between them, but that was not it there was a much greater attraction between them.

"Ladies and gentlemen, it is time for our break, but never fear the entertainment will continue. At this time, please, allow me to present, Mike Arne, a young and upcoming star who will play his guitar for you while we are away. Please, give him a huge welcome!"

The band leader motioning toward Mike. His introduction indicated he was giving the bar patrons an unexpected gift which they should appreciate. Mike bowed then spoke to the crowd most of whom were applauding out of courtesy they did not know whether he was talented or not.

"Ladies and gentlemen for your listening pleasure, I shall play several classical Spanish guitar pieces while the band takes a well-deserved break."

Most of the patrons cheered, and a few stood clapping their hands none of them had heard Mike play before, but they wanted him to feel welcome to demonstrate his talent.

"For my first number I will be playing *Flamenco Malaguena* with which most of you are familiar, enjoy," said Mike as he thrummed his guitar. He played *Malaguena* and several other classical Spanish songs to the delight and applause of the crowd who appreciated both his selection of musical scores and his outstanding presentation of them. Mike won the admiration of the audience with his ability which was far superior to that of most artists performing in hotel bars. Rising from his seated position Mike addressed the audience once more.

"Ladies and gentlemen for my last number I will be playing a selection from *El Amor brujo* which I hope you will find to be interesting and entertaining. Before I begin, I would like to introduce you to my instructor and mentor, Miss Martha Schuber! Martha, would you please stand?"

Martha arose to the cheers of the patrons taking a bow before returning to her seat next to Alan. Mike was not finished he had a special presentation in mind for his next number.

"Ladies and gentlemen, with generous applause from all of you, I think we could persuade Martha to perform the *Falla* Ritual fire dance that accompanies my last selection. Let's hear it for Martha."

The crowd went wild, they were all standing and cheering as Martha removed her shoes and walked barefooted to the center of the dance floor before bowing to Mike. He began playing his selection from *El Amor brujo* which began slowly. Barefooted, Martha began her dance to the slow beat around an imaginary bonfire in the center of the dance floor. She moved freely with the music her supple body bending and swaying as she became a part of the music itself. As the tempo picked up Martha's movements increased to a near frenzy before the dramatic climax of her dance. She slid to the floor as the piece ended her head was bowed on her outstretched leg with her right hand extended to her toe, her left arm and hand were raised straight up in the air. Mike rushed to Martha helping her to her feet with his extended free arm. They jointly took a bow amid the cheers and *oles* from the audience all of whom were on their feet applauding. The music and Martha's dance had been breathtaking and electrifying. The delirious crowd was very appreciative of the performance they had witnessed, it was extraordinary for free entertainment in a bar. Martha and Mike retreated to Alan's table as the patrons continued to cheer. Alan grabbed Mike's hand which he shook briskly.

"What a performance young man, you were great, I really appreciated your treatment of classical Spanish you are a master with your guitar."

He then picked Martha off of her feet kissing her vigorously on the mouth while swinging her around slowly.

"And you young lady were absolutely marvelous, I have never seen such dancing perfection. Are you aware that was a wonderful sexy dance you just performed?"

Mike stayed only long enough to hear Martha's critique of his performance he could see that he was in the way of something special.

"I must say, all of us enjoyed the music your presentation was impeccable, Mike. I liked the way you handled the audience too, smooth and friendly, they liked the idea of me dancing thanks to your skill in offering the option. Good job Mike, I'll see you tomorrow."

Watching Mike walk toward the exit Alan could not help thinking.

"How in this world did this happen. Martha is beautiful, talented and sexy as hell. I don't know who to thank for this, Jim, Yoko or lady luck, but I am sure grateful that I came!"

Martha and Alan listened to the band play a couple more numbers while holding hands before deciding to leave. They walked to the parking lot hand in hand and upon reaching Martha's car they embraced kissing goodnight not once but twice. Alan was reluctant to leave, yet he had the good sense and presence of mind to say good night while maintaining control of his mounting desires. Intrigued by the promise of an added dimension to his work dominated existence he added in parting.

"Martha, I would like very much to see you again, is there somewhere I can call you?"

Martha responded by handing Alan her business card and kissing him on the cheek replying softly.

"I would like that very much."

She drove away leaving Alan alone in the parking lot with his empty car. He waved as she eased past him then stood motionless for a moment watching her taillights disappeared around the corner.

"What a mysterious and talented woman she is, beautiful and sexy almost beyond belief. I have to see her again and the sooner the better!"

343

Alan was up early the following morning, preoccupied with his thoughts of Martha, he drove to the office without noticing he had skipped breakfast. He was so enthralled with Martha that the thought of her overshadowed his normal mental process he could not think of anything else. Alan sat looking at his computer screen for several minutes attempting to immerse himself in JUMBO, but to no avail. He could not concentrate on the project and its many complicated pieces. His thoughts kept returning to Martha, the more he thought about her, the more convinced he became that he had to spend more time with her. After struggling to work for most of the morning, he gave up then began searching his billfold for Martha's business card where he had stashed it for safekeeping the previous evening. Alan entered the number on her card into his cell phone call list and after making certain it had been saved pressed dial.

"TDI. How may I be of service?"

"Martha, this is Alan Strong we met last evening. I was wondering if it would be possible for us to get together for lunch or dinner."

"Alan, it's so good of you to call. I can't tell you how much I enjoyed sharing your table last night, I will never forget the fantastic evening we spent together. I can't go to lunch today I will be working with a client until two, after that I have something to do at three this afternoon. Why don't you pick me up at my office at half past two and go to the event with me? You will enjoy it and we can talk, afterward we can consider dinner."

Alan could not accept quickly enough.

"Martha it's a date. I will see you at two thirty."

He smiled as he locked the door to the office and went home to shower and change clothes. While in the shower, Alan thought about being with Martha again then said to himself.

"This may turn out to be a great day after all."

Alan checked his watch every minute or two, he was anxious to see Martha again and did not want to miss even a moment with her. His condo was not far from Martha's office, but to be on time he left early and was waiting in his car near the entrance to her building when Martha appeared. Jumping out of his car he rushed toward the entrance, Alan met her on the steps as she descended toward the parking lot saying.

"You are even more beautiful in the sunshine than you were last evening in the dim light."

Martha took his hand and gave him a peck on the cheek.

"Thank you, Alan, I hope you don't say that to all the ladies."

"Only to you, Martha, only to you. Who's driving?"

"Since I know where we are going, it's probably best that I do unless you are afraid to ride with me." Replied Martha jingling her car keys in the air. She pulled out of the parking lot and was speeding toward downtown before Alan asked. "Where are we going, to some special event?"

Martha giggled with an air of mystery as she replied, "We are going to see the Sirens play."

"Who are the Sirens and what instruments do they play?" asked Alan who was completely baffled following Martha's brief explanation.

"Who are the Sirens, anyway?"

"It definitely is a special event, to clear thing up, the Sirens are a female volleyball team at UT. I was a member of the team for three years while I was in school and I seldom miss one of their games."

"Are all the Sirens as beautiful and in as good of shape as you are?"

"I'll let you be the judge of that, we will be there in a few more minutes," answered Martha smiling in anticipation of Alan's upcoming surprise.

Holding Alan's hand, Martha led him to their seats in the bleachers before she went to the Siren's sideline. Martha and the Sirens exchanged pleasantries and high hands then talked for a while before the team returned to their bench ready to start the match. Their coach spoke with Martha briefly before the first serve then Martha returned to her seat next to Alan as the game got under way. Alan watched in amazement he had never seen female volleyball players in action they were much more athletic than he had imagined. They were slim, trim and tall and very attractive. All of them were taller than Martha which brought Alan to inquire.

"How did you compete with all of these tall women? Most of them are three or four inches taller than you."

"It wasn't easy, but I am a high jumper. I can jump higher than any of the people you see on the court."

"How is that possible?"

"It is a natural talent reinforced by my physical training as a classical dancer. I do some rigorous physical workouts, aside from a lot of dancing, to stay in shape. It's the part of classical dancing no one sees."

"Is there anything you are not good at?"

"I hate to disappoint you, Alan, there are many things I can't do well. How about you, what do you do for fun?"

"I've always stayed in good physical condition even though I didn't play sports in college. One thing I really like is saltwater fishing."

"That's strange, I grew up in Corpus Christi where fishing is a way of life, yet I have never gone fishing. My parents weren't interested, so I never thought about fishing."

"Martha, before I fall in love with you, there is a question I have to ask. Do you have a boyfriend or a significant other?"

"Alan, I am unattached. I had a fiancée, and we were about to be married, but tragically he was killed in a plane crash in China. That was two and a half years ago, I have been alone ever since."

"I'm so sorry Martha, I know exactly how you feel. I was engaged to be married to my long time soul mate, unfortunately, she was killed in an automobile accident in Waco just two weeks before our wedding. I have been very much a loner since then, you are the only woman I have danced with in the past two years."

"Another odd coincidence, Alan. We each have known the pain the other has endured. Before today, I haven't had a date since the plane crash."

"Me either, Martha another odd coincidence we share."

The volleyball match ended early. Martha congratulated the Sirens on another win and as they were leaving the court she glanced at her watch then at Alan.

"It's early, Alan. If you're game, I know a really neat place on Lake Travis where we can have dinner."

Hearing her proposal, Alan squeezed her hand gently.

"You are driving I'll go wherever you go."

Martha was unerring, she drove to The Oasis on Comanche Trail without missing a single turn. They were walking toward the restaurant when Martha said urgently.

"Before we go in, come with me there is something I want you to see."

She led him on a small trail which came to an opening at the edge of the brush providing an unsurpassed view of Lake Travis. Many of its islands were visible on the near side of the lake and with the unobstructed view provided by the overlook, the panorama of the lake and its surroundings was a magnificent sight to behold. A purview not often available except from inside the many restaurants located on the hills surrounding Lake Travis.

"Isn't that among the most beautiful sights you have ever seen?" asked Martha as they looked across the lake toward the setting sun.

"It is beautiful indeed, but it doesn't compare with you. Martha, you are even more beautiful than the lake or the sunset."

Alan pulled her against him kissing her full on the mouth, Martha did not resist instead she kissed him back her lips trembling slightly as they stayed on his for an extra moment. Following the unintended amorous kiss, they walked swinging their joined hands as they made their way to the entrance of the restaurant. Once inside, they selected a table with a view of the lake so they could enjoy watching the sunset as the sun sank below the horizon on the other side of the lake.

Martha pulled into the parking lot at her office near midnight, the lights in the building were still on, but the parking lot was empty except for Alan's car. She enthusiastically thanked Alan for the wonderful afternoon and dinner then kissed him as they were about to depart.

"Alan, I think we should get together again whenever we have some free time. I enjoyed the afternoon and dinner very much, you have made me happier than I have been in a long time. Thank you."

"Martha, can we please go on another date later in the week? I can arrange my work so that I can get away early at least for one evening, let me check my schedule tomorrow then I'll call you?"

"Please do, Alan, let's see how our schedules work out we may be able to get together later in the week. I would like that Alan."

Alan drove out of the parking lot a happy man, he followed Martha's car until he was sure she had safely turned to enter the main highway.

He then turned toward his condo which was in the opposite direction. Alan wished they were both heading in the same direction to spend the night together in his condo, but it was not going to happen today.

Alpha-4 sent an urgent message to Abe.

"Martha and Alan have met and appear to be dating. What are your instructions?"

Alpha-2 Sent a high priority Red Alert message to Abe.

"Alan is dating Martha. Please send you instructions."

Abe sent an identical reply to both requests.

"Continue 24 hour surveillance."

Alan did not go to his office on Sunday as was his custom instead he slept late getting out of bed about 9:00 o'clock. Once he was up and about Alan, reflected on the last two days and their impact on his life. Meeting Martha was definitely a major event in his mundane existence, he found her to be irresistible, someone he enjoyed being with. He was drawn to her by some unknown force that kept urging him to make her happy and be a part of his life. He couldn't explain what was happening, all Alan knew was that he and Martha were destined to be together. Since Betty's death, he had ignored women completely none of them interested him romantically and certainly not in a sexual way. Martha was different, she was exciting to be around both sexually and mentally. Aside from being a beautiful woman with a magnificent body, there was something magic about Martha which drew Alan to her. He could tell she was brilliant with a probing mind and had a strong determination to accomplish her goals. Being around her stimulated his mind and his imagination they seemed to be perfectly suited for each other. Considering how little time they had spent together, Alan was somewhat shocked that he felt it was natural for he and Martha to be together. He spent the remainder of the day thinking about the best way to insure their relationship would flourish in the coming weeks.

"Go slow and easy, keep sex in the background and let nature take its course and above all make Martha happy."

Monday morning Jim unlocked the office door which was unusual. Alan normally was there an hour before him and was busy working when he showed up. Jim was not concerned just surprised that he had arrived first. Alan came in a few minutes later with a broad smile on his face.

"I'm sorry to be late Jim, something unusual came up over the weekend which caused me to get very little sleep last night."

"What could have happened that caused you to have a sleepless night?" asked Jim looking at Alan somewhat startled by his comment.

"I took your advice and went out for a change last Friday night. Somehow, I wound up at the New Place Hotel bar where I met this beautiful woman named Martha. At first, I thought she was a prostitute coming on to me, since I was alone, but that was not the case at all. She turned out to be the owner of TDI, a training company for professional entertainers. She was there to observe the first public appearance of one of her clients. We shared a table and the live entertainment for the evening, Jim, she is exceptionally smart and talented. We spent most of Saturday together too and have agreed to see each other in the future."

"From the way you are talking about her, you must really like this Martha. What did she look like?" responded Jim smiling at the thought of Alan becoming actively involved with a woman.

"She is beautiful with black hair, big brown eyes and the most exquisite olive colored skin you have ever seen. Jim, I more than like her. Believe me, I will never be able to thank you enough for urging me to go out for an evening. My friend that was the best advice I have ever had."

"Do you think you can forget Martha long enough to work on our project we are running out of time?"

"You know me, when it comes to work I can shut out anything and everything maybe even Martha."

"Then let's get to it old buddy, we have a lot to accomplish and little time to spend on other things. By the way, I like seeing a smile on your face it's good for you, you are like the Alan I have always known. Congratulations on an enjoyable weekend you deserved it."

The employees at TDI could not help noticing Martha was even more exuberant than usual, she had a bit more of a bounce in her step and a happy lilt to her voice when she arrived at work on Monday. She seemed happier than usual although there was no apparent reason. Martha was convinced her chance meeting with Alan had not only changed her outlook it might change her life. She enjoyed his company and conversation immensely, in addition touching him had awakened dormant romantic feelings she had not experienced since Jimmy's untimely death. She liked touching and kissing Alan, he was exciting and a talented person who made her feel alive. She had an almost uncontrollable desire to be in his arms as if she belonged with Alan. Unlike Alan, Martha had no close friend to tell about her feelings, so she turned to her mother, Rachel. Martha called her later in the evening after Rachel and Phil had finished dinner.

"Mom, a strange thing happened this weekend, I met a man named, Alan Strong who interests me. I find him very fascinating, almost irresistible, I feel wonderful when we are together."

"That is interesting. What kind of man is Alan?"

"He is a tall blond, exceptionally smart and a scientist businessman."

"How did you happen to meet him, was it through your work?"

"Sort of, I met him at the New Place Hotel bar where one of my students was performing publically for the first time. We shared a table."

"So why are you captivated by this fellow, Alan?"

"We talked at length and found we have a lot in common, and when we danced feeling his body close to mine really excited me. That has not happened in a long time. I wanted to kiss him and stay in his arms. But what is really important I have this overwhelming feeling of happiness when we are together."

"Martha, I am so glad for you. It sounds like you have found someone you could love."

"I am almost sure that is what happened too, it's as if our meeting was directed by some higher power. Mom, our meeting was no accident, I have the feeling it was meant to be."

Rachel and Martha continued to talk mostly about how things were going in business in Austin and in Corpus Christi. Both businesses were expanding at a rapid rate the owners were enjoying their success and were happy with their prospects for the future. Rachel and Phil were quietly growing a large mid-stream oil and gas company becoming moderately wealthy in the process. As a reminder and a bit of encouragement to Martha, Rachel repeated an old Schuber family adage she had learned from her mom.

"Every day you spend being unhappy is a day of your life wasted."

To reinforce the idea, Rachel added.

"Whatever you do, Martha, don't forget what your grandmother said because it's truly the secret of life."

The next morning Martha called Alan early.

"Good morning Alan. How are you today?"

"Now that I'm talking to you, I am fantastic. How about yourself?"

"I'm doing great I just wanted to talk with you for a moment. I was wondering, would it be possible for us to get together for a while after work?"

"Can you believe it? I was thinking the same thing. Of course we can. Where and when? I'm available and open to any suggestions you might offer."

"Why don't you pick me up at my office at five thirty, you can select a destination."

"Being with you again will make my day Martha, I'll be there at five thirty sharp."

Jim noticed that Alan was preparing to leave the office on time. He paused at the door to Alan's office thinking something unusual was going on with Alan.

"Are you OK Alan, you are not sick or feeling bad are you?"

"I'm fine, Jim I just have something important to do this evening. I'll see you in the morning at the usual time."

Alan could see Martha on the steps as he drove up. He left his car and walked toward her taking her hand the moment they met.

"You are so gorgeous! How do you do it?"

"You look great Alan, I am so glad you could come I just had to see you. I couldn't wait any longer."

Once in the car, he kissed her gently on the lips savoring the excitement, he was alive with love for Martha. Driving out of the parking lot Alan asked, "Where would you like to go Martha?" He then added, "The one thing I want to do is make you happy."

"Anywhere you like Alan, I'm going with you."

"Then we are going to the New Place Hotel bar."

"I found it interesting and sort of eerie that you want to make me happy. I talked with mom last evening and she quoted an old family precept which goes like this."

"Every day you spend being unhappy is a day of your life wasted."

"That is very interesting, I'll remember it the rest of my life. But believe me, Martha I truly do want to make you happy."

"Alan, just being with you makes me happy, can't you tell?"

"I hoped that was the case because knowing you for this short time has changed my perspective dramatically, my greatest pleasure is being with you and seeing you smile."

Alan had intended to sit at the table where they first met, but it was occupied when they arrived. Undaunted, they selected a table next to the dance floor some distance away, Alan ordered drinks which were delivered quickly by the waiter who was anxious to get a hefty tip at the end of the evening. Realizing that neither of them had eaten, Alan persuaded the waiter to bring a selection of snacks to tide them over. There was no band playing instead they were playing taped music for dancing. After a few sips of her *margarita* Martha insisted they dance, the moment their bodies touched Martha became engulfed in a warm soothing feeling. She could feel Alan's hand on her back, the sensation it created made her very happy. Having Martha in his arms was very much to Alan's liking as well, she fired his sensual feelings the more they danced the more excited Alan became. Touching Martha's warm body and the signal it was sending turned him on, yet he made no move or advances that could be construed to be sexual or pushy. Alan enjoyed their being close, but he wanted first and foremost for Martha to be happy and he had no intention of spoiling her evening. They had two drinks each and danced several dances before Martha reminded him.

"Tomorrow is a work day and as much as I would like to stay, I think we should be going."

When Alan stopped his car near Martha's, she leaned over kissing him hotly on the mouth.

"You can't believe how much I enjoyed being with you this evening, I thank you very much for your invitation."

"The pleasure was mine. Can we do it again tomorrow and the next day and the next day?" asked Alan as he pressed Martha's hand.

"I'd like to, I'll have to call you in the morning after I check my schedule."

Over the next few months, Martha and Alan enjoyed each other's company during the week and on most weekends they became inseparable spending as much time together as possible. On a warm day in early June they were enjoying an early dinner at a nearby restaurant when Alan asked.

"Do you remember me telling you that I really liked to fish?"

"Sure, and I said I had never been fishing."

"What would you say, if I told you one of my friends who has a boat and condo in Palacios has offered to let me use them next weekend?"

"Are you asking me to go fishing with you?"

"I definitely am, we could drive down after work on Friday, go to dinner that evening then fish Saturday and Sunday morning. What do you think?"

"Alan, I would be delighted to go fishing with you, but you have no idea what you are getting into I know absolutely nothing about fishing. You will have to teach me how it's done."

"With your talents, I'm sure learning to fish will not be difficult, I promise to teach you everything I know about the sport."

Friday after work, Alan arrived at Martha's condo to pick her up along with her luggage so they could be on their way to Palacios. The drive would take two and one half hours provided they didn't make too many stops and weren't unnecessarily delayed. Although he had picked her up there several times in the past, Alan had not been inside of Martha's condo she has always met him at the door and for some reason had not invited him inside. This time was different, when the doorbell rang, Martha opened the door wide ushering him into her lair smiling broadly as she did.

"Welcome to my humble abode, Alan. Stay put while I get my bags from the bedroom."

Alan looked around transfixed by the sight before him, her work room walls were covered by large posters of the Sirens in action plus several gigantic photographs of Martha dancing. The remainder of the condo was decorated conventionally with a touch of Martha's musical taste added, it was subtle, yet definitely reflected her personality. Alan noticed the minute details which others missed, these fine points characterized the woman he loved. He could not refrain from commenting.

"Martha, I like the way you decorated your condo, it's perfect in every detail just like you. I love it!"

"I'm so glad you like it, Alan. I did it myself. Thank you for the compliment."

Martha had packed a small vanity case and one small travel bag which she sat down near the front door for Alan to put in his car. She was ready to go. She checked the condo security system making sure it was operating properly then checked to made sure her smart phone was in her purse before telling Alan.

"Lean over, I need a big kiss before we leave just to make sure all of this is real."

Taking her in his arms Alan kissed her hotly before responding.

"Will that do?"

"Yes, we are ready to go."

He picked up her bag as Martha set the alarm and locked the door behind them while holding her vanity case in one hand. Alan had on a T-shirt with no sleeves and shorts which displayed his muscular frame in much greater detail than Martha had previously witnessed. He took Martha's travel bag in one hand and her hand in his other leading her to the car where he stowed her belongings in the trunk. Martha wore blue shorts, sandals and a light blue and white tie around halter which gently caressed her beautiful breasts without completely covering them. Alan reached to turn on the ignition, but before he could start the car Martha hugged him kissing him with hot moist lips before giggling loudly and starting to sing.

"A fishing we will go. A fishing we will go."

She placed her left hand lightly on Alan's thigh as he drove away saying in a magical voice.

"We're on our way to a weekend of fishing, I'm sure it will be a memorial experience."

Alan could not help replying.

"Don't fry your fish before you catch them."

He laughed to himself at the thought of Martha catching more fish than an experienced angler like himself, yet stranger things have happened. His friend's condo was located next to the water between the street and Palacios Bay it had a covered boat dock which was equipped with an electric hoist to lift the boat out of the water for storage when the boat was not in use. The landing pier and the storage area were covered to protect the boat from the elements when it was not in use and stored out of the water. The condo had two bedrooms and a large adjoining bathroom with a huge shower large enough to accommodate two people at a time. The featured amenity of the condo was a luxurious lounging area equipped with stuffed chairs, a table, a large screen television and a computer area. In addition, the condo had a small fully equipped kitchen which was filled with food, drinks and supplies of every description. The lounging area was highlighted by a fully stocked bar located adjacent to the interior wall while the bay side of the lounge featured a clear glass wall which provided an excellent view of Palacios Bay. Sliding glass doors opened from the lounge onto an outside veranda that had two anchored round tables with collapsible umbrellas and eighth heavy wrought iron chairs. The chairs were heavy by design to keep them from blowing away in the strong winds which frequented the bay area. Except for those days having very high winds, the veranda provided an ideal place to enjoy a cold drink and the sea breeze. On high wind days it was much more enjoyable to stay inside and take advantage of the air conditioned lounge area.

"Which bedroom do you prefer, Martha, the pink or the blue?" asked Alan jokingly.

"I had best take the pink, it's too late to change now," said Martha as she carried her travel bag into the pink bedroom.

"You friend must have a lot of money to own a weekend place like this," commented Martha while she was unpacking. She placed the folded small items in the dresser the larger items she hung in the walk-in closet. The contents of her vanity were placed in the bathroom beside one of the two counter top sinks.

"Yeah, you're right, he founded the company where I worked before Jim and I teamed up to start our company. He has made a lot of money doing something he really enjoys. That is what Jim and I are trying to do. We have been working together since we were kids and we love what we are doing. It's not like my loving you, but it is very satisfying."

Martha rushed across the room, she pulled Alan's head to her level then standing on her tiptoes she kissed him lavishly her lips hot on his.

"Alan, did you just say you loved me?"

"I thought you knew, I've loved you from the first time we met at the New Place, when you kissed me I knew why I had come there. It was no accident, it is our destiny to be together."

Martha put her hands under the back of Alan's T-shirt before she answered.

"I love you too Alan, call it what you want luck or destiny. I love you with all of my heart, we are two people who are meant to be together."

Alan picked her off of her feet holding her firmly against him he kissed her passionately before lowering her onto one of the stuffed chairs.

"I suggest we pour a celebratory drink from the bar to toast our future together," said Alan stepping toward the bar.

"What is your preference?"

"I'll have what you are having."

Alan poured two Irish whiskeys over a little ice then took two folding recliner chairs to the veranda where he placed them next to each other. After sitting down and leaning back to a near horizontal position they touched their glasses.

"Here is to a long life of love and happiness together."

They held hands and talked for nearly an hour as they sipped their drinks and looked across the bay as twilight descended. Finishing his drink Alan asked.

"Are you hungry? I'm starved!"

"So am I. Do you have some place in mind?"

"If we go now, we can get a seat at the Outrigger Restaurant for some great seafood. You do like seafood don't you?"

"Yes, I love good seafood. Do we need to change?"

"No, anything goes so far as attire is concerned, people come here to relax."

The Outrigger proved to be an excellent choice Martha had her favorite seafood dinner, baked flounder with all the trimmings, while Alan opted to have fried shrimp and fried onion rings. The food was excellent, although the place was so noisy it was difficult to talk without yelling, it definitely was not a place to carry on a quiet romantic conversation. The restaurant filled to capacity with people waiting outside for a table by the time Martha and Alan finished their meal. They did not tarry after eating, they went directly to the condo to refresh themselves and prepare for Saturday's fishing trip.

"We will need to be up and on the water early in the morning it is going to be clear and hot tomorrow according to the local weather forecast. With my fair skin, I don't want to be out there in the afternoon and you probably prefer not to get sun burned either. Why don't you take a shower first while I check out the boat to make sure everything is ready to go in the morning?"

When Alan came back inside, Martha had finished her shower and was seated in the lounge dressed in a short nighty which left little to the imagination her magnificent body was barely covered and her long black hair hung below her bare shoulders creating a very intriguing picture. Upon seeing Martha waiting in the lounge, Alan rushed through his shower to join her. He put on a pair of colorful fishing shorts, but no shirt before hurrying to the lounge.

"Should we have a nightcap or should we go to bed now?" asked Alan towering over Martha who was curled up in an overstuffed chair.

"Let's have a nightcap first to relax us for the night."

Martha was seeing Alan's bare upper body for the first time, she was overjoyed he was essentially free of body hair, except for a small collection of fine hair in the middle of his belly there was no hair at all. Martha could not have been happier he was just as she had pictured him naked, perfect. She approached Alan with her drink in hand then touching him on the shoulder Martha said smiling as she did so.

"I wish to propose another toast. Here is to the most handsome body in the world."

Alan was astounded that she would say such a thing, but accepted her toast responding.

"And here's to you, beautiful."

They finished their drinks in short order then retired to their rooms for the night. The sun had not broken the horizon when Alan lowered the boat into the water. He checked the fuel and tested the engine to make sure it would start before he drove in his car to the bait stand at Grassy

Point where he bought a quart of live shrimp. They were just right for bait, two inches long and their shells were hard and crisp a sure sign that they were fresh. Upon his return to the condo, he transferred the shrimp to the boat's livewell to keep them alive and frisky until later when they would be used for bait. He put ice, drinks and sandwiches in the cooler before going into the pink bedroom to wake Martha who was curled up under the sheet with only her head uncovered. He leaned over kissed her on the cheek then yelled.

"Time to get up my sleeping beauty. It's fishing time!"

Martha was startled, yet she bounced out of the bed smiling and began kissing Alan. He could not resist he pulled her hard against his chest, but then he relaxed asking.

"Are you ready for some breakfast?"

Alan was finishing the last bit of his bacon and eggs when Martha asked.

"What should I wear fishing?"

"You can wear what you have on, if you want to, or maybe wear a bathing suit if you want more of a tan. Whatever you decide, be sure to bring something to cover your upper body a little later in the morning. The sun can be brutal on the water when there are no clouds to protect you."

Martha went inside to change clothes and to put sun tan lotion and sun screen in her bag along with several items she thought might be needed during their fishing trip. Alan moved the boat to one side of the slip where he tied it off in the in front and in the back against the walkway to provide a stable platform for Martha to come aboard without the danger of slipping. Alan left the four stroke engine idling while he went inside to get several white hand towels he had stowed in his travel bag and to check on Martha to see if she was ready to go.

Martha had changed into a bright yellow bikini, she was standing majestically in front of one of the glass doors to the veranda facing the sun. Its rays flooded her with a soft glow which outlined her body in a halo of bright sun light accentuating her finer attributes. Alan stood silently behind her admiring her beautiful sensuous body all the while thinking, "I have never seen anyone so beautiful, the Gods must have delivered her to this place and to me."

"If you are ready, we need to go," said Alan not fully ready to abandon the awe inspiring sight before him.

"I have my things, let's go fishing!"

Two Abe agents witnessed Alan's return to the condo with the bait shrimp, afterward, they drove to the marina where they had arranged for a fishing guide to assist them in their task of following Alan and Martha.

"Are you ready?" asked the guide as the agents approached.

Charley, the senior agent replied, "Start you engine, game on."

They rounded the point and were in view of the condo when Charley instructed the guide who was idling along at a slow rate of speed.

"Anchor several hundred yards off of the condo toward the public loading ramp where we will appear to be fishermen getting ready to make the bay run. When they shove off, wait until they are a half mile away then follow them, but don't get too close. We don't want them to suspect we are following them or spying on them either."

The air was still, and the bay was glassy when Alan pulled away from the condo slip headed toward the open bay at a slow pace. Once the depth finder indicated there was sufficient water depth for the boat to plane out, Alan pushed the throttle forward revving the engine to near top speed while pointing the bow directly into the sun. After making minor adjustments to find the best speed and motor tilt necessary to produce a smooth ride Alan turned to Martha who was sitting by his side saying.

"There are a number of good fishing places we could try, such as Pilkington or the *Tres Palacios*, but since it is calm, we will hit the big bay first. I know some good fishing reefs near the shoreline where we might limit out on trout and redfish. It gets rough out here after the diurnal wind starts blowing off of the Gulf around nine o'clock once it starts the wind will increase throughout the morning producing some large waves in the middle of the bay by afternoon. Should it look like the bay is going to get rough, we will head back to the more protected water. Until it does, let's catch some trout and redfish."

"I'm glad you know what you are doing because I don't have a clue," quipped Martha who was enjoying the breeze created by the boat's speed. The relative humidity was over ninety percent making her hair damp and clammy when the boat was not moving. Once the sun warmed the air, the relative humidity would drop substantially allowing the dampness to go away making conditions more pleasant for their fishing trip. The guide and the Abe agents followed at a discreet distance keeping Alan's boat within sight without getting close enough to raise any suspicion that they were being followed or watched. Unknown and undetected by any of them a second set of Abe agents and their guide were shadowing their movements from another boat located some two miles to the south. They kept their distance, but did not lose sight of either of the other boats.

After running at near full throttle for thirty minutes. Alan slowed the boat then eased it into shallow water near the shore where he dropped the front anchor. Once satisfied it was holding, he maneuvered the back of the boat into position then dropped the back anchor. He explained to Martha.

"By positioning the boat properly, we can both fish on the reef without either of us facing the sun."

She was dazzled by his knowledge of boats and Palacios Bay, hopefully, his fishing instructions would be equally inspiring. They were anchored in five feet of water just inside of Oliver Point Reef. If one looked hard, the Palacios water tower could barely be seen on the horizon when looking toward the far side of the bay. The main channel which carries most of the boat traffic between Palacios and Matagorda Bay, lay two to three miles south of their location. Alan looked around the reef to see where other people were fishing, to his surprise he found they were alone, there were no other boats anchored nearby.

"Anchor a couple miles away, so they can't see what we are doing and make it a location where we have a clear view of their boat and the surrounding area," said Charley speaking to the guide. A few minutes later the guide dropped his anchors.

"How is this chief?"

"This will do just fine. Don, you take the area surrounding the boat first. I will watch what's going on in the boat and our guide here will keep an eye out for approaching boats, we don't want anyone slipping up on us without our knowing about it. Don, you and I will switch every thirty minutes to maintain a fresh pair of eyes at all times. You know how a person's eyes get accustomed to the same scene after a while, then they miss things they would normally see."

Unlike being onshore, the agents had only rudimentary surveillance equipment available, binoculars and high powered telescopes. Their intervention capabilities were still high they were fully armed and the guide's boat had a top cruising speed of 55 miles per hour. Should an emergency arise, they could reach Alan and Martha in a matter of minutes and easily overtake anyone threatening them.

"Martha, the first thing we need to do, before I get out the fishing tackle, is put on our sun screen and sun lotion so we don't get sun burned. If the fishing is good, in the excitement we may forget to put it on, so to be safe let's do it now."

Alan reached into his bag for his sun screen and palm oil which he used in combination. Martha removed her protective shirt and began putting tanning lotion on her shoulders and legs. After a while, she tapped Alan on the shoulder handing him her tube of sun tan lotion.

"I could use a little help, Alan. I can't reach my back to put this stuff on."

Alan was sitting on the cushioned ice chest with Martha standing to one side in front of him as he took the lotion from her hand and began gently applying a small amount to her back. She immediately responded to his touch becoming excited and aroused to the point she unfastened the top of her bikini dropping it to the floor of the boat while telling Alan.

"As a dancer, I can't have any tan lines it would be unprofessional."

Alan continued applying sun tan lotion to her back his nimble fingers touching her softly, but his technique changed to a light massage as his hands gently rubbed her neck and shoulders. Martha turned facing him.

"I can't have any tan marks on the front either."

Alan put tanning lotion on the front of her shoulders then moved to the area around her navel and the top of her bikini bottom. He did her left breast first before moving to the right one where he slowly worked his way to the nipple. At that moment Martha deftly untied the bottom of her bikini which she laid on the ice chest next to Alan. Alan wiggled out of his shorts then pulled Martha against him he was still seated on the ice chest with his legs together. Martha stood there naked in the morning sun for a few moments before Alan untied her hair letting it fall in all of its glory to her shoulders and back. Martha faced him kissing him wildly then she pulled his lips against her breast as she leaned back neither of them rushed they timed their slight movements to coincide with the boat's gentle back and forth motion as it swayed with the rhythm of the waves. After a while, the waves increased in size rocking the boat vigorously, as the tempo increased, Martha began to gasp her breathing became harder, she began to wiggle wildly then shake uncontrollably as she released a scream of absolute pleasure. Suddenly her entire body began to quake, an uncontrollable rapture swept over her consuming her consciousness as she melted into Alan's arms still facing him with her arms around him. Then her lips were on his. They did not stop, they lingering for several minutes until the last wave of pleasure was complete. Standing face to face they, kissed each other over and over with their arms around each other and their bodies pressed together. At that moment they both knew their love for each other had been sealed and it was eternal. Martha looked up into Alan's blue eyes smiling.

"I love you Alan, I always will. You can't imagine how happy you have made me."

Alan pulled her even tighter against him until they were almost one. He didn't want to let her go. He caressed her gently on the back as they stood naked in the morning sun.

"I love you Martha, we were destined to be to be together from the first time we met. I love you and we will always be together for each other."

"Yes, we will be, Alan, I promise," replied Martha.

"Jesus Christ," shouted Charley suddenly bolting to a standing position.

"It looks like they are having sex in the boat. Take a look to make sure I'm not seeing things."

Focusing his telescope on the anchored boat swaying on the waves Don replied, "They are not just having sex, they are screwing with him sitting on the ice chest."

Don handed his telescope to the guide.

"Want to have a look?"

"Sure. Exciting stuff, huh?"

Handing the telescope back to Charley the guide remarked.

"Couples fucking in their boats is not all that unusual out here in the bay. Shit, I see it all the time. You ought to see what goes on when the rich guys take out their party boats on weekends, I've seen four or five gals on board running around buck assed naked drinking wine and champagne on some of their outings. Hell, I saw this one gal and a guy having oral sex on the deck like they were the only ones around there was a whole boat load of people on board. But listen to this, a guy I know from Wharton sold his boat because every time his girlfriend went fishing with him all she wanted to do was to screw in the boat. She got so hot, he never could fish, he didn't catch any redfish or trout when she was along and she wanted to go every time he did. He fishes with me now! She doesn't come along any more it turned out she doesn't like fishing at all, just gets sexed up when she's out on the water! He still takes her on a boat ride sometimes just to keep her happy."

Charley was taking his thirty minute turn watching Alan's and Martha's activities when he commented to Don his assistant.

"You know what? If my wife knew I was doing this, she would swear I am a pervert of some kind. She would never understand I am only doing my job. Hell, I didn't tell them to have sex in the damned boat, but I have to watch, anyway. It's our job to protect Martha from harm. Some crazy bastard might see them and pull up beside the boat, pull his pistol and rape her at gun point. If we were not watching, how in the hell could we prevent that from happening? Or they might fall over board from exhaustion and drown. See what I mean? We have to keep watching. But hell, my wife would never understand."

He turned to the guide yelling.

"My God, can you believe it? They are at it again only this time she is on the ice chest. Don't they know they will get sun burned screwing naked out here?"

He handed the telescope to his assistant Don saying during the exchange.

"I hope to hell they don't keep this up all day, we'll both go blind if they do!"

Alan looked around and for the first time considered the possibility that there might be people watching, but he saw only two distant boats which were in opposite directions from them and a couple of miles away. They were of no consequence he breathed a sigh of relief as he and Martha put their clothes back on. Earlier the heat of passion had ruled his senses to the point nothing else mattered except pleasing Martha while satisfying their mutual sexual desires. Martha retied the

363

bottom of her bikini in place then smiled at Alan holding out her top toward him. He tied her it in back caressing her shoulder as he slowly turned her around then kissed her tenderly on the lips.

"It's a good thing I insisted we put on the sun screen before we started fishing, or else we would be sun burned all over. Right now, I am a little tender on my butt and a couple of other spots that normally do not see the sun because I didn't put sun screen on them. How about you?"

"Oh, I'm OK no sun burn at all. You know, Alan. I really like this fishing maybe we should do it again, sometime? You are such a good teacher, in fact, you were magnificent, I had no idea how much fun fishing could be!"

"I must say Martha, you proved to be a fast learner. You have turned into an excellent fisher person your first time out, there is no telling how good you will be next time," said Alan grinning all the while.

"Since we have fished up most of the morning, why don't we go back to the condo, shower and go to lunch?"

"That sounds like a refreshing idea to me, Martha. We can fish from the condo this afternoon, only this time I am going to show you my fishing technique."

Alan started the engine and headed straight across the bay toward the condo which was invisible in the distance because of the earth's curvature, but they could see the water tower which was a nearby landmark Alan used as a guide on his return trip. They paid little attention to the building waves as they raced across the bay with two boats following them in the distance. While Martha showered, Alan cleaned up the boat putting it on the lift, he considered leaving the boat in the water overnight for a possible trip up the *Tres Palacio* the following morning, but decided against it. He had a feeling they would not be using the boat again this weekend. He and Martha sampled the finer techniques involved in fishing off and on until late Sunday morning when they reluctantly packed up and headed back to Austin leaving Palacios behind as a fantastic memory which neither would ever forget. It cemented their love for each other they were a perfect match ideally suited to making a happy life together.

Martha kept her hand on Alan's right leg most of the way back to Austin she commented as they were driving through El Campo.

"Alan, this was my first fishing experience, I shall remember it for the rest of my life. I can't recall enjoying a weekend so much as this one, you were wonderful teaching me how fish and I love you for it."

Alan thought a moment before replying.

"Martha, you are magnificent, you have made me the happiest person on the planet, come hell or high water I will always love you with all of my heart."

Alpha-4 assigned to Martha reported to Abe.

"Red Alert, Martha and Alan are in a sexual relationship, they had sex in the boat while fishing on Palacios Bay. No videos are available they were out of range of our video equipment. Their engaging in sex was confirmed by multiple visual observations using our long range telescopes. They were naked in the boat for a good part of the morning before returning to the condo where they stayed for the rest of the weekend. Except for going out to eat they remained in the condo until they headed back to Austin Sunday morning."

Alpha-2 also reported the sexual encounter to Abe.

"Alan and Martha are definitely having a sexual affair, we observed them naked and in the act of engaging in sex using our long range manual equipment. They had sex in their boat more than once while anchored near Oliver Point. They did not wet a line or get out the fishing tackle before they headed back to the condo, it was one hell of a fishing trip for both of them. Not one they will soon forget. They only left the condo to eat the rest of the weekend."

Frank read both reports several times before reacting.

"God damn it, how can two such brilliant and gifted individuals get themselves into such a fucking predicament as this? I know George wanted his children to be happy that's why we set up Abe and ADAM in the first place. What the hell am I going to do with them? They have both suffered heart break and sorrow on a massive scale for us to force them apart now will condemn them both to a life of abject misery. I need to think carefully before making any decision concerning Martha's and Alan's future."

Frank sent the same message to Alpha-2 and Alpha-4.

"Continue surveillance, but do not interfere with their relationship."

Monday morning Alan came to the office early he had new vigor in his work surprising even Jim who had long ago accepted Alan's unrelenting dedication to their projects.

"What happened Alan? You seem engrossed with the project today."

"Martha and I went fishing this weekend. We are a mutual admiration society not only that we are in love. I think you and Yoko should meet her, she is beautiful, brilliant and will be an integral part of my life from now on."

"In that case, I will make it a point to meet her. Let me talk to Yoko this evening maybe we can get together for dinner this week."

"Let me know early, so I can make arrangements with Martha, no wait I'll call her right now to check her schedule for the week."

Martha was free for either Tuesday or Thursday evening. They settled for Thursday at The Oasis on Lake Travis. Alan and Martha arrived first, but did not wait for Jim and Yoko before being seated. They ordered their usual drinks which now consisted of Irish Whisky over a little ice, they were amused that Yoko had picked The Oasis for dinner it had been Martha's selection on their first date. Could Yoko be psychic or was it just another odd coincidence?

When they arrived, Jim and Yoko greeted Martha and Alan warmly, Jim paid particular attention to Martha making sure that she understood she was welcome and considered a permanent part of the group. Alan, who hardly knew Yoko, made a point of making her feel she was part of Cyber Resource's team as well, they were all in this together. He also emphasized in his discussions with Yoko that he expected Martha to become a permanent part of the team in the near future.

During dinner Alan asked Yoko.

"What is it that you do? Jim told me you were a medical professional, but he never really explained what you actually do at work."

"I am a psychiatrist specializing in the treatment of people suffering from schizophrenia, it's a difficult endeavor considering the few patients who are ever able to live semi-normal lives. There is no cure, we can only moderate the condition, sometimes to a great degree and sometimes not at all, but the effort is worth it for the people we do help."

Yoko smiled then turned to Martha asking.

"While we are on the subject, what is your profession Martha?"

"Nothing as noble as yours, Yoko. I'm a classical dancer by training and I own and operate a company specializing in training entertainers of all types to become professionals. Our graduates are sought after by Hollywood and Television agents as well as recording companies, stage companies and live entertainment agencies. We are very proud of the accomplishments of our ex-students."

"That is very interesting, I have always had a yen for classical dancing myself maybe you could instruct me."

"When you have the time I'll make myself available, just give me a few days advance notice so that I can manage my schedule."

Yoko started lessons with Martha the following week, she proved to be a dedicated student making more than adequate progress in both dancing and muscle toning. Over time she and Martha became close friends exchanging confidences as only friend do. At the end of an especially difficult workout Yoko confided.

"Martha, I cannot thank you enough for teaching me muscle control it has increased Jim's pleasure tremendously when we make love, I thank you for this gift and so does Jim. Hopefully I can return the favor sometime."

Jim and Alan finished JUMBO before the end of their first year in business, it consisted of a new wireless method of safely transmitting huge bundles of information anywhere in the world. In addition, the core system was adaptable to meet special needs for companies requiring certain types of data collection and transmission to one or more super-computers for processing. Companies conducting large scale 3D seismic surveys in remote areas of the world were considered prime candidates to license and adopt the technology. Following a full scale demonstration of the system's capabilities by Alan and Jim, the Imperial Enterprises representatives were prepared to patent and market the system as soon as possible it was far superior to anything currently available anywhere around the globe.

The young entrepreneurs received a letter of congratulations for a successful first project from Mr. Jerry Schneider President and Chairman of the Board of Imperial Enterprises. He also declared his confidence that their next and future projects would be equally successful. Alan was about to email to his ex-boss in Houston using his personal computer, but at the last minute decided to conduct a scan of his computer using their company developed Malware Catcher Program. To his shock he found a spyware program imbedded in his personal computer. Someone had hacked it and was monitoring his personal correspondence as well as his personal information.

"Hey Jim, come look at this? Haven't we seen something like this somewhere before?"

It took only a minute before Jim replied.

"That's the same sort of crap that showed up on your computer back when we were in high school. Want me wipe it out?"

"No, there is something screwy going on here I need to think about it first."

Alan was disgusted with himself because he had not installed Cyber Resources' protection system on his personal computer to protect it from hacking in the first place, he had been too busy. Now it was too late.

Alan arranged to get together with Martha at her condo after work to run the Malware Catcher Program on her computer he suspected it might also have been infested with the same spyware. Sure enough the same spyware program was imbedded on her computer. Upon completing his check of her computer Alan looked at Martha with a scowl saying.

"I don't know what is going on, someone is spying on both of us. We have the same spyware imbedded on our personal computers."

"Why would anyone be interested in us?" Asked Martha perplexed at the thought of a stranger reading her email.

"I don't know why anyone would want to spy on us, but they could have compromised all of our means of communication including our phones and cell phones. I have no idea how long this has been going on or who is doing it, but I will find out. It may take a while, but these guys can't hide now that I know they exist."

Alan changed the subject, he did not want to alarm Martha any more than necessary and he had something more important he wanted to talk about.

"Martha come with me I have something to show you, first let's check out the view from your balcony."

"Sure, Alan. It's a beautiful sight this time of the year."

Martha stepped out on the balcony first followed by Alan, who came up behind her putting his arms around her waist then kissing her on the neck.

"Oh that feels good. What are you up to Alan?"

He turned her round kissing her softly. When the kiss ended Alan held her tight so that he could feel her warm body against his.

"And what is it that you want Mr. Strong?"

"Martha, will you marry me?"

"Yes, Alan I love you."

Martha snuggled against him kissing him. Alan produced a small box from his pocked it contained a large solitaire diamond ring which he deftly removed. Smiling he placed the ring on Martha's finger then held out a matching wedding band, extending it toward her he said.

"This could be on your finger this weekend if you like."

"I would like that very much. How can that be accomplished in such a short time? We can't get a marriage license that quick!"

"I am proposing that we elope. We can be married in one day in Oklahoma. There is no blood test requirement and no waiting period all we have to do is buy a marriage license at the County Court House and find a Justice of the Peace."

"Why don't we celebrate our engagement with an Irish whisky then go to dinner?"

Martha took his hand leading him inside giggling all the way.

"Are you aware this is going to be a very short engagement? Just four days in all."

For their engagement dinner they elected to go to a nearby restaurant which served drinks and a mixed fare of western dishes. During dinner, Alan suggested they tell no one of their plans and that they not communicate by computer or phone prior to their departure. Alan produced two burner cell phones handing one to Martha he explained.

"Martha, we can talk to each other using these phones, but do not call anyone other than me with your burner phone, temporarily these are reserved for us alone."

Martha was in full agreement, they would communicate with each other only in person or using the burner phones until they returned to Austin as man and wife.

Alan worked out a plan to insure they were not traced or followed by whoever was spying on them. As a part of the plan, Martha arranged to borrow Yoko's Explorer for the weekend without revealing the purpose. Jim picked them up on the street facing the back entrance to Martha's condo from there he took them to a taxi stand where they took a cab to Jim's home where they transferred to Yoko's Explorer. Jim assumed this maneuver was a part of Alan's plan to unmask the culprits spying on his and Martha's personal computers. To aid their secret plan, Alan called Martha using his regular cell phone setting up a weekend rendezvous at her condo. They left their regular cell phones at Martha's condo and parked both of their automobiles in her garage, anyone tracing their GPS locations would think he and Martha were at Martha's condo. They were unobserved leaving from the inconspicuous back entrance to Martha's condo Abe's video cameras had an unknown blind spot there because the back entrance was totally obscured by two large oak trees left in place by the builder.

Everything went as planned, Martha and Alan were married in Durant, Oklahoma the following day. They spent their wedding night at a motel in Paris, Texas and arrived back in Austin late Sunday afternoon. They reentered the condo as they had departed unobserved through the back entrance.

Several days lapsed before Abe received two urgent messages.

Alpha-2 reported.

"Alan and Martha were secretly married in Durant, Oklahoma last weekend, we last saw them entering Martha's condo on Friday morning. There was no visual or video of them until Alan drove away in his car late Sunday evening."

Alpha-4 presented a similar report except it added the critical information.

"They may suspect we are watching, their elusive actions indicate a well-planned exit and return to Martha's condo."

Frank read the reports with anguish he had devised a plan for Alan and Martha, but this new development was going to make it much more difficult, maybe impossible, to implement under the guidelines George Angleton had set for ADAM.

"Damn it Alan, you and Martha are screwing up my plan for you! Hopefully, for your sakes, I can adapt it and still make it work, anyway. It's difficult to protect smart people, they keep coming up with ideas of their own."

Chapter 15 Passing the Baton

Kevin had been expecting the attorney to arrive any minute when the doorbell rang he opened the door to see a short, balding man standing at the entrance to his condo.

"Mr. Goodhall, I am James Hunt. We spoke by phone on Wednesday."

Extending his hand, Kevin motioned for the man to enter saying.

"I'm pleased to meet you Mr. Hunt, please come in."

Kevin led the lawyer upstairs to the living area where he offered him coffee. After getting acquainted over coffee, Mr. Hunt addressed the reason for his visit.

"Let me explain why I am here Mr. Goodhall. I am with Powell, Kimble and Hurst one of the larger law firms in Houston we represent a wide range of individual clients as well as corporations and multi-national ventures. Before I begin our discussion, I must ask, are we alone? I can divulge my mission to you and no one else, I'm sure you will understand the reason as we proceed."

"That's not a problem we are the only ones here my wife is meeting with a friend at UT and will not be back until late this afternoon."

Kevin was taken aback by the cloak of secrecy presented by Mr. Hunt it was akin to his days at Abe where everything was kept under wraps because of the nature of their work. He listened with cautious reservation as Mr. Hunt continued.

"Great. Then let's get to it. Kevin, do you know a man named Frank Stram?"

"Of course, he was my mentor and former boss at my last place of employment."

"I am sorry to be the one to inform you that Frank passed away last week from a massive heart attack."

"My God, he wasn't that old I thought he was in perfect health."

"Actually, he had known his days were numbered for the last two years. He was aware that he could go at any time and that it was just a matter of when not if. He didn't tell anyone other than me, he insisted on working the last few months because there was some unfinished business he wanted to take care of himself. He never told me what it was, but it was important to him. He did tell me a week ago that his work had been finished and that he expected a satisfactory resolution of the problem even though he might not be around to see it happen."

"Mr. Hunt, are you familiar with Frank's professional career?"

"Yes, I am aware he headed up some sort of secret agency called Abe among other things and was a top executive at Imperial Enterprises for a number of years. Actually, I probably know more about Frank than anyone, I have helped with his estate planning for years. You know he never married."

"He mentioned to me, more than once, that he was a confirmed bachelor although he never elaborated about his marital status beyond that. What does any of this have to do with me?"

"You are probably uninformed concerning the colossal wealth Frank accumulated over his years with Imperial he died an exceedingly wealthy man. Frank left his entire estate to you and a foundation he established to aid women in distress. He set up the foundation because of his mother, who committed suicide at an early age, Frank wanted to make it possible for troubled women to have an opportunity to find help and not wind up miserable and dead like his mother. His primary objective in creating the foundation was to give these women a chance at happiness. He gave his brain child the name, Women First Foundation. Frank named you the permanent and sole Director of the foundation, you have complete control of the foundation's income and its selection of programs as well as the allocation of funds to the projects undertaken by the foundation."

"I am overwhelmed. I knew Frank liked me, but I never considered his doing anything like this! I am honored by his confidence and trust."

"Frank more than liked you, Kevin. He admired you, he considered you the son he never had. He not only loved you, he loved Verona as well. Are you aware that Frank had a plan for you two long before you met? I have never seen a happier man than Frank when he received confirmation that you two had married. He didn't say much about your marriage, but for the next week he smiled all the time and seemed dedicated to our working out his plans for you and Verona and the future of his foundation."

"Several months ago, Frank called me out of the blue with a request for me to meet him in Pflugerville the following day. During our visit, he asked me to do him a personal favor, which to my astonishment, was to marry Verona as soon as possible. He left without any further explanation."

"Let me clear this up for you, Kevin. He had visited with his cardiologist a few days earlier learning his heart had deteriorated to the point he could die at any moment. The cardiologist advised him to wrap up any loose ends he might have right away. His number one goal was to see you and Verona married before he died."

"I wish I had known he was ill, I would have insisted on our spending more time together before he left. Frank and I were friends, I have tried to be as much like him as I can he was my idol."

"Frank left you individually, $22,000,000 in cash to be delivered to your bank or any banks you select. The foundation's investments are managed by a fellow named, Zane Kraft, you probably will never meet him, although his signature will appear on the monthly checks to the Women First Foundation. It looks like the foundation will receive around $8,000,000 per year or about $670,000 per month for operating expense and grants. All the necessary paperwork will be ready for your signature next week. I suggest we do it in our office in case we have to make some minor changes or corrections. We'll also have a Notary nearby. Bring Verona if you like, there will be no discussion of Abe or your and Frank's former association or positions there. We will never mention Abe again, but explaining Frank to Verona without revealing any classified facts will be your chore. Frank and I both know you can handle the situation satisfactorily and in keeping with your covenant with Abe and Frank."

Kevin sat down after the lawyer left to consider the effect Frank's bequeath would have on his and Verona's future.

He said out loud.

"I'll miss you Frank, you taught me well, but why in the hell did you do this? Why me? This is going to change a lot of things for Verona and I!"

After considerably more thought Kevin put two and two together.

"Now that I look back, Frank always expressed a keen interest in Verona more so than any of the other Gentex children. It's clear now that he knew all along I was attracted to her he was probably delighted when I quit Abe to be with her. I think he knew he could trust me to do the right thing with both Verona and his fortune."

Kevin thought for a while about what Frank had done. He was very appreciative of the faith frank had in him and his abilities.

"Frank I make this vow to you, your trust was not misplaced, your fortune will be used in a manner which will make you proud and so shall Verona and I."

Kevin recalled Frank's favorite axiom which Frank said he learned from George Angleton his longtime associate and friend.

"If something is worth doing, it's worth doing right."

He silently pledged that he and Verona would do their best to abide by that dictum. Kevin was still sitting in the den trying to come up with a way to tell Verona what had happened without breaking his vow of secrecy to Frank when he left Abe. When he heard Verona drive into the garage, Kevin sprang out of his chair then rushed down the stairs to open the door for her. She held two packages under her left arm which he quickly set on the floor before embracing her and showering her with kisses.

"And what have I done to deserve this?"

Once upstairs, Kevin took her hand leading her to the couch where he seated her before sitting down beside her.

"That was because you are you, and I love you. It's going to take a lot of faith on your part to accept everything I am about to tell you because I can't give much of an explanation for some of it."

Verona looked at him blankly she was mystified by his remark, yet said nothing. Instead she motioned for him to continue.

"My meeting with the lawyer this morning was a monumental shock. My former boss and mentor at my last job died suddenly last week leaving essentially his entire estate to me. I really can't discuss him with you for reasons you might not understand, but the estate is huge! I had no idea this was coming, it was a complete surprise to me I didn't even know he had a lot of money!"

"Sweetheart, you are confusing me please, slow down a bit so I can understand what you are saying. What do you mean by a lot of money?"

"He left $22,000,000 in cash to me and sole control of the Women First Foundation which has an income of around $8,000,000 per year."

"Holly molly, Kevin that is a mountain of money. Who was this guy?"

"His name was Frank Stram, he was my former boss and coworker before I returned to UT. You need to understand and trust me because I can't say much more about, Frank, other than he was a successful businessman who liked me and was my mentor."

Verona wrinkled her nose then replied.

"Honey, I have always trusted you. Even though I am very curious and would like to know more about your benefactor, there will be no more questions from me about Frank Stram, if he must, then he will always remain a mystery to me."

She would have liked to know much more about Frank, but Verona understood that had Kevin been able to discuss Frank he would have told her all about him.

"We will need to go to Houston next week to sign the final papers after that you and I have to decide what to do next. I have an idea about what to do with our part of the cash, but the Women First Foundation needs more than me, it will require your talents and attention to accomplish the goal Frank set when he created the foundation!"

Verona's eyes lit up at the mention of her participating in Women First Foundation's operation. She didn't need to know Frank to realize the foundation offered her an opportunity to help people become happy and reach their goals in the process. Verona thought a minute before remarking.

"How odd that Frank and I never crossed paths, we had similar ideas and the same objective. Very strange, very strange indeed."

All the involved parties reviewed and executed the papers related to Frank's estate and establishing Kevin as the sole Director in charge of Women First Foundation. Once that task had been completed, Mr. Hunt arranged for deposits into Kevin's bank accounts in the amount of $22,000,000. In his discussion of the status of the foundation, Mr. Hunt pointed out that in its present form it was a paper organization which had no offices or employees only a monthly income from its investments. Frank had stipulated that only the income from the investment fund could be used by the Women First Foundation. The fund itself could not be touched or spent by the Director, the investment fund was to be permanently managed by Zane Kraft, or his successor, at Offshore Enterprises for the sole purpose of funding the foundation from the income it generated. It would be up to Kevin, or his assigned manager, to organize and set up the physical facilities and programs for the foundation. When, where and how to accomplished this was left completely to the Director's discretion.

Kevin was acutely aware of Zane's investment skills from his days at Abe, he along with the other Abe agents, had followed Zane and Peggy's story until he resigned to pursue Verona. Kevin had never met Zane, but he knew about his association with the *Bastardos Locos* and his brilliant success in investing their money. Kevin found himself in a difficult position he could not reveal what he knew about Zane, yet he would be the perfect person to manage his inheritance from Frank.

"How can I handle this properly and still have Zane manage our money? I can't let on that I know about him, so what the hell am I going to do. He's the perfect man for the job."

Kevin mulled over the situation for several minutes then settled on a plan he thought would help him get what he wanted.

"Mr. Hunt, would there be any objection to me meeting Mr. Kraft, the guy who manages investments for the foundation? I think Verona and I will need someone trustworthy to manage and invest our $22,000,000."

"I have no objection to your contacting him, here is his phone number, be sure to tell him I told you to call, it might help."

Kevin called Zane the following day inquiring about his managing the $22,000,000 he had received from Frank. He requested a one-on-one meeting, but Zane turned him down explaining that Offshore Enterprises did not usually manage investments for individuals rather they made investments for their own account. He emphasized that Offshore Enterprises was involved in acquiring companies and assets not managing other people's investments except when the individuals bought a substantial interest in one or more of their companies.

"We are managing the investments for Women First Foundation because Frank was a major stockholder and Chairman of the Board of Directors of Offshore Enterprises. His holdings included stock in many other companies and some hard assets all of which are now owned by the foundation, but held in trust and managed by Offshore Enterprises.

Since you are Frank's beneficiary, and I am already managing the investments for the foundation, I may be able to get the Board's approval to manage your assets as a piggy-back to managing the foundation's assets. I'm not making any promise, but I will put your request before the Board and let you know what they decide."

Zane's response was music to Kevin's ears, should the Board approve his request he and Verona would be able to devote their full time to the foundation without worrying about managing their own investments. Jerry Schneider, Frank's longtime friend and associate, had become Chairman of Offshore Enterprises following Frank's untimely death. Upon hearing Kevin's request, he took little time in obtaining the Board's approval. Zane notified Kevin within days of their original contact that he would be able to manage Kevin's inheritance as a piggy back to his work for Women First Foundation. Zane made arrangements for Kevin to transfer the $22,000,000 into a joint investment account at Offshore Enterprises with Kevin and Verona named as co-owners with exclusive right of ownership by the survivor. Terms of their agreement required Offshore Enterprises to distribute 10% of the account's monthly earnings to Kevin and Verona the remainder was to be reinvested in the monetary instruments selected for purchase for Women First Foundation. Zane's past record virtually guaranteed their account would be safe and that it would increase in value over time.

Verona resigned from her job to devote full time to organizing Women First as a free private center where women could receive help. One of the first calls Verona made was to her ex-roommate Amanda, who had moved to Oklahoma City after graduating from UT. At her father's insistence Amanda had joined his company as manager of personnel and benefits. She and Robert had parted company before she left Austin, but she was dating a young vice-president of her father's company whom she had met at work. According to Amanda, they were a perfect match like Verona and Kevin. Verona was excited when she spoke to Amanda.

"Amanda, can you believe that Kevin and I are managing a super-rich foundation called Women First Foundation? Kevin is its sole Director and has complete control of its income and its programs. The objective of the foundation is to aid women who are distressed and to help them to become happy."

"I am so happy for you Verona, I can't think of anyone more qualified than you. Your talents can help a lot of women to happiness and a better life. Congratulations I think you have found your life's work."

"Yes, Amanda, I think you are right. I can hardly wait to get started helping Kevin with the foundation. I'll keep you posted on our progress."

 Kevin appointed Verona President and General Manager of Operations for the foundation putting her in charge of creating an organizational structure and delineating the foundation's objectives and its requirements for individuals to qualifying for the foundation's programs. Verona leased space in a prominent downtown building for the initial Women First Foundation's site, most of the tenants in the building were professionals with a smattering of local investment firms and stock brokers. Women First Foundation located its office on the eight floor adjacent to the elevators, their suite was considered prime space it was visible to all who came to the eight floor. The entrance had double glass doors with Women First Foundation written in large gold letters across them. Inside the receptionist was seated behind a high custom built desk which was attached to the wall on one side. It enclosed her within an arc which was closed except for a small entrance next to the inner wall. The waiting area was well lighted and decorated with cheerful paintings of women in action. The furnishings were functional, yet inexpensive they presented a fresh and wholesome atmosphere. It was a happy place, a lighted displayed on the wall behind the receptionist showed Women First Foundation's motto in large gold letters enclosed in quotation marks.

"Every day you spend being unhappy is a day of your life wasted."

Verona had heard the phrase from Kevin the day they met, she never forgot the statement because it perfectly expressed her personal feelings on being happy. It became a tool she used often in dealing with people who were having a hard time getting their lives together.

A second glass door led from the reception area to the office proper where three interview rooms were lined up down the right side of the hallway. All the rooms were informally decorated with the walls painted a light blue, a color reputed to create a feeling of tranquility and trust for those being interviewed. The paintings on the walls depicted scenes of happy women laughing and participating in activities with children. Further down the hallway were two larger offices both of which were decorated in the identical motif as the others. The office at the end of the hall belonged to Verona while the other one was occupied by her assistant. Verona spent three months interviewing potential employees and hiring her staff before Women First Foundation was ready to commence operations. Two weeks before opening day, the staff conducted a massive ad campaign to alert women in the greater Austin area of their free services and location. Aside from giving their location, telephone number and email address the ads had a simple message.

"Beginning December 1st. If you are a woman in an unhappy situation, please, contact us by phone or email. We can help and our services are free."

The first day of operation proved to be hectic beyond description, the staff was inundated with phone calls and by necessity many calls went unanswered. Those callers who did reach a staff member were asked to call back at a later date. The assistant who operated the foundation's website, was so swamped with emails that she could not respond quick enough to prevent a huge backlog of appointment requests. By the end of the day, all callers and email responders were being requested to contact Women First Foundation after the beginning of the New Year because all interview times had been filled through the end of the year. Those women who had been unable to make an appointment were advised to be patient, Women First Foundation was there for them and no one would be left out, an appointment would be scheduled as soon as possible.

Women First Foundation accepted women into their program based on personal need and their reason for seeking help. Their services were intended to be all inclusive not specifically for the under privileged, but for all women without respect to their socio-economic status. During their first interview with the staff, each applicant was asked to describe their particular problem and as a corollary they were also requested to indicate how dedicated they were to helping find the right solution for their problem. Most applicants, who were unhappy because they did not have enough money, or those looking for a hand out, were dismissed with the response that Women First was not a welfare organization. Sometimes lack of money was considered if it was the result of a lack of skills or opportunity rather than a lack of trying.

The first applicant approved for the Women First Foundation program was a black lady who was upset and unhappy because, for some unknown reason, her two teenaged sons were no longer communicating with her. This had never been a problem before they had always talked with her freely about what they were doing and where they were going. Since they no longer confided in her, she feared they could be swept into the world of crime and drugs unless she could reach them soon, but no matter how hard she tried they were unresponsive. After hearing the woman's story, Verona was determined to help the single mother reestablish contact with her sons before she lost them completely.

"Let's talk about your boys for a while, what do they like to do?"

"They used to like to play sports, but now they don't play on any of the teams anymore they have quit all sports."

"Did you ask why they aren't playing anymore?"

"Yes, but they didn't say. Right after they quit is when this problem first started."

"What are they doing now? Do you know?"

"No, they won't tell me what they are up to. They don't get home for four or five hours after school. This happens every day. They stay gone all day Saturday and Sunday too! I can't get nothing out of them and it scares me. I'm afraid they may be in trouble, you know what I mean?"

"Let me think about this for a while, you come back next week at the same time. By then, we will have had time look into your problem and come up with a plan to help you and your boys."

Verona discussed the lady's problem with Kevin that evening, he listened intently before volunteering to give her a little expert help with the boys.

"Honey, I will hire someone who can secretly check out the boys without their ever having a clue that they were being investigated. It will be interesting to find out what they are doing that needs to be such a secret. It may take several days, so don't get in a rush for answers."

Kevin called the new director of Abe, a person named Aaron, who was unknown to him he had never met anyone by that name while he worked at Abe. Aaron had been one of the five original founders of ADAM and Abe and since becoming head of Abe he had learned the details about Kevin's relationship with Frank and Abe. After hearing a brief description of Kevin's problem, Aaron recommended a private investigator who could be trusted to deliver information on time and at a reasonable cost. Kevin made contact with the private investigator, right away, giving him the boy's names, ages and address. He requested a full visual and video surveillance of the boys around the clock to determine what they were doing and who they were associating with. He contracted for a full investigation into their past histories and current activities with all information reported directly to him as soon as possible. Two days later, Kevin received an email report from his investigator.

"The boys are clean they are not involved in dope or associated with any gang. They quit sports and took jobs at nearby car wash to earn enough money to buy their mother a new washer and dryer for Christmas. It is to be a surprise which is why they are not talking, they're afraid they might inadvertently give away their secret before Christmas and ruin the surprise. Their uncle, their mother's brother, is holding the money they have earned and is in on the deal. Other than a few friends at school the uncle is the only one the boys are talking to, but they are great kids."

Knowing this bit of information would make Verona very happy, Kevin could hardly wait to pass on the information his operative had relayed to him. Kevin had the following day off and Verona was going to be away most of the morning, so he decided to talk with the uncle. After introducing himself, Kevin explained to the uncle the reason for his visit, he wanted him to persuade the boys to let up a bit on not talking with their mom. They were unwittingly making her very unhappy she was sick with worry about them because she was afraid something was wrong. The uncle was more than obliged to help after hearing his sister was unhappy and worried about the boys. Kevin was about to leave before he thought to ask.

"How are the boys doing with their money raising efforts?"

The uncle shook his head then replied.

"I think we are going to be about $500 short unless they put the stuff on sale just before Christmas."

Kevin handed the uncle two $500 bills.

"Buy the boys something for Christmas with what is left over."

Driving home Kevin heard himself saying aloud.

"Thank you Frank, a person can do a lot of good things when they have an unlimited supply of money."

Later in the afternoon when Verona arrive home, she was still concerned about the boys. After Kevin told her what he had done she replied.

"My love, you have made my day."

She kissed him before adding.

"Honey, you may be better at this than you realize."

"I'm at your service for all of your needs." Said Kevin before kissing her while giving her an endearing pat on the rear.

On Christmas day, mom and the boys were having breakfast when their uncle pulled his pickup in front of the house. The boys were excited and full of joy as they begged their mother.

"Come outside mom, see what Santa brought."

She opened the door to see a new clothes washer and dryer with big red bows tied around them. They were in the back of her brother's pickup along with a large sign which read MERRY CHRISTMAS MOM from your boys. Tears streamed down her cheeks when she realized her sons had not shut her out after all it was all about their big Christmas surprise. Over Christmas dinner, which Mom had prepared for them, her brother and the boys discussed the hush-hush plan which the boys had devised as a special surprise for their mother on Christmas day. She was the happiest person at the table. Even though the boys had each received a new pair of Air Jordan shoes and workout suits, their Christmas joy did not come close to matching that of their mother, her boys were home again and talking.

Mom called Verona the day after Christmas to thank her. She was the happiest mom in the world her sons had really been in touch all along she just didn't know it.

"Mam, we were glad to be of service and are pleased you are happy with your boys again. Should you know anyone who needs our help, please, have them contact Women First Foundation we may be able to help them."

It did not take long for Kevin to figure out that he could not manage the affairs of Women First Foundation and continue his quest for a PhD.

He withdrew from the PhD program and opened the Women First Foundation's headquarters office near their townhouse. The headquarters office was crisp and clean it was much larger than the downtown site and it was user functional with new furniture, individual computers and an intercom system. Each employee had their own private office, yet could communicate with the other employees without leaving their desk by using the intercom system which allowed secure private conservations as well as open discussions among designated individuals.

The corner office, which Kevin occupied, was spacious as well as functional it was adjoined by a similar office reserved for Verona who expected to move to headquarters once the downtown facility was running smoothly and could be turned over to her assistant. Initially there were eleven employees making up the headquarters staff, aside from Kevin and Verona, all of whom had been screened to meet the same standards used by Abe in selecting its employees. Kevin was confident his entire staff was competent and honest and shared his and Verona's dedication to Women First Foundation and its programs.

Frank, would have been pleased by Kevin's thoroughness and dedication to protect the foundation and its integrity while providing the best service possible for those who sought its help. Foremost among the new employees was a CPA with a background in accounting for privately financed foundations, he set up a system whereby the financial status of the overall foundation and its individual branches could be viewed and monitored on a daily basis. Three people were working in accounting where they shared a single receptionist. Another seven employees were specialist in planning and implementation who took care of the operational needs of Women First Foundation providing whatever was required to keep the foundation operating smoothly on a day-to-day basis. This group also provided planning and the facilities necessary for future expansion. Overall, the staff was equally divided between males and females all of whom were college graduates with a few having advanced degrees. None of them were more than thirty five years old the staff was young, well-educated and well paid. Kevin knew how to keep employees happy and on board he tried to make sure that each employee enjoyed his or her work at Women First Foundation. Through Kevin's foresight, Women First Foundation took an option to lease additional space in the building should it become necessary to expand in the near future.

Verona's assistant at the downtown facility identified a young single mother among her applicants who she thought might warrant financial aid. The young mother was sixteen years old and a sophomore in high school when she became pregnant, circumstances forced her to drop out of school when the baby was born. Her boyfriend refused to marry her, instead he went back to Honduras, leaving her to raise the boy alone. She was an American citizen, but she had been unable go back to school, her father was dead and her mother was on welfare. She worked part time cleaning houses to help pay her and her mother's bills. The young mother was deeply concerned that she was condemning her son to a life of poverty, or worse, unless she could somehow find a way to educate herself and get a good paying job. She was determined to provide her son a chance to break the out of the rut of poverty her family had been in for years. She did not come to Women First Foundation seeking a financial handout, she was looking for some way to educate herself while she worked.

After hearing of the young woman's predicament, Verona was very sympathetic, she agreed with her assistant's assessment of the girl's plight and her determination to better herself and her son through education. Together they devised a program for Women First Foundation to provide a way for the young mother to complete her high school education and to obtain a college degree. Continuation of the program was contingent upon the young mother remaining single and her successful completion of the required courses to graduate from high school. The young lady was overjoyed when the assistant explained their proposal to her.

"Women First Foundation will pay you a monthly stipend large enough to support you, your child and your mother while you continue your education. We will pay your way to a private school where you can get individual instruction and tutoring, if necessary, until you graduated with a high school degree. Upon receiving your high school diploma, Women First Foundation will then pay your way to a State University where you can earn a BS degree or its equivalence."

Upon hearing their proposal, the young mother broke down sobbing, then said.

"You have given me and my son a new life. We both thank you. I will not disappoint you, you will be proud of me and you will always have my gratitude for this opportunity."

Those words were satisfying to both Verona and her assistant, but not nearly as satisfying as seeing the young mother graduate with a BS degree in Geology from Texas A&M a few years later. Hers had been a remarkable story from the beginning a success story which Verona and her staff expected to build on in the future at Women First Foundation.

Women First downtown Austin continued to have a steady stream of clients after they worked off their initial backlog. After six months, Verona turned over the operation of the downtown location to her assistant whom she promoted to Manager. The new Manager's old office was filled by one of the other original employees and a replacement was hired to fill the resulting vacancy. Verona moved to headquarters where she and her staff began surveying other cities with the idea of opening new Women First Foundation offices to expand the scope of coverage for their services. Dallas, San Antonio and Houston were at the top of the list, much to Verona's dismay, the main hold up was finding qualified people to operate the new sites. Funding additional sites was not a problem for Women First, their monthly income far exceeded their expenditures and they were building a surplus in their operating account.

Kevin insisted that all Women First Foundation employees be held to the same standards he had set at headquarters which made selection of new hires time consuming and difficult in areas where Women First Foundation had not yet established a reputation. Verona appointed her original employees from the Austin operation as managers for new sites as they opened. As planned, the downtown Austin site was the manager training center for new facilities because its employees had been screened for management skills as a part of Verona's initial plan. Later managers were selected from all of their operating sites as the foundation expanded encompassing a wide variety of skilled people in various parts of the State.

At the end of their second year of operation Women First Foundation had facilities in four major Texas cities with tentative locations planned for seven more. Women First Foundation was operating with a sizeable monthly cash flow surplus and their income was increasing each month. Kevin and Verona discussed the surplus issue at length, according to the accounting forecast, even after opening the seven new sites there would still be a surplus of funds flowing into the foundation's account.   Obviously there were a limited number of population centers in Texas to support additional outlets another approach to applying the funds was needed. Verona made a request to the four site managers asking for their employee's ideas in expanding the scope of their operations including new services to be offered. Verona and Amanda had stayed in touch and visited on the phone regularly. Amanda was kept in the loop, often contributing ideas to improve the services offered by Women First Foundation.

Kevin solicited ideas from his entire staff concerning expanding the offerings of Women First to the public. His email read in part.

"Any and all ideas are welcome and will be considered by your management team please, do not hold anything back. Thanks Kevin."

In his interaction with Women First Foundation's employees, he was known simply as Kevin, not Mr. Goodhall or by the title Director. Employees thought of Kevin as one of their own not some distant manager tucked away in a fancy office somewhere that no one ever saw.

He and Verona were scheduled to meet in his office to review the suggestions from the employees at headquarters and the operating sites, there were hundreds of suggestions, it seemed everyone had an idea and was interested in making a contribution. Verona had an earlier appointment and was expected to arrive in her office within the hour. When she arrived, Verona unexpectedly closed the door behind her when she entered Kevin's office, which he thought was unusual, since they did not operate behind closed doors.

"Before we get into this, I have a little surprise for you," said Verona with a smile and a hint of mystery.

"Have you come up with a fantastic idea of some kind?"

"Well, yes and no."

"Come on let's not be coy about this, out with it."

"Darling, I'm six weeks pregnant we are going to be parents."

"That's the greatest news ever! It's an exceptional idea."

Kevin leaned over kissing Verona as she sat in her chair then whispered in her ear.

"You look wonderful mommy. When did you find out?"

"This morning, for certain, my appointment was with a specialist dealing with early stages of pregnancy. I liked him, he was very thorough in explaining the tests he ran and he assured me that I am not only pregnant I am also in great physical condition to become a mother. He offered his congratulations to both of us on commencement of our great parental adventure as he called it. My next appointment is not until next month."

"I'm excited about becoming a father and embarking with you on the great parental adventure. By the way when did you quit taking the pill?"

"Actually, I stopped several months ago, after that I let nature take its course to see what would happen. We can talk about this at home, let's get back to Women First's dilemma."

Kevin opened the office door before they began reading the employee's suggestions and ideas to improve the foundation and its services. One suggestion, which caught their attention, came from the Houston location. They proposed adding more locations in Houston, Dallas, Ft. Worth and San Antonio to better serve these high density population centers. Another idea was to create several centers in the *Rio Grande* Valley which had no real population center, but rather consisted of a narrow band of towns and cities stretching from Mission to Brownsville along and parallel to the *Rio Grande* or Mexican border. It was also suggested that Women First Foundation's services be expanded to include neighboring States. There were a multitude of suggestions for ncw and expanded service to those qualifying for help from Women First. Many of them dealt with increased educational aid for both the women and their children. A number of ideas pertained to helping those women who were financially secure, but were having other problems which required counseling or personal guidance to overcome. One such idea, which was adopted, created voluntary lecture and open discussion sessions made up of women who shared similar situations. These sessions were designed to create a, you are not alone, atmosphere while offering a variety of solutions to the participants.

Women First Foundation expanded its presence in the major Texas cities to multiple locations and opened four locations in the *Rio Grande* Valley at the same time they concentrated on increased educational opportunities for those who qualified. One of the most popular new programs, offered training in computer and technical skills to upgrade the employment opportunities for mothers who were raising children alone. Most of the applicants were high school dropouts who became pregnant or married early. Women First Foundation had a high success rate in enabling these women to increase their incomes and improve the opportunities for a better life for their children and to lead happy and productive lives themselves many remarried or married educated coworkers who shared their ideals. Not all the qualified participants completed the program some dropped out while others failed to maintain the standards required to remain in the program. Some married while others became pregnant again and were unable to complete the required courses.

Many of these women and their families avoided becoming part of the enslaving social welfare system which for generations had trapped many of their relatives and contemporaries. Women First Foundation was highly successful where the government run programs failed miserably. This was partly due to Women First's sound screening of applicants, but mostly because of the dedication of the people who worked at Women First Foundation who were genuinely interested I aiding women to better themselves rather than becoming professional welfare recipients and slaves of the government. Their personal commitments to helping their clients reach their goals of independence and self-sufficiency was critical to the foundation's success as was Verona's and Kevin's leadership and visionary concept they were dedicated to helping people to be happy. Frank, had chosen well with Kevin and Verona, under their management Women First Foundation expanded its services across the nation utilizing its funds to save thousands who would otherwise have spent their lives being unhappy, unproductive and miserable.

The blue eyed baby arrived on time, he had a head of black hair and was a beautiful, robust and healthy boy who looked a lot like Kevin. In remembrance of Frank, he became Frank Kevin Goodhall. Verona glowed, no longer a mother in waiting, she was a mother with a newborn cuddled in her arms she loved the tiny boy she and Kevin had created. Verona and Kevin were starting the great parental adventure the same way they had started their life together as lovers committed to raising their family with love and understanding.

Frank's name sake would not be the only Goodhall offspring to grace the world, he was joined by two siblings, another boy and a girl. Verona gave up her position with Women First Foundation to become a stay at home wife and mother after the birth of Frank. She followed in the footsteps of Clare whom she idolized as the perfect mother. Verona's relationship with her children was filled with love and openness they were encouraged to discuss any problems they might have with her and she in turn guided them toward a solution without being critical or domineering thereby allowing them to come to their own solutions. Kevin was equally adept at rearing children in an open and loving environment while promoting individual responsibility and happiness. He emphasized to all.

"Every day you spend being unhappy is a day of your life wasted."

Frank's secret plan for Kevin and Verona had worked to perfection although it had taken several twists and turns along the way. They found each other just as Frank had envisioned in his scheme to unite them. Although the circumstances and settings strayed far from Frank's original plan, Kevin and Verona completed his dream for them.

Kevin remained the leader of Women First Foundation after Verona became a full time mother, her skills and counsel were still available when necessary. Kevin kept her informed concerning operation of the Foundation he seldom made a major change without seeking her input. This served two purposes for Kevin, both of which were dear to his heart, Verona was a full time mom to their children and her extraordinary skill at helping people was still being used. She was a happy mother and a happy wife who loved and appreciated her husband and children she thrived as a stay at home mother.

Chapter 16 Selected

Katy entered Southern Methodist University in the fall leaving Peggy and Zane with an empty nest except during Katy's random visits home. They were free of family obligations restraining their ability to come and go as they pleased, which made travelling with Zane on business trips a refreshing new option for Peggy, they could spend his travel time together. Sometimes, Zane's business obligations required him to be on the road for a week or more at a time which was longer than Peggy wanted for them to be apart. At Zane's insistence, Peggy began accompanying him on his longer trips out of town particularly those outside of the country. Travelling together turned out to be romantic and relaxing for both of them they were staying in the best hotels with dining and dancing in the evenings with sightseeing for Peggy during the day while Zane took care of business. For Peggy it was reminiscent of the time they spent as young lovers sharing exciting *rendezvous* in strange hotels in and around Houston. Something about spending the night with Zane in a strange hotel turned Peggy on, her libido soared to an enormous high creating a sustained rhapsody of excitement and pleasure. Zane, who was well aware of Peggy's idiosyncrasy, took great care to magnify her pleasure during their out of town trips together. It made him happy to be able to give her such pleasure which also added to his own enjoyment. He loved travelling with Peggy she added excitement to otherwise mundane business trips, there was no pressure to keep their location secret as was the case during Zane's tenure with the *Bastardos Locos*. They relaxed and enjoyed themselves without fear of disastrous consequences. There was no reason for them to hide, nor were they in any danger other than that of all travelers. The days of danger and intrigue were far behind, yet Zane was very careful when they ventured outside of the U.S. Due to habits formed years earlier, he remained cautious leaving little to chance. He was equally careful in his business dealings with foreigners, just as he had been while with the *Bastardos Locos*, their personal backgrounds were routinely checked before conducting any business with them or their companies. The years together had been good to Zane and Peggy they had amassed a huge fortune rivaling that of most old line Texas families including those who had become enormously wealthy in oil and real estate. The Offshore Enterprises' company jet flew Zane and Peggy to Panama on their first foreign trip together. Through a Costa Rican associate, Zane arranged a conference with six wealthy Central American investors, who were interested in buying large stakes in successful American companies or partial ownership in new American startup companies. The potential investors were a diverse group with one thing in common, they each had a strong desire to move part of their wealth outside of their native country for one reason or another. Their motives were varied and not easily discernible, but what interested Zane was their universal willingness to pay a premium fee to Offshore Enterprises in order to take advantage of his expertise and ability to provide first-rate investment opportunities. His reputation as an investment manager was well known in his native Costa Rica and throughout Central and South America as well as over most of the business world. Zane, on behalf of Offshore Enterprises, dealt with each potential investor individually affording them the opportunity to fulfill each of their objectives and requirements. One investment program did not fit all, fortunately Zane had the freedom to match investment opportunities to the individual investor or investors. During his offering to the Central Americans, Zane assured each of the six conference attendees that Offshore Enterprises could and would provide suitable investment opportunities for each of them within the next quarter. In concluding his presentation, Zane made a reassuring statement to the group.

"Gentlemen, I'll be in touch with each one of you shortly with an investment opportunity specifically designed to meet your individual situation. I appreciate your attendance and look forward to fulfilling your needs."

Zane called his hired limousine driver before he left the meeting room, once the driver arrived, Zane directed him to return to the *Casa Libertador* hotel where he and Peggy were guests during their brief stay in Panama. They celebrated his successful conference by having an early dinner and dancing for a while afterwards. Unknown to them, two Abe agents were watching and recording their every move as they had done for years. Peggy and Zane were as one when they danced, very graceful and beautiful to watch, the passage of time had only made them better. Their unwavering love for one another had grown stronger over the years and was obvious to those watching.

"Honey, it has been wonderful, why don't we slip off to the suite before it gets too late?" Whispered Peggy as they were leaving the dance floor.

"An excellent idea my dear, Peggy. Do you have something special in mind?"

"Wait until we get to the room, you'll see." Said Peggy smiling over her shoulder as she had done many years ago during their courtship. They did not rush to the elevator as they had done years earlier they took their time, yet were gone in less than a minute or two. Turning to his partner, one of the agents remarked in admiration.

"It's refreshing to see they are still as much in love as they were when we were tracking two young lovers. You know that was a few years ago, wasn't it? Damn, we are all getting older, but it doesn't seem to have changed them."

"Yeah, you are right. They seem as young as they were when we were watching them back in Houston before they were married, but this time there are no cameras in the suite."

"We need to send the pictures of the six rich Latinos to headquarters right away, they will want to check them out as soon as possible. These two will be safely in bed within the next hour, so we can relax and have a night cap before starting our surveillance in the morning."

Zane was standing in the bathroom shaving when Peggy surprised him putting her arms around him and pushing her bare breasts into his back.

"Honey, you feel hot. Hurry up with the shaving, I can hardly wait to get you in bed." Said Peggy as she rubbed Zane's lower belly with her soft hands.

"Don't get me too excited, I might cut myself." Replied Zane wiping the shaving cream from his face. Turning in Peggy's arms he pulled her body next to his excitement before kissing her. They stood there in each other's arms for a moment before going to the bed. Peggy pulled Zane down beside her then began kissing him ravenously as she put her leg over his.

At Abe's headquarters the special agent assigned to Peggy began his review of the pictures and identities of Zane's new Panama investors. Most of them were well known and appeared on the Abe's list of cleared foreigners. In the final analysis only one of the Panama group proved to be unknown to Abe or their contacts with the FBI. A full scale international investigation of the individual calling himself Ricardo Schmelling was initiated using all of Abe's worldwide sources. The investigation proved fruitless, neither Interpol, nor Abe's foreign sources were able to provide any detailed information concerning Ricardo Schmelling's activities other than he was a rich Nicaraguan. The disappointing results moved Jerry to have an Irish whiskey at the Tmex bar with his old friend, Joe. They were on their second drink before Jerry posed the question.

"Joe, have you ever heard of a fellow called Ricardo Schmelling?"

"I don't know that name. I'm sure he is not involved in the drug trade or I would have heard of him. I'll ask around, if you like."

"I would appreciate it very much, we have been unable to determine exactly who he is and what he does. We do know he is rich and is from Nicaragua."

Joe called early the following week.

"Jerry, I think we need to have another drink at the Tmex."

With their first Irish whiskey almost finished, Jerry could stand the suspense no longer.

"Joe, you going to wait until the second drink, or can you tell me now?"

"I can tell you now, if you want."

"Then who the hell is he?"

"Mr. Schmelling is not what you think."

"You mean he is not a drug smuggler?"

"He is even worse. Ricardo Schmelling is a wealthy Nicaraguan who is also a long time Sandinista sympathizer and informant. Over the last twenty years, he has been responsible for the deaths of many landowners in his country. He posed as an anti-Sandinista for many years, when in fact, he was actually a government agent. Once he learned a landowner was anti-Communist, Mr. Schmelling reported him to the Sandinistas, who subsequently murdered the landowner and his family. The Sandinistas confiscated the land, presenting Mr. Schmelling with a portion or cash for his services to the government. He is nothing more than another crooked communist bastard stealing from his own people."

Joe added. "I'd like to kill the son of a bitch myself."

"If you feel that strongly, why don't you? All I wanted was to find out who and what!"

"Who knows, Jerry? I just might. People like him really piss me off!"

Jerry's private phone rang several weeks later, to his surprise it was Joe.

"It's time for an Irish whiskey. Meet me at the Tmex at one."

He hung up without any explanation. When Jerry arrived, Joe had already finished his first drink and was working on the second.

"What the hell is this, Joe? Are you so thirsty you couldn't wait for me?"

"No, Jerry. I'm just celebrating!"

"Celebrating what, Joe?"

"Remember that guy Ricardo Schmelling you were asking me about? Well that poor son of a bitch disappeared last week. I have a feeling his body is buried in the deep jungle and will never be found. Care to join in the celebration?"

"Joe, let me catch up on my whiskey. We may be celebrating the rest of the afternoon, so the drinks are on me. By the way, how many Irish whiskeys do you think you can drink in an afternoon?"

"We'll see, Jerry. We'll see. Here's a toast to the dead."

Zane couldn't make contact with Ricardo Schmelling he had reportedly disappeared and was no longer available, consequently he was dropped from Zane's group of Panama investors at Offshore Enterprises. Zane thought nothing of Ricardo's disappearance it was something that happened regularly in Central America no one ever really knew what happened to these people one day they didn't show up. So far as Zane was concerned, Mr. Schmelling may as well have been dead. Zane subsequently furnished the remaining five investors varied opportunities to buy American, mostly in companies owned or controlled by Offshore Enterprises and Zane. These companies, although very successful, often needed capital to expand their businesses. One popular method to obtain an infusion of capital without increasing their corporate debt was to sell new corporate shares through a private offering thereby keeping their balance sheets in order. Zane served both his Central American investors and the companies he controlled well, earning huge fees and profits for Offshore Enterprises in the process, while growing the companies and providing solid investments to his clients. Zane was so successful in directing the Central American's investments that they earned an average annual dividend of five percent while their original investments appreciated in value at twelve percent the first year. Several of the Panama group requested that Zane or Offshore Enterprises manage their U.S. investments on a permanent basis reinvesting their dividends and other profits in America. After his acquisition from the *Bastardos Locos*, Zane became the number one trader at Offshore Enterprises returning many times over the cost Jerry had paid the *Bastardos Locos* for his release. His investments at Offshore Enterprises had quadrupled the company's value during his tenure. Jerry's association with Joe as a result of the trade for Zane also proved to be invaluable to ADAM over the ensuing years. Jerry and Joe became business associates and friends who respected each other and enjoyed the other's company.

Over time, many of Zane's wealthy business contacts urged him to take an active interest in making contributions to worthy causes such as hospitals and medical research. As a group they were familiar with Zane's investigative abilities and well-documented talent for evaluating companies and their managements. Several people in the group knew Zane personally, they sought his counsel to determine those charitable organizations which were honest, had competent management and whose goals were worthwhile. Four of his colleagues requested a meeting with him for a drink at the Tmex to discuss a proposal which they thought he might find interesting. All four of them were seated at a table in the bar when Zane arrived, he was dismayed when he noticed none of them had a drink.

"Gentlemen, I am at your service." Said Zane as he shook each of their hands.

"Before we start, allow me to order a special round of drinks."

Motioning for a waiter, Zane ordered.

"Waiter five Irish whiskeys please, with ice if you don't mind."

The drinks were delivered right away as the last glass was placed in front of Zane one of the others said.

"Gentlemen a toast. May, Zane, unconditionally accept our proposal."

There were ayes around as they toasted. After sipping his drink, the leader began outlining their proposition saying to Zane.

"We, and a number of our friends, have decided to set up a nonprofit to fund worthy institutions, organizations and research projects. We would like for you to head up our nonprofit and to invest our contributions, either personally or through Offshore Enterprises, to fund those donations. Further, it is our desire that you determine the organizations to which these donations are to be made. Our primary concern is that our contributions are actually applied as promoted by organizations rather than being used to enrich the managers and their staffs."

"I appreciate your confidence in me and my ability. Peggy and I have been working toward making a sizeable charitable donation ourselves. It's possible we could join forces in establishing the nonprofit you just described."

"We would be delighted to have you aboard. So far, we have commitments for over $100,000,000 to put in the nonprofit's investment fund. The returns should provide ample funding for donations to the selected charities for years to come. If you are agreeable, we will set up the nonprofit and start accepting contributions."

"Gentlemen, let's get started. Peggy and I will make an initial contribution of $10,000,000 to the nonprofit."

"Now, that we have settled that problem, I'm ordering another round of drinks. We are not finished yet." Said the group leader as he motioned to the waiter.

The participants enjoyed their second Irish whiskey relaxing a bit before taking up their second project. The leader sipped his drink niggardly savoring every taste of the enticing elixir. Clearing his throat, he addressed the others and Zane in particular.

"Zane, we have another project in the making which needs your help and input. As you know there is a national election coming up soon, we would like to set up a super PAC to support conservative candidates nationwide. The fund will be governed by five directors who will determine which candidates receive our indirect support. We would like for you to be our lead director which means you will be in charge of all the meetings and be influential in making the selections of candidates for our funding."

One of the others added before Zane could answer.

"We need someone with your ability to determine truth from fiction when it comes to analyzing people, or to be more precise, politicians and aspiring politicians."

"Gentlemen, you may be overestimating my abilities. I will do my best to guarantee we support the best conservative candidates available. Peggy and I will also make a sizeable donation to the super PAC we want to see the best possible people in government and the courts."

To an outside observer, it appeared Zane had suddenly emerged on the political and charitable stages in one afternoon, nothing could have been farther from the truth. Years of hard work and success at Offshore Enterprises had focused many wealthy individual's attention on his abilities which in turn resulted in their trust and support for making him their investment manager and a candidate for public service. Zane put his extraordinary talent and knowledge to work investing the nonprofit's funds in reasonably safe dividend paying companies. He also proved to be a prudent dispenser of the income generated by the charitable nonprofit. During its first year, the fund donated to deserving programs and individuals including schools, hospitals, research and veterans aid. Zane was very appreciative of those who had fought for their country and particularly those who had suffered debilitating wounds and loss of limbs in fighting our terrorist enemies. The nonprofit supported not only research in rehabilitation it also funded research to develop new and innovative artificial devices to restore mobility and quality of life for those who had sustained injuries while serving their country.

His introduction to politics on the national scene was more arduous. He had been an invisible player in Texas politics for several years rather than a national player before creation of the super PAC. Once it became known that the super PAC had raised over $900,000,000, it became the darling of every conservative politician and aspiring politician in Texas and every quarter of the country. Several weeks of constant calls requesting campaign contributions for politicians from all parts of the country caused the super PAC to limit incoming calls to those wanting to make contributions. After a while the candidates got the message, no amount of pleading or self-justification for support would get them on the approved list. Their records alone would determine the degree of the super PAC's support, if any.

Upon Zane's selection as lead director of the super PAC, Jerry made a large cash contribution and volunteered to make his investigative resources available to Zane in screening candidates for the PAC's support. This became important in excluding those who were charlatans and those who were morally unacceptable. From its inception the super PAC, known as AFIR (Americans for individual rights) was continuously attacked by the liberal media as being directed against the poor and most of all directed against the children! Branding an organization as being an enmity against the children has been a ploy of the liberal left for generations. Whether or not it is true makes no difference, all is fair in love, war and politics. A candidate or an organization perceived to be against the children, automatically becomes the archangel of the devil with little chance of being politically successful.

In his quest to understand conservative politics, Zane made a point to meet many of the conservative politicians in Texas to talk with them up close and personal in order to get an idea of the size of their political organizations and the basic ideals of their supporters. Right away, he found two distinct groups of Texas conservatives, religious conservatives and fiscal conservatives. Their beliefs and doctrines do not always complement each other and sometimes are directly opposing forces. They mutually support smaller government, lower taxes and efficiency in government, immigration control, personal rights and freedom of religion. And both groups oppose labor unions, but have differing views on abortion, gay marriage, socialized medicine and welfare in general. Zane learned early that one must carefully tip toe through the bluebonnets to become a viable statewide candidate in Texas whether a Democrat or a Republican. He had no political ambitions for himself, since he had been born in Costa Rica, he was certain he could not be elected to a political office in Texas. Bruce, on the other hand, was a native Texan, born in the Lone Star State. Should Bruce become interested in politics, Zane was in a position to give him his support as well as that of the larger political organizations in the State. When Zane mentioned Bruce's possible interest in politics to Peggy she commented. "We'll see. Maybe you should encourage him."

Chapter 17 The Awaking

Rachel rarely visited Tex Con's rural work sites her work consisted mostly of negotiations and evaluations which were performed in the office. Phil handled the design and installation of the physical facilities in all projects they undertook for Tex Con and their partners. Upon completion, each new facility became a part of the company's ongoing operations making them a part of Phil's full time responsibility. Sometimes he was required to be on site during construction and often he was needed to solve operational problems which could not be done from the office as a result Phil spent a lot of his time in the field. He managed all company personnel outside of the Corpus Christi office which required him to visit the various company locations on an ongoing basis. Among other duties, he was responsible for explaining company benefits and company policy to their employees, but his primary focus was keeping them happy and productive in their jobs. It was up to Phil to set the pay scale for all field employees including the supervisors, technical and non-technical workers the company employed in their operations. He set Tex Con's pay scale considerably higher than that of their competitors, their employees were well paid and happy in their jobs. Due to his efforts, the subject of unionism never came up at Tex Con or at any of its work locations, their employees trusted Phil to look after their best interests.

Rachel insisted on accompanying Phil on a field trip to start up a newly completed pipeline and gathering system so that she would have a better understanding of what was involved and the amount of expertise required to start up similar projects. They left their home several hours before sunrise in order to be at the first meter site at 7:00 a.m. when the producers were scheduled to turn their wells into the gas gathering system. After a rough and grueling two hour drive from the paved highway, they arrived at their first stop, Rachel rolled down the car windows and was instantaneously greeted by a hot scorching wind blowing across the low rolling hills and mesquite covered anticlines. She got out of the car following Phil to a large natural gas meter run before turning to Phil saying.

"I didn't expect anything like this when I arranged to accompany you on this field trip."

"I didn't either. It must be over a hundred in the shade out here and that torrid wind must be blowing at least twenty miles an hour."

"Can we make this fast? I'm going to be burn up if I stay in this all day."

"You should stay in the car as much as possible," said Phil pointing to his Ford Explorer.

Rachel heeded his suggestion she wasted no time getting into the Ford Explorer once inside she started the engine then turned on the air conditioner. In a few minutes she rolled up the windows then watched Phil inspect the remote gas metering station from the comfort of the cool Explorer. Phil took notes and photographs of the metering station using his smart phone before walking to the car. He wiped his forehead with a handkerchief as he opened the door.

"Am I glad you have it cooled off in here, I might have a heat stroke if I stay outside much longer it's hot out there."

"Did you get what you came for?"

"Everything is in order and operating as expected, all the equipment meets our specifications, and the construction crew did a good job. I've got four more of these remote metering stations to inspect before our final stop at the compressor station which should be up and running by the time we get there."

Over the next two hours Phil checked out four other metering stations all of which he found to be operating properly and built to his specifications. Rachel remained in the Explorer the entire time with the air conditioner running, she followed Phil's instructions keeping a close watch on the temperature gauge to make sure the engine did not overheat. From her comfortable vantage point Rachel paid close attention to Phil and his meticulous inspections. She marveled at his ability to concentrate under these horrid conditions. While watching Phil, she put her hair up in a ponytail and removed her bra in an effort to stay cool and comfortable. The wind was furiously whipping the Mesquite trees and dirt was flying all around the Explorer filling the air to the point it was nearly suffocating outside as Phil finished his inspection of the last meter installation.

"What a time to bring you on a field trip, another time would have worked out a lot better."

Phil brushed away as much dirt from his shirt as he could before getting into the cool comfort of the Explorer. He was gritty, but at least it was reasonably cool once he got inside.

Looking at Rachel, he noticed her blouse was unbuttoned and her well rounded breasts were partially exposed.

"Well, maybe not," said Phil as he leaned over kissing Rachel between the two open buttons at the top her of her blouse.

"Hey, it's beginning to get hotter in here," quipped Rachel before she asked.

"How far is it to the compressor station? Can we get out of this stifling heat and dust when we get there?"

"It's about eighteen miles as the crow flies, but due to the rough terrain it will take us just under an hour to get there and yes you will be pleased to know there is an air condition building there."

"Ok, let's put his thing in gear and make a run for it before we choke to death or worse."

The Explorer bounced over the dirt road leaving a huge dust cloud in its wake. Phil drove as fast as possible on the narrow winding road without endangering Rachel and himself. He had to slow down on all the blind turns because it was possible another vehicle could be coming from the other direction. As they were nearing the compressor station, Phil reminded Rachel it was a manned facility with only male employees there.

"You should probably button your blouse, it would not be appropriate for the field hands to see a vice- president's boobs. They might get the wrong idea."

"Do I have to get out? I am a mess, I would rather not be seen like this."

"I think it would be a problem if you refused to talk with our employees. Not only that we may be here for quite a while, so button up, but leave your bra in the Explorer that way they won't notice what a mess you are."

The wind subsided just as Phil and Rachel arrived at the compressor station, they entered through the control center which was a separate air conditioned building adjoining the compressor building. All four of the employees manning the facility were inside the cool control center as Phil and Rachel entered. Phil introduced each of workers to Rachel calling them by name. This was something he practiced and prided himself on he knew all of company's employees by their first and last names. The guys shook hands with Rachel, but none of them could keep from peeking at the top of her blouse the sight was too inviting. With the introductions over, Phil, Rachel and the operator walked into the compressor building so Phil could inspect the compressors and the piping system along with the overall operation of the facility.

The noise inside the compressor building was so loud and constant Rachel had difficulty hearing what the operator was saying even though she was only a few feet away. The three stage, double acting compressors were driven by four identical direct coupled 1,200 horsepower internal combustion engines. Each of the units were fueled with natural gas they were aligned perpendicular to the long axis of the building allowing the piping to be orientated along the long axis. Through the outlet piping system, the natural gas discharged by the compressors was interconnected with a single header which delivered the compressed natural gas to a pipeline which transported it to a gas processing plant located several miles away. Although the engines were equipped with mufflers, they were still extremely noisy. The floor of the building vibrated slightly from the interaction of the engines and the compressors they were driving, giving one an eerie feeling while walking within the building. The floor consisted of polished grey plastic coated concrete which was super clean. The soles of their shoes produced a slight squeaking noise as they walked on the smooth surface. Rachel began to sweat slightly, it was extremely hot inside the building because of the high temperature outside and the additional heat generated by the compressor units. As they continued their inspection, she felt a trickle of perspiration moving slowly down her back. She assumed their tour of the compressor installation would be short, otherwise, she would be forced to retreat to the small air conditioned metal building to keep from becoming drenched in sweat. Much to Rachel's relief, Phil, and the operator completed their inspection allowing the three of them returned to the control center and its life saving air conditioning. The building served as a control and communication center as well as a refuge from the noise and heat. By monitoring its instrument panel, the station operator could remotely observe all the critical information from both the engines and the compressors from inside the control center. An alarm on the control panel was designed to sound, should an instrument reading be outside of a preset acceptable range, alerting the crew to a possible problem. Certain controls automatically flared incoming gas should one or more of the compressors go down unexpectedly or the incoming gas volume exceed their capacity. Automation had been a large part of Phil's design for low operating costs and minimum personnel requirements. The compressor station and gas gathering system were automated and designed to be fail-safe using the most modern technology available. The communication center was used to make contact with the gas producers' field personnel when it was necessary to cut or increase production and to notify the downstream gas processing plant of any loss of gas production or problems which might cause an upset in their processing unit.

Fully convinced that the new gathering system was functioning as planned, Phil congratulated his team on their efforts. Startup of the entire system had been flawless, Phil was proud of his design work, but even prouder of the performance of his employees. There had been no problems loading the compressors, no excessive flaring of gas and no dangerous situations created everyone involved had done their jobs properly. Phil was more than pleased, he had spent many hours training the employees for startup of the gathering system and compressor station. It had taken more than an ounce of prevention, but in the end it was worth the extra effort. The men at the compressor station were a small part of the overall team which included field personnel working for the gas producers, Phil's superintendent of pipeline operations and his field men plus the supervisor and operators of the gas processing plant. This new addition to the gathering system increased the gas volume to the processing plant to a total of 500,000 MCF per day. The Rachel Plant, as the gas processing facility was known, was one of three plants Tex Con had constructed for themselves and their investors. Rachel had negotiated the contracts while Phil had designed and constructed the gathering and processing facilities and the processing plant.

After a couple of hours at the compressor station, Phil asked Rachel if she was ready to head home.

"Yes sir, Mr. Jensen, I am ready whenever you are."

Phil shook the four employee's hands and thanked them again for their excellent performance as he and Rachel departed. Once they were out of sight, Jose, said to the other three employees.

"Did you see the tits on that woman? My God she is hot."

The station operator stared at Jose then barked.

"Jesus Christ. Jose, don't you know who she is? She is married to Phil that's Rachel, the processing plant is named after her for God's sake. She owns half of Tex Con and is an engineer like Phil, she finds and makes the deals for Tex Con. Believe me, she is one smart lady, and she pays your salary. Don't you understand she could have your job for saying shit like that?"

"I don't give a damn. She is one sexy *Chiquita* I'd give an arm to get between that hot bitch's legs for just an hour," replied Jose making idiotic gestures at the other three.

Driving on the narrow bumpy road surround by mesquite brush on both sides, Phil suddenly pointed ahead.

"Look at those roadrunners would you? I haven't seen many of those in the last few years. Aren't they magnificent?"

"Yes, but their plumage blends in with the mesquite so well it makes them very hard to see. When they get off of the road, you can't see them at all."

"Yeah, Rachel, it's easy to lose track of them once they get off of the road. I love that long stride they make when they are running and, interestingly, every once in a while they make a noise just to let us know they are here."

"When I was a girl in Orange Grove, we saw a lot of them on the farm. We called them *Paisanos* instead of roadrunners and some people called them *Chaparrals* after the brush country. Whatever you call them, they are good birds they eat all kinds of bugs and small snakes including rattle snakes, not only that, they are fun to watch."

By late afternoon, Phil and Rachel reached the main highway tired and hungry and happy to be on a smooth road at last. Phil suggested they drive on to George West where they could get a motel for the night and enjoy a good meal at the Café.

"Did you pick George West for its historical significance, or for some other reason?" asked Rachel.

"I don't know about its history only that it has a good motel and the best chicken fried steaks in Texas."

"In that case, we must take a slight detour through downtown, so I can enlighten you about the origin of George West,"

"What could be so important about George West that I need to learn about it?"

"To begin with, the town is named after George Washington West, whose family like many Texas citizens of the time, they came here from Tennessee. You do know that a lot of early Texas immigrants came from Tennessee, don't you? George's family settled north of here in Lavaca County. You didn't know his middle name was Washington, did you?"

"I had no idea, but it's interesting."

"It was his father, Washington West, who brought the family to Texas to begin with, he was looking to find cheap land on the frontier and expected to establish a cattle empire here in Texas."

"The name Washington seems to have been popular in the West family. Were there more family members named Washington?"

"Not that I know of, but to continue my story George joined several cattle drives north after the Civil War eventually making a deal with the Federal government to drive a herd of 14,000 Texas longhorns to Montana. He and his cow punchers succeeded in getting to Montana with that herd and in the process George West established the longest cattle trail in North America. Did you know that?"

"No, I didn't. It's strange we have heard about the Chisholm and the Goodnight-Loving trails most of our lives, I don't know if the longest of them all even has a name."

"If it does, Phil, I am unaware of it. To complete your enlightenment, in 1880 after his cattle drive to Montana, George West purchased a ranch in Live Oak County where he and his wife made their home. Over the years George became wealthy from his cattle operations and other enterprises, so in 1915 he decided to build a complete town on the ranch, he provided utilities, streets and a Court House. George had earlier made a deal with the railroad for a right-of-way through his ranch and as you might expect he located his new town nearby, so that the inhabitants would have access to the railroad. Slow down please. Look there is the Court House, and this is the center of the town that

George West built. Don't you feel better now that you know how the town of George West was started and how it got its name?"

"I'll have to admit I will think about the town differently from now on. Let's check into the motel and go eat I'm hungry as a dog. Aren't you?"

"Yes, we can shower later."

"By the way, I didn't know you were such a history buff."

"I'm not really, just about South Texas. I have some other talents you might be interested in after we shower."

"Really! I can hardly wait. If I were not so hungry we could skip dinner."

The Café was packed with transient oil field workers, a few locals and travelers on their way to and from Laredo and from the Rio Grande Valley to San Antonio. George West is also a stopping place for travelers between Corpus Christi and San Antonio. There are few eating places between George West and Laredo only open spaces and oceans of mesquite brush and beautiful scenery. The Café is the last place travelers know for sure they can get a meal before reaching Laredo.

"Two chicken fried steaks with French fries please," said Phil to the waitress who was wearing a standard light yellow-orange work dress with a white apron.

"You get another side if you want it," she replied pointing to the menu.

"I'm OK with just fries," said Rachel.

Phil added green beans as his other side dish. By the time their orders were delivered, a waiting line had formed in the café entrance every table in the place was occupied because a Laredo bound bus had stopped for its passengers to get a meal and go to the bathroom. They finished their chicken fried steaks in short order with little talking between them. Rachel left most of her French fries while Phil left only a cleaned plate and a tip. As they were leaving the Café parking lot, the Laredo bus blinked its lights three times then blew its horn signaling its passengers it was time to re-board to continuing on their journey.

Rachel commented.

"I'll have to admit that was among the best chicken fried steaks I have ever eaten. I'm glad you remembered."

"Are we going to flip a coin to see who showers first or shall I concede to you now?"

"There is another alternative, which I prefer, we could shower together." Replied Rachel patting Phil's leg. He gunned the engine burning rubber as they sped away from the Café parking lot.

Phil and Rachel were up early the next morning with the intention of driving to Corpus Christi before breakfast. Phil had just finished showering and shaving when he noticed Rachel standing naked just outside of the bathroom door.

"Aren't you getting dressed?"

She put her arms around him pulling him against her body then kissed him hotly. Phil let go of the towel around his waist letting it drop to the floor as Rachel pulled back.

"Since you are freshly shaved and we do not have to check out until eleven, I think we deserve a repeat. Last night was wonderful and I think this morning will be even more fantastic since we are rested."

They laughed as they jumped back in bed, Rachel was beside him lavishing him with kisses as she felt the warmth of his waiting body.

The Board of Directors of Tex Con met the following week in Corpus Christi. As President and co-Chairman, Phil opened the meeting with a presentation summarizing the results of their latest venture which recently began delivering gas to Tex Con's Rachel Gas Processing Plant. The joint venture consisted of a major expansion of their pipeline and gathering system located in the highly productive Karnes County sector of the Eagle Ford Shale Field which made it one of the more lucrative projects undertaken by Tex Con. Rachel served as Vice-President and co-Chairman of Tex Con as well as its Treasurer. The Board of Directors consisted of three other members: an outside bank president, an independent attorney and Jerry, head of Imperial Enterprises. Aside from Rachel and Phil, Jerry was the next largest owner in Tex Con's ventures which included their gas gathering systems and gas processing plants. Although he did not own stock in Tex Con itself, Jerry played an integral part in the various ventures promoted by Tex Con because of his personal investments and his ability to attract other wealthy outside investors. His input was sought in determining each new venture to be undertaken by the company. Rachel and Phil made it their practice to invest only in those projects he actively supported they valued his opinion equally with their own. Phil wrapped up his report making way for Rachel to take center stage to put forth a new project for the Board's consideration. The Board discussed the merits of the new venture for two hours without reaching a decision on whether Tex Con should proceed or put the project on hold. Jerry decided to end the impasse.

"The venture proposed by Rachel is a very interesting high risk project, but we must remember that the first one on the ground makes all the money. I think we should expand Rachel's proposal extending our area of investigation to explore ways to make it profitable in the long term rather than right away. For instance, if we can we make construction of a new pipeline and gathering system contingent upon producers committing their processing rights prior to our commencing construction, we will have the processing rights tied up should a processing plant become a viable venture sometime in the future. I vote to accelerate and expanded the study to including a possible processing plant in the overall plan."

The entire Board agreed with Jerry, and at his suggestion. They added funding to hire outside consultants and engineers as needed for the expanded study. Jerry stayed on after the Board meeting adjourned for a private talk with Rachel and Phil. Before Jerry had an opportunity to speak Phil voiced his concern about the new expanded project.

"Jerry, the very size of the expanded project, if it proves to be feasible, may cost more than Tex Con can handle financially."

"I know, Phil, that's why I stayed behind so we can discuss some options for you and Rachel should we decide to move forward."

Rachel spoke up.

"The one thing we do not want to do is become over leveraged by taking out excessive loans which might endanger our company in case of a downturn in the economy. We would also like to maintain control of our company rather than sell stock to raise money. What other options are available, Jerry?"

"I'm glad you asked, Rachel because I know a lot of wealthy investors who would jump all over a high risk venture like this provided the potential returns are great enough. What I am saying is that when the time comes, I can bring enough investor money to do the deal in such a way that you and Phil can promote a share of the venture to these people keeping Tex Con financially sound should the project not work out, but we need your expanded evaluation before we can take the next step. I just want the two of you to know in advance that we can work out a method to do the project where your interest in Tex Con will not be at risk."

"Thank you, Jerry. I'll feel out the producers on terms for processing rights, I am almost certain we can make a great deal if it is connected to construction of a gathering system and pipeline. The producers in the study area are in a financial bind they need to market their gas to stay in business."

Rachel was eager to accept the challenge of negotiating a gathering and transportation agreement with the producers which included processing rights. She was confident she could obtain very favorable terms.

"Rachel, the contracts are going to be critical to our success in putting this thing together, of course, you already knew that. As far as I am concerned, we need the expanded evaluation first then if the results justify the project long term I will come up with a plan to promote and sell the deal."

In the final analysis the economics of the project hinged on whether or not drilling would continue at the current rate over the next few years, which in turn depended directly on the price of oil. Jerry's investor friends were more than willing to assume the risk that the price of oil would be relatively stable going forward, consequently the venture was fully subscribed in the first offering.

From start to finish the new gathering system and pipeline were constructed and operational in five months. Rachel executed contracts with all the producers in the area obtaining dedication of their developed and undeveloped acreage to the processing agreement assuring the feasibility of constructing a gas processing plant should developmental drilling continue over the coming years. Once all the invoices had been paid a final accounting showed the project came in 10% under budget which made the outside investors very happy with Tex Con. They had expected just the opposite based on previous experiences with other companies. Tex Con sent each of them a check for their over payment with their notification the gathering and transportation system was in service and operating as planned. Within a year the system was delivering enough gas to justify construction of a full processing plant capable of recovering most of the ethane, propane, butanes and essentially all the heavier hydrocarbons from the produced gas. After the second year of operation Tex Con began negotiating with the other intrastate and interstate pipelines to deliver residue gas to them as a service to producers in the area. This increase in capacity to deliver gas to new purchasers allowed expansion of the entire system and the processing plant. Tex Con's investors were pleased with the return on their investment and ready to make further investments when the opportunity arose.

Rachel and Phil were enjoying an after dinner glass of *Cabernet Sauvignon,* while overlooking Corpus Christi Bay when the ring tone of Rachel's cell phone broke the silence. It was Martha.

"Mom, do you remember me telling you about Alan Strong, the blond guy that I met? We got married last weekend in Oklahoma. It was sort of strange, we eloped."

There was momentary silence before Rachel responded.

"I am so happy for you Martha."

"Mom, I'm sorry you and Phil didn't get to meet him first, he is fantastic, and he makes me happy."

"When do you think we might meet your husband, Mr. Strong?"

"Mom, that's why I called. Are you and Phil free this coming weekend?"

"I'll make sure that we are. When do you plan to arrive?"

"About noon, you are going to love Alan and so will Phil. He's a genius."

"I'll tell Phil sweetheart, we will be anticipating your arrival and meeting your husband. Congratulations dear, Martha, as always we wish you happiness."

"Thanks mom, we'll see you Saturday, bye."

Rachel sank onto the sofa next to Phil then picked up her glass holding it up she said to Phil.

"My love, let's drink a toast to Martha, she is married."

Phil almost spilled his wine, recovering in time to touch his wine glass to Rachel's before taking a sip.

"Please tell me more about Martha's being married. When did this happen?"

411

"Last weekend, she and Alan Strong eloped to Oklahoma. That's all I know except he makes her happy and he is a genius."

"You just said the keywords, he makes her happy."

"Yes, I know. I just wish we had met him first."

"Do you think it would have made a difference?"

"I don't think so, she has been in love with him for a sometime now. I suspected that when she first mentioned him, but their marriage was a total shock to me. We will have a close-up look at him this weekend I'm very interested in meeting a genius aren't you?"

The newlyweds arrived a few minutes before noon. Both Phil and Rachel were on hand to welcome them into their home and to get their first look at Martha's new husband, Alan. To Rachel's delight he was tall, blond and handsome with a big smile and a firm handshake. After shaking Rachel's hand Alan proceeded to give her a big hug.

"In my family we hug the women and shake hands with the men. I hope you don't mind my hugging you Mrs. Jensen, Martha's mother deserves much more than a hand shake from me."

He turned to Phil offering his hand in the process. Phil grasped Alan's hand pumping it once as a sign of acceptance before inviting him into the living room. He already liked Alan because of his demeanor with Rachel and his friendly approach to meeting his new in-laws. The specter of an awkward first meeting had been deftly put aside by Alan's actions. Rachel and Martha followed seating themselves opposite Phil and Alan, so they could all see each other while they talked. This was important to Rachel and Phil because they were evaluating their new Son-in-Law. Alan was doing his own evaluation, but knew in his mind that he had to like Phil and Rachel, no matter what he thought, because of Martha. Martha began the conversation saying to no one in particular.

"Are you aware that it takes only one day to get married in Oklahoma?"

"I never really thought about it. Is that important in some way?"

"Sure mom. That's why we were married in Durant. Alan asked me to marry him. I said yes, and we agreed to do it straight away. Alan was aware of the requirements in Oklahoma, so we slipped away on Friday after work. We didn't tell anyone we were getting married or going out of town."

"Was this a spur of the moment decision?"

"Not exactly, I had decided to say yes months earlier, should Alan ask. It was very deliberate, we love each other. Why wait?"

Alan added in his straight forward manner.

"I have been in love with Martha since we accidentally met in a bar one Friday night. After our first official date, I was sure we were destined to be together we seemed to have a special feeling for each other. And I was right, we have much more in common than most couples. We like the same things and think the same way on most important life topics."

"You mentioned to me earlier that you met Alan in a bar, just how did that happen again."

"I went there to critique one of my client's performance and Alan happened to be sitting at the one table directly in front of the stage where I could have a clear view. So I asked Alan if I could join him since he appeared to be alone. We couldn't sit there just looking at each other all evening so we had a drink and talked for a while then danced once or twice while we waited for my client to appear on stage. Alan was very gracious to allow a total stranger to share his table. After the performance, Alan walked me to my car, and we parted as fiends."

"Actually, I was so fascinated by Martha that I called the next day to make a formal date. After that I was totally captivated by her beauty and brain, she is an extraordinary person you know. "

"Over the following months we got to know each other and as a consequence each of us became dedicated to making the other happy. I must say Alan has a talent for making me happy all the time. He is marvelous as a husband and I might add a brilliant innovator and business person."

Phil motioned to Alan to come with him to the patio. The sea breeze was brisk with a fresh smell to it as they seated themselves at the patio table overlooking Corpus Christi Bay.

"Alan, is it too early in the day for a drink?"

"That sounds like a good idea to me. Do you have Irish whiskey? No, wait I'll have whatever you are having."

Phil returned with two large frozen *margaritas* and two shot glass filled with *Jose Cuervo* gold *tequila*.

"I have found this to be the ideal way to drink a frozen *margarita*. Sip about a third of the frozen drink to get accustomed to the *tequila* taste then add the shot and stir briskly until well mixed. The result is a drink promoting a great outlook and an ease of existence."

The first third of Alan's *margarita* had a delicate taste very pleasing to the pallet. Alan poured in the shot and mixed it well before taking a taste of the new concoction it had a sharper taste, but was amazingly smooth.

"Phil, I have never had anything like this, it is smooth as silk and has a very delicate taste."

"I'm glad you like it. Tell me, Alan just what is it that you do for a living?"

"My partner and I own and operate Cyber Resources, Inc. which is a pure research enterprise. We are supported by a large investment company which pays all of our costs and in turn has the right to market all of our products. Cyber Research Inc. retains 25% interest in those products and shares in 25% of the net income generated from their sale and or leasing."

"My God, what a deal. You will have to tell Rachel about this, she is our negotiator and deal maker. Who negotiated the agreement?"

"That was the arrangement they offered, if we were willing to start a research company. They found us, we didn't find them. My partner, Jim Running Horse, and I have been friends since we were kids in Waco. His mother and father are professors at Baylor as is my dad. When we were kids, Jim, and I worked on our own personal research projects outside of school. After a while, my dad became our mentor and advisor. Dad's name is Randall Felton, but I have always called him Professor."

"Is the name of the company backing Cyber Research a secret or can you tell me their name?"

"It's no secret. The company backing us is Imperial Resources out of Houston. Have you heard of them?"

Startled by Alan's answer, Phil sat there muted as he processed the information. For Imperial Resources to seek out and finance two individuals to start a research company was indeed support for Martha's genius assessment of Alan. Phil replied with a question.

"Do you know a fellow with Imperial named Jerry Schneider?"

"I don't exactly know him. I have not met him in person, but he sent us a letter of commendation following completion of our first project at Cyber Research."

"How many projects have you finished to date?"

"We are nearing completion of our fifth right now. Imperial has already marketed the other four."

"One more question Alan, who comes up with these projects?"

"Jim and I. We have the freedom to work on anything we choose."

"You and your partner have the best arrangement I have ever heard of, but enough about business. Let's go inside we need to decide where we are going for dinner this evening."

Phil inquired of Martha and Rachel.

"Ladies, what is your desire for dinner, shall we go to the Oasis?"

Martha responded before Rachel could answer.

"That would be nice Dad, but could we go to Kings Inn instead?"

"If that's what you want, let me see if I can get us an early reservation."

Rachel spoke directly to Martha to indicate her approval.

"What an excellent idea. Back when I was going to Texas A&I that was our Friday night hangout. A group of us would go early and dance to the juke box music which was mostly western and popular swing. We would have two beers which we nursed for the entire evening because we couldn't afford to eat there it was too expensive. The dance floor no longer exists they needed the space to handle their increasing number of dinning customers. Without a reservation there is a long waiting line on weekends."

"We are in luck, I have a reservation for four at 5:45 p.m. All the later times are filled."

"I am so glad. Alan has heard about the food at Kings Inn, but he has never been there. It will be a treat for him! What time will we have to leave?"

"It will take about an hour and a half depending on the traffic."

Kings Inn has been in business since 1945 and is located on Baffin Bay north and west of the old resort known a Riviera Beach. Early on, many of its customers were from the Naval Air Station located just south of Kingsville, but over the years it became a premier seafood dining establishment known throughout South Texas and beyond. Their avocado salad and fried onion rings are famous as is their secret tartar sauce. Their shrimp and fish platters are treats for those who savor seafood.

The parking lot was almost filled when Phil eased into the only remaining open space near the entrance. One couple was waiting to be seated when Phil and his party entered the restaurant. The building itself was nothing to brag about, a person who had never been there would be disappointed before going inside because the exterior was rather weather beaten and in need of minor repairs. The waitress who had worked at Kings Inn for a number of years, directed their party to a window table in the dining room where they had a view of Baffin Bay, unfortunately the wind had been blowing hard for several days making the water chocolate brown ruining the otherwise scenic view.

"I think it would be a good idea for everyone to select their main dish and to allow me to order the sides, but first everyone needs a drink."

Phil motioned to the waitress who responded quickly taking their drink orders.

"This is a far cry from when I was in college. They have upgraded the interior a lot, the one thing that has not changed is their excellent food. It was good back then, but we seldom came to eat because of the high priced menu."

"It's amazing, half of the people calling on me in Corpus Christi want to come here to eat," added Phil.

"People think nothing of driving fifty to a hundred miles to come here to eat. If you don't like the food, Alan, we may have to throw you back," jested Phil.

They ate until they were stuffed talking all the while about the great seafood and how efficient the waiters were in replenishing their bar drinks. Alan made several inquiries concerning Tex Con and its operations which were answered by both Phil and Rachel they appreciated his interest and were impressed by his knowledge of the technical issues involved. Phil ate the last morsel of his fried shrimp declaring.

"We can't leave without an after dinner drink, one more for the road. While I order, everyone go to the bathroom, we won't be making any pit stops on the way back to Corpus Christi."

Phil turned on to FM 628 heading for U.S. 77 while the rest of the diners settled into their seats for the long ride home. Alan remarked to Martha.

"You know, I think the food was even better here than at the Outrigger in Palacios."

"Yes, I agree their seafood is outstanding. Speaking of the Outrigger, maybe we can eat there on the way home tomorrow," replied Martha rubbing Alan's arm and kissing him on the neck.

The group sat around talking for an hour or so before deciding to shower and go to bed. Rachel turned off the night light in their bedroom then asked Phil.

"Well what is the verdict?"

"Alan is indeed a genius if that is what you asking about," answered Phil turning slightly to face Rachel.

"It turns out that, Jerry Schneider, and Imperial Resources sought out Alan and his partner Jim to form Cyber Resources. Imperial is financing Cyber Resources one hundred percent, we'll have to ask Jerry about this the next time we are together."

"That's good to know, my real question was do you like him?"

"How could I not like him? He is smart, tall, good looking and really good at interacting with people."

"Is there more?"

"Alan adores Martha, and the feeling is mutual. Can't you tell they are very right for each other?"

"Yes my love, I wanted your thoughts to make sure it was real. After her previous experience, I was afraid Martha might never find another man she could love."

"You mean like us?"

"Yes, just like us!"

Alan and Martha departed a little before noon on Sunday. They had arranged to have Monday off and were spending the night at Alan's friend's condo in Palacios on their way home. They arrived in mid-afternoon, but did not take the boat out. The wind was blowing hard making Palacios Bay dangerously rough. Instead they spent the rest of the afternoon inside before going to dinner at the Outrigger. Conditions had not improved by Monday morning there was little prospect for improvement throughout the day. Martha expressed her disappointment as they prepared to leave.

"I was so looking forward to another fishing trip. I found the last one to be exhilarating, I had my heart set on a repeat performance."

"Me too. I know how much you liked our first fishing trip. You are a natural, unfortunately we will have to wait for another time when the weather cooperates."

They made the drive to Austin thinking about what might have been, but they had not given up on fishing in Palacios. Another trip was planned in the fall.

Chapter 18 Calling

Estelle worked for two years after she and Bruce married and returned to Stanford where Bruce continued his studies toward a medical degree. After six years at Stanford they still felt out of place living in the land of California where they were conservative thinkers in a society over run by socialist ideas. They were outcasts in a forbidden land occupied by left wing liberals and a few hardline communists. To their relief, upon graduating from medical school, Bruce was selected to do his internship at a prominent neurological research hospital located in San Antonio, Texas. San Antonio was not far from Junction and within easy driving distance of Houston making their parents accessible for periodic visits. Bruce's internship at the hospital proved to be a near perfect training situation for him and Estelle.

Unknown to Bruce and Estelle his internship at the hospital came about because of Zane's intervention, he exerted extreme pressure on the hospital's board of directors to offer the internship to Bruce rather than one of the other four graduates recommended by the by research department. For years, Zane had been among the hospital's largest monetary supporters a distinction he achieved the year he and Peggy married, in the ensuing years he and Peggy made substantial private donations to support its ongoing research programs. In addition, Zane became the hospital's prime solicitor for outside aid he worked tirelessly on their behalf raising millions of dollars to support the hospital and its research programs. Without Zane's efforts and support, the hospital would have been unable to conduct the many research programs which had made it famous worldwide. The hospital's reputation for excellence in developing new neurological methods and treatments to solve devastating pain problems and nerve related illnesses would not have come about without Zane and his associate's long term monetary commitment.

Bruce had little free time during his internship, but after he became a full staff member as a neurological MD things changed for the better. He had free time on the weekends allowing him and Estelle to lead a somewhat normal life. They joined the Country Club where many of their friends and acquaintances were members and took up golf as a weekend hobby. Estelle also joined the ladies tennis club becoming an excellent player after a short while. She excelled at the game making numerous new friends among the club members. Estelle continued painting in her spare time producing beautiful western scenes as well as other outdoor pictures. She was very adept at painting scenes featuring towering cumulonimbus clouds at twilight and sunrise. Her combinations of color along with her use of light and shadows made her paintings individualistic and in great demand at the local art shows. She found her place in the art world she continued to paint the remainder of her life selling her paintings for thousands of dollars each. As her reputation grew so did the price of her paintings.

At the hospital, Bruce became involved in a new neurological research program which satisfied his desire to create new techniques and treatments in his chosen field. His research work did not interfere with his weekend time with Estelle who had put up with the inconveniences of being associated with the medical profession ever since they became a couple. She was happy that they could finally participate in the society of the upper middle class like normal people. Estelle had no desire to enter the elite society reserved for the idle rich she was just a country girl who had come to town, she had no desire to become a socialite

They had finished their Saturday round of golf and had showered and changed into their street clothes before having a snack at the Country Club. As they were entering the house Bruce said.

"Don't you think it is about time for us to start thinking about having children?"

"I've been thinking about it ever since we got married. We can't wait much longer, or we will be old before they grow up. I don't want our children to think we are their grandparents."

"Then why don't we start now?" Said Bruce putting his arms around Estelle lifting her in his arms and carrying her toward the bedroom. Estelle replied, "How could I refuse a proposal like that?" She kissed Bruce on the neck before he released her near the bed where she immediately began undressing. Bruce quickly removed his clothes and began kissing Estelle before she was half undressed. He started with a passionate kiss on the mouth then kissed each part of her body as it became exposed. By the time she was totally naked Estelle was stimulated to a near state of euphoria, she pulled Bruce to the bed putting her legs around his waist. She kissed him passionately as he caressed her.

"Bruce that was absolutely fantastic, shall we say just what the doctor ordered. You realize, I have to get off the pill before I can become pregnant."

"Yes, I know, but that doesn't mean we can't practice."

He laughed then added, "I don't want you to become bored."

Their first child, born a little over a year later, was a blond girl like her mother and very active, she wiggled most of the time she was awake. Once she was walking, she was into everything exploring each new thing she contacted looking it over from top to bottom and feeling its parts over and over. She was an extremely curious and bright child who quickly expanded her world beyond eating and sleeping. This gifted girl was named Estelle Verona Wilkerson as a tribute to Verona who played a special role in the lives of Estelle and Bruce, without her, they probably would not have met and their love for each other would never have materialized instead it would have never existed at all. Eighteen months later she was joined by a brother who was also a blond and every bit as bright as his sister. Bruce and Estelle produced two more boys before they called it quits. They continued to practice on a regular basis remembering what Estelle said to Verona years earlier.

"Love and sex go together and they had better both be good."

Bruce and several of the other research doctors were having coffee in the hospital cafeteria during their morning break when the subject of politics came up. The lead doctor in the neurological department mentioned the upcoming election which was nine months away.

"What we need is a young, well educated person to run on the conservative ticket to represent the hospital and this district on the city council. We and the hospital are getting kicked around like dirt by those liberals downtown, they don't give a damn about the valuable work we are doing all they care about is staying in office."

Bruce was dismayed by the comment although he had little interest in politics, yet he felt compelled to speak.

"I don't understand. What's going on?"

He listened attentively as they explained how the hospital was expected to treat illegals and indigents free while the city was increasing their taxes and supporting unionization of their employees making the hospital's operation more difficult and expensive.

"Something has to be done to protect the hospital from these leaches before we have to close our doors. You understand, we do not turn anyone away, but now they are urging their voter base to come here because it's free. We can't treat all of their freeloading supporters in this hospital for free and remain a viable institution. We do not receive any funding from the City, State or the Federal government, we are totally supported by private donations and the fees we charge for our services."

A week later, Zane came by to visit Bruce during one of his periodic conferences with the hospital management team and its board of directors. Zane was in town to discuss a large-scale statewide fund raising campaign for the hospital. Although the lead doctor's comments interested Bruce, he had given their discussion about a candidate little thought. He mentioned the conversation to Zane only because of his association with the hospital.

"I think that is a great idea. Bruce, why don't you run for the position?"

"Me, run? Zane, I don't know anything about politics."

"Think about it for a while before you say no, there is a real problem for the hospital that needs to be taken care of right away. Do you know anyone who might be able to fix this?"

"Not really, but I can't run. Estelle and I don't have enough money to pay for a campaign. Not only that, I don't know anything about managing or running a political campaign, I wouldn't know where to start."

"Bruce, my associates and I can fund a first class campaign and we can provide the best campaign manager in Texas. Should you run for the office, I can guarantee a cadre of wealthy San Antonio supporters who will work hard for your election. Go home and discuss this with Estelle, her reaction to my proposal may surprise you."

After putting little Estelle Verona to bed Estelle looked at Bruce frowning.

"Ok, honey, out with it, what is bothering you?"

"I talked with Zane today and he sort of dropped a bomb on me."

"What kind of bomb, sweetheart?"

"The other day one of the doctors at the hospital said that we needed a young conservative to run for city council to protect the hospital from the liberals on the council. I was telling Zane what the doctor said when he proposed that I seek the office. I tried to tell him I knew nothing about politics, but he had an answer for all of my short- comings. Zane wanted me to discuss his proposal with you. I am not sure that I want to do this even though Zane promised funding and management for a campaign."

"Honey, do you remember all the time we spent in California and how disgusted we were with liberal ideas that permeated the entire social order there. Do you want Texas to become another California where everyone is entitled to a good living at tax payer's expense even if they are just too lazy to work?"

"You know that I don't."

"Then what is the problem? We should do our part to preserve the Texas we know and love for our children. Where else can an individual start a small business and not be taxed to death to pay for all the socialist entitlement programs run by the State? I think we should do the right thing. Don't you?"

"I see your point and I sure as hell don't want Texas to become another California or bankrupt like Illinois. Did you know there are more people on welfare than there people working in Illinois?"

"Then you are going to run for the City Council?"

"With your support, I don't see how I could refuse. Let's do our part to save Texas, this will be our first contribution toward keeping the world safe for our children."

Zane almost jumped off of his chair when Bruce called telling him that Estelle was enthusiastic about his proposal and they were ready to get started. Within minutes, Zane put the wheels in motion to organize Bruce's campaign, he hired an acclaimed publicist and an expert campaign manager before the day was over. Bruce and Estelle had been thrust upon the stage of politics.

Two separate Alpha-3 reports came into Abe, one from the group assigned to Bruce and Estelle and the other from the group assigned to Peggy and Zane. Both reports recounted the fact that Bruce was entering politics running as a conservative for a position on the San Antonio City Council. The campaign finances and management were to be controlled by Zane and his associates. Aaron read the reports with interest then thought about this turn of events for a couple of days before making a decision concerning the campaign which would involve Bruce and Estelle and Peggy and Zane. His instructions to the on-site Abe agents doubled the size of the surveillance team assigned to Peggy and Zane with extra coverage for Bruce, Estelle and their daughter. Bruce was to be treated as, endangered, by his political opponents. All political adversaries were to receive the full Abe treatment as they became known, so that Aaron would know everything about each of them past and present. He also ordered Abe's complete spy package applied to all of those councilmen opposed to Bruce's election. Aaron intended to know what and who Bruce was up against in seeking the office of city councilman. Abe's best agent in headquarters was assigned the task of compiling and analyzing all information gathered for possible use in the campaign or in determining who were Bruce's political enemies and their stake in the election. Aaron had not decided whether Abe would become actively involved in the campaign and election behind the scenes, but he made sure they would be prepared should Abe's help become necessary.

The campaign manager and his staff set up a strategy session to address a possible fatal campaign issue that would undoubtedly be exploited by the opposition. According to the public records, Bruce was born out of wedlock. How was this to be averted as an issue in the election?

"I would rather not run for office if it embarrasses mother publicly. In fact, I will not run unless we find a solution to this problem."

Bruce made it clear that embarrassing his mother was not something he would do even if it meant giving up the race before it began. He had been reluctant to enter politics in the first place. Bruce was unaware of Peggy's involvement with Gentex, but he did know that Zane was not his father and Peggy had not been married before she married Zane. Zane let it be known to the group that he had a perfect solution to the problem, but before it could be implemented, he needed to talk with Peggy to get her approval. With that bit of information the campaign manager charged ahead.

"In the meanwhile, let's lay out a campaign platform and a publicity program for our candidate and get him into a fast track public speaking program before he says something he shouldn't," said the manager taking up where Zane had left off.

Peggy listened carefully as Zane laid out the necessity of explaining how Bruce was born out of wedlock in such a way that it would be acceptable to the public. Although it was a non-issue to her, Peggy appreciated how it could be exploited by unscrupulous reporters and politicians.

"I can solve the problem if you agree," said Zane.

"You know I will not refuse Zane, I'll do whatever it takes to help Bruce in this endeavor. That is the way it has always been, if it makes you and Bruce happy, it makes me happy. Both of you have my full support."

"Here is my plan to avoid involving you and the Gentex program in a lot of unwanted scrutiny because of Bruce's candidacy. I will have a Costa Rican marriage certificate recorded in the legal archives showing a marriage between you and a nonperson named, Jimmy Stout. The story will be that after your honeymoon together in Costa Rica, you came back to the States where he was to join you. He never showed up and could not be found in Costa Rica, he had disappeared, so you had the marriage annulled before you discovered you were pregnant. I can arrange to have your annulment recorded in the archives as well. The records will show it happened just as I stated, people will feel sympathetic toward a young bride abandoned by her new husband. You will be regarded as heroic by the news media and voters. Problem solved."

"I must say you are clever, I like the idea and cover story."

Zane took care of the problem of Bruce being born out of wedlock in the normal way, a little money was placed in the right hands and suddenly Peggy's marriage and subsequent annulment became a matter of public record in Costa Rica. Her involvement with Gentex was never discovered or brought up by the reporters covering the campaign or by any of the opposition. Peggy had been saved the embarrassment of trying to explain Bruce without involving Gentex. Aaron noted with pride the skill and effectiveness of Zane's tactic to protect Peggy and her connection to Gentex from the news media while solidifying Bruce's candidacy. In an effort to get Bruce into an accelerated public speaking program, the publicist researched private companies offering well-qualified training in public speaking and public presentation. He found Talent Development, Inc. (TDI) located in Austin to be among the highest rated of the Texas companies it was the most recommended by entertainment professionals leading him to enroll Bruce for one week of intensive training in public speaking and the art of handling interviews by the news media.

Bruce came to Martha's office for an interview focused on determining the state of his public speaking ability. In order to help him, she needed to determine those areas in which he required additional training before embarking on a program to make him a public figure whose speeches people enjoyed. It was clear to Martha, following a short speech given by Bruce, that he already possessed some of the qualities required to be a great public speaker, his style made him believable by its directness, plus he possessed a natural ability to make the subject interesting. Martha concluded this was due in part to his being a doctor who took unusual care to explain things to his patients. She agreed to train Bruce herself for a fixed fee of $80,000. In her judgement, he could become a great public speaker with the right kind of guidance and she was prepared to provide that guidance. Martha introduced Bruce to the speech studio and its features before they began their first session. She explained.

"To become a great public speaker it is necessary to have a good memory, the one thing you do not want to do is use a Teleprompter, it gives your audience the impression you are only reading a speech written for you by another person and it makes you appear to be lacking in facts and unsure of yourself. Some speakers, highly acclaimed by the news media, have been revealed to be complete dunces incapable of thinking on their feet when forced to speak without their Teleprompters."

Bruce nodded his head in agreement then asked.

"Where do we start?"

"In your case, the first thing we need to work on is learning to have a plan for every speech and for every interview conducted by reporters following its conclusion. In making a speech, you will have control of the subject and the length of the speech, so planning is required on your part to make your point without boring your audience. Remember, the opposition has no input in what you say or how you say it. For you to be a really good public speaker you must have a pleasant delivery, stay on the subject, make it interesting and most of all do not talk too long. The number one thing people dislike is a speaker who talks forever and never says anything other than a bunch of meaningless words. Keep it short and have a clear message!"

Martha continued emphasizing those qualities and abilities she felt were important.

"At the conclusion of a speech is when things can get out of hand because the speaker has limited control over the questions reporters ask. The cardinal rule in after speech question and answer sessions is: DO NOT ANSWER ANY QUESTION NOT RELATED TO THE SUBJECT OF THE SPEECH, IGNORE THE QUESTIONER. Rule number two is: DO NOT ANSWER ANY QUESTION YOU DO NOT WANT TO ANSWER, BUT DO NOT PASS UP AN OPPORTUNITY THAT PLAYS TO YOUR STRENGTH. And rule number three is: BE DECISIIVE IN YOUR ANSWERS THERE IS NOTHING WORSE THAN GIVING THE IMPRESSION THAT YOU ARE NOT SURE OF YOUR POSITION ON AN ISSUE. We will be working on these rules the rest of the day. I want you to make a short speech on any subject you chose. You will then have a mock question and answer session with my staff to see how you handle the interview. Both the speech and the interview will be recorded on video for our joint reviewed and critique. Then we will do another and another until you have mastered the techniques required, we may be here well into the night."

The first short speech proved enlightening to Martha, Bruce was a natural in his presentation he followed all the rules of good speech making. It was in the mock question and answer session that he was woefully lacking. Martha had four experienced coworkers playing the parts of reporters. They were brutal in their repeated questioning and insisted that Bruce give an answer to their embarrassing questions. Some questions were, by design, totally unrelated to the subject of Bruce's speech. Bruce had that good old boy malady, he disliked a confrontational attitude which led him to answer several of the questions he should have ignored. During a joint analysis of the questions and the techniques employed by the reporters to extort answers his errors were pointed out to Bruce as were his proper responses. The question and answer session was repeated, the second time around Bruce responded much better in keeping the questions on the subject. He completely ignored many of the questions asked, deftly changing the subject and directing the interview to where he wanted it to go. It was difficult for Bruce not to answer a direct question because of his upbringing, usually an answer was given if it came from a parent or a person of authority. Throughout the day and well into the evening Martha repeated her theme concerning reporters.

"Plant this firmly in your brain and never forget it, reporters are not your friends, they are potential enemies if you are seeking any kind of elected office. Their attempts to change the attitude of readers and viewers depend on their political orientation not necessarily what is factual or newsworthy. Never trust a reporter. I repeat, never trust a reporter. They are almost exclusively left leaning in their personal views!"

Martha emphasized over and over again.

"There is no such thing as an off-the-record comment, among reporters nothing is sacred. If it makes a news story or supports their own position, it is in play!"

Bruce stopped by the hotel bar for a drink following the first grueling day at TDI ordering a frozen *margarita* with salt. His first sip of the drink took his breath away it was heavy on *tequila,* just what he needed to wind down the tension generated by Martha's intense learning session. Sitting alone at the bar he sighed then thought.

"How in the hell could I be so stupid at my age? I didn't realize how vulnerable I am to being questioned by reporters. I'll have to learn how to overcome this fault, if I am to succeed in public life."

He finished his *margarita* enjoying the last drop of its calming qualities before heading toward his room to call Estelle.

"How was your first day in training?" Asked Estelle in her sexiest voice.

"It was tough, I didn't know how difficult being a public figure was going to be for me and maybe for you too."

"Are you just finishing up for the day?"

"Yeah, we spent twelve hours working on just one of my problems and there are probably many more. How are you and Estelle Verona doing?"

"She is doing fine, but I am already missing you. I think we should come over and spend the night Wednesday. Don't you?"

"That's a good idea, I think I'm going to need a little practice in order to last out the week. Like my instructor here keeps saying, practice makes perfect."

"Yes, dear you read my mind, we'll see you Wednesday."

Estelle Verona was glad to see her father she jumped at Bruce's feet asking to be held in his arms. He picked her up then gave Estelle a warm kiss as he hugged the youngster who had her arms around his neck. She said in her small voice.

"Daddy, when will you be home? I miss you!"

"I've missed both of you. Honey, we will all be home together next week I have to stay here through Friday to finish my work. After that I promise to rush home to be with you and mommy."

Estelle waited her turn then gave Bruce a hug and a kiss saying softly in his ear. "I've missed you too daddy in a big way. Can we practice after Estelle Verona goes to bed after dinner?"

"You'll have to fight me off. I'm in desperate need of some relaxation after three days of speech training it has been tough to say the least." Replied Bruce playfully patting Estelle on the bottom.

"Speech therapy will not end when I get home, you and I will have to repeat parts of the program over and over to ensure that I am ready, comfortable and prepared when the time comes for my debut. It's what the instructor calls practice, she doesn't know what practice is around our house."

The necessary forms were filed, and the fees paid making Bruce an official candidate for city council. Campaign signs and placards announcing Bruce's candidacy appeared overnight throughout the area followed by a well-planned media blitz featuring a short speech to his supporters, Bruce also made an appearance on the local conservative television network. He did interviews with reporters from all the San Antonio television stations in which he vowed to work hard to provide fair treatment by the city for the voters in his district and to fight to preserve the hospital for posterity. Saving the hospital became a center piece of his campaign, one that Bruce repeated at every opportunity.

"The hospital is an asset to both the district and the City of San Antonio, both should be working to insure its continued ability to serve the community and continue its outstanding research programs."

He promised to change the city's position on several of its socialist inspired programs currently targeting the hospital. The die was cast, Bruce had successfully stated his platform in a clear and simple manner. His challenge to the city and its overtly liberal council was clear. Bruce represented a viable alternative in his district to the entrenched liberals running San Antonio. The progressive liberals at city hall responded to the challenge issued by Bruce and his supporters using every avenue available to discredit Bruce and his campaign. Soon there was a venomous rumor circulating in San Antonio purporting that Bruce Wilkerson was born out of wedlock and was indeed a bastard in the true sense of the word. The source of the rumor was never disclosed although it allegedly originated with a liberal female writer working for a daily Houston newspaper. As planned, Peggy came forward with her story clarifying the circumstances surround Bruce's birth. Her marriage and annulment in Costa Rica were quickly verified by the news media and much to the liberal's disgust the rumor died without damage to Bruce's reputation or his candidacy. The airways were filled with campaign ads on radio and on TV touting Bruce's message and his qualification for a seat on the San Antonio City Council. Bruce became well known among the San Antonio citizens and particularly well known among those in his district who voted.

As the campaign progressed, it became apparent there were other hurdles to overcome, the entrenched liberals fielded a candidate who had never lost an election since he appeared on the San Antonio political scene some twenty years earlier. He currently held no elected office he had been out of local politics for six years serving as President of an investment firm specializing in making investments for rich Mexican clients. The liberal's selection, Juan Carlos Salinas, was a formidable candidate long associated with liberal programs and a proven vote getter in previous elections. The liberals were well organized with support from national labor unions and the liberal clique which occupied the White House and had control of the U.S. Senate. They had unlimited monetary support from the national neo-socialist organizations from the east coast who viewed this election as a direct challenge to their continued dominance in the city of San Antonio and the Democrat party. A loss here to an unknown conservative could damage their national image as the party of the people. San Antonio had been a liberal stronghold for many years, its elected officials regularly advocating for more benefits for those criminals who had violated our laws by entering the country illegally, those receiving welfare and those on the public dole while at the same time reviling those who paid taxes to pay for these socialist programs.

Aaron studied all the reports Abe's agents sent to headquarters regarding both Bruce's preparation for the election and the opposition candidate and his supporters. Abe agents in Houston ran an investigation into the activities of Juan Carlos Salinas, Bruce's opponent. They found nothing suspicious in his activities either in the U.S. or in Mexico, yet there was a lingering doubt that he was legitimate based on his rapid accumulation of wealth after leaving office as an elected official. Remembering Jerry's success in using Number Three at the *Bastardos Locos* to take care of the Muslim agents stalking Martha a few years earlier, Aaron prevailed on Jerry to contact Joe to inquiry about Juan Carlos Salinas.

Jerry was reluctant to use information obtained from the *Bastardos Locos* in a political campaign, but out of necessity he put his concern aside then called Joe his contact from his previous encounters with *Bastardos Locos*. To his dismay, he found Joe was no longer available at his old phone number. Following an arduous discussion with the person answering the phone, Jerry was informed Joe could be reached at Marine International Investments. A little research on Jerry's computer produced a phone number which he punched into his cell phone.

The operator answered, "Marine International, to whom do you wish to speak?"

"I need to speak with Joe," replied Jerry.

"Sir, we do not have a Joe listed, but we have a Joseph. Would you like to speak to him?"

"Yes, but tell him it is an old friend from the Tmex," replied Jerry hoping that would get him through to Joe.

"Hello my friend, I didn't expect to hear from you again. What's up?"

"Joe, you are one difficult guy to find. How have you been?"

"Things have changed a lot since we last talked. What do you have on your mind?"

"How soon could we meet at the Tmex?"

431

"For you my friend, I can be there within an hour."

Jerry was seated at a table when Joe walked up his hand extended in greeting. Joe was wearing an expensive suit and tie which startled Jerry, Joe had always been casually dressed in their past encounters. Jerry stood up and after shaking Joe's hand admired his attire from head to foot before inviting him to sit for a drink.

"Will an Irish whiskey do? Or have you switched?"

"Irish whiskey is always good *Amigo*, that's the only thing I haven't changed."

"Really, what's been going on with you? Why are you all dressed up?"

"I'm sure you are aware that I became Number One at *Bastardos Locos* following the untimely deaths of Number One and Number Three who were killed a plane crash in Columbia."

"Was it a planned crash or an accident?"

"It was an accident, there was no foul play involved. Lucky for me, I was in a position to take over *Bastardos Locos*. I was even luckier after taking over as the new Number One, I had absolute control of the cartel and its investments. I remembered how you structured the deal when you bought Cross Border I&E Company from the cartel. I solidified my position by appointing a Number two and a Number Three I could trust. Following your example, I spun off the investment arm of *Bastardos Locos* into an untraceable offshore company which eventually became Marine International Investments now owned by me and my family. I gave the *Bastardos Locos* cocaine business to my Number Two and Number Three along with all the cash in the investment account they were grateful to get it. I am no longer associated with *Bastardos Locos* in any way. Thanks to you, I am a businessman just like yourself and have no connection to the cocaine trade. I can never thank you enough, my friend, without your recommending me to Number One this would never have been possible. I thank you and my family thanks you. We are now a normal American family working to get ahead in the business world."

"Joe, I'm impressed by you and your accomplishments it's refreshing to see success in today's world."

"Aside from a having drink, what else do you have on your mind?"

"I was wondering if you could shed some light on a Juan Carlos Salinas who runs an investment company located in San Antonio? He reportedly serves rich Mexicans with their American investments."

"I know the son of a bitch, he launders money for one of the big Mexican drug cartels. They are involved in smuggling drugs and under aged girls for the sex trade in the U.S. Check out the Angels that's who he works for. We kept our distance from these guys they are brutal and will stop at nothing to have their way. Be careful if you are thinking of taking them on. I hope this helps because I know nothing more about Juan Carlos except he is one cunning bastard with political connections in San Antonio."

Jerry ordered another round of Irish whiskey without ice, he had become a purist over the years since first being exposed to its benefits. Their glasses touched as they raised their arms to salute, their eyes met in mutual admiration as they sat back to enjoyed their drinks and each other's company.

"My friend, it was good of you to call maybe we should meet more often."

"Joe, you are right we should get together more often, say once a month. I'll give you a call. If you like, we can have a standing monthly get-together here at the Tmex. It will be interesting to compare notes and visit while we share a couple of drinks."

"Look, if you need anything from me you know where to reach me. My friend, I await your call."

"Joe, should you need any kind of help in your business give me a call. You know you can depend on me."

They left the Tmex bar anticipating their next regularly scheduled session between friends. Armed with the information Joe provided, Jerry called Aaron at Abe requesting an immediate all out investigation of Juan Carlos Salinas and his connection to the Angels. Aaron moved quickly summoning the Abe agents in charge of investigations to a meeting in his office. He opened the meeting by declaring!

"Gentlemen, this is a maximum efforts project requiring mobilization of all of Abe's capabilities. Our earlier investigation of Juan Carlos Salinas turned up nothing, but we have since discovered he has a connection to the Angels cartel. As soon as possible, I want to know everything there is to know about Juan Carlos Salinas and his connection to the Angels. In addition, you are to identify those people in politics and business who are the source of Juan Carlos' influence in local government. Once you have identified those parties of interest, all of them are to be subjected to the full array of Abe's resources. This includes individual surveillance, bugging all communication media and recording of all of their activities around the clock. Juan Carlos and any members of the Angels residing in Texas are to be subjected to Abe's most intense scrutiny without arousing any suspicion that they are being investigated. Are there any questions?"

"Sir, where are we going to get the people required for this assignment?" asked the lead agent in charge.

"If you can't borrow agents from the other Abe groups, then you are free to hire outsiders on the approved list. I am making everyone here at headquarters available for this project, it's up to you to select those people you need. Let me impress upon all of you that failure in this operation will be considered a failure of the entire Abe organization. Cost is no obstacle, you are to use all of Abe's assets and resources for a successfully completion of this project in the shortest time possible. If there are no more questions, let's get on it now!"

At Aaron's request the lead agent remained behind while the other agents rushed to their assigned areas in preparation to put Aaron's plan into action.

"I want you to put together an organizational plan for your leadership team on this project today, so we can get started. I will inform all supervisors that you have *carte blanche* use of their agents so feel free to select anyone you want for this project. Your best work will be needed to make this project work, should you need anything more or encounter any internal roadblocks, give me a call."

Aaron then ushered the lead agent out of his office with a smile and a pat on the back as he was leaving.

With three months remaining before the election, Juan Carlos began to make inroads into the early lead Bruce held in the polls. Support was waning for Bruce among some of the businessmen in his district they had suddenly switched to Juan Carlos and were actively advocating his election. This loss of support among the business group was both disturbing and puzzling. Some of them had previously been strong supporters of Bruce in his bid for city council. Bruce's campaign manager sought to offset this loss of support by having Bruce make more public appearances. Bruce and his aides stressed his conservative agenda and what it meant to his district as well as for San Antonio and all of Texas. These appearances were well received Bruce was a natural speaker and had learned to evade the entrapment questions put to him by the media. He deftly over shadowed his opponent in speaking ability and crowd response, yet he was losing support in the polls an enigma which was hard to explain.

Estelle contributed to the campaign as well, she was depicted by the conservatives as a concerned homemaker and mother who stood for better education and healthcare for all children. Her handlers were aware that all elections are about the children this theme never gets old in politics. She had revived this theme among conservatives usurping the liberal's favorite campaign tactic, which irritated the national leftist advisors to Juan Carlos. Saving the children belong to the left this upstart conservative had encroached on their hallowed message, it wasn't fair that she was using the children against them!

Entering the final month of the campaign Bruce had fallen farther behind in polls of probable voters. Juan Carlos had gained support from many of the incumbents on the City Council including two prominent businessmen who were also city councilmen. Unless a miracle occurred, it appeared Bruce's election bid was going down the tubes and his political career was destined for oblivion. At best it would be a close race, he was well liked by many voters and had proven to be an excellent campaigner and public speaker who aroused his supporters. If the election was close and a vote recount become necessary, it was a foregone conclusion that his opponent would win. All the vote recounts in recent years had ended with the liberal candidate winning through manipulation of the recount tally, reminiscent of Lyndon Johnson's notorious box 13 recount victory in Duval County which clenched his first election to the U.S. Senate.

In a shocking turn of events, the Evening News reported two of the councilmen, who were also prominent businessmen, supporting Juan Carlos had ties to money laundering for the Mexican drug cartel known as the Angels. The source of the report was never released, but the evidence it contained was irrefutable and incriminating. According to the report in the paper, the FBI had also received a copy of the report and the supporting evidence enhanced the Federal case they had been building against the two men for several months. Since receiving a tip from one of their informers in San Antonio, the FBI had started an active investigation looking into the finances of the two men and their families. Revelation of the on-going investigation by the FBI was a blockbuster event causing massive defections among business supporters of Juan Carlos. The following week the Evening News reported a connection between the two prominent city councilmen, who supported Juan Carlos, and a kickback scheme with contractors to defraud the city of San Antonio. According to the Evening News the FBI was also actively investigating both of them for fraud. Several contracts that had conveniently disappeared from the city files suddenly turned up in the hands of the FBI solidify their case against them. Both men resigned their positions as city councilmen following a release to the news media, by an unknown source, of damaging evidence supporting the fraud charge against them. Backlash from the breaking news stories caused Aaron to pay Juan Carlos a visit. He made an appointment under the pretense of having a large sum of cash he wanted Juan Carlos to invest on his behalf. Aaron entered Juan Carlos' opulent office expecting to meet a towering specimen of a man instead a short diminutive person held out his hand as Aaron approached.

"Aaron, it's always nice to meet new clients, what can I do for you today?"

"Before we get to that, I need a little background information on your company. What kinds of securities do you invest in, mostly? I always like to check before putting my money in for the long haul."

"No problem, it's always a good idea to ask before investing. We invest in large capital companies who have a history of increasing dividends over at least the past fifteen years. These are solid, safe companies with anticipated growth and increased dividends going forward."

"Then you have nothing to do with laundering drug money for the Angels?"

Juan Carlos looked at Aaron in shocked surprise. He sputtered slightly as he replied.

"What are you talking about?"

Aaron produced a copy of Abe's report from his briefcase laying it face up on Juan Carlos' mahogany desk. Clearly rattled by Aaron's question, Juan Carlos looked at the cover briefly before starting to read the report which contained a wealth of damaging information concerning his operation. The details of every transaction he had made over the past ten years were listed as were copies of Juan Carlos' signature authorizing each cash transfer to the Angels corporate front. His corporate disguise was laid bare including its integrated use of shell companies to shield the Angels from governmental scrutiny. The evidence was overwhelming and well documented it clearly showed a long term financial connection between Juan Carlos and the Angels. His wealth was directly tied to his money laundering activities for the Angels. Juan Carlos blinked as he looked up.

"What do you want from me?"

"Just a small favor," replied Aaron smiling because of the obvious capitulation of Juan Carlos when confronted by the overwhelming evidence presented in the report. The following day Juan Carlos withdrew from the race for city councilman without explanation. Although there was much speculation in the news media concerning his sudden withdrawal, Juan Carlos did not consent to an interview or make a public statement he quietly and permanently withdrew from public life. Bruce went on to win the election garnering 96% of the votes cast in his district. The local and national news media proclaimed his election a political masterpiece resulting in a landslide victory upsetting the political establishment and creating a new dynamic force to be reckoned with in San Antonio politics. According to the media, Bruce would have swept the election by a wide majority, even had Juan Carlos remained in the race, his campaign had appealed to the voting public like none other in recent history. Bruce was a political genius, a new political juggernaut had been born in San Antonio. At a post-election party hosted by Zane and the many backers who contributed to Bruce's campaign success, Bruce and Estelle were applauded as the new faces of conservative politics in San Antonio, if not all of Texas. Discussing the race with Bruce, Estelle voiced her reaction to his win.

"This whole thing was exciting, I enjoyed my small part in the campaign immensely. How do you feel about politics, now that you have won your first election?"

"If you agree, this will be the first of many campaigns to come, I think we can do a lot of good for Texas and Texans."

Much to the delight of the hospital and the electorate in his district, Bruce went on to fulfill his campaign promises, the city withdrew its support for unionizing employees at the hospital and agreed to lower the hospital's tax base the following year. Aaron, armed with Abe's research made several visits to San Antonio's elected officials successfully collecting favors to support Bruce's agenda during his two year term in office. With two months remaining on his second term as city councilman, Bruce, Zane and his supporters were actively engaged in an aggressive campaign for Bruce to win a seat in the Texas Senate. Following a successful term in the Senate he would be a natural for Governor. After that?

Chapter 19 Clare's Place

Clare and Ned had become accustomed to being grandparents they enjoyed Verona's and Kevin's children when they were together, but they were alone most of the time since Angel had gone away to college at TCU. It was the beginning of a new lifestyle for them having no children at home left a void in their lives. Clare retained her classical beauty and perfect figure plus a walk that drove men mad her magnificent brain was intact and functioning well she definitely wasn't ready to retire to the sideline with the old folks. Her inquisitive nature made her want to experiment, to do something different with the rest of her life. Clare had no intention of sitting around doing nothing for the next thirty years she was receptive to new ideas and expanding her horizons in new and exciting ways. Ned had spread a little in the midsection, yet he was still a fine specimen of a man whose interests were boundless. A tinge of grey showed in his hair adding a sexy touch to his appearance making him a distinguished male in his late fifties the personification of experience and knowledge not too old to be actively engaged, yet old enough to be well versed in life experiences.

The Board of Directors had elected Ned President of MyTeeTech several years earlier and with his outstanding management and development of new products the company gained a leadership position in cloud storage and new data storage technology. Their new developments for business applications forced the older and larger established companies to revise their product lines due to MyTeeTech's superior technology and fierce competition in pricing of their products. As a result Ned and Clare had become wealthy through the generous stock options and bonuses he earned as the valuation of MyTeeTech increased under his leadership. During his career as chief executive, Ned had invested wisely acquiring a substantial ownership in MyTeeTech and several other unassociated tech companies. He and Clare were financially secure with an annual income placing them in the upper 1% of Americans. Ned delighted in telling Clare.

"This is our butt money, if I hadn't seen your rear through that glass door I wouldn't have gone to work at MyTeeTech. It's amazing how a simple glance on the way to the John profoundly changed our lives and a lot of other people's as well."

Over time Clare's stock answer to Ned's observation became a classic.

"But for a butt we would never have become lovers and lived this wonderful life together. Kiss me so I know it's real."

In their circle of friends and acquaintances Clare and Ned were known for their upbeat and cheerful demeanor they made a point not to argue, at least not in front of others, they did not correct each other over trivial facts during casual conservations as did many of their friends. Their love for each other was evident to those around them, it was obvious that they were more than lovers they were also friends who respected each other. Ned was the only man in the world for Clare she adored him and Ned had eyes for Clare only, she was beautiful, sexy and brilliant the love of his life. Together they were an admirable couple an example of true love at work. While having an after dinner glass of wine on the patio, Clare happened to mention to Ned.

"It's a strange thing, but a few of the women among our acquaintances ask me for advice about their children and their married life."

"What kinds of advice?"

"Such as how to get their husbands to be more considerate and to make sex more enjoyable for them, or how to handle discussions about sex with their children?"

"Interesting, but how do you answer these questions?"

"It's a little tricky, since we have never had any problems between us, I have to stop and think before giving an answer and even then I have to be careful how I respond. I don't want to make any of them mad."

"Could I make a suggestion? These women should tell their husbands what they need, what turns them on. Show him. If their husbands love them, they will learn how to make sex better for both of them. I can't imagine married people not knowing what their spouses like. Don't they talk?"

"Ned, you and I do, but some people don't get it. I'll try to figure out how to pass that information on. For now let's take a shower and make some of our own magic."

Clare took Ned by the hand and led him inside. Afterward lying in bed Clare put her arm across Ned's chest caressing him softly saying.

"You know what? We are going to have to decide what to do with the rest of our life. The kids are gone and we have plenty of money. What would you like to do?"

"It's uncanny how you read my mind, I have been considering retiring as President of MyTeeTech the time has arrived for new and younger thinking in the leadership role. If the company is to keep its young people, which is necessary to stay ahead of the competition, our young fertile minds need to be allowed to face the challenge with one of their own as leader of the company. I don't intend to retire completely, I plan to remain on the Board of Directors and stay connected to the management of MyTeeTech. We have too much invested for me to sit idly by without making a contribution I still do have some good ideas, you know."

"Yes, I love your Ideas like the one you had a while ago. I also know you will need to have something to occupy your time after you retire, otherwise I will have a wild man on my hands all the time rather than just when we are in bed together."

"I haven't thought about what to do beyond staying on the Board of Directors, but I know you are right I'll need more than being a board member to keep me occupied."

"Let's sleep on it and discuss our options in the morning,"

With breakfast over Ned sat at the kitchen table sipped his coffee for a few minutes before saying to Clare.

"I noticed you did not wake me this morning, but got up and fixed breakfast instead."

Clare changed the subject posing a provocative question on a completely unrelated subject.

"Do you remember Verona's friend, Estelle, who came to visit several times when they were in school at UT?"

"Of course, she was the tall good looking blond from Junction. What about her?"

"She is happily married with kids and lives in San Antonio. What I wanted to mention though was her formula for being happily married. You may not have heard it, but Verona and I did. It went something like this. Love and sex go together and they had both better be good for a happy marriage. Is there some way you and I can get this message across to people without pissing them off?"

"I had not heard her formula before, however, I agree it is excellent advice that most people should hear. Clare, you and I could very well have written it for her. To answer your last question. I don't know, but I promise to give it some thought. Maybe I can come up with something that will work."

Ned knew that some men never mastered the art of love or sex, either because they were stupid, or just didn't give a shit about their partner's desires. He first learned about this unfortunate situation in his youth while serving as a male escort during his last two years at UCLA. Some of the women, who commissioned his services, complained that their husbands, most of whom were dead, never learned how to satisfy them in bed. It was the greatest disappointment of their lives to have a loving mate who could not or would not take care of their sexual needs. A few of the women went so far as to propose having sex with Ned to satisfy their desires. Ned politely refused all of their requests, while noting the importance of good sex to women in general, it was necessary for a happy marriage. With repeated comments on the subject from his clients Ned came to embrace the idea that women needed more than just love to be truly happy, they need to have a satisfying sexual relationship as well. He resolved to make sexual satisfaction for his partner a primary objective in his future relationships with the women, who became a part of this life. His attention to these primary details had worked beautifully for him and Clare, the question was how could he and Clare get this across to strangers? A week of thinking on the subject led Ned to the idea of establishing a website dedicated to answering people's specific questions related to rearing children, sex and marriage. Outlining his concept to Clare, Ned suggested.

"We could call it Clare's Place."

Clare immediately embraced the idea with enthusiasm, proclaiming!

"Ned, you are brilliant, as usual, I would never have thought of this approach in a million years. I think there is a growing and ongoing need for this kind of website, particularly among young people starting a family, those with teenaged children and those having problems in their marriages. Then there are those people who are not married and are having difficulties with sex in their lives. I think there would be a great interest in getting answers to sticky questions provided the people asking the questions can remain anonymous. A little guidance could make a big difference for some of these people. Who knows? It might save some marriages and change a few lives for the better."

"Clare, I think we would be good at it, look at us! How could any couple be happier than we are? We were happy from the start because we love each other very much and are fantastic together in the sex department. For some people fantastic is out of reach, but good is a must for a happy and long lasting relationship. Just think how much happiness would be created if we were able get one out of five people to cross over the line from being marginally unhappy to enjoying life."

"Ned, we will want to limit questions to three or four categories otherwise we will be overwhelmed, maybe we should limit the questions to sex and marriage to start with in a trial run. We can add other categories later if the website turns out to be a viable vehicle for helping people with their problems."

"Let me check into constructing a website, I think it will probably require some unusual techniques to protect the identities of those asking questions. That is an issue we can overcome, but technically it may be very complicated. After all, the Russian hackers have been able to hide their identities from detection for years. We can use the same technique they do except we will have to do it legally. I'm going to arrange a conference with the owner of Squidz Ink Design in, Houston to determine how we should set up the website and how we can protect the users' identities.

"Mr. Stanley, I understand you are in need of a special website. Exactly what are your requirements?"

"Please call me, Ned. Well, I am not sure, but first things first. The website is to be called Clare's Place and I want it to be attractive as well as functional. Secondly, I need a website which will provide total identity protection for those users requesting anonymity. I envision creating a free website offering advice to users limited to two, three or possibly four categories of personal questions. Without their identities being protected, I'm sure people will be reluctant to ask sticky questions concerning their private lives."

"What kind of questions are we talking about?"

"For example. How do I get my wife to be more involved in sex? Or, my teenaged daughter is dating a married man, how should I handle this?"

"Yes, I see what you mean. Users probably would not want their friends and neighbors or anyone else to know they are asking such questions. Are you planning to answer all inquiries?"

"Yes and no. We want to answer all questions within the categories specified on the website. We also want to respond to those who ask questions outside of our limited categories by acknowledging their question while letting them know it was beyond the scope of acceptable questions answerable on the website."

"We can design and produce a website which will allow access to anyone who signs in for the free service. The users will be allowed to select a privacy or not icon before they pose a question. That way the option is up to them whether or not their identity is protected. Believe it or not, a lot of people don't really care or don't know any better so they put their identity all over the internet. We can also create and include a program within the website which will automatically send your desired response to any questions found to be outside of the categories permitted. This feature will save a lot of your time while responding to those asking questions outside of your approved categories. The real problem will be in protecting the identities of those making a privacy request. Do you have access to a number of internet servers?"

"No, but if necessary I can set up as many as needed. Why do you ask?"

"There is no such thing as total identity protection on the internet, by piggybacking the question and response on several foreign programs through different servers we can provide the best identity protection available for those requesting it."

"Do you think we should go for four categories on the initial website or maybe try two to begin with?"

"It doesn't make that much difference, but I recommend we include all of them that way you will have a complete website from the beginning and not have to make revisions later. It's a lot easier to do the whole thing to start with as opposed to going back and making a bunch of planned or unforeseen revisions. If the site is a hit which I think it will be, you are going to need a staff to read all of these questions on daily basis and to decide which require an answer and which receive your automated reply. I suggest you post a question of the day and your answer on the website daily. It will promote viewership and interest, especially if the questions have widespread appeal to younger people. A lot of viewers will sign in just to see the question of the day and its answer if they like the website they will urge their friends to take a look."

"That is a great idea, I wish I had thought of it myself. Clare will be pleased with your suggestion."

"Ned, there is one more thing I would like to suggest. I think your idea is going to be a winner with hundreds of thousands of viewers within a short time. The website should be designed to display advertisements for a fee. This could ultimately become a huge source of income to pay for the cost of running the website. What do you think?"

"Another great idea, let's do it. What are we looking at time-wise before you can have the site up and running?"

"We can do our part in a month provided you have your server network operational within three weeks. The first thing we have to agree on is the design of the webpage for Clare's Place and the operational features to provide user access. I will email you a proposed website design within two days."

"Ok, I'm going to set up four servers, all of which will belong to Clare's Place, but they will be individually named and housed at other locations. There will be no obvious internet connection to Clare's Place. We will be running other sites and programs on them which will also belong to us and our affiliates. I will furnish you the information on each server so you can use them to make Clare's Place as secure as possible for its users."

Two days later Clare viewed the proposed webpage for Clare's Place on her computer. She loved the graphics and was intrigued by the artistic use of complementary colors, the webpage was Clare personified. Without requesting any changes, she embraced the design making it the official face of Clare's Place. Ned enlisted several of the MyTeeTech experts to help set up his system of internet servers, websites and programs for the piggyback operation. All were operating as planned at the end of the second week. To no one's surprise, Ned stepped down as president of MyTeeTech at the end of the month having named his young vice-president as his heir apparent. The following week, he and Clare embarked on their new career operating

Clare's Place for those internet users seeking answers to their very private questions. Ned, in conjunction with Squidz Ink Design, conducted an on line publicity campaign announcing the official opening of Clare's Place and its website. Response to Clare's Place reverberated across the internet the website had over a thousand hits on its first day in service with the number of viewers increasing exponentially each succeeding day. Shortly, Clare's Place became a favorite destination for internet users with thousands regularly signing in to view the question of the day and its answer. Many of the viewers sent their personal questions to Clare's Place and were delighted to receive a meaningful and personalized answer the same day. Within a few months, the site had gone viral encompassing the entire internet world with viewers numbering in the hundreds of thousands daily.

At the end of a very successful first year of operation, Clare's Place had become one of the best known and most used websites on the internet. The demand for advertising created thousands of dollars in monthly income providing more than enough cash to support the entire operation. Although Clare and Ned were more interested in the services Clare's Place provided to the public than its money generating ability, they were pleased to see it make a profit while providing a free service designed to help others live a more enjoyable life.

Angel was fascinated by the purpose of Clare's Place and how it functioned, she worked at the office as an aide to Clare during her first summer break while she attended TCU. She fell in love with the website embracing its purpose and success. Angel liked the idea of offering free useful advice to the public she appreciated what her parents were doing and loved them all the more for it. Angel decided to follow in their footsteps by joining them at Clare's Place after she graduated from TCU. She took over management of personnel and advertising to free up more of Clare's time allowing her to concentrate on doing the thing she enjoyed most, helping other people to be happy.

"My God, Clare, who would have thought your desire to help people would have led to our making another fortune in the process?"

"Well, not me Ned. All I wanted was for us to do something useful. We have more money than we need."

"I agree. What do you want to do with all the profit Clare's Place is generating?"

"I don't really know what to do with the money, Ned. I do know that had it not been for the Gentex program and you, I would probably have led a miserable unhappy life and never accomplished anything worthwhile. I would like to give something back because I have you, Verona and Angel. I am grateful for what Gentex did for me."

"Don't be ridiculous Clare. Gentex may have been the catalyst that focused you, but you are the one responsible for being who you are. It was you who made the commitment, and it was you who made your life no one else did that. You are still the same person, one of the most brilliant people I have ever known as well as the most beautiful women in the world! I love you for being you, nothing more is required."

"I love you for being you as well, Ned. You have made me a happy woman with your love and understanding. Let's wait a while before deciding what to do with Clare's Place's profits."

Eventually, Clare's Place became one of the most popular websites on the internet, with billions of viewers and subscribers worldwide. Advertising became expensive and in great demand because of Clare's Place's policy of limiting the number of ads run daily. Clare and Ned continued to answer all new questions posted which were cleared by the staff and the website's screening program. This was possible because of continued additions to their staff and a data base cross-reference feature which provided their previous replies to similar questions. The number of unique questions dwindled to a trickle, with time, making it difficult to present a new question every day. Much of the system was automated, nevertheless the staff still had to read all the unique incoming questions which were not repeats picked up by the screening system and were within the established website parameters. Clare replied to those questions posted by females while Ned handled those posted by the males. When the sex of the poster could not be readily determined Clare answered the question.

Ned and Clare devised a program for Clare's Place to provide monetary help and assistance to some of its users who were determined, by a selection committee, to be worthy recipients. The premise of the program was simple, those who submitted questions and who were in need of help and fit into one or more established categories which included military veterans, couples with disabled children, those trying to escape poverty, those seeking to improve their education or to better themselves by any method of self-improvement were eligible for the program. A grant-in-aid or gift was to be made each month to a deserving individual following a detailed investigation and screening to determine the person most deserving of that month's award. The program was to be anonymous and nameless. Clare had essentially completed setting up the program when she recalled the screening technique Gentex had used in selecting the women to participate in their genetic study. She was in need of a method to screen the potential recipients under the Clare's Place program, so she contacted Gentex asking for advice on how to set up a similar screening program for her project. She was referred to, Randy, who was apparently in charge.

"My name is Clare Stanley. I am seeking advice on how to set up a screening and selection program for aid to people trying to improve their lives."

"Do I know you? Clare."

"Probably not. I was one of the women selected to participate in the Gentex genetic study program years ago which is why I am calling."

"In that case, I will have to get back with you later. Leave your number and I will call back tomorrow."

It wasn't the answer Clare had expected although it was a start. Randy, seemed shocked when she mentioned being in the Gentex genetic study program.

"I'm sure his call tomorrow will be interesting, I just hope he can be of help in our selection process."

Clare's phone rang as she sat down at her desk at Clare's Place's main office.

"Hello, this is Clare, how may I help you?"

"Clare, this is, Jerry Schneider. You talked with Randy, yesterday. I believe you mentioned that you were one of the participants in the Gentex program. My congratulations. How can I be of service to you Clare?"

Clare thought for a second before she answered, she had expected a call from Randy and was a bit wary of talking with someone else.

"Are you associated with Gentex, Mr. Schneider?"

"I am not with Gentex, but I have absolute control over the screening program they used in making the selections for their research project. You see, it is proprietary and was leased from one of our companies. I understand you have a need for such a program and I think that I can be of help to you. Why don't you and Ned meet me in Houston tomorrow evening at the Tmex Hotel? We can go over the selection program and I can explain how it will work for you. I will be waiting for you in the bar at 6:00 p.m."

"You know my husband's name?"

"Yes, Clare. I know about MyTeeTech and Clare's Place as well. You and Ned will find me to be very useful in setting up your screening program."

"You know about that too? You are full of surprises Mr. Schneider. How will we recognize you in the bar?"

"It won't be a problem, I'll introduce myself when you show up. You and Ned have a safe trip. I'm looking forward to seeing both of you at 6:00 p.m. tomorrow."

Clare hung up then rushed into Ned's office closing the door behind her.

"I just had the strangest conversation with a Mr. Jerry Schneider. He claims to have control of the screening program Gentex used to select the women who participated in their genetic study program and says he can help us with our program. I called Gentex yesterday and asked for help in setting up a screening program. I don't understand what's going on here, a guy named, Randy said he would call me today. Instead I got this call from Jerry Schneider. Ned, I have a real surprise for you now!"

Ned looked at Clare amused.

"Clare not here in the office. It's too risky."

"No, no. Ned. That not the kind of surprise I was referring to. You and I are meeting Mr. Jerry Schneider in Houston at the Tmex Hotel tomorrow at 6:00 p.m. He says he can be helpful in developing a screening program for Clare's Place."

"How does he know about that?"

"I have no idea, but he seems to know a lot about us. Do you know him?"

"Not that I know of, but I'm spending the rest of the day checking him out. I suggest you do the same, Clare. If I come up with anything I will come to your office. You do the same, but don't use your phone or cell phone come to my office."

Ned came into Clare's office later motioning frantically for her to close the door. Ned spoke slowly and clearly.

"Clare, Jerry Schneider, heads up Imperial Enterprises one of the largest and most successful companies in the country. How in the hell did he get involved in this?"

"I have no idea, he did say he is not associated with Gentex, but controls the screening program they used. That is the only connection I can think of. I guess we will find out tomorrow."

They left Austin early to avoid the mid-afternoon traffic arriving at the Tmex in time to check in and refresh themselves before their appointment. Clare was trying to make up her mind what to wear to the meeting with Jerry and after a few moments of frustration inquired.

"What do you think I should wear to this meeting?"

"Honey, wear the sexiest and most charming thing you brought with you. We need to dazzle this Jerry with your beauty maybe you can distract him enough that we have an advantage. We probably need all the help we can get."

Clare and Ned walked into the Tmex bar hand in hand they looked around searching for an empty table, but there was none. Before Jerry approached, the regulars gave Clare the once over offering their approval in a standing toast.

"Cheers."

Rang out as they raised their glasses in salute which had become their custom when an exceptionally attractive women entered their domain. Clare waved her hand in acknowledgement of the toast just as Jerry approached the two of them.

"I saw you two come in, but I didn't rush to greet you because I didn't want to spoil your toast, Clare. I knew it was coming, so I waited until the regulars had made their salute. I would like to add my own, Clare you are absolutely stunning. I am happy to meet both of you in person, over the years, I have heard a lot of good things about both of you, please follow me to our table. It's over in the corner where it is a little quieter, so we can talk without raising our voices."

Once they were seated, Jerry announced.

"I'm having an Irish whiskey, what would you like?"

"Really, I've never had Irish whiskey. I'll have one too," replied Clare looking toward Ned.

"I've never had Irish whiskey either let's make it unanimous."

Jerry was beaming as he looked at Clare and Ned. He raised his glass saying.

"Here is to a beautiful and happy couple. May there be many more like you in this world."

Clare accepted the compliment at the same time realizing the importance of the second part of his toast. It was Jerry's tacit approval of their program in progress and Clare's Place itself. She already liked this guy even though she knew next to nothing about him. Jerry continued.

"Before we get started, we need to have an understanding, there will be no questions concerning Gentex or its program except as related to its screening techniques, OK?"

"That is not a problem with me," replied Clare.

"Now, that we understand each other, let's get to your problem, but before we go further, Ned, I want to congratulate you on the excellent job you have done in building MyTeeTech into a leader in the field of data storage. You may not be aware of it, but one of our subsidiaries was an original investor in MyTeeTech. We have continued to acquire more shares and today we are the largest single shareholder in your company."

"I appreciate your comment and interest," said Ned somewhat shaken by Jerry's congratulatory statement concerning his career. He had not delved into the stock ownership of MyTeeTech in detail while serving as President because there had never been a need, there had been no disputes between him and the Board during his tenure and he had enjoyed strong support among the stockholders and Directors

"I understand you are in need of a superior screening method to aid in selecting those people most qualified to receive grants, gifts or aid from the benevolent arm of Clare's Place. Is that correct?"

"Yes. That is why I called Gentex in the first place because of the screening program they used in selecting the participants in their genetic study."

"Clare, I can offer you and Ned access to our investigative arm's resources which are far superior to anything on the market. We can provide you with a complete background check on everyone who has posted a question on Clare's Place. Our program can automatically eliminate those who have questionable honesty and integrity issues and screen the remainder to determine the most needy or deserving."

Ned was quick to react, the program was exactly what they needed, however he had some reservations.

"Jerry, if we use your program. How are we going to protect the identity of users of Clare's Place?"

"Ned, my people were impressed and fascinated by your network of servers and your piggyback system to protect the identities of those Clare's Place users who want to remain anonymous. Let me assure you our protection is even better, none of your user's information will be vulnerable in our system. Because of your philanthropic endeavor I'll make the program available to you free of charge."

Under terms of the finalized agreement, the identities of all users of Clare's Place were to be automatically fed into Jerry's system which in turn would screen and selected the ten most deserving users each month. On Jerry's recommendation, Clare and Ned set up a committee of five consisting of themselves, Angel, Verona and Kevin which would select that person from the ten candidates who would receive that month's award. Ned and Clare thanked Jerry for his help before leaving the bar to return to their room to prepare for dinner with a couple of their friends from Houston. Jerry remained in the Tmex bar treating himself to another Irish whiskey for a day's work well done. Sipping the fresh drink he leaned back in his chair closing his eyes thinking.

"Clare, when we selected you, I never dreamed you would become the wonderful person you are today. That was a side effect that neither, George nor any of the rest of us considered when we set up ADAM. We were only thinking about George's offspring. Our system has worked much better than we foresaw at the time. You are a fine example of collateral improvement, or unintended benefits resulting from an action taken to reach another objective. My hat is off to you, Clare, you are a magnificent person of your own making. You have far exceeded my expectations."

Chapter 20 First Class

Sitting at their back yard table enjoying a fresh glass of ice tea and a glorious sunset, Darlene and Randall were laid back without a care in the world life was great and the going was easy. The Professor was nearing retirement and Martha's business was prospering. Darlene pointed to the sunset in the west.

"This may be a reminder to us that one part of our life is about to come to an equally glorious end. You will be retiring shortly and so will I. I've decided to sell my real estate business, so we can start travelling the world and visit all of those places we keep talking about. It's time, before we get too old to enjoy it let's do what we always planned."

"I am more than ready, once I retire there will be no more daily schedules to meet or disruptive students to put up with we can travel as much as we like."

"Since Alan and Martha married, I am no longer concerned about Alan he is in great hands with Martha. I can almost feel the love flowing every time they look at each other. Seeing Alan happy again gives me great confidence in the power of love and divine intervention. I don't think anyone, other than Martha, could have provided him with the love he needed in the way she has. They have a great life together and are happy just like two other people I know. I need to start working on selling my business before you retire. If I don't get with the program, we may be stuck here after you retire while I try to find a buyer."

Darlene had three outstanding sales agents working with her in her real estate business, she made the deals while the agents sold the finished products on a combination salary and commission basis. They worked well together and were friends aside from being business associates. Darlene considered offering to sell the business to her three sales agents, but after considerable thought decide it was not a good idea none of them had any business experience outside of sales. In order for the company to remain a viable and ongoing business, it needed a leader who understood the business side of real estate, someone who had experience in building and development. Darlene chose to look for potential buyers among successful real estate companies that might be interested in expanding into the Waco market. Competition from pure real estate companies was almost non-existent because of the special niche Darlene's company filled in the Waco market. A few independent builders offered new homes for sale which competed directly with that part of Darlene's business, in the upgrading and refurbishing sector she had little competition because of the higher risk involved. An error in the purchase price or the renovation cost could spell disaster for smaller companies dependent on a steady, uninterrupted cash flow stream from their current projects to stay in business. They could not withstand a major loss on a single project and the larger companies shunned this higher risk part of the business.

At one of her presentations at the Builder's Association's annual meeting in San Antonio, Darlene had met a builder-developer from Austin who operated on a business plan similar to her own, he came to mind first when she thought about potential buyers for her company. She set up an appointment to meet in his office the up-coming Tuesday to explore his interest in entering the Waco market. Darlene had not seen Alan and Martha in a while, prompting her to arrive in Austin a day early to visit and to spend the night, before her meeting. Martha had just returned from work when Darlene arrived at the condo while she and Martha were greeting one another, Alan called informing Martha that he had been delayed and would be arriving home later than usual. Alan's delay provided an opportunity and ample time for a rare woman to woman discussion between Darlene and Martha a situation which did not happen often. Martha made coffee while Darlene unpacked her things in the guest room and refreshed herself before returning to the den. They had hugged earlier, so Martha offered her mother-in-law a fresh cup of hot coffee.

"Darlene, aside from visiting with us, what brings you to Austin?"

"As you know, Randall will be retiring soon, so I am retiring as well. Afterward, we will be free to travel and see the world like we have planned for years. Tomorrow, I am meeting with a potential buyer for my real estate business, but we can talk about that later when Alan gets home. Right now, I would rather we talk about you and Alan before he arrives."

"Is there anything in particular you have on your mind?"

"Not really, I just want to tell you how pleased Randall and I are that you and Alan found each other and married. We think it must have been divine intervention that brought you two together you are so well suited for each other."

454

"I'm honored to hear you feel that way. We have felt from the beginning that our meeting was no mere accident that we were meant to be together for a reason. Our marriage and love for one another gives us a feeling of completeness in our lives that was not there before."

"I can tell. Martha, you not only make Alan happy, you make me and Randall happy too. We love you, Martha, and we want you to know that."

"You don't know how much that means to me, I love you both and so does Alan. There is no power on this earth that could ever separate Alan from me, our love for each other will never end. Our meeting was no accident we were destined to be together! If you were to ask Alan he would tell you the same thing."

"I'm glad we had this talk Martha, it solidifies my conviction that you and Alan were deemed to be together as eternal partners in love and happiness. You complement each other in every way."

Alan showed up as Darlene ended her statement, after he hugged Darlene, she changed the subject to her desire to sell her real estate business.

"How much do you think it is worth mom?" Asked Alan as he poured himself a cup of black coffee.

"I don't know really, I made a profit of $250,000 last year which would put the value of the company at around $1,250,000, if I sell its assets as well; it would be worth much more. I'll probably get a better idea of its value tomorrow."

The next morning, Darlene was helping Martha with breakfast when she mentioned how happy she and Randall had been together even though they never had children of their own.

"Alan filled Randall's life with love and joy and became his son, Randall has always been happy that Alan accepted him as his own dad because he loved him. Randall was the ideal male role model for Alan while he was growing up, and to his credit, Randall did more than a good job of keeping Alan focused and on track during his formative years. If you were to thank anyone for Alan's being Alan, it should be Randall. He helped mold him into the person you love so much today."

Martha stored this bit of information in her memory bank then asked Darlene.

"What time is your meeting in the morning?"

"I plan to be there around ten thirty the owner said any time before noon would be OK he planned to be there all day."

Preparing to leave for work the following morning Martha said.

"I hate to leave like this, but I have to meet with a client for his public speaking and elocution training at eight thirty. He is running for a seat on the City Council in San Antonio. It's sort of a strange situation, he is a doctor named, Bruce Wilkerson, and is about Alan's age. It's a crash course to prepare him for the up-coming campaign. When you leave just latch the door I can set the alarm remotely from my office later. We love you Darlene, good luck with your meeting. We plan to come and visit you and Randall soon."

The two women put their arms around each other and Martha was about to depart when Darlene responded.

"We'll be expecting you and Alan in Waco in a week or two. Love you, Martha."

Martha said good bye before closing the door behind her and rushing to the office to begin Bruce's instruction for the day.

Darlene tidied up the guest room making sure she had not left a mess or any of her things behind before leaving for the builder's office, which happened to be located on her homeward route to Waco making it unnecessary for her to return to Martha's and Alan's condo following her meeting. When she arrived at the builder's office, Darlene was greeted with enthusiasm by the owner who knew her casually and more by reputation than in person. They had met only once when she made a presentation to the Builder's Association on refurbishing older homes for resale. He was familiar with her stature in the real estate business, as were many of his contemporaries, Darlene's reputation as an astute realtor was well known across Central Texas.

"Mrs. Felton, it is a pleasure to see you again. As I recall, we met at the Builder's Association's convention last year in San Antonio where you made a great presentation which most of us considered the highlight of the convention."

"Thank you very much. Yes, that's where we met. It was in October, if I remember correctly, but please call me Darlene."

"OK, Darlene, call me Abel. My full name is Abel Watson, I prefer just plain Abel."

"Abel it is. May I ask how things are going with you here in Austin?"

"Very well, as a matter of fact, last year was good for me and my business one of the better years in a long time I might add. I hope you are not planning to move into my territory."

"On the contrary, I was wondering if you might be interested in expanding into the Waco market."

"I am very interested with the right kind of deal, I plan to have a presence over the entire state before I am finished. This might be the first step. What can I do for you?"

"I am looking for a reputable buyer for my business. My husband will be retiring soon from his teaching job at Baylor and I would like to join him in retirement. My business recently closed the books on its latest fiscal year, I brought a copy of the company financial statement with me, if you are interested in looking at it."

Removing the report from her briefcase Darlene offered it to Abel.

"You are free to examine it, if you like, all of our current financial information is in there."

"Let's move to my conference room, so we can spread out. In the meanwhile, I'll have my secretary hold all of my calls that way we are not interrupted."

Abel analyzed the report carefully noting those items of interest on his yellow legal tablet as he went through the report. Neither of them spoke until he finished.

"Darlene, I see here that your company has no outstanding long term debt and has $550,000 in cash. Is that still the case?"

"Yes, Abel that is still the case. We are a Sub-Chapter S Corporation meaning we pass all profits and losses on to the stockholders, which in this case means me and my husband. The Company maintains a cash account sufficient to pay off our short term debt at any time without borrowing money. In other words we are solvent at all times."

"Yes, I see that. How many building projects do you have in progress right now?"

"We have two new homes being built and three others which are completed and paid for which are currently on the market. We also own several prime building sites which are also paid for."

"A remarkable accomplishment, Darlene. I notice on the Balance Sheet that you have a very small number in your goodwill account that's the first thing I check when looking at financial statements. It's a fudge factor account used to disguise the facts by some companies. In your case it is a positive."

"Abel, I have not contacted any other companies about selling my business, your reputation for honesty and fair dealing prompted me to give you a first look. Tell me, Abel, do you have an interest in making me an offer?"

"Give me an exclusive right to purchase for two weeks, which is long enough for my people perform a due diligence study of your operations and company, I will then make you a fair offer or decline all together."

"Good enough, Abel. Our books, titles and operation will be open for you or your representative's inspection starting Monday. If you need anything more from me. Let me know."

"Darlene have a safe trip home, I'll have my representative in your office Monday morning. Thanks for giving me the first look."

Abel's accountant arrived Monday morning to commence her evaluation after three full days of inspecting the company books, records and land titles, she left without giving any indication of what she thought or what her assessment of the company might be. Another week passed before Abel called saying he was prepared to make an offer to purchase Darlene's company.

"If it is alright with you, Darlene I would like come to Waco to make you an offer in person and to explain some steps needed to complete the trade in the best interest of both parties. How would tomorrow morning fit your schedule?"

"That sounds good to me, Abel. Any time after 8:00 a.m. would be great for me."

"Darlene, I will see you around 10:00 a.m. tomorrow morning."

Abel arrived at Darlene's office alone, he had only his brief case and his cell-phone with him, Darlene escorted him to her private office which contained a small conference table she used for negotiating and closing transactions. Following their corrigible greetings, Darlene offered him coffee or tea which Abel declined.

"Darlene, I think you are going to like my offer, it's fair and a good deal for both of us."

Abel made himself comfortable then opened his briefcase producing a one page offer-sheet which he handed to Darlene. She read the entire sheet before responding.

"I think we can work with these numbers, Abel. I will need to consult with my attorney on the matter of converting to a regular corporation before I can agree to that requirement. You do understand, Abel, that it's more of a tax matter than a legal issue."

"Then pending his approval we have a deal, right?"

"Yes, we do have a deal, I find your offer to be fair and adequate I will put this issue to my attorney today and give you his answer tomorrow or no later than the day after tomorrow. Is that OK with you?"

Abel and Darlene shook hands on the deal before Abel departed leaving Darlene alone at the conference table holding the offer-sheet in her hand. She read it again hardly able to believe her eyes, Abel had offered $2,150,000 for the company and its assets after it was converted to a regular corporation. The offer sheet contained a special provision requiring that prior to the conversion to a regular corporation, all the company cash was to be distributed to the stockholders. The cash at the time of distribution amounted to $500,000 plus any additions or subtractions to the cash account up to the date of conversion. Darlene was quick to conclude she and Randall would come out of the deal with roughly $2,650,000 before federal income taxes. It was in excess of what she had expected, in her view, Abel had offered more than a fair price, his reputation for honesty and fairness was well deserved. He had also requested that all three of her agents remain on the company payroll, if they were so inclined, he liked the way Darlene had taught them to operate straight up and above board.

Darlene called Abel the following day giving him the go ahead to prepare the necessary legal documents to complete the sale. A total of $550,050 was distributed from the cash account to Darlene and Randall before converting the Company to a regular corporation. Abel explained his reason for the conversion to Darlene after presenting her with a cashier's check for $2,150,000. He planned to retain Darlene's company as a wholly owned subsidiary to take advantage of its excellent reputation among the home buying community in Waco. The company was known for fair dealing and honesty which are qualities sometimes abused in the real estate business. Abel had been able to retain the three agents who previously worked for Darlene, he believed her training them in honest representation set them apart from most agents he knew. He felt that he needed them on board in order to maintain the business's reputation and to make a smooth transition to a new owner. Darlene presented each of her former agents with a check for $50,000 in appreciation of their excellent performance during their long association with her business. Darlene closed out her business career on a high note of self-esteem and satisfaction. She was ready to begin a life of retirement and travel with Randall at her side.

She thought.

"What a long way I have come from the Sabine bottoms and the café in Joaquin. Thanks to Alan, my friend the widow, Gentex, hard work and Randall I have been able to make the journey to this point. Randall and I are starting a new journey together which will be all our own."

Randall retired at the end of the spring semester saying goodbye to his fellow educators at his retirement party sponsored by Baylor University and its faculty members. In the ensuing months, he and Darlene directed their efforts toward planning their future. Their first order of business was to invest the net proceeds from the sale of Darlene's real estate business in reasonably safe dividend paying stocks and other investment vehicles such Master Limited Partnerships traded on the New York Stock Exchange. They were very selective in making their purchases mixing a number of stocks and MLPs. They spent hours in research before making each purchase eventually building a diversified portfolio yielding an average return of 5% per year in dividends. They were able to produce this rate of return by investing in companies which had proven track records of consistently increasing their dividends year over year while expanding their annual incomes. Using some of the money from the sale, they also invested in raw land located in and near the Waco city limits, but kept a cash reserve equal to approximately 20% of their total worth. Income from their investments, Randall's retirement and Darlene's Gentex stipend plus her retirement account allowed them do anything they wanted within reason. They had plenty of money to travel wherever they wanted.

While planning their first trip, Darlene meticulously searched the travel brochures for the best deal available. Randall picked up the brochures crumpled them up playfully then tossed the lot into the air saying.

"My dear, Darlene, there is no need for this, we will be travelling First Class from now on, we have plenty of money, so let's enjoy it. Our retirement is a whole new life and money is not a problem let's make our retirement First Class. What do you say?"

"Our entire life has been First Class, Randall, and I love you for making it that way, but you are right we are going to have a First Class retirement in every way. I'll start looking for good First Class deals I hear upgrading at the last minute is the best way to go First Class. I'll check it out."

Chapter 21 Franks Final Plan

Frank's untimely death required a dramatic leadership change at Abe which had been under his command since its inception. Aaron, one of the two remaining survivors from the original five founders of ADAM, out of necessity, became Frank's successor. Jerry, the other survivor and leader of ADAM was anxious to resolve their problem with Alan and Martha, their marriage created a new urgency which could not go unattended he wanted Frank's plan for Alan and Martha implemented as soon as possible. The normal course of events between these two young married and highly sexually active people could create irreversible damage with dreadful results. Frank chose not to interfere in their courtship instead he devised a plan which would allow them to be together without unwanted ramifications even though George Angleton was their common father. The other organizers of Abe, Gentex and ADAM had joined George Angleton in the hereafter and as caretakers of George's offspring both Jerry and Aaron were advancing in years. Jerry felt it was his duty to conclude ADAM the way George Angleton and the founders planned, yet he felt an even stronger moral obligation to protect Alan and Martha from themselves and from the harsh moral mores prevalent in society.

"They are the two of George's children who need my help the most, and I damned well intend to do my duty no matter what happens. I'm going to see that they are happy and together. I don't give a damn what other people might think and nothing on this earth is going to stop me."

He selected Randy, his protégée and heir apparent at Imperial Enterprises and its worldwide subsidiaries, to present Frank's program to Martha and Alan. Jerry considered it imperative that they be convinced to adopt Frank's plan and be persuaded that the plan was in their best interest. A task which he did not expect to be an easy sell.

Since he and Martha married, Alan had searched off and on in his spare time for the source of the spyware he had found on his and Martha's computers before they eloped eventually tracing it to an internet server located in Houston. He could not get beyond the server itself to find the owner of the program, each time he attempted to identify the owner, he was routed back to the server it was an endless cycle which frustrated Alan to no end. Finding the owner presented a challenge which Alan refused to put aside. Now and then, when time permitted, he resumed his search for the culprits.

"If the person or persons who installed the spyware didn't want their identity known, why did they use such an easily detectable spyware program in the first place? It doesn't make sense."

Alan had removed the spyware then installed Cyber Resources' anti-malware program on his and Martha's computers to safeguard them against hacking in the future, but this process provided no clues as to who had hacked them in the first place. Alan and Jim were engrossed in developing their largest project ever which involved nanotechnology applications to communication satellites. Their work left little time for Alan to spend looking for the hacker, in disgust, he put the project aside temporarily.

A stranger called on Alan at Cyber Research and after introduction himself as, Randy, requested a private conference behind closed doors. Alan was hesitant to take time out from their project to talk with him until Randy brought up the subject of spyware.

"Mr. Strong, you will find what I have to say both interesting and enlightening with respect to the spyware which you recently blocked on your and Martha's computers."

Following Randy's opening comment concerning the spyware, Alan could not resist he invited him to have a seat then closed the door to his office before asking.

"And what can I do for you, sir?"

"My full name is Randy Talbot, I'm pleased to meet you, Mr. Strong. I am here because of what I can do for you rather than what you can do for me."

"What do you mean by that? Mr. Talbot."

"Let explain, Alan. Is it OK, for me to call you Alan? My clients commissioned a company called Gentex Research to conduct a genetic study a number of years ago. You Alan are a product of that study."

"Yes, I know about Gentex I remember all the tests they performed while I was growing up. Wasn't that part of the Gentex study?"

"Yes, it was. Among other things they also paid all the medical bills for you and your mother."

"What does that have to do with the spyware?"

463

"I'll get to that. Alan, are you aware that as part of the program you were conceived by artificial insemination with your mother's permission?"

"Sure, she told me when I was a young boy. It wasn't a problem then, and it is not a problem now. So what's this all about?"

"Your wife Martha, was also a product of the same program. Did you know that?"

"I had no idea until now, it never came up in any of our conversations. Is that significant in some way?"

"Very much so, Alan. You and Martha have the same father, you are half- brother and half-sister."

"Oh my God! This can't be happening. I'll never give up Martha, we love each other. I don't care what you say, it can't be true! After all the pain and misery we suffered in the past, we deserve to be happy. We were destined for each other don't you understand that? I can't and won't live without Martha. Do you hear what I am saying?"

Alan was much more distraught than he appeared, he was sick to his stomach and his mind was churning with fear that he and Martha could somehow be separated he was frightened and desperate. The fact that he and Martha were related was irrelevant, he loved Martha, and she loved him. He was never going to be separated from Martha. Life was nothing without her.

"Why in the hell are you telling me this?"

"Look, Alan. I understand you and Martha are married and love each other deeply, nevertheless, what I told you is true. A simple DNA test would show that the two of you share a common father."

"I don't give a damn! I don't want to hear any more of your nonsense! What do you want from me?"

"Let me emphasize that I'm not here to break you and Martha apart or cause either of you despair or unhappiness, far from it, I came to help. I'm very much aware of the love you share together as are the people I represent. I'm here to outline a method whereby you and Martha can remain together without creating any unwanted repercussions. Do you understand Alan? We are trying to help you and Martha. Both of you are important to us."

"Has anyone told Martha about this? Does she know?"

"I would never do that without you being there, she is completely unaware of the facts I just presented, but she needs to know. No one has approached Martha on the subject and no one will without your approval. Take a few minutes to digest what I just told you, then with your consent, I suggest we tell Martha together. After you have thought the situation over why don't you call her? We can go to her office together, so I can explain the situation to her. I'm sure you agree it has to be done. I can then explain how you two can stay together without doing unintended harm."

Alan was shaken, but after thinking over the situation for a few minutes he called Martha insisting on an immediate meeting in her office.

"Martha, there is a man here in my office, named, Randy, who you need to meet as soon as possible, it's important. Cancel whatever you are doing we will be there right away. I love you, Martha!"

Martha sensed the reason for Alan's call was urgent by the sound of his voice he sounded distressed which was very unusual he was normally a perennial happy face. Martha ushered the two of them into her office then kissed Alan.

"What's wrong, dear?"

"Martha meet, Randy. Please sit down then he will explain everything."

Randy repeated the same presentation of facts to Martha. When Randy told Martha that she and Alan were half-bother and half-sister. Martha shouted.

"Oh God. No, no it can't be. I won't accept it!"

Sobbing frantically, she staggered to the door of her office then ran down the hall into the ladies room locking the door behind her. Rushing to her aid, Alan shoved aside his own anguish and heart felt sickness in an effort to persuade Martha to unlock the door. He could hear her crying which nearly tore his heart apart, he hurt inside hearing Martha's uncontrollable sobs and wailing. Despite Alan's repeated pleadings, Martha refused to unlock the door her crying increased in intensity to the point Alan could hear her gasping for breath. He was in a near state of panic himself when Randy handed him the key he had obtained from Martha's assistant. Alan found Martha on the floor at the far end of the restroom her head crammed in the corner face down on the tile floor she was sobbing uncontrollably and shaking violently as if having a seizure. She did not respond to his pleading instead she began convulsing as her crying became louder.

"Martha, please look at me?"

Upon hearing his voice, her crying became even louder. Alan leaned over and gently lifted her in his arms whispering.

"I love you, Martha. I love you."

She put her arms around his neck saying between sobs.

"I love you Alan. I love you. Please save us. Alan please save us!?"

"I'll never let you go Martha. I love you. You are everything to me!"

Alan carried her to her office consoling her the best he could.

"I love you, Martha. We will always be together no matter what happens! I promise you I will always be here for you!"

Alan placed a wet towel on Martha's forehead and moistened her lips with cold water. After her panic subsided somewhat, Martha regained her composure enough for Alan to convince her to listen to Randy's proposal.

"Martha, it is in our best interest, please listen to what he has to say."

Randy was quick to comfort Martha talking to her in a soothing and reassuring voice he explained.

"Martha, we do not want to separate you two, we are trying to keep you together our only interest is making sure you spend your lives together. I am here to help you make that possible, but there are steps we must take now to prevent a possible disaster for both of you."

In his explanation to Martha, Randy emphasized.

"There are only two people, other than the three of us, who know you are half-brother and half-sister and there is no reason for any of us to tell anyone else, but it is vital that you and Alan know the truth. Now that you do know, it is important that you both keep this information to yourselves."

He then added.

"It will probably be impossible, at some point, to prevent your mothers from discovering they were both a part of the Gentex program, but there is nothing to suggest their children were conceived using sperm from the same donor. I want to stress again that only you, myself and two other people know that the two of you are related. For you to remain together it is an absolute necessity that it remain that way. Our main concern right now and the reason we felt this meeting was urgent, is that you're having children together could produce disastrous results. We know you do not want a mentally or physically handicapped child. That would not result in a lifetime of happiness for anyone."

"Are you saying we can never have children?"

"No, that is part of my mission to present a way for you to have children. The immediate problem is to make certain Martha does not get pregnant as a result of your sexual activity. There are several ways that can be accomplished one is by abstinence, which we all know is out of the question, or use of the pill, or by Alan submitting to a vasectomy. Martha can't be sterilized because that would ruin Frank's plan and take her out of the equation for having babies which is an essential part of his program. Consider this, we can collect sperm from Alan before he has a vasectomy then store it preserving his ability to produce babies well into the future. We have evidence that continuous use of the pill could be detrimental to a woman's health and wellbeing and for safety a vasectomy is a simpler and more effective method of preventing conception. It will present a minor inconvenience to Alan and is much safer for the two of you."

"Then how do you propose we have children of our own?"

"We refer to it as Frank's plan, it involves our locating a suitable surrogate mother to impregnate with Alan's sperm. This will produce a baby related to both of you through your father. Our experts will also select a suitable male to provide sperm to impregnate Martha by artificial insemination producing a baby related to both of you through your father. The babies will also be related to each other through your father, they will be his grandchildren just as you are his children. The whole process will be free of cost to you for as many babies as you might like to have. What do you think? Shall we implement Frank's Plan?"

Alan and Martha talked for a few minutes before Martha responded.

"We like Frank's Plan and certainly do not want to create a handicapped child, could we wait a year or two before we start a family? We would like some time to ourselves first. How does that work?"

"That's not a problem we can store Alan's sperm for years, maybe indefinitely, all you have to do is call us when you decide to have babies. We will need some time to locate a suitable surrogate mother and father so a certain degree of forward planning is need for either of you to produce a child. The first step in Frank's Plan is to confirm that both of you are capable of producing children, if that is not the case and only one of you prove to be fertile the plan will have to be altered. Should both of you be sterile, we no longer have a problem you will have to adopt. Alan, a vasectomy doesn't diminish one's sexual performance in any way in case you are wondering."

Randy was pleased he had been able to convince Alan and Martha that he and his clients were interested in helping them stay together. He knew out of necessity that they were half-brother and half-sister, but he had no idea they were the children of George Angleton only Jerry and Aaron were privy to that information. Alan failed to ask Randy about the spyware before he left, somehow it was no longer relevant.

Both Martha and Alan tested to be highly fertile necessitating a no sex moratorium while Alan made sperm contributions over several weeks preceding his vasectomy. During the procedure, he was surprised to learn that it was reversible in most cases. He had always been under the impression vasectomies were permanent, he felt better knowing that it could be reversed, but he didn't know why.

Several months later, Martha and Alan were sharing a joint Christmas with their parents at their condo in Austin both set of parents had accepted their invitation to join them for the holidays. There was no mention of Gentex by any of the parties although the subject of grandchildren came up on more than one occasion. Neither Rachel and Phil or Darlene and Randall had children of their own Martha and Alan had been born through the Gentex program before their mothers met their future husbands. Rachel and Darlene were mutually interested in when they might become grandmothers. Throughout their conversations, Alan and Martha remained tightlipped giving no indication of when or if they were planning a family. After listening to several evasive answers, Rachel could stand it any longer she asked directly.

"Martha, are you and Alan planning to have a family?"

Martha had anticipated the question and had planned her answer in advance.

"We have discussed the subject several times, but as yet we have not established a timetable."

Using one of her negotiating ploys to force an answer, Rachel replied.

"You do know it becomes more difficult to have children after you are thirty?"

"Well yes, I have been told that, but I am only twenty eight!"

"That doesn't leave much time before you are thirty does it?"

"If you put it that way I guess it doesn't." Replied Martha who changed the subject by asking Darlene.

"Where are you and Randall planning to go first?"

"Our first trip will be a cruise to the Caribbean on Carnival Cruise Lines to celebrate our meeting when Alan was a youngster. After that, we intend to see the world. Next year, we are planning an around the world cruise meaning we would appreciate any advanced notice on the expected birth of a grandchild, so that we are not out of the country when the event happens."

Darlene refused to allow Martha to change the subject completely. Still Martha held her ground giving no indication of when or if there would be a grandchild in the foreseeable future. Following the traditional turkey dinner Alan served after dinner drinks to those wanting them. Much to his shock and surprise Darlene requested an Irish whisky.

"Mom, when did you start drinking this?"

"Today. Jim and Yoko were in Waco visiting his parents last week and while we were all together, he mentioned it was your favorite drink, so I am going to give it a try."

"What else did Jim have to say?"

"That Cyber Research had completed its fifth successful project and as a result the two of you were well on your way to becoming rich. He also mentioned Cyber Research had a new project nearing completion which would greatly increase your income over the coming years."

"I wouldn't say we are getting rich, but it's a start. Getting rich is immaterial to me beyond a certain point money becomes meaningless. Martha is all I need to be happy, without her all the money in the world wouldn't mean anything."

"Jim, also had another interesting bit of news. Yoko is pregnant they are having twins."

"I wonder why he didn't tell me they were expecting. I had no idea."

"I'm sure he wanted to tell his parents first. Wouldn't you?"

"Well yes. When we are expecting you will be the first to know."

"It's good to know you are planning to have children, Alan. Please pour my drink I am anxious to try your Irish whisky."

The Christmas guests had gone all the leftovers were stored in the refrigerator and the dishes were washed and put away as were the pots and pans. The condo was quiet and restored to its normal neatness when Martha and Alan sat down to relax. Alan put his arm around Martha's shoulder as they sipped their drinks.

"It was great having our parents here, I really enjoyed the way they interacted everyone seemed to have a good time."

"Mom and Darlene were really putting the pressure on us to start a family, but I guess that is what moms do. I was thankful that the name Gentex did not come up during their visit hopefully it never will."

They sat in silence for several minutes before Alan leaned over kissing Martha then whispered in her ear,

"Let's go fishing, we can talk about babies later."

Over breakfast the next morning Martha said, "I guess we should do more than fish, maybe it is time for us to think about having babies."

"No one said we have to give up fishing to have babies at least not permanently. Actually, I have given some thought to the subject of babies since yesterday."

"Really, overnight you've suddenly been thinking about having babies? What prompted that?"

"Mom's mentioning that Yoko and Jim are having twins gave me, what I think is a really neat idea. I hope you agree. Why don't we have twins like Jim and Yoko?"

"Alan you are a genius, I would never have thought of having twins. I love the idea."

Martha was so anxious to kiss him she smeared cereal all over his mouth, but he didn't care she was so happy he kissed her again.

"When shall we get started on this little project?"

"Right away, it's going to take a while to check out and test possible surrogate mothers and donors. We need to give them the green light to get things started. I'll call Randy, when I get to the office to inform him of our plan."

"Alan that's fantastic!"

Exclaimed Randy upon hearing Alan's revelation that he and Martha had decided to have twins and that they were ready to start a family.

"Congratulations to both of you, I'll get our people started right away. Keep in mind this can't be accomplished overnight. They will find the best possible matches for this project, which will not be easy, our experts will screen a lot of people searching for the perfect genetic match for you and for Martha. I'll let you know when they have made their selections. Give my regards to Martha."

Randy was satisfied with the Strong's decision, it meshed perfectly with Frank's Plan, he was indeed a genius as everyone said. Randy called Abe to alert Aaron and Jerry that Frank's Plan was in play and that their expertise was needed to find and enlist the services of a suitable donor and surrogate mother as outlined in Frank's plan.

Aaron assembled the Abe supervisors in his office that afternoon.

"Gentlemen we have a new and urgent assignment which requires each of our full attention. Starting today, we are to locate and perform a full background workups on the nearest female relatives of Rachel Donna Schuber Jensen formerly known as Rachel Donna Garcia. These girls or women must be unmarried and of child bearing age. We are also charged with finding the nearest male relatives of Alan Charles Strong who are sexually mature and their backgrounds are to be checked as well. All of our research and investigations are to be clandestine without the knowledge of any of the subjects. Cost is not a problem, so let's get started. All reports are to be sent directly to me. Is there anyone who does not understand the assignment?"

It was known from Rachel's dossier that her four brothers returned to the Rio Grande City area of South Texas with their parents the same year Rachel went missing in Indiana. The Abe agents had a starting point in finding Rachel's close female relatives, subsequent investigation indicated that none of the brothers currently lived in Rio Grande City, but they had not moved far. Two lived in Corpus Christi, one lived in Brownsville and the other was located in nearby McAllen.

Rachel's brothers had been a prolific bunch producing among them a total of seventeen female children all of whom were of child bearing age. Only six were unmarried and of those only three proved to be desirable candidates as surrogate mothers.

Darlene's two older brothers were much more difficult to locate. James had settled in Midland, Texas and married a local girl with whom he had two girls, but no boys. He had acquired a local workover rig company with his life savings and was operating six old rigs which he was in the process of upgrading as company finances permitted. He and his family were respected members of the community who were well liked by the townspeople and neighbors. The girls were both blonds, but were of no value in implementing Frank's plan. Sid, on the other hand, had been stationed at Marine Corps bases in the United States and Europe as well as the Middle East and Asia. He retired from the USMC as a Master Sargent and was currently making his home in San Diego, California. He and his wife had four boys, all of whom lived in the San Diego area they ranged in age from twenty seven to nineteen and were fair skinned with curly blond hair. Their mother was also a curly haired blond with fair skin. The older two sons were married and had children while the younger pair were single and working their way through college. The youngest who was tall and lean had finished his freshman year at San Diego State and had his sights set on obtaining a degree in Business Management. He was flipping burgers part time at a McDonalds to earn money for tuition and to pay his living expenses. He and a fellow student shared a cheap apartment in a seedy part of town to make ends meet while attending San Diego State. It was a tough grind, still he was determined to complete his education no matter how difficult the task or how long it took. His brother had it a little easier, he was a junior with work related support in the form of time off and a monetary reimbursement program to pay for his books, fees and tuition. He worked at a tech company committed to upgrading their employee's educational levels so they could progress within the company. The company had discovered that these employees made a larger contribution to its success than employees who earned their degrees before coming to work for the company.

Karl, Darlene's youngest brother remained at the Strong Plantation after their parents died even though he and Frieda had married and completed their college degrees. They originally contemplated leaving

East Texas for good once they married, but her parents needed them nearby as they were no longer able to take care of themselves and the farm. There were no other brothers or sisters to help since Frieda was an only child she and Karl stayed on out of a sense of duty. After marrying, Frieda and Karl moved into the Strong house since both of his parents had passed away the previous year. They were serving as caretakers for the family eventually buying out the other sibling's interests to become the sole owners of the Strong Plantation. Karl adopted the name Strong Plantation which Alan had bestowed on the place during his high school visit many years earlier. Karl and Frieda taught at Joaquin High School after earning their degrees, within a few years Karl became superintendent of schools for the entire County, while Frieda continued to teach English at the high school. Teaching was well suited to their needs they had the summers off which allowed time for Karl to oversee farming of Frieda's land and to make improvements at the Strong Plantation. Karl enticed the electric company to build a power line to the Strong Plantation which allowed modernization of the house and the lifestyle there. Gradually, Karl restored the house to its original grandeur making it an outstanding example of early twentieth century architecture. He, Frieda and their two boys loved the place it provided them all the amenities of living in town plus absolute privacy. For Karl and the boys it had the added allure of the Sabine its wildness and mysteries were boundless. Both of the boys were in their early teens too young to be considered as sperm donors except in an emergency situation.

Aaron, marveled at the speed and efficiency of his agents in locating possible surrogate mothers and sperm donors for Alan and Martha from among their close relatives. The prospects had been narrowed to three women and two men with two possible emergency alternatives for the men should the primaries not be available. The next step in Frank's Plan was ready to begin, Aaron selected his best two agents to approach the potential players in Frank's scheme to produce children for Martha and Alan who would be as closely related to their parents as possible without them actually having children together.

Marie Garcia, Rachel's niece, had lived her entire life in McAllen ten miles from the American weekend playground of Reynosa, Mexico. She had graduated from high school two years earlier, but she had no apparent interest in going to college. Marie was employed by an oil company in McAllen which paid well above the average wage and she was happy working there. Marie was dismayed when the agent contacted her by phone inquiring about her interest in serving as a surrogate mother. She thought it was some kind of warped joke being played on her by one of her fellow employees. His second contact was viewed in a more professional manner Marie agreed to meet the agent in person at a local restaurant after work. He identified himself as a tall guy with a red tie. The agent took his time explaining the program its requirements and monetary benefits should Marie be interested. Marie, a tall black haired young lady explained to the agent.

"A year ago, I might have been interested in participating, but now I have to say no."

"May I ask why you are saying no?"

"It's this way, Sir. I'm dating a young engineer where I work. We have been together for six months he professes to be in love with me and I am in love with him. When he proposes, I will accept. Marrying him will provide me with a great future as his wife and mother of his children. He is what I really want we will be happy together."

"I see, Marie. I wish you well."

He checked Marie off of his list of three then decided to drive to Brownsville to interview his next prospect. Upon his arrival in Brownsville, the agent presented himself as a representative of Gentex when he contacted Yolanda Garcia another of Rachel's nieces. After reviewing the screening information from all the candidates, Yolanda had been Aaron's first choice for a surrogate mother for Alan. She stood out from the others for two reasons. First, she graduated from high school near the top of her class and she was taking college courses at night while working at a Mexican restaurant during the day. Second, her background check revealed an exceptionally high IQ. Yolanda demonstrated a strong work tradition and her desire for a higher education indicated a determination to better herself through her own efforts. The agent initially engaged her while ordering beef *enchiladas* with a *guacamole salsa* he then expanded the conversation to Gentex's program which economically supported certain people in getting their college degrees. She expressed an immediate interest saying.

"Wow, I could use some help myself."

The agent gave her a large tip and his card telling her he would be happy to discuss the Gentex program in detail after she got off work.

"I get off at four, but have to be in class by seven. Is that enough time?"

"That's great, I'll meet you outside at four. We can have our discussion in the lobby of my hotel which is across the street."

"OK, I'll be looking for you at four."

They found an empty table with comfortable chairs in an obscure corner of the lobby which provided them with reasonable privacy for their discussion. Yolanda was apprehensive meeting with a man she didn't know. Sensing her discomfort the agent quickly dispelled her fear.

"Yolanda we at Gentex have your best interest at heart we do not want you to do anything against your moral code or that you do not willingly want to do. Simply put, we have need of a surrogate mother for one of our programs and our investigation shows that you would be ideal provided you are willing. In exchange Gentex will provide you with free housing and living expenses in another city while you carry the baby. There will be no sex involved the baby will be conceived by artificial insemination with sperm from our client. Gentex will pay all cost of a college education for you at any Texas university or college you chose. You can attend school while carrying the baby if you want. It's entirely up to you. You will be provided a generous monthly payment for a period of ten years and you will have free medical care for life. After you graduate, we will purchase a new home for you wherever you chose in Texas. Before we go further, are you interested?"

"I must admit it sounds too good to be true, but giving up a baby is not something I have thought about before. It would be very difficult for me. I need some time to think about it before I can give you an answer."

"Take you time and think carefully before deciding this is not an issue to be taken lightly. One other thing to keep in mind the entire project will be conducted in secret no one, other than you and Gentex, will ever know you had a baby. You will also be required to keep our monetary support secret as well. I'll meet you here at the same time three days from now we will proceed from there whichever way you decide."

Yolanda left the meeting somewhat dazed by the proposal and its ramifications. Upon entering her parent's house she looked around at the miserable living conditions cringing to think she would spend her entire life living like this. She went to class that evening hoping to put the Gentex offer out of her mind. No matter how hard she tried, she kept thinking. "I need to get away from this life, but can I give up my baby?"

Two days and nights of mental turmoil and self-examination led Yolanda to conclude the only way she could accept would be to convince herself the baby would not be hers. She kept telling herself over and over.

"The baby would not be mine it would belong to the father and his wife."

The agent greeted Yolanda with a smile and hug before motioning toward the dining room where a buffet breakfast was being served.

"Would you like to have breakfast?"

"No thank you, I'm too nervous to eat. I would appreciate a cup of black coffee though."

He returned shortly with two cups of hot coffee.

"Cream and sugar," he offered.

"I'll have mine plain, thank you," replied Yolanda feeling much calmer than when she first arrived.

"Me to, I like the taste of coffee not cream and sugar," allowed the agent.

Sitting down next to Yolanda he was very comforting as he touched Yolanda's hand.

"I know it has been a tough three days for you Yolanda. I hate it that you had to go through this, unfortunately for this project to succeed, we all have to be committed from the beginning. You must realize that the baby will not be yours, it will belong to the father and his wife."

Those were the words Yolanda needed to hear.

"The baby would not be hers."

"It has been very difficult for me. I have decided to accept Gentex's offer, in fact, I would like to get away from here as soon as possible."

"Congratulations, Yolanda you have made the best possible decision for yourself and my client. If you do not want to return home we can leave now, Gentex will take care of you from now on."

"I can't go back, if I see my family again I might not be able to go. Let's leave now."

Three weeks later, Yolanda was living in an apartment near the University of Houston campus and was enrolled as a second semester student. All the necessary agreements had been signed by the parties and Gentex's doctors had cleared Yolanda for conception. She was very happy in her new surroundings although she missed her family when things slowed down. In a strange way, she was looking forward to having a baby as a surrogate mother it would make her happy and it would make the father and his wife happy. But, it would to be their baby.

Yolanda was determined to be a conscientious student she aimed to master each subject and to make the best grades possible. Studying relaxed her while she waited. Gentex indicated they would let her know when it was time, the agent checked on her frequently to make sure she was OK and had everything she needed. Yolanda was happy she had made the right decision she could look forward to a satisfying life for herself and her future children.

Signing up the male donor was less traumatic than getting Yolanda on board, it proved to be a simple task. Gentex's agent approached Ralph Strong, the San Diego State student, who was working part time at McDonalds.

"Son, how would you like to have the rest of your college education paid for by my employer?"

"Mister, are you kidding me? What would I have to do?"

Responded Darlene's young nephew who was also Alan's first cousin.

"By the time I get my burger and fries, your shift should be over. Why don't you meet me at that table near the door so I can explain our program?"

A few minutes later, Ralph Strong hung up his apron and hurried to the agent's table anxious to hear more about a free college education.

"Sir, my name is Ralph Strong," said the young blond man holding his hand toward the agent.

The agent extended his hand saying.

"I'm Tom, have a seat, Ralph. My employer would like to make you a proposal that I think will interest you."

"I'm listening, Sir. If it's legal, I'm interested."

"Here is the deal, we are in need of a male sperm donor with your particular characteristics to impregnate a married woman. Should you provide us your sperm for this purpose we will pay all of your costs to complete you degree. These costs will include an upscale apartment near the campus, a monthly educational and living cost payment in the amount of $2,500 plus all fees, tuition and equipment costs. In other words the remaining cost of your degree will be free and you will have $2,500 a month to spend as you like and that's not all, should you decide to pursue an advanced degree, we will pay for that too."

"Sir, when can I sign up?"

"Tomorrow, if you like. I'll pick you up when you get out of class."

Ralph quit his job at McDonalds before leaving for his apartment. At that moment, he made up his mind to never eat another burger the rest of his life. Ralph enjoyed a pleasant drive to his apartment in his old pickup humming the Marines' Hymn all the way to the parking lot. The papers to become a sperm donor were signed the following day as was the educational agreement with Gentex. Over the next three weeks, Ralph made multiple sperm donations and moved into his new apartment which featured a modern study room along with a large bedroom with two closets, best of all, it was only a block from the campus. Ralph was elated by his good fortune and had a renewed dedication to his studies. Since he no longer worked six days a week, his grades improved markedly and with free time available for other activities he began dating a female student who had caught his eye the previous semester. He kept saying to himself from time to time.

"A little sperm can create wonders."

Ralph explained his new found affluence to his friends and relatives as payment for participating in a genetic experiment being conducted by a large scientific company. Under the terms of his agreement with Gentex he was forbidden from disclosing the nature of his contribution. He gave no thought to who received his sperm only that he had made them happy and provided himself with a free education.

Aaron called Jerry announcing that the final piece of Frank's plan was ready for implementation.

"All the pieces are in place. Frank's plan can be completed whenever Alan and Martha are ready."

Jerry was pleased with Abe's speedy completion of its assignment. He passed on his congratulations.

"A fantastic job, Aaron. Give all of your people at Abe my regards and praise for a job well done. Before we inform Alan and Martha, I think you and I should have a face to face, say at the Tmex Hotel bar tomorrow at noon. We need to discuss their future and that of Gentex, Abe and ADAM."

The two remaining originators of ADAM were seated at a secluded table in the bar area, without thinking, Jerry automatically ordered two Irish whiskeys as had become the custom between him and Frank.

"What's this?" Asked Aaron when his drink arrived.

"Irish whiskey, I ordered it out of habit that's what Frank always had," replied Jerry embarrassed by his error.

"It had great significance to Frank and me because it was associated with two of our greatest accomplishments at Abe and at ADAM."

Aaron picked up his drink then suggested.

"In that case, we should drink a toast to Frank who was a friend and a great man."

"You are right, here is to Frank he was indeed a friend and great man."

The two of them agreed that the successful culmination of Alan's and Martha's saga would be the zenith of Abe's, Gentex's and ADAM'S efforts on behalf of George's children. Alan and Martha being happily married and having children of their own against near insurmountable odds was a miracle made possible by their collective efforts.

"If he were alive, George would be proud of Frank's innovative solution."

Both Jerry and Aaron agreed ADAM would commence winding down when Gentex's and Abe's responsibilities to George Angleton's children expired on the 30th birthday of his youngest child which would be coming up in less than two years. After that all surveillance, monitoring and protection would end except that for the mothers of George's children who had lifetime protection and benefits. Abe and Gentex had almost unlimited funding available from the investments originally set up by George Angleton to finance their operations. It would be up to Aaron and Jerry to come up with a use for the growing income which would be in keeping with the wishes of George

Angleton. They decided to concentrate on Alan and Martha until they produced children then tackle the bigger problem.

Randy, notified Alan and Martha that all was ready for them to start their family with a set of twins. With their agreement, Martha's next fertile period would be determined so that she could be inseminated by the Gentex expert at the proper time to insure she became pregnant. Martha was elated she wanted to get started and so did Alan they were going to be parents of twins. Although he had nothing to do with the timing of Yolanda's pregnancy and had no idea of her identity, Alan insisted on being informed as soon as it was definite she had conceived. By happy coincidence Martha and Yolanda had their fertile periods within a week of each other which meant, provided everything went according to plan and both women became pregnant on the first try, the children would indeed be twins or nearly so. Alan was beside himself once he learned Martha and the surrogate were both pregnant, he could not wait for the nine months to pass, he buried himself in his work to keep himself calm and sane during the gestation period.

Martha began to show by the fifth month after that it was obvious to anyone who looked that she was pregnant. This did not present a problem to anyone they knew since it was well known she and Alan were married, her pregnancy was an expected and natural event nothing out of the ordinary. No one else cared, Martha was just another among thousands of young pregnant women in Austin. Having children was a high priority among the young techies, who made up a large portion of the Austin working community. The pregnancies of Martha and Yolanda were under the control of Gentex as prescribed in Frank's Plan and although Yolanda was located in Houston her doctors and Martha's doctors were in constant contact by computer and by phone to co-ordinate the births of the babies.

A day prior to Martha's due date, she began showing signs of giving birth, at Gentex's insistence, she was airlifted by helicopter to Houston. Her friends and relatives were told that due to unforeseen complications she required special care available only in Houston. The next day she delivered a blond boy baby who from all appearances could have been Alan's child. Yolanda was located in another private facility attended by her own doctor. On the same day Martha gave birth, Yolanda's doctor induced labor producing a beautiful dark haired girl baby. By design, Yolanda, never saw her child or knew its sex, she was sedated at the time of delivery and the baby had been removed before she awoke.

The helicopter flew Alan, Martha and the two babies back to Austin where the happy couple joyfully announced the birth of twins, one boy and one girl. Martha was excited, she was the mother of twins while Alan was the proudest father in Texas. He delighted in showing off pictures and videos of the twins on his internet page where he posted new pictures almost daily. The twins were named Rachel Darlene Strong and Alan Jim Strong in honor of the two grandmothers and Alan's closest friend and business partner.

Frank's Plan had worked to perfection the twins were as nearly related as possible under the circumstances. They were blood related ¼ from Rachel's family, ¼ from Darlene's family, ¼ from George Angleton and ¼ others. The difference in blood line between the twins was the makeup of the ¼ others, they shared three quarters of the same blood line. Alan and Martha were unaware of the true relationship of their twins, but it made no difference to them so far as they were concerned they were brother and sister.

Shortly after the twin's second birthday, Martha and Alan concluded they would not be having any more children, two were enough. They informed Gentex of their decision implying that the stored sperm could be destroyed since it would no longer be needed. Gentex chose to keep the sperm just in case they changed their minds, or if for some unforeseen reason, Alan should desire to have children in the future. Gentex's concerns proved to be unwarranted, Martha, Alan, and the twins were a happy family that lived by the family motto borrowed from Martha's grandmother Martha Schuber.

"Every day you spend being unhappy is a day of your life wasted!"

ADAM came to an end leaving Abe and Gentex intact to fulfill the mandate originally established by George Angleton and his five advisors to provide an annual income, free medical care and protection for life for the final four. Protection and surveillance of George's children ended upon their reaching thirty years of age the last of which occurred on Martha's thirtieth birthday. Once the final four passed away there was no established program for using the funds of either Abe or Gentex. Jerry and Aaron spent months working on a plan to utilize the huge volume of cash pouring into the coffers of the two organizations. Their first consideration was preserving the secrecy pledged to George Angleton that there would be no way to connect either organization to him or to Imperial Recourses and that his identity as father of his children could never be traced.

Aaron had originally set up Abe and Gentex as offshore companies to shield both their income and the origin of their invested capital from detection. After operating for thirty years without incident, Aaron decided to add a layer of protection for Abe and Gentex to keep them safe from prying eyes well beyond his own death. Through third parties, he arranged for Abe to be merged into Gentex with the surviving offshore company to be known as Adam, Inc. which in turn had two divisions Abe and Gentex. The point was not to hide Abe and Gentex, but rather to distance them even farther from their original source of funding and its purpose which they had given the code name of ADAM. ADAM, itself, never had an official identity nor did it exist in the business world. ADAM was purely fictitious, it existed only in the minds of George Angleton and his five advisors.

Jerry and Aaron established a new mission for both Abe and Gentex. Abe directed its resources toward locating teen aged boys and girls who were on the verge of being drawn into gangs, drugs, prostitution and petty crimes or becoming permanent dropouts from civil society. Abe's agents and resources were to be used to steer these individuals toward rewarding and productive lives and to protect them from harm when necessary. After establishing the status and identity of an endangered teenager, Abe furnished the parents anonymous reports including pictures and videos showing what was going on with their children and what was implied for their futures. In those instances where the parents refused or were unable to take steps to help the children on their own, they were made aware of military type camps where their child could get a free education and training. Under Jerry's plan, Abe established and operated military style campuses across Texas. Secret intervention by Abe's agents on behalf of the participants in these camps was taken when they were threatened by outside sources. These boys and girls were afforded complete protection equivalent to that provided to George's children until they reached the age of thirty. For those incorrigibles whom Abe could not reach, Abe sent their records to the local police to aid in their prosecution and incarceration to remove them from society before they could do irreparable harm to other teenagers.

The new assignment for Gentex was not nearly so difficult, the Gentex organization was charged with conducting genetic studies aimed at isolating good genes which could be beneficial to mankind. Their agenda was wide open with no restrictions other than keeping costs within their budgeted funding. A strict review of spending was conducted annually by an independent accounting firm selected by the five Directors of Adam, Inc. who had been picked by Jerry and Aaron to manage their plan and assure that it continued for coming generations. Gentex's budget for each following year was to be determined based on the previous year's allocated income from Adam, Inc. and its actual productive use as determined by the accounting firm.

"Two Irish whiskeys please," said Aaron to the Tmex barmaid, who was new at the job. She was a young blond with a huge smile and a friendly disposition, she reminded Jerry of someone he had encountered in the past. He and Aaron were celebrating the end and the beginning of ADAM, George Angleton's creation to facilitate producing his four children.

"Aaron, I hope George knows how many lives he has impacted for the better with his funding of ADAM."

After downing his drink, Jerry ordered two more then asked.

"Aaron, are you aware that George did not leave any of his fortune to his children?"

"No. I would have thought otherwise, surely he would have wanted them to share in his riches. He could have found a way without their ever knowing the money came from him."

"George gave all of his personal fortune to charity, not one, but hundreds of them. His stock in Imperial and its subsidiaries he gave equally to all the employees, who had been on the payroll for at least a year, at the time of his death. He confided in me just before his death that he thought giving his fortune to his children would ruin their lives. The last thing in the world George wanted was for his children to become Trust Babies. More than anything, George wanted them to be happy and successful on their own he insisted they be allowed the opportunity, as he put it, to make their own lives and careers without his interference. That is why he didn't want to know his kids, he was afraid he would inadvertently ruin their lives. If he could see his children today, George would be pleased with his creations, they all have proven to be gifts to humanity. George Angleton was brilliant in more ways than just making money as he always said."

"If something is worth doing, it's worth doing right."

About the Author

C. P. Schweikhardt was born December 29, 1929 in Allen, Oklahoma the second son of Forest and Ailene Schweikhardt a young couple who eventually had three sons. He attended various schools in Oklahoma, Indiana and Illinois graduating from Mt. Carmel High School in Mt. Carmel, Illinois where he lived alone his senior year in high school, his parents had moved to Texas at the beginning of the school year. After moving to Texas following graduation, he worked for a year before enlisting in the U. S. Air Force. He was assigned to the weather service and was stationed at Rhine Main AFB during the Berlin airlift. Four years later he returned to Texas and enrolled at Texas A&I University where he met and married his beautiful wife Patricia during his second year there. The following year he graduated with honors receiving a B.S degree in Petroleum and Natural Gas Engineering.

He worked for major oil companies for the first fifteen years of his career moving from one location to another as the job required. Over time he became a supervising engineer then moved into various management positions while working at the company headquarters in Houston, Texas. In 1972 he resigned to form an engineering consulting company with two friends and later formed an exploration and production company. Over the years he has served as president of two oil companies and has been involved in organizing and forming several companies some of which are unrelated to the oil business.

Mr. Schweikhardt and his wife have three grown children, four grandchildren and one great grandchild with another one on the way. He and his wife live in Houston where Mr. Schweikhardt has spent most of his long career during which he has written hundreds of engineering reports, studies and evaluations which are restricted to facts, conclusions and occasional opinions. ADAM is his first novel and is pure fiction, an attempt to let his imagination create an unusual and interesting set of circumstances for reading entertainment.

Cast of Characters

Patriarch-George Angleton
Advisors-Frank, Jerry, Aaron, Ed and Harry
Final Four (mothers)-Rachel, Peggy, Clare and Darlene
George Angleton's children-Alan, Bruce, Martha and Verona
Couples-Rachel, Phil; Peggy, Zane; Clare, Ned; Darlene, Randall

Comments and Reviews

Send all comments and reviews for the author to
matagorda29@yahoo.com

www.ingramcontent.com/pod-product-compliance
Lightning Source LLC
Chambersburg PA
CBHW080721020726
47503CB00010B/2748